THE
DIABOLIC

THE
DIABOLIC

S. J. KINCAID

SIMON AND SCHUSTER

First published in Great Britain in 2016 by Simon & Schuster UK Ltd
A CBS COMPANY

First published in the USA in 2016 by Simon & Schuster BFYR,
an imprint of Simon & Schuster Children's Publishing Division

1 3 5 7 9 10 8 6 4 2

Simon & Schuster UK Ltd
1st Floor, 222 Gray's Inn Road
London
WC1X 8HB

www.simonandschuster.co.uk
www.simonandschuster.com.au
www.simonandschuster.co.in

Simon & Schuster Australia, Sydney
Simon & Schuster India, New Delhi

A CIP catalogue record for this book
is available from the British Library.

HB ISBN 978-1-4711-4714-2
Export PB ISBN 978-4711-4838-5
ANZ PB ISBN 978-4711-4839-2
eBook ISBN 978-1-4711-4716-6

Printed and bound by CPI Group (UK) Ltd, Croydon, CR0 4YY

MIX
Paper from
responsible sources
FSC® C020471

Simon & Schuster UK Ltd are committed to sourcing paper
that is made from wood grown in sustainable forests and support the Forest
Stewardship Council, the leading international forest certification organisation.
Our books displaying the FSC logo are printed on FSC certified paper.

To
JAMIE
(a.k.a. Poosen)
and
JESSICA
(a.k.a. The Real Yaolan)

Having one lifelong friend
I could absolutely trust and rely upon
is a blessing,
but I have been lucky enough
to have two.
You guys mean more
to me than you know.

Did he who made the lamb make thee?
—WILLIAM BLAKE, "The Tiger"

EVERYONE believed Diabolics were fearless, but in my earliest years, all I knew was fear. It preyed on me the very morning the Impyreans viewed me in the corrals.

I couldn't speak, but I understood most words I heard. The corral master was frantic in his warnings to his assistants: the Senator von Impyrean and his wife, the Impyrean Matriarch, would be arriving shortly. The keepers paced about my pen, surveying me head to toe, searching for any defect.

I awaited this Senator and Matriarch with my heart pounding, my muscles poised for battle.

And then they came.

All the trainers, all the keepers, dropped to their knees before them. The corral master reverently drew their hands to his cheeks.

"We are honored by your visit."

Fear shot through me. What manner of creatures were these, that the fearsome *corral master* dropped to the floor before them? The glowing force field of my pen had never felt so constrictive. I shrank back as far as possible. Senator von Impyrean and his wife strolled over and looked in at me from the other side of the invisible barrier.

"As you can see," the corral master told them, "Nemesis is approximately your daughter's age and physically tailored to your specifications. She'll only grow larger and stronger over the next several years."

"Are you quite sure this girl is dangerous?" drawled the Senator. "She looks like a frightened child."

The words chilled me.

I was never supposed to be *frightened*. Fear earned me shocks, reduced rations, torment. No one must ever see me afraid. I fixed the Senator with a ferocious look.

As he caught my eye, he looked startled. He opened his mouth to speak again, then hesitated, squinting, before his gaze broke from mine. "Perhaps you're right," he muttered. "It's in the eyes. You can see the inhumanity. My dear, are you very certain we need this monstrous thing in our household?"

"Every great family has a Diabolic now. Our daughter will *not* be the only child to go unprotected," said the Matriarch. She turned to the corral master. "I wish to see what our money will pay for."

"Of course," replied the corral master, turning away to wave at a keeper. "Some chum . . ."

"No." The Matriarch's voice was whiplash sharp. "We must be certain. We brought our own trio of convicts. They will be a sufficient test for this creature."

The master smiled. "But of course, Grandeé von Impyrean. You cannot be too careful. So many substandard breeders out there. . . . Nemesis won't disappoint you."

The Matriarch gave a nod to someone out of my sight. The danger I'd been anticipating materialized: three men were being led toward my pen.

I pressed back against the force field again, the tingling vibrating along the skin of my back. An icy pit opened in my stomach. I already knew what would happen next. These were not the first men who had been brought to visit me.

The corral master's assistants unchained the men, then deactivated the far force field to shove them inside with me before raising it again. My breath came in gasps now. I did not want to do this. I did not.

"What is this?" demanded one of the convicts, looking from me to their impromptu audience.

"Isn't it obvious?" The Matriarch linked her arm through the Senator's. She cast a satisfied look toward her husband and then addressed the convicts in a most pleasant tone: "Your violent crimes have brought you here, but you have an opportunity to redeem yourselves now. Kill this child, and my husband will grant you pardons."

The men goggled at the Senator, who gave a disinterested wave of the hand. "It is as my wife says."

One man swore violently. "I know what that thing is. Do you think I'm a fool? I'm not going near it!"

"If you don't," replied the Matriarch with a smile, "you will all three be executed. Now kill the child."

The convicts surveyed me, and after a moment, the largest of them broke into a leering grin. "It's a little girl. I'll do it myself. Come here, girl." He stalked toward me. "You want this bloody or do I just break her neck?"

"Your choice," the Matriarch said.

His confidence emboldened the others and set their faces ablaze with the hope of freedom. My heart punched against my rib cage. I had no way to warn them away from me. Even if I had, they would not have listened. Their ringleader had declared me only a girl—and so that was what they saw now. That was their fatal mistake.

The big one reached down to grab me very carelessly, his hand so close that I could smell his sweat.

The smell triggered something within me. It was the same as every time before: the fear vanished. Terror dissolved in a swell of rage.

My teeth clamped down on his hand. Blood spouted, hot and coppery. He shrieked and tried to pull back—too late. I seized his wrist and threw myself forward, twisting his limb as I went. His ligaments crackled. I kicked at the back of his leg to knock him down to the ground. I leaped over him and landed with a stomp of my boots on the back of his head. His skull splintered.

There was another man, who'd also been too bold, moved in too close, and only now realized his error. He yelled out in horror, but he did not escape. I was too fast. My palm thrust into the cartilage of his nose and drove it straight into his brain.

I stepped over the two bodies toward the third man—the one who'd had the sense to fear me. He shrieked and stumbled back against the force field, cowering as I had done earlier, when I was not yet angry. He held up his shaking hands. Sobs convulsed his body.

"Please don't. Please don't hurt me, please no!"

The words made me hesitate.

My life, my whole life, had been spent this way, fending off aggressors, killing to ward off death, killing so I would not be killed. But only once before had a voice pleaded for mercy. I hadn't known what to do then. Now, as I stood over the cowering man, that same confusion filtered through me, rooting me in place. How was I to act from here?

"Nemesis."

The Matriarch was suddenly standing before me, separated only by the force field. "Can she understand me if I speak?" she asked the corral master.

"They've got enough human in them to pick up language," the corral master said, "but she won't learn to respond until the machines do some work on her brain."

The Matriarch nodded and turned back to me. "You've impressed me, Nemesis. I ask you now: Do you wish to leave here? Do you wish to have a precious thing of your own to love and protect, and a home with comforts beyond your dreams?"

Love? Comfort? Those were strange words. I didn't know their meaning, but her tone was coaxing, full of promise. It wove through my mind like a melody, drowning out the whimpers of the terrified man.

I could not look away from the Matriarch's sharp eyes.

"If you wish to be something more than an animal in this dank pen," she said, "then prove yourself worthy of serving the Impyrean family. Show you can obey when it matters. Kill this man."

Love. Comfort. I didn't know what those were, but I wanted them. I would have them. I closed the distance and snapped the man's neck.

As the third corpse dropped to the floor at my feet, the Matriarch smiled.

Later, the keepers brought me to the laboratory, where a young girl waited. I was restrained for her safety, my arms and legs encased in thick iron with an outer ring of glowing electricity. I couldn't stop staring at this odd little creature, small and trembling, with dark hair and skin and a nose that had never been broken.

I knew what this creature was. This was a *real* girl.

I knew, because I'd killed one before.

She drew a step too close to me and I snarled at her. She flinched back.

"She hates me," she said, her lower lip trembling.

"Nemesis doesn't hate you," the doctor assured her as he double-checked my restraints. "This is how Diabolics behave at this stage of development. They look like us, but they aren't truly human beings like you and me. They're predators. They can't feel empathy or kindness. They simply don't have the capacity for it. That's why, when they're old enough, we have to civilize them. Come closer, Sidonia."

He crooked a finger. Sidonia followed him to a nearby computer screen. "See that?" he asked.

I could see the image too, but I didn't find it interesting. I'd broken open enough skulls to recognize a human brain.

"That's called a frontal cortex." He fell silent a moment, and there was a flicker of fear in the look he darted at the girl. "I haven't researched that for myself, of course, but in my line of work, you simply learn things from watching the machines."

Sidonia's brow flickered downward, as though his words had puzzled her.

Flustered, he went on in a rapid tone, "As far as I understand it, these machines are going to make this part of her brain bigger. Much bigger. They'll make Nemesis smarter. She'll learn how to speak to you and how to reason. The machines will also begin the bonding process."

"Then she'll like me?"

"After today, she'll be your best friend."

"So she won't be so angry anymore?" Sidonia's voice sounded small.

"Well, that aggression is simply how Diabolics are engineered. But Nemesis won't direct that toward you. In all the universe, you'll be the only person she will ever love. Anyone who tries to hurt you, though—they better watch out."

Sidonia gave a tremulous smile.

"Now, honey, I need you to go stand where she can see you. Eye contact is critical for the bonding process."

The doctor positioned Sidonia before me, carefully out of reach. He avoided my biting mouth and applied stimulating nodes to my skull. After a moment, they buzzed and hummed.

A tingle through my brain, stars prickling before my eyes.

My hatred, my need to smash and shred and destroy—it began to calm. Began to fade.

Another fizzling of a current, then another.

I gazed at the small girl before me, and something new stirred inside me, a sensation I'd never felt before.

A constant roar within my skull now, changing me, shifting me.

I wanted to help this girl. I wanted to protect her.

The roaring went on and on, and then it faded away as though nothing else existed in the universe but *her*.

For several hours as my brain was modified, the doctor ran tests. He let Sidonia move closer to me, and then closer still. He watched me as I watched Sidonia.

Finally it was time.

The doctor withdrew to a distance, leaving Sidonia alone before me. She rose to her feet, shaking all over. The doctor aimed an electricity gun as a precaution and then flipped open my restraints.

I straightened up and extricated myself from the bonds. The little girl drew a sharp breath, her collarbone standing out below her scrawny neck. It would have snapped so easily. I knew that. Yet though I could have hurt her, though I'd been released upon her just like all the others I'd slain, the very idea of injuring this delicate creature made me recoil.

I stepped closer so I could look at this girl in full, this being of

7

infinite value whose survival now meant more to me than my own. How small she was. I wondered at the feeling inside me, which glowed like warm embers in my chest. This marvelous glow came from looking at *her*.

When I touched the soft skin of Sidonia's cheek, she flinched. I examined her dark hair, such a contrast to my pale, white-blond shade. I leaned close to examine the irises of her large eyes. Fear flooded their depths, and I wanted that fear gone. She still trembled, so I placed my palms on her frail arms and stood very still, hoping my steadiness would calm her.

Sidonia stopped trembling. The fear faded. Her lips tipped up at the corners.

I imitated the gesture, forcing my lips to curl. It felt unnatural and strange, but I did it for *her*. It was the first time in my life I'd acted on behalf of someone other than myself.

"Hello, Nemesis," Sidonia whispered. She swallowed loudly. "My name is Sidonia." A line appeared between her brows, and then she pressed her palm over her chest. "Si-doe-nya."

I imitated her, patting my own chest. "Sidonia."

Sidonia laughed. "No." She took my hand and pulled it over her chest. I could feel the frantic thump of her heartbeat. "I'm Sidonia. But you can call me Donia."

"Donia," I repeated, patting her collarbone, understanding her.

Donia broke into a smile that made me feel . . . warm, pleased, proud. She looked back at the doctor. "You're right! She doesn't hate me."

The doctor nodded. "Nemesis is bonded to you now. She'll live and breathe for you all the days of your life."

"I like her, too," Donia declared, smiling at me. "I think we'll become friends."

The doctor laughed softly. "Friends, yes. I promise you, Nemesis will be the best friend you'll ever have. She'll love you until your dying day."

And at last, I had a name for this feeling, this strange but wonderful new sensation within me—this was what the Impyrean Matriarch had promised me.

This was *love*.

1

SIDONIA had made a dangerous mistake.

She was carving a statue out of a great stone slab. There was something mesmerizing about the swiping and flashing of her laser blade, bright against the dark window overlooking the starscape. She never aimed the blade where I expected, but somehow she always produced an image in the stone that my own imagination could never have conjured. Today it was a star gone supernova, a scene from Helionic history depicted vividly in rock.

Yet one swipe of her blade had extracted too large a chunk from the base of the sculpture. I saw it at once and jumped to my feet, alarm prickling through me. The structure was no longer stable. At any moment, that entire statue was going to come crashing down.

Donia knelt to study the visual effect she'd created. Oblivious to the danger.

I approached quietly. I didn't want to warn her—it might startle her into jerking or jumping, and cutting herself with the laser. Better to rectify the situation myself. My steps drew me across the room. Just as I reached her, the first creak sounded, fragments of dust raining down from above her as the statue tilted forward.

I seized Donia and whipped her out of the way. A great crashing exploded in our ears, dust choking the stale air of the art chamber.

I wrested the laser blade from Donia's hand and switched it off.

She pulled free, rubbing at her eyes. "Oh no! I didn't see that coming." Dismay slackened her face as she looked over the wreckage. "I've ruined it, haven't I?"

"Forget the statue," I said. "Are you hurt?"

She glumly waved off my question. "I can't believe I did that. It was going so well. . . ." With one slippered foot, she kicked at a chunk of broken stone, then sighed and glanced at me. "Did I say thanks? I didn't. Thanks, Nemesis."

Her thanks did not interest me. It was her safety that mattered. I was her Diabolic. Only people craved praise.

Diabolics weren't people.

We looked like people, to be sure. We had the DNA of people, but we were something else: creatures fashioned to be utterly ruthless and totally loyal to a single individual. We would gladly kill for that person, and only for them. That's why the elite imperial families eagerly snatched us up to serve as lifelong bodyguards for themselves and their children, and to be the bane of their enemies.

But lately, it seemed, Diabolics were doing their jobs far too well. Donia often tapped into the Senate feed to watch her father at work. In recent weeks, the Imperial Senate had begun debating the "Diabolic Menace." Senators discussed Diabolics gone rogue, killing enemies of their masters over small slights, even murdering family members of the child they were assigned to protect to advance that child's interests. We were proving more of a threat to some families than an asset.

I knew the Senate must have come to a decision about us, because this morning, the Matriarch had delivered a missive to her daughter— one directly from the Emperor. Donia had taken a single look at it and then thrown herself into carving.

I'd lived with her for nearly eight years. We'd virtually grown up side by side. She only grew silent and distracted like this when worried about me.

"What was in the missive, Donia?"

She fingered a slab of the broken statue. "Nemesis . . . they banned Diabolics. Retroactively."

Retroactively. That meant current Diabolics. Like me.

"So the Emperor expects you to dispose of me."

Donia shook her head. "I won't do it, Nemesis."

Of course she wouldn't. And then she'd be punished for it. An edge crept into my voice. "If you can't bring yourself to be rid of me, then I'll take the matter into my own hands."

"I *said* I won't do it, Nemesis, and neither will you!" Her eyes flashed. She raised her chin. "I'll find another way."

Sidonia had always been meek and shy, but it was a deceptive appearance. I'd long ago learned there was an undercurrent of steel within her.

Her father, Senator von Impyrean, proved a help. He nursed a powerful animosity toward the Emperor, Randevald von Domitrian.

When Sidonia pleaded for my life, a glimmer of defiance stole into the Senator's eyes. "The Emperor *demands* her death, does he? Well, rest easy, my darling. You needn't lose your Diabolic. I'll tell the Emperor the death has been carried out, and that will be the end of the matter."

The Senator was mistaken.

THE DIABOLIC

◊

Like most of the powerful, the Impyreans preferred to live in isolation and socialize only in virtual spaces. The nearest Excess—those free humans scattered on planets—were systems away from Senator von Impyrean and his family. He wielded his authority over the Excess from a strategic remove. The family fortress orbited an uninhabited gas giant ringed by lifeless moons.

So we were all startled weeks later when a starship arrived out of the depths of space—unannounced, unheralded. It had been dispatched by the Emperor under the pretext of "inspecting" the body of the Diabolic, but it was no mere inspector onboard.

It was an Inquisitor.

Senator von Impyrean had underestimated the Emperor's hostility toward the Impyrean family. My existence gave the Emperor an excuse to put one of his own agents in the Impyrean fortress. Inquisitors were a special breed of vicar, trained to confront the worst heathens and enforce the edicts of the Helionic religion, often with violence.

The Inquisitor's very arrival should have terrified the Senator into obedience, but Sidonia's father still circumvented the will of the Emperor.

The Inquisitor had come to see a body, so a body he was shown.

It simply wasn't mine.

One of the Impyreans' Servitors had been suffering from solar sickness. Like Diabolics, Servitors had been genetically engineered for service. Unlike us, they didn't need the capacity to make decisions, so they hadn't been engineered to have it. The Senator took me to the ailing Servitor's bedside and gave me the dagger. "Do what you do best, Diabolic."

I was grateful he'd sent Sidonia to her chambers. I wouldn't want her to see this. I sank the dagger under the Servitor's rib cage. She didn't flinch, didn't try to flee. She gazed at me through blank, empty eyes, and then a moment later she was dead.

Only then was the Inquisitor allowed to dock with the fortress. He made a cursory inspection of the body, pausing over it merely to note, "How odd. She appears . . . *freshly* dead."

The Senator stood bristling at his shoulder. "The Diabolic has been dying of solar sickness for several weeks now. We'd just decided to end her suffering when you arrived in the system."

"*Contrary* to what your missive said," the Inquisitor stated, swinging on him. "You claimed the death had already been carried out. Now that I see her, I wonder at her size. She's rather small for a Diabolic."

"Now you question the body, too?" roared the Senator. "I tell you, she was wasting away for weeks."

I watched the Inquisitor from the corner. I wore a new Servitor's gown, my size and musculature hidden beneath voluminous folds. If he saw through the ruse, then I would kill him.

I hoped it wouldn't come to that. Concealing an Inquisitor's death might prove . . . complicated.

"Perhaps if your family was more respectful of the Living Cosmos," the Inquisitor remarked, "your household would have been spared a ghastly affliction like solar sickness."

The Senator ripped in an angry breath to reply, but at that moment the Matriarch darted forward from where she'd been lurking in the doorway. She seized her husband's arm, forestalling him.

"How right you are, Inquisitor! We are immensely grateful for your insight." Her smile was gracious, for the Matriarch didn't share her husband's eagerness to defy the Emperor.

She'd felt imperial wrath firsthand at a young age. Her own family had displeased the Emperor, and her mother had paid the price. Now she appeared electric with anxiety, her body quivering with eagerness to placate their guest.

"I'd be ever so pleased if you'd observe our services tonight, Inquisitor. Perhaps you can note what we are doing wrong." Her tone dripped with sweetness, the sort that sounded odd in her usual acrid voice.

"I would be glad to do so, Grandeé von Impyrean," replied the Inquisitor, now gracious. He reached out to draw her knuckles to his cheek.

She pulled away. "I'll go make the arrangements with our Servitors. I'll take this one now. You—come." She jerked her head for me to accompany her.

I didn't want to leave the Inquisitor. I wanted to watch his every movement, observe his every expression, but the Matriarch had left me no choice but to follow her as a Servitor would. Our steps brought us out of the chamber, far from the Inquisitor's sight. The Matriarch picked up her pace, and I did as well. We wound together down the corridor toward the Senator's chambers.

"Madness," she muttered. "It's madness to take this risk right now! You should be lying dead before that Inquisitor, not walking here at my side!"

I cast her a long, considering look. I'd gladly die for Donia, but if it came to my life or the Matriarch's, I'd put myself first. "Do you intend to tell the Inquisitor what I am?"

Even as I spoke, I visualized the blow I'd use to kill her. A single strike to the back of the head. . . . No need to risk her screaming. Donia might emerge from her chambers if she heard anything. I'd hate to murder her mother in front of her.

The Matriarch had the survival instinct her husband and daughter lacked. Even my mild tone sent terror skittering across her face. The next moment it vanished so swiftly that I wondered whether I'd imagined it. "Of course not. The truth would condemn us all now."

15

So she would live. My muscles relaxed.

"If you're here," she said darkly, "then you'll make yourself useful to us. You'll help me conceal my husband's work before that Inquisitor inspects his chambers."

That I could do. We plunged into the Senator's study, where the Matriarch hiked up her gown and shuffled through the debris strewn about the room—blasphemous database fragments that would instantly condemn this entire family if the Inquisitor laid eyes on them.

"Quickly now," she said, gesturing for me to start swiping them up.

"I'll take them to the incinerator—"

"Don't." Her voice was bitter. "My husband will simply use their destruction as an excuse to acquire more. We simply need to clear these from sight for now." She twisted her fingers in a crack in the wall, and the floor slid open to reveal a hidden compartment.

Then she settled in the Senator's chair, fanning herself with her hand as I heaved armful after armful of shattered fragments of what looked like computer debris and data chips into the compartment. The Senator passed days in here, repairing whatever he could salvage, uploading information into his personal database. He avidly read the materials and often discussed them with Sidonia. Those scientific theories, those technological blueprints. All blasphemous. All insults against the Living Cosmos.

I stashed the Senator's personal computer in with the debris, and then the Matriarch crossed to the wall again and twisted her finger in the nook. The floor slid closed. I heaved the Senator's desk over so it covered the hidden compartment.

I straightened again to find the Matriarch watching me narrowly. "You would have killed me back in the hallway." Her glittering eyes challenged me to deny it.

I didn't. "You know what I am, madam."

"Oh yes, I do." Her lips twisted. "*Monster.* I know what goes on behind those cold, soulless eyes of yours. This is exactly why Diabolics have been banned—they protect one and pose a threat to all others. You must never forget that Sidonia needs me. I'm her mother."

"And you must never forget that I'm her Diabolic. She needs me more."

"You cannot possibly fathom what a mother means to a child."

No. I couldn't. I'd never had one. All I knew was that Sidonia was safer with me than with anyone else in this universe. Even her own kin.

The Matriach loosed an unpleasant laugh. "Ah, but why even debate you on this? You could no more understand family than a dog could compose poetry. No, what matters is, you and I share a cause. Sidonia is kindhearted and naive. Outside this fortress, in the wider Empire . . . perhaps a creature like you will be the very thing my daughter requires to survive. But you will never—*never*—speak to anyone of what we've done today."

"Never."

"And if anyone seems ready to find out we've spared our Diabolic, then you will take care of the problem."

The very thought sent a sizzling, protective anger through me. "Without hesitation."

"Even if taking care of it"—her eyes were sharp and birdlike—"starts with yourself."

I didn't condescend to answer. Of course I would die for Sidonia. She was my entire universe. I loved nothing but her and valued nothing but her existence. Without her, there was no reason for me to exist.

Death would be a mercy compared to that.

2

THAT VERY EVENING, the entire household—people and Servitors alike—gathered in the heliosphere, the clear dome at the top of the orbiting fortress. As much as the Matriarch pleaded with him, the Senator never bothered with services unless there were visitors. Today he attended for appearances' sake, but he didn't bother to hide his insolent smile from the Inquisitor.

The Inquisitor, after all, had just thoroughly inspected the fortress. He'd found nothing worthy of reporting to the Emperor. A clever man would not gloat, but the Senator was a fool.

The Matriarch had accorded the Inquisitor an honored seat just behind the family for the service. We all watched in thick silence as the star rose over the curvature of the planet below us. The windows were crystalline, refracting light in just the proper way to send it scattering to certain points of the room where mirrors were positioned. For a split second, the bright rays all converged upon a single point: the ceremonial chalice at the center. It ignited the oil within. We gazed at the burning chalice as the perfect angle to the star shifted, dispelling the blinding glare of the lights. The blessing began.

"And so," spoke the vicar, lifting up the burning chalice, "through our birth star, Helios, the Living Cosmos chose to spark life on planet Earth and gave rise to our most revered ancestors in that ancient era when the stars were but distant points against the infinite dark. Humanity was veiled in ignorance in those days, devoting themselves to worship of deities imagined in their own likeness, unable to recognize the true divinity of the universe itself all about them. . . ."

My gaze crawled the room, passing from the intent vigilance on the Matriarch's face to the ill-concealed disdain on the Senator's. Next I looked to the Inquisitor, who was staring intently at the Senator's back. Then I looked to Donia, whose wide brown eyes were fixed on the chalice as the vicar recited the story of homo sapien genesis. Sidonia had always possessed a strange fascination with the tale of the solar system of human origin, and the sun, Helios, that had nourished the first human beings.

She was devout. She'd tried to convert me to the Helionic religion as soon as I was acquired, and she'd brought me to a service to entreat the vicar to bless me with the light of stars. I didn't quite grasp the concept of the Living Cosmos or souls yet, but I hoped to be blessed because Sidonia wished it for me.

The vicar refused. He informed Donia that I had no soul to bless.

"Diabolics are creations of mankind, not of the Living Cosmos," the vicar told Donia. "There is no divine spark in them to illuminate with Cosmic light. This creature can observe the blessing as a gesture of respect to your family, but she can never participate in it."

As he spoke, there was a strange expression on the vicar's face and on the Matriarch's. I'd just begun to figure out facial expressions, and

I recognized it even then: total revulsion. They were disgusted by the mere notion a Diabolic might be favored by their divine Cosmos.

For some reason, the memory of the looks on their faces made my stomach clench even now as I listened to the vicar. I chose instead to resume watching the Inquisitor, the man who would report the details of this visit to the Emperor. His word could condemn Senator von Impyrean if he found the Impyreans insufficiently pious. Worse, his words could condemn *Sidonia.*

If anything happened to her, anything, I would hunt this man down and kill him for it. I memorized his proud, cold features—just in case.

The vicar's voice droned on until the nearby star mercifully sank behind the curvature of the planet. Then the lights dimmed within the heliosphere but for the burning chalice. The vicar drew an earthclay lid down over the top of it to extinguish that fire.

A deep, hushed silence followed in the darkness.

Then one of the Servitors turned the lights back to full. The people left the heliosphere first—the Impyreans, the Inquisitor, and then the vicar. After that I filed out along with the Servitors.

The Senator escorted the Inquisitor toward the bay doors, not even offering him the courtesy of a night's sleep at the fortress. I followed them at a careful distance, my keen hearing able to pick out their parting words from a corridor behind them.

"So what's the verdict?" boomed the Senator. "Am I sufficiently pious for the Emperor's taste? Or do you, too, wish to call me 'the Great Heretic'?"

"It is your *manner* that offends the Emperor," the Inquisitor replied. "And I don't believe the Emperor will find it improved. How boastful you almost sound about that hateful name you've acquired! Well, heresy is dangerous, Grande, so I'd advise you to watch your step."

"*Senator.* You will call me that."

"Of course, Senator von Impyrean." The words were spoken as a sneer.

With that, the Inquisitor and the Senator parted.

I found Donia, where she'd planted herself by a window overlooking the bay doors. She refused to move until the Inquisitor's ship pulled out and disappeared into the black. Then she ducked her head in her hands and dissolved into tears.

"What's wrong?" I demanded, my alarm mounting.

"Oh, Nemesis, I'm so relieved!" She raised her tearstained face and laughed. "You're safe!" She hurled herself forward and threw her arms around me. "Oh, don't you see? He may be mad at Father, but *you're* safe." She buried her head against my shoulder. "I could never live without you."

I hated when she spoke like this, as though I meant everything to her when in reality, she was the one who meant everything to me.

Donia continued to weep. I wrapped my arms around her, a gesture that still felt unnatural and strange to me, and contemplated the oddity of tears. I had no tear ducts and was totally incapable of weeping, but I'd seen tears often enough to know they were about pain and fear.

But it seemed they could come from joy as well.

As the sole heir of a Galactic Senator, Donia would be expected to take her father's seat after he retired. That meant she had to cultivate political instinct now and learn to speak to others among the Grandiloquy, the Empire's ruling class. Her social skills would fashion the future alliances of her family and ensure their continued influence. The virtual forums were her only means of practicing social niceties. I'd never seen these forums myself, but Donia had explained to me that they were set in a virtual reality where people used avatars to interact with one another.

Twice a month, Donia was forced to attend formal gatherings on the forums, where she'd meet other young Grandiloquy in far-off star systems who were destined to inherit power in the Empire. The meetings were a painful necessity for her. As she prepared for the day, her shoulders were slouched, dejection in every line of her body.

The Matriarch, as always, ignored her gloom. "The Emperor will have a report of the Inquisitor's visit by now," she told Donia. "If your fool of a father has created any new problems for us—"

"Please don't call him a fool, Mother. He's really quite visionary in his own way."

"—if he *has*, then the Emperor will have told his confidants. Their children will have heard. You need to *listen*, Sidonia, both to what they say and what they don't say. The survival of our family may depend on the information you gather in these forums."

The Matriarch prized these gatherings so dearly, she always sat next to Donia and tapped into the feed with an add-on headset of her own. In that manner, she monitored her daughter's interactions and hissed advice—or rather, orders—in her ear.

Today they settled by the computer console and pulled on their headsets to begin observing a world only they could see. I listened as Donia stammered nervously through small talk. Occasionally she made some social blunder, and the Matriarch pinched her in punishment.

It took all my self-restraint not to stride forward and break the Matriarch's arm.

"What have I told you about avoiding certain subjects?" the Matriarch hissed. "Do not even ask her about the nebula!"

"I just asked if it was as beautiful as I'd heard," Donia protested.

"I don't care *why* you asked. The Great Heretic's daughter can't afford to ask anything that could be misconstrued as scientific curiosity."

Then the Matriarch said, "That's the avatar of Salivar Domitrian.

Everyone will soon be fighting for an audience with him. Go pay your respects before he is swarmed."

Then, a few minutes later, "Why are you at the edge of this crowd, Sidonia? You are flanked by nobodies! Move lest someone think you belong here!"

At one point, both Donia and the Matriarch tensed up. I straightened, watching their backs, wondering who they'd just seen to put them both on edge. The Matriarch's hand whipped over and clenched Donia's shoulder.

"Now, tread very carefully around this Pasus girl. . . ."

Pasus.

My eyes narrowed as Donia nervously conversed with the girl who had to be Elantra Pasus. I knew her family well because I'd made it my mission to acquaint myself with all the Impyrean enemies—Sidonia's enemies. I'd watched the Senate feed live a year before as Senator von Pasus gleefully denounced Sidonia's father. Pasus and his allies were the most ardent Helionics in the Senate, and they'd had enough votes to formally censure Senator von Impyrean for "heresy." The Impyreans suffered a dreadful blow to their reputation, for which the Matriarch still couldn't forgive her husband.

Privately, I resented Senator von Impyrean as well, for he'd endangered his daughter by publicly speaking on those matters that were supposed to be left unvoiced. He questioned the wisdom of forbidding education in the sciences. He possessed strange ideals and an absurd devotion to learning. It was one reason he collected old databases containing scientific knowledge, those databases the Matriarch and I had hastily concealed from the Inquisitor. He believed humanity needed to embrace scientific learning again, and he never gave a second thought to how his actions would impact his family.

He was reckless.

And now because of him, Donia had to interact with Senator von Pasus's daughter as though their fathers weren't rivals.

Donia did not converse long before hastily making her excuses to walk away.

Surprisingly, the Matriarch patted her shoulder. "Well done." It was rare praise.

It seemed an eternity before Donia could tug off her headset, dark shadows of exhaustion under her eyes.

"Let's discuss your performance," the Matriarch said as she rose imperiously to her feet. "You were very good about evading forbidden subjects, and your interactions were most cautious, but what did you do wrong?"

Donia sighed. "I'm certain you'll tell me."

"You sounded meek," the Matriarch railed. "Self-deprecating. I even heard you stammer several times. You are a future Senator. You can't afford to be weak. Weakness is a sign of inferiority, and the Impyrean family is not inferior. One day you'll lead us, and you will squander everything your ancestors have won for you if you don't learn to show some strength! There are other members of the Grandiloquy slavering to take what we have thanks to your father's idiocy, covetous Grandes and Grandeés who would rejoice to see the Heretic's family fall! Your father is set on bringing this family to ruin, Sidonia. You will not take after him."

Donia sighed again, but I watched the Matriarch from where I lurked, forgotten, in the corner of the room. Sometimes I suspected I valued her wisdom more than her daughter did. After all, Donia had very little instinct for self-preservation. She had never required it, growing up sheltered as she had. The idea of enemies creeping in from the dark remained foreign to her.

I was not like her. I had not been sheltered.

As ready as I felt to tear apart the Matriarch and break her every bone when she slapped or pinched her daughter, I also recognized the cold, merciless wisdom of her warnings. I knew she believed she was acting for Donia's own good when she was harsh and brutal with her. Donia's father had placed the family in danger with his brash and opinionated conduct, and the Matriarch had the survival instinct to know it. She was the only one of the Impyreans who seemed to appreciate the threat that the Inquisitor's visit had posed.

The Matriarch hauled Donia from the room so she could critique her in front of Senator von Impyrean—hoping, no doubt, to show her husband that he was failing to teach his daughter sense. Usually I followed them, but today I had a rare opportunity.

Donia's retina was still scanned into the computer console.

One look, I thought, moving toward the console. It might be the only time I'd get to see the avatars of these aristocratic children for myself. . . . The one chance I'd have to gauge the dangers on Donia's horizon with my own firsthand judgment. I would avoid speaking to anyone.

I pulled on the headset, and disorientation swept over me as my environment shifted. I snapped into a new scene, Donia's avatar standing on one of a series of glass platforms—totally surrounded by bare space.

A swooping sensation filled my stomach. I swallowed hard, shaking off the feeling. As the strangeness receded, I grew aware of the other avatars. . . . The finest-dressed young Grandes and Grandeés of the Empire were scattered about me, laughing in a void that would kill them in real life, the starlight artificially bright to bring out the unnatural beauty of the computerized personas they'd chosen for themselves.

Acutely aware that I was using Donia's avatar, I slowly mounted the crystalline stairs between platforms, moving wherever my mind willed me to go, passing avatars that seemed oblivious to me. I remained silent, hoping to avoid attention. Apart from a few surprised greetings at Sidonia's abrupt return, none seemed the wiser.

Snatches of conversation floated to my ears:

". . . the most enticing intoxicant . . ."

". . . embedded lights have to be tastefully implanted or they cross the line from flattering to gaudy . . ."

". . . such a crude avatar. I can't imagine what she was thinking . . ."

Relief rippled through me as the vapidity of their conversations registered. After several minutes of eavesdropping, nothing reached my ears that alerted me to any unusual cunning or craft. These were children. Spoiled, vapid children from powerful families, glorying in their rank.

If there were vipers among these young Grandiloquy, they'd either cloaked themselves so cleverly that their fangs remained invisible, or they hadn't grown into their venom yet.

And then a voice spoke from behind me.

"How intently you observe everything, Grandeé Impyrean."

I jumped in real life, startled, because I'd believed myself at the edge of the crowd. I never would have missed someone creeping up like this in the real world, but my virtual senses were undeveloped, totally askew.

I turned to behold an avatar very unlike the others.

Very unlike them.

This young man was totally naked.

He smiled at my shocked appraisal, sipping languidly at a goblet of wine that had to mirror whatever his real-life body was drinking.

His avatar didn't resemble the others' sheer gleaming perfection. Instead, it was an exhibition of flaws: his hair a messy mop of copper, his eyes a startling, almost unnerving pale blue, his face lightly blotched by sunspots. *Freckles*—the word came to me as I stared. Even his muscles were unfashionably crafted, their slight asymmetry detectable after a hard moment's study. His beauty bots had failed him . . . or he'd earned his muscle through actual physical exertion.

Impossible. None of this empty-headed lot would willingly choose to exert themselves.

"And now, Grandeé," the young man noted, amusement in his voice, "you stare so intently at *me*."

Yes, I was doing that behavior Diabolics were known for: fixing him with an intent, predatory gaze, too unwavering for a real human's. My eyes were empty and absent of feeling unless I faked it. The Matriarch claimed this look made the hair stand up on the back of her neck. Even with Sidonia's avatar, my true nature had slipped through.

"Forgive me," I said, stumbling over the unfamiliar phrase. No one ever required apologies of a Diabolic. "You must realize it's difficult *not* to stare."

"Is my outfit so mesmerizing?"

That confused me. "You're not wearing anything."

"Ridiculous," he said, and he sounded genuinely outraged, as though I'd insulted him. "My technicians have assured me they programmed this avatar in accordance with the finest imperial fashions."

I hesitated, truly baffled—an unfamiliar, thoroughly unpleasant feeling. Surely he could just look down and see that he was naked. Was this humor? Was he joking? Others must have told him he was naked already. It had to be a jest.

I did not trust myself to mimic laughter; the sound did not come naturally to a Diabolic. So I settled on a neutral remark. "How fine a performance you put on."

"Performance?" A sharpness had stolen into his voice, but it smoothed away as he continued. "Why, whatever do you mean?"

How would Sidonia reply? My mind came up blank, so I forced a smile, wondering if I'd misread him. "Someone so eager to attract the eye is surely performing." A strange notion crept over me from what I'd learned of battle, of killing people. Feinting to one side often exposed weakness in an opponent's other side. "Or maybe you wish to draw the eye in one direction so no one will look in another."

An odd look passed over his face—narrowing his pale eyes, tightening his expression so the strong bones of his face became more prominent. For a moment, I glimpsed how he would look as a full-grown man. He reminded me of someone, though I could not say who.

"My Grandeé Impyrean," he said very mildly, "what intriguing notions you have of me." His avatar leaned negligibly closer to mine, unblinking. "Perhaps some who are close to you should embrace such tactics themselves."

The statement snapped me to attention, and a demand leaped up in my throat. What had he meant by that? Was that an insinuation? A warning? But I dared not ask. Donia wouldn't, and if I was wrong . . .

And I never had a chance to speak further. At that moment, several avatars descended upon us. They dropped to their knees before the naked young man, drawing his knuckles to their cheeks. Their simpering words reached my ears:

"Your Eminence, how wonderful you've paid us the honor of your visit!"

"What a magnificent outfit you've chosen for your avatar."

"Such fine clothing!"

Suddenly I realized how I recognized him. He resembled his uncle—the Emperor.

Here before me, naked and unashamed, was *Tyrus Domitrian.* Tyrus, the Successor Primus. . . . The young man who would one day inherit the throne.

Even I knew about Tyrus. The Matriarch and Senator von Impyrean chuckled over evening meals as they discussed his latest antics. He was the disgrace of the Empire because he was utterly insane. In his madness, he probably hadn't realized he was naked—and because of his rank, no one had dared to point it out to him.

No one but *me*.

I eased myself back from the scene, prickling all over with the awful realization of what I had done.

Long minutes after I had logged out, horror still beat through me.

I had thought to learn more of the spoiled young Grandiloquy, the better to protect Sidonia. Instead, I'd won her the attention of an infamous madman—one who had the power to destroy her.

3

"PERHAPS *some who are close to you should embrace such tactics themselves. . . .*"

Tyrus Domitrian's words rang in my ears over the following days, so much like a warning, and yet . . . And yet I wasn't certain whether I could credit the words of a madman.

The Domitrian family was called "sun-scorned" because so many of them died young, but the truth was one of those secrets everyone knew and pretended they did not: the Emperor and his mother had murdered most of his rivals for the throne. Tyrus was the only survivor from his immediate family. Perhaps that was what had driven him mad: witnessing the murders of most of his family by others in his family.

I told Sidonia of Tyrus's warning that evening after she'd returned from her father's study, but she shrugged it off and told me, "Tyrus is a lunatic. You can't take anything he says very seriously. And please stop worrying about whether he'll remember anything about your manner that was strange. . . . He never seems to recall anything from the forums." She gave a wry smile. "Too bad you can't always go in my place. Then I could skip socializing and spend all my time studying the stars."

She was in one of those strange dazes that came over her after poring over the old scientific databases with her father. Such evenings always left her dreamy, optimistic, those mysteries of the universe unfolding with answers for her.

Despite my desire to keep her focused on Tyrus's words, on the threats facing her, I couldn't help but give in when she patted the mattress next to her. I sprawled out next to her, an odd, warm feeling settling over me at the familiarity of this. From my first days at the fortress, Donia had nestled up next to me like a . . . like the way I'd imagine sisters did, to tell me things. Like two people, two friends, speaking to each other as equals. Stories, sometimes. Once she'd begun showing me images of letters, determined to teach me to read. I'd learned within a few weeks.

Today she related to me some of what she and her father had read in his study. "I told you how our bodies are made of tiny atoms, these things called 'elements,' didn't I? Well, it's most incredible, Nemesis. Do you know where those elements come from?"

She leaned her head against my shoulder, and I felt that odd indulgence I only felt toward her. "I couldn't begin to guess. Tell me."

"From within *stars*! Think of it." She stretched her arm up above us, marveling at it. "Every single bit of us comes from this process called nuclear fusion that only happens inside stars." She stifled a yawn. "Strange to even think of it. We are all of us but stardust shaped into a conscious being. The Helionics and the old scientists really do agree, even if no one realizes it."

I pondered her words, weighing them. If what she said was true, this bed, the fortress walls about us, everything came from those glowing lights outside the window.

Donia smiled at me sleepily. "I told you that you have the same divine spark I do. I was right all along, Nemesis."

She fell into a slumber at my side, and I watched her chest rise and fall for a while before slipping off her bed to my place on my own pallet. A strange pit settled in my stomach as I turned over her words. Donia had the temperance of her mother and the curiosity of her father, but she was kinder than both of them.

She could be great one day. She could do what her father never could and bridge those two factions in the Senate, unite the Helionics with those who wished a return of scientific pursuits . . . if she survived long enough to do so.

And she would survive.

A sharp determination spiked through me.

As long as I had breath in my body to defend her, *she would survive.*

I'd heard the tale from Sidonia and the vicar many times. It was one of the central Helionic myths. Centuries ago, there'd been five planets dedicated solely to storing all the accumulated scientific and technological wisdom of humanity on massive supercomputers. A great supernova had wiped away all of them at once. It was an important event to all Helionics. To them, the stars were the means by which the Living Cosmos expressed its will. The Interdict—the spiritual leader of the Helionic faith—declared the destruction wreaked by that supernova a divine act.

The Empire suffered a devastating blow. The Emperor of that day united his domain in common cause by declaring a Helionic crusade. The faithful systematically destroyed other repositories of scientific and technological knowledge. Education in sciences and mathematics was banned as blasphemy. And ever since then, no new technology had been created. The only starships and machines in existence were those constructed by human ancestors before the supernova. The starships still functioned because machines repaired them, and other machines repaired those machines, though all of them were deteriorating. This technology rested solely in the hands of the Grandiloquy.

The Excess, those humans who lived on planets and obeyed imperial rule, had to content themselves with only the machines they were lent by their Grandiloquy betters. Because it was blasphemy to learn sciences, they would never be able to build starships of their own.

The stability of the Empire hinged on this basic divide between the Excess and the Grandiloquy.

In rallying members of the Senate to challenge the ban on scientific education, Senator von Impyrean had threatened the very balance of power. The Inquisitor's visit signaled growing royal impatience with his actions.

It was a warning the Senator did not heed.

A transmission came from the Emperor one evening. The shouting that ensued jerked me from my sleep. Donia slept through it, unable to hear as well as I could. I slipped from my pallet and rushed down the corridor. Just inside the Senator's atrium, I found them: the Matriarch in her nightclothes, striking at her husband's arms, and the Senator cringing back from her blows.

"Fool! *You FOOL!*" she screamed. "Did you think no one would find out? You have destroyed this family with your actions!"

I closed the distance and wrenched the Matriarch away from her husband. Sturdy as she was, the woman proved no match for my strength. The Senator stumbled back, straightening his tunic.

"Idiot! Miscreant! We are all undone!" screamed the Matriarch, still struggling against my grip.

"My dear," said the Senator, spreading his arms, "there are things more important than whether one person lives or dies."

"And our family? And our daughter? We will lose everything!" She turned and seized me. "You." Her wild eyes found mine. "You, take me from here. I can't bear to look upon him a moment more!"

I cast the shaken Senator a long, measured look, then drew his wife away. The Matriarch shook where I held her. I led her like an invalid toward her chambers, where she promptly collapsed onto a chair, clawing at the fabric with her hands. "Undone . . . We are all undone. . . ."

"What's happening?" I demanded. "Tell me at once."

No one issued orders to the Matriarch, but if Sidonia's life was in danger, I needed to know immediately.

"What do you think is happening?" she said. "My husband made a move against the Emperor! The fool thought he was being crafty. The Emperor would not loosen his restrictions on scientific education, so my idiot husband took the roundabout way—and sent information from those ridiculous old databases to some members of the Excess."

"The Excess," I repeated, shocked. Was the Senator *insane*? "Is he hoping to be executed?"

Her lips twisted. "He's imbecile enough to believe he can force the Emperor's hand. He thinks that if the Emperor's worst fears come true and the Excess begin to develop their own starships, then the Emperor will insist the Grandiloquy follow suit and create new ones of their own. He thinks this will lead to the Emperor seeing matters his way." She gave a bitter laugh. "He miscalculated, of course. The Emperor had those Excess killed. He just notified us that he's aware of my husband's role in the debacle."

I drew a sharp breath. "Madam, the Senator is becoming a threat to all of you. Let me—"

"You are not to kill him." She launched herself to her feet. "Don't you

see it's already too late? Our necks are under the Emperor's blade now. It's done. And as usual, it falls to *me* to clean up my husband's mess." She closed her eyes, drawing several bracing breaths. "All we can do is wait. Whatever happens next, you and I will protect my daughter's interests—at any cost."

"At *any* cost," I agreed. If it meant I had to spirit Donia away from this place, I'd do so.

Her grip clamped my wrist. "You will tell Sidonia *nothing* of this. She has a social forum coming up. She *must* have no stain of guilt on her conscience. If she seems totally ignorant, word will filter back to the parents of the other children. If Sidonia knows of this matter, she won't be able to fool them. My daughter is many things, but a skilled liar she is not."

I nodded slowly. Donia's innocence was her only protection. Her ignorance would shield her as nothing else could, not even me.

"I'll tell her nothing," I assured the Matriarch.

Donia was no liar.

Luckily for her, *I* was.

She stirred when I returned to her chamber that evening, and rubbed at her sleep-clogged eyes. "Nemesis, is something amiss?"

"No," I answered soothingly. "I was restless. I left to exercise."

"Don't . . . ," she said, yawning, "pull . . . a muscle."

I made my lips smile. "That never happens to me. Go back to sleep."

And she did, plunging back into a slumber of total innocence.

I didn't sleep again that night.

The Emperor's next move came quickly. I received a summons to the Matriarch's chambers.

It was rare that she requested me directly. The summons put me on edge. When I stepped inside, I found the Matriarch lying in her low-gravity bed, a beauty bot coloring her gray roots and smoothing the wrinkles from her face. At a glance, the Matriarch looked to be in her twenties. False-youth, it was called. Only her eyes betrayed her age. No young person could look at me the way she did now.

"Nemesis. I was partaking of an opiate rub. Have some."

The offer surprised me. My eyes found the jar at her elbow. The opiate was a lotion applied to the skin. The Senator was fond of it, but it was rare for the Matriarch to partake. She scorned it as a weakness. The recreational chemicals she abused were those that made her sharper, more alert.

"It would be wasted on me."

She shoved away the arm of the beauty bot with an impatient gesture. "Of course, you Diabolics metabolize narcotics too quickly. You'll never know the thrill of a good intoxicant."

"Or the burn of a lethal poison," I reminded her.

She propped one high-cut cheekbone atop her fist as she studied me. The drug had made her pupils tiny and put an uncharacteristic sloppiness in her manner. I waited, painfully alert, to discover the reason she'd called me here.

"A pity," she said at last, dipping her finger in the opiate rub and smoothing it onto the pulse point of her wrist, "that you can't feel this. I suspect you'll shortly require it as much as I do."

"Why?"

"The Emperor has ordered us to send our daughter to the Chrysanthemum."

The words were like a fist to my gut, an impact that drove the breath from me. For a moment, all I could hear was my own heartbeat, thrumming wildly in my ears.

"What?" I whispered. "He wishes her to go to the Imperial Court?"

"Oh, this is how it works," she said bitterly. "My grandfather displeased him and he executed my mother. The Emperor rarely strikes directly—it's the influence of that wretched mother of his. The Grandeé Cygna believes in striking at the heart to inflict more damage. . . ."

Before I knew it, I had crossed the room. My hands closed on the Matriarch's shoulders—more solidly formed than Sidonia's, but no greater challenge for me to crush.

"Sidonia won't go." My voice was low and bestial, cold dark anger like ice within my heart. "I will kill you before I let her go to her death."

She blinked up at me, looking curiously unmoved by the threat. "We have no choice, Nemesis. He demands her presence within three months." Her lips curved in a sluggish smile, and she snaked a hand up to cup my cheek, her long fingernails pinching my flesh. "That's why I intend to send you to the Chrysanthemum in her place. *You* will be Sidonia Impyrean."

It took me a moment to understand her words, and even when I did, they made no sense.

"W-what?"

"How stunned you look!" The Matriarch's laugh was unsteady, but her pinprick eyes bored into mine, unblinking. "Must I repeat myself?"

"*Me?*" I shook my head once. I had no great fondness for the Matriarch, but I had always supposed her to be intelligent. *Sane.* "You truly mean to suggest that *I* will pose as Sidonia?"

"Oh, it will require some modifications, of course." Her gaze raked down my body. "All that's been seen of Sidonia is her avatar, which resembles her as little as you do. Your coloring, your musculature . . . We can fix that. As for your disposition, I've summoned my Etiquette Marshal to come teach you the essentials that she taught me in my own girlhood—"

I reared back a step. This woman had lost her mind. "An Etiquette Marshal can't give me humanity. You can tell just by looking at me that I'm not a real person. You've said so yourself numerous times."

The Matriarch tipped her head, her eyes glittering maliciously. "Oh yes. That cold, pitiless gaze . . . so utterly devoid of empathy. The very mark of a Diabolic! I rather suspect you'll fit in better than you expect in that pit of vipers." She laughed softly. "Certainly better than Sidonia ever would."

She rose with a swish of her gown, still smiling.

"The Emperor wishes me to send my innocent little lamb to the slaughter. No. Instead, I'll send him my anaconda."

4

SIDONIA was in her art room when I returned, sketching a bowl of fruit. My eyes picked out her frail form silhouetted by faint starlight spilling in from the windows. I gazed at this frail entity I was going to impersonate, trying to imagine myself posing as her.

It was total and utter madness. Like a tiger playing a kitten. No, not a tiger—something more monstrous and unnatural.

My thoughts reached back to the thing I'd once been, the creature I'd been before I knew my own name, before I was civilized.

I remembered the relentless hunger and fear. I remembered the anger at finding the world so confined, the walls a trap. I remembered when they released me with another creature for the first time. I was so hungry I killed it and consumed its flesh. All of it. I knew that was the right thing to do because my food rations increased after.

I didn't understand much back then, but I noticed cause and effect. When the weaker Diabolics were to be weeded out, they gave them to the stronger ones. Sometimes they simply gave us something pitiful and weak to kill, just to be certain we would show no mercy. I remembered the girl who was shoved into my corral with me. She cowered in the corner. It enraged me when she tried to drink my water, to eat my food. I killed her just like I killed everything else.

A girl who could have been Donia. Just as small, just as weak.

That had been my existence. Death and fear. I was afraid all the time. I feared the next second, the next minute, the next hour. Nothing beyond that, because there was nothing beyond that for me then.

My life had no shape or form or purpose or dignity until the day Sidonia materialized in it. There'd been no compassion, not a hint of meaning, until I was bonded to her and learned to love something for the first time. I had a future now, and it was *her* future. Donia was the reason for anything good or worthy about me.

Now I would have to *be* Sidonia. That seemed inconceivable, impossible. I felt revulsion at the mere suggestion that a creature like me could pose as something so wonderful as her—the mere suggestion was *profane*.

When she looked up from her drawing, she gave a small jump. "Nemesis! I didn't hear you come in. . . . Is everything okay?" Her worried eyes searched my expression.

She was the only one who could pick up on my subtle changes of mood. I swallowed against a sudden knot in my throat. "Yes. I'm fine. Everything will be fine," I told her.

I had no soul and very little heart, but what heart there was belonged to her.

The Emperor wanted Sidonia to come to him, so I would go in her place. There was no terror in that, no fear. I was grateful I could do so.

Posing as Sidonia would save her, so I had no alternative.

I would go.

◊

The Etiquette Marshal arrived within two weeks. Sidonia and I watched the ship slide through the bay doors of the fortress. Sidonia still didn't know about her summons to the Chrysanthemum, so she had come to her own conclusions about the new visitor.

"Mother must intend me to visit with another family," Donia muttered. "There's no reason she'd make me undergo etiquette training now. I hope she doesn't want to marry me off to someone."

She retreated to her chambers in protest when Sutera nu Impyrean arrived, but I did not. The Matriarch summoned me to her side. It was most important, after all, that I listen to and learn from this woman.

Sutera nu Impyrean was one of the Excess, and not one of the Grandiloquy. Unlike most of the Excess, though, she was a devout believer in the imperial system and had given her sworn allegiance and willing service to the Impyrean family. She'd earned the honorary "nu" appellation as well as the family name.

I waited with the Matriarch in her antechamber as the woman swept into our presence. For a moment, she stood in the doorway, jeweled hand clutched over her heart in a show of allegiance to the Matriarch, and just gazed at her old pupil lovingly.

My first thought was that surely this "Sutera" creature wasn't an *actual* human being.

Her skin wasn't a smooth brown like the color preferred by the Matriarch and the Senator, but rather a patchwork of different colors as though her beauty bots had neglected some areas and saturated others when administering melanin. Not only that, but her skin looked worn, like it was oversize for her frame, even creased and spotted in parts.

Even the Matriarch appeared taken aback by her appearance, just blinking at her for a moment. Then she reached out her hands. "My dear Sutera."

41

Sutera nu Impyrean dutifully crossed the room and took the Matriarch's hands, dipping to her knees to bring them to her cheeks. "Oh, Grandeé von Impyrean. You look as fresh as the day I met you. And me—look at the ravages of planetary living."

"Nonsense," said the Matriarch with a polite laugh. "A session with my own beauty bots, and a telomere treatment should—"

"Oh, no. The wind, the dirt, the solar radiation. It's a sun-scorned existence, dwelling planet-side." She rose to her feet, her lips quivering. "The smells, they're everywhere. And humidity! Oh, you can't imagine what it is like, my Grandeé. If it's too low, your skin cracks and bleeds, yet too high and every breath becomes an effort. It's positively bestial. Oh, and the way the planet-bound breed uncontrollably, so many families with two or even *three* children . . . No wonder they are always strained for resources! I could tell you such stories. . . ."

The Matriarch's smile had grown thinner, more brittle. "Perhaps you should not. Maybe you should rest up before we speak again to recover from your long trip."

The warning in the words was clear: Sutera nu Impyrean was not here as an equal, as a guest, but rather to provide a service. Fond as she was of her old Etiquette Marshal, the Matriarch was now tired of hearing her go on about herself.

The Etiquette Marshal remembered herself then. She lifted her chin, pride and professionalism evident in her demeanor. "Of course, I wouldn't dream of slumbering before I've seen Sidonia and learned what we have to work with. Will you fetch her—" Her eyes moved to me, and she stuttered into silence.

I stared directly back at her, and the Matriarch seemed amused, watching her old Etiquette Marshal try to figure out what I was. Clearly no Servitor, but no way was I Sidonia Impyrean.

"What manner of creature is this one?" Sutera said.

"This is Nemesis," said the Matriarch.

Sutera's eyes narrowed as she tried to connect the name with a type of creature. I watched her closely, because the Matriarch had told me the Excess knew of Diabolics—we were a vague, threatening myth to them. They wouldn't be familiar enough with the naming conventions or how we looked, so Sutera shouldn't be able to figure out what I was.

The Matriarch spoke again, pulling Sutera from her musings. "She is my daughter's most beloved pet and her close companion. Sidonia is . . ." She groped a moment for the proper way to characterize her. "She is a willful child, very given to strange quirks."

"I will drill them out of her."

"No, alas. She's not like I am. She's timid yet very stubborn. No, you will use Nemesis."

"Nemesis?" Sutera echoed blankly.

"You will teach Nemesis as you teach Sidonia."

"This one?" said the Etiquette Marshal, trying to fathom the meaning of this. "And the Senator wishes this too?"

"My husband's wishes are irrelevant. He is leaving this matter entirely in my hands. And you know my wish. Train them both."

The Matriarch looked at me, her eyes drilling into mine, our secret lurking dangerously between us. Sutera nu Impyrean was loyal to this family, and what was more, married to a low Viceroy on a moon in the next system. She posed no threat and could be trusted to conceal the minor secrets like the strange class of humanoid she'd encountered in her mistress's household. . . .

But sending me as hostage to the Emperor in Sidonia's place was far beyond that. It was directly circumventing the will of the Domitrian family. It was high treason.

The Etiquette Marshal could never know.

"Nemesis and Sidonia will both undergo your training. When Sidonia sees Nemesis learning and refining herself, then my daughter will curb her rebellious impulses and be inclined to cooperate as well."

"Train them both." Sutera looked me up and down. "I can do so, but . . ."

"You've objections?" said the Matriarch.

"None to your proposal, madam." She inched forward and nudged my arm tentatively. Then, emboldened, she began to grope up and down my arms. "Such a sturdy thing."

I stared down at the odd little creature manhandling me, as perplexed by her saggy skin and irregular coloring as she was by my muscles, my size.

"She is remarkably . . . large. I can't imagine her mastering the graces I'll require of her."

The Matriarch laughed. She took Sutera by the shoulder and led her toward the door.

"Have you ever observed a tiger? A true breed like the ones in the Chrysanthemum. Not those kittenish sorts like those in our cloisters. They're all muscle and sinew, with jaws powerful enough to break the strongest man, yet if you see them stalk prey, if you see them hunt— the sheer strength gives them more grace than the most refined of delicate creatures. That's Nemesis."

The next morning the Etiquette Marshal arrived in Donia's chambers. The beauty bots had been at work on Sutera the night before. She'd given herself a new look, a showcase of recessive physical traits— single eyelids instead of double eyelids, blue irises in place of her old amber ones, and a new shade of scarlet red hair. Her wrinkles had been smoothed down as well, but nothing could truly hide the wear. This had to be what the Matriarch meant when she said people "looked old."

Sutera nu Impyrean must have expected the worst, because her face lit up when she beheld Sidonia, a delicate beauty and a far cry from me.

"Why, Sidonia, this is a great honor. I remember when it was your mother's time to travel the stars—"

"I'm traveling somewhere?" Donia said shrilly. "I knew Mother wanted to send me away!"

Sutera paused, taken aback. "Eventually, you must leave this place. You can't expect to molder here your whole life."

"I don't want to go anywhere."

"But you have a role in the Empire."

"My parents have a role in the Empire. I don't care about politics at all."

Sutera frowned and withdrew her fan, waving it at herself. "Your mother warned me you were quite . . . stubborn."

I found my gaze riveted to the fan.

It's a weapon, whispered my thoughts. My eyes never left it. I couldn't help the thought. This tool could be for nothing else. Grandes and Grandeés of high birth weren't supposed to lower themselves by openly carrying weapons, so Donia had told me they concealed them in innocuous objects. Because Sutera had spent her life learning and teaching the habits of the Grandiloquy, she must have imitated this aspect too.

What could be within it? A blade? A whip?

"I think we'll start with your appearance," said Sutera, recovering. "Now I trust you know the basics of styling and self-modifications. You need to decide on your signature features."

Because I was the one who ultimately needed to know this, I interrupted, "What are those?"

Sutera slanted me an irritated look. Although she had to teach us both, she obviously considered my attendance a waste of her time and talents.

"In Grandiloquy circles, every physical aspect can and will be modified as fashion demands. No one knows anyone's true age, skin color, hair color, lip shape, weight, eyelid composition, or other features. A child of a great family has the means to modify his or her appearance at will, but one learns quickly that changing everything all the time is highly frowned upon. For instance, once must always display the gender you identify with. It's positively gauche to undergo chromosome resequencing just on a whim or for a party. Additionally, for delicacy's sake, a few features must always remain the same to keep you identifiable. Those are *signature* features. Mine, for instance, are my lips and my chin." She waved a graceful hand to herself, her plush lips curving into a smile. "I never change them."

I peered closely, studying her lips and chin, wondering what about these features made them her point of pride.

"I'll help you choose yours, Sidonia Impyrean." Then, after a moment, Sutera said, "And of course, yours, Nemesis dan Impyrean."

"She's not 'dan,'" Donia said suddenly. "You have to have noticed she isn't a real Servitor."

"That's ridiculous, child," twittered Sutera. "*Everyone* owned by your household is a dan, girl, Servitors and other humanoid creations alike."

Donia clenched her small hands into fists. "Nemesis is different."

"Is she?" Her eyebrows shot up. "She was bought by your parents. She was fashioned for you. She serves a function. She is no different from a Servitor in that respect; therefore, she is Nemesis dan Impyrean."

"Stop using the 'dan' or I'll tell Mother I'm through here," Donia said, her voice shaking with anger.

"Donia . . . ," I warned her. This wasn't the time to get worked up defending me.

But this was one battle Donia always fought. She tilted her chin up. "Nemesis Impyrean. That's what you'll call her in my presence."

Sutera gave a huff of laughter. "Oh, so now she's an immediate blood relation of yours?"

"That's not—"

"Well, while we're inventing things, let's just call her Nemesis *von* Impyrean and deem her head of your household, too. Have you any instructions for me, Madam von Impyrean?" Sutera dipped a mock bow toward me.

"I'm done," Donia announced. "I won't tolerate this."

And then she turned around and stalked out.

Sutera blinked after her, astonished. Then she murmured, "By the stars, this already looks quite hopeless."

I followed Donia, thinking grimly that if the Etiquette Marshal thought the Impyrean heir was utterly hopeless, it was a good thing she didn't realize she was actually here to drill graces into a Diabolic.

5

DONIA AND I both lay awake that evening. Donia was clearly stinging from the tongue-lashing the Matriarch had given her over storming out on Sutera nu Impyrean. As for me, I couldn't forget what Donia had said earlier about me.

Finally I broke the silence.

"I am."

"What?"

"I *am* Nemesis dan Impyrean."

"No, you're not." Donia twisted in bed to face the window.

I stared at her frail shoulder blades. "I am a creature owned by your household. I don't know why you deny this."

"You *are* Nemesis Impyrean." Sidonia sat up and glared at me in the starlight. "Simple as that."

"Only a fool would battle the Etiquette Marshal over so small a matter as my name. You know what I am. I am not a person. I'm a

Diabolic. This is just like when you tried to take me to the blessing! Haven't you gotten it through your head yet that I'm not like you?"

"But, Nemesis—"

"I don't want you doing this anymore!" I roared at her. Suddenly I was furious. "Stop dangling these things in front of me when we both know I can't have them! I can't get blessed, and I can't be called Nemesis Impyrean. There's no reason to teach me to read or to insist I am of the stars just as you are. . . . There's no dignity in trying to force me into a mold I will never fit."

"No dignity?" Donia echoed. Then tears sprang to her eyes. "I'm not trying to humiliate you."

Humiliation. I realized the word for the awful emotion that swelled within me whenever I saw the heliosphere and remembered that first meeting with the vicar. It was humiliation over my predicament, over *myself.* It had nothing to do with Sidonia, and I didn't wish to feel more of it.

"I am *not* your equal. I am your Diabolic and that is all. Never forget that again."

Her lips wobbled. Then, "Fine, Nemesis *dan* Impyrean. If I own you, then obey me and stop talking so I can sleep." With that, she whipped around in bed and buried her face in her pillow to muffle her tears.

I listened to her weep softly as the dark side of the gas giant formed a massive black gulf out the window. Donia was attached to me. It would hurt her once the Matriarch's deception was known. She would order me not to go to the Chrysanthemum in her place. She'd fear for my safety. I knew the pain my actions would cause her.

Yet her feelings for me mattered less to me than my feelings for her.

For a moment, the contradiction sat there in my mind as I stared up into the darkness. It had never occurred to me before that there was something profoundly selfish about devotion. Because of what I was, I was supposed to have no ego, no needs of my own. Even now, I only needed to sleep three hours a night, yet I lay here on the pallet by Sidonia's bed because *she* needed eight hours of sleep and felt comforted knowing I was here.

A Diabolic was meant to be utterly without self-interest where a master was concerned.

Yet it seemed I had self-interest. How could that *be* when I wasn't a real person? This humiliation, this selfishness, it was all unnatural in a creature like me. It shouldn't exist.

I turned on my pallet. It seemed easier just to listen to Donia's slow breathing and put it out of my mind.

And then I heard a footstep scuff outside the doorway. I instantly sharpened to alertness.

"Come out here, Nemesis."

The whisper was so soft, Sidonia never could have heard it even wide awake. I bounded to my feet and crossed the room, then stepped outside.

The Matriarch waited, arms folded. "Come."

She turned and I followed her soundlessly, unquestioningly. We retreated to her wing. I'd never seen the Matriarch's chambers and was surprised to find myself in a place of clunky relics. I stared down at a clumsy sculpture shaped like a doughy human form, chiseled entirely out of stone. Why would she value such a thing?

"That figurine was crafted before the first agricultural civilizations on Earth," the Matriarch remarked, seeing my scrutiny. "It's priceless."

"How could that be? It's not very impressive. Donia could carve a better one."

"You truly have no concept of value." She withdrew an iron box and slid the lid off. Out buzzed a swarm of tiny metallic machines, all smaller than the tips of my fingers. As I watched, needles emerged from them, one from each.

"Sutera was correct," said the Matriarch, studying me. "You are too large to ever pass for a natural human. We'll have to pare down your muscles and shave in your bones. That's where these machines come in."

I stared up at the bots swarming like the insects of the garden. The needles flashed in the light. "So many are needed?"

"They'll each inject a substance in a targeted area of your skeletal structure to begin the process of breaking down what's there. We need to shrink you rapidly. I told Doctor Isarus nan Impyrean they were for my husband—that he'd become unfashionably bulky and I wished to pare him down to a more attractive size. The doctor says this process needs to be repeated over many nights. It's fortunate we have three months before you need to be at the Chrysanthemum. We'll need them. Every two nights after Sidonia is asleep, you'll come here for your injections."

I drew a breath, not afraid, exactly, but my heart had picked up its tempo. Adrenaline. "This sounds painful."

"Excruciating, I'm told," the Matriarch answered. "I'd offer an anesthetic, but we know that would be quite useless."

For Sidonia, I thought.

I slipped off my outer garments and held out my limbs. I was determined she wouldn't see me so much as flinch. "Then let's begin."

The next several nights I dreamed of swarming insects, jabbing and stabbing and tearing into me. When I awoke, it was to a twisting, grinding sensation all through my arms, and faint swelling over my calves, my thighs. It was difficult hiding my discomfort from Donia. I felt drained, and every time I relieved myself, I knew molecules from my muscles were leaving me.

For Sidonia, I reminded myself, tugging down my sleeves to hide the splotches of bruising all along my arms. Each step hurt and my bones felt like large splinters, but I tried to hide my discomfort.

My faltering strength made me more normal, perhaps, but made things difficult during the next sessions with the Etiquette Marshal. Sutera nu Impyrean recovered from the insult of Sidonia storming out on her and began drilling us in the Grandiloquy gait—the style of approach one was to take when meeting the Emperor. Normally I'd find any physical task effortless, but my formidable strength was languishing. I perfected the gait before Donia, but just barely.

Then we moved on to the tedious task of mastering our chemical substances. This was most difficult for me because I felt none of their recreational effects, so I had to fake whatever effect they seemed to have on Sidonia.

"Remember," Sutera told us, her own eyes dilated as she swayed under the effect of the vapors she'd just inhaled, "relaxation without . . . what?"

"Sloppiness," Donia said, her voice slurred.

"Laughter without . . . ?"

"Mania."

"And always, always use moderation. Recreational chemicals, but never neurotoxic ones," Sutera said, twirling herself around in time with whatever chemical impulse she was following. "Addiction is a most unattractive quality. You'll need med bots to fix your brain, and in the meanwhile everyone will whisper about the scandalous Impyrean girl. And neurotoxins, well, the best med bots in the galaxy won't be able to fix you after you're through with those."

Donia didn't handle all the drugs well. Anything that gave her energy made her anxious and jittery. Anything that caused euphoria made her delirious. On one occasion, I had to force Sutera nu Impyrean to end the lesson so I could put Donia to bed.

Her weight was too much for me amid the muscle reduction treatments, so I drew her down the hallway with an arm over my shoulder.

Donia smiled at me lazily the whole way. She sprawled across her bed, grinning at me, trilling nonsense like, "You're glowing from within."

"I'm not," I assured her.

"You are. You glow like a star, Nemesis. A beautiful star." She reached out and ran her fingers over the skin of my arm, entranced. "You're a supernova."

"That would be very dangerous for you, then," I said, pulling off her shoes.

"You do have a divine spark." Her eyes flooded with tears that spilled over, happiness giving way to melancholy. "I wish you'd believe it."

I sighed. What a dreamer she was. "Go to sleep, Donia."

"I love you more than I can bear sometimes. You're a wonder and you don't even know it." She spoke so earnestly, almost sadly, that I reached out and put my hand on her arm, following a tender impulse I rarely felt, and only for her.

"Please go to sleep," I urged her softly.

"You're really wonderful, Nemesis. I wish you could see that. I wish I wasn't the only one who knew it. I wish you knew it."

What a strange idea she always insisted upon, *me* having a divine spark. I stroked her arm, disturbed by how much the notion appealed to me. What use did a Diabolic have for an afterlife? Donia would not require my protection once she'd perished. Wherever her soul journeyed next, the entrance was barred to a creature like me.

"You speak nonsense," I said. "Sleep now."

Donia drifted off, and I sat there listening to her breathe, trying to will away the odd weight in my chest. I had no use for delusions—still, it was strangely comforting to know that one person in this universe believed sweet lies about me. Were I less disciplined, I might even have taken pleasure in pretending to agree.

6

AFTER we passed through the array of chemicals, we moved on to memorizing dances. There were all types of them for different occasions, with varying gravitational conditions. I always took the lead because I was larger and stronger than Donia, but it made no difference which position I danced. I learned and perfected both just from watching Sutera nu Impyrean demonstrate them.

One day we practiced a rendition of one of the more complicated dances at the Imperial Court called the Frog and the Scorpion. The women performed the quick, lashing movements of the scorpion, and the men the great sweeping throws and repositions of the frog. After the first section of the dance, the scorpion was supposed to spend most of the dance entirely supported by the frog. The dance was performed in zero gravity, but the Impyreans had no zero-gravity dome. We made do as best we could in the low-grav chambers of the fortress, which only dipped to one-third standard gravity. I tossed Donia into the air and made to catch her as she soared down toward me, but she slipped from my arms.

It wasn't a disaster. She stumbled and caught my arm for balance, gaining it easily in the low gravity, but I experienced an ugly shock. My arms shook from the strain of throwing her even in the low gravity, and when Donia's eyes met mine, I knew she hadn't missed it either.

I'd been sleeping more on the nights I wasn't treated because my body needed rest to recover. That evening after I dropped off into slumber, Sidonia shook my shoulder to wake me.

That, in itself, was unusual. Usually I snapped awake instantly at the slightest sound.

"Are you sick?"

"Sick?" I mumbled.

"You've been so listless lately. And I didn't want to say anything, but your clothes are all looking baggy on you. Nemesis, you're wasting away."

"I'm fine."

"I think we should call Doctor Isarus here."

"All I need is sleep."

But Donia eyed me with more worry every day. The Matriarch finally decided I'd pared down my muscles and bones to an acceptably fragile size. No longer did I have the sturdy frame of a tiger, but something longer and leaner, like a lynx. I could at last pass for a normal girl. An unusually tall one, but certainly not a Diabolic.

I was relieved to end the injections. My strength rebounded more than I could have hoped. I couldn't comfortably exercise in the high-gravity chambers, but I *could* walk through them again. Even with my skeletal muscles systematically shrunk, I was far stronger than a normal human.

"This will make it more difficult for you," remarked the Matriarch as I lifted myself into a handstand over the arm of her couch. "It would have been easier if we'd weakened you further. You'll have to fake it. No more displays like this."

"You asked to see what I was capable of," I reminded her, slowly releasing my grip and lifting up an arm, balancing on a single palm. Though I wasn't so strong as before, my body was lighter, compensating somewhat for the muscular changes. "Should I have lied to you about my capabilities?"

She watched me lower myself toward the couch, then push myself back up. She looked strange and almost old when viewed upside down. "No more exercising even in private. There are eyes everywhere in the Chrysanthemum, and we'll have wasted all this treatment if you simply bulk up again."

I gazed at her from beneath my dangling hair, my arm burning gloriously, but . . . but shaky. It never used to shake when it held me up like this. "I know all of this, madam. I'm no fool."

"Starting now. Get down."

I swung my legs down and landed on the ground. My arm ached, so I rubbed it, holding her eyes. "Starting now."

I'd now experienced weakness, and between hiding my strength or possessing genuine frailty, I vastly preferred to hide.

So I would.

The Etiquette Marshal had found cosmetic work pleasing enough to perform on both of us to the best of her ability, not just Sidonia. Now Donia and I both possessed carefully applied glow and shade pigments under our skin, and even effervescent essence woven into our hair, nourished by the beauty bots into flowing, elaborate manes. We'd wake in the morning with our hair down, and with a single command, the mechanized stilts woven into our hair tightened and rearranged themselves, pulling our locks into any hairstyle we chose, no matter how elaborate. Another command, and certain threads morphed from a shade that matched our hair into glowing strands like gold or silver, or anything that might match a garment. They could even cast a light that artificially altered our hair color without the need of beauty bots.

Sidonia sat up several nights tinkering with the settings of the hair stilts, turning her hair blue, making it all stand on end, giving herself tight ringlets that temporarily morphed into her natural frizzier texture with a single electric jolt. Another jolt and her hair smoothed again. She then amused herself manipulating my hair, and decided raven brown with light waves was her favorite style for me.

Sutera nu Impyrean had finally exhausted her decades-old knowledge of the Imperial Court. Her final session, she showed us off to the Matriarch and Senator with pride. "And for the benefit of my Grandeé, I propose that your daughter Sidonia's signature features should be those beautiful eyes of hers, and you should darken her skin two shades to really complement them. Perhaps a lovely golden brown? Oh, and that long, graceful nose . . . Glorious. Whatever modifications she makes, she should always first think of how to draw attention to her eyes and her nose."

"And Nemesis?" the Matriarch said.

Sutera was silent a moment, caught off guard by the question. She glanced at me, startled to realize we were going to keep up the pretense of training me until this very end. She had no idea. "Well, I suppose she could pick and choose. She's completely symmetrical, as all humanoid creations are. It doesn't really count as true beauty when it's engineered in a laboratory, I don't think, do you?" She looked at the Matriarch for agreement.

The Matriarch just looked at her, waiting with mounting impatience.

Sutera said, "Well, engineered creatures are always meant to be physically inoffensive, so there's nothing objectionable about her other than her nose. *That* I'd fix. At least shave down that unsightly bump on the bridge."

I touched my nose, thinking of how I'd broken it more than a few times in skirmishes before I was civilized.

"The eyes and the cheekbones, I should say," the Matriarch chimed in, studying me. "What do you say, Sutera?"

"I . . . I suppose. Again, you can pick and choose any of them." Sutera laughed and patted her hair. "Perhaps I'd alter her coloring?"

"Hmm, yes," the Matriarch said. "We never add melanin enhancements to our humanoid creatures, just to keep them physically distinct from the family, but Nemesis could use some more pigmentation. Don't you agree?" She looked to the Senator.

For the first time, he chimed in, "Oh yes. Whatever it is you wish."

"I still can't envision in what capacity Nemesis would serve at the Chrysanthemum," Sutera said, "but whatever my Grandeé says, I would maintain you can't go wrong with eyes, and sharp cheekbones are highly in fashion, always."

Sutera moved on to exhibiting our knowledge. She fired question after question at us, and I answered everything correctly. Donia was distracted and nervous about the hawk-like scrutiny of her mother and faltered several times. The visages of the imperial royals were flashed before our eyes, and Donia mixed up Cygna and Devineé Domitrian.

But I missed nothing. That was all that mattered.

"Excellent," the Matriarch said, clapping her hands together elegantly. "Bravo, Sutera. They are well prepared."

"Very well prepared," the Senator agreed.

The Matriarch's eyes drilled into me, a ruthless smile on her face. Her anaconda.

Sutera glowed under her mistress's praise and dipped into an elaborate Grandiloquy gait until she was clutching her heart down at the Matriarch's feet. There, she drew the Matriarch's knuckles to her cheeks, and then the Senator's.

"I am so pleased to serve another generation of your family. I hope to see Sidonia's child one day when she has returned from the stars."

The Matriarch gave a brittle smile. "Yes, well, we will hope for the very best."

It wasn't until Sutera was dismissed that Donia turned on her parents. "Why are we really doing this?"

The Senator and Matriarch exchanged a look.

"I know something is going on," Donia said, her voice rising. "I thought perhaps you were going to marry me to someone, or send me away, but . . . but just now, I missed some answers. I *missed* them, Mother, and you haven't even scolded me. What's going on?" Tears sprang to her eyes. "Oh no, Father, are you in trouble? Am I being groomed to replace you?"

"No, no," the Senator said. "I am safe, my dear."

"I don't believe you! What's—"

"Oh," huffed the Matriarch. "Tell her the truth."

The Senator sighed, lines standing out on his face. He hadn't refreshed his false-youth since Sidonia's summons. "Very well. I am in some disfavor with the Emperor, but I'm not in danger—"

"You are, Sidonia," the Matriarch said.

Donia flinched back, shock blooming on her face. "M-me?" She threw me an urgent look.

I drew toward her. "Don't be afraid."

"*I* am in danger, Mother?" Donia cried.

S. J. KINCAID

"You've been summoned to the Chrysanthemum to face the Emperor," said the Matriarch. "To be held accountable for your father's idiocy, naturally. But you won't be going."

Donia wasn't a fool. She connected it all in a moment—the change in my appearance, my training alongside her, and now . . . this.

"No," she breathed.

The Senator stepped forward and clapped his daughter on her frail shoulder. "Your mother's got a plan to keep you safe from the Emperor. We won't send you. We would *never* risk you like that, sweetheart. Instead, we're sending her."

"No," Donia said again, shaking her head fiercely. She rushed over to me, clasped my hands. "No," she told me.

"It has to happen," said the Matriarch. "Sidonia, don't you see this is precisely why we ordered you a Diabolic? We bought Nemesis so we could protect our daughter. Our heir. And now, here Nemesis is, ready to help us do that."

"I am," I assured Donia.

"So . . . so Nemesis will be the Emperor's hostage?" Donia said, her grip tight on my hands.

"We hope she'll be a ward of the court. We hope she'll come to no harm."

"And if he summoned me for my death?" cried Donia. She turned to me. "What about then?"

"Then *you* will be safe with your family," I said simply.

"Sidonia," said the Senator, "see sense: Nemesis is not our heir. She's our property."

Donia looked between her mother and me, horrified. "No. No! I won't let this happen! Even if you fool them at first, what if someone finds out *what* you are?"

"How?" I said, looking down at myself. I didn't resemble a Diabolic anymore.

"They won't even imagine what she is," the Matriarch said. "They will never fathom someone could have the audacity to keep a Diabolic alive, much less send one in their daughter's place to the heart of the Empire. Nemesis is clever enough to pull it off. It's the perfect scheme."

"Unless she dies!" shouted Donia. She shook my arm. "You can't go. I order you not to go. I won't let you risk this for me! Mother—" She turned on her mother, tears streaking down her face, but she saw the cold, iron-hard look on the Matriarch's face, then her father's careless ease. "No! No, this can't happen!"

Donia spun around and ran from the room.

I gave her time to process what she'd learned, and then tracked her down in the fortress gardens right by the tiger enclosures. The large cats were gathered in a cluster at the edge of the enclosure, mewling for her attention, but Donia just stared at them like she couldn't see anything.

"How could you?" she said as soon as she noticed me. "How could you conspire with my parents behind my back? How could you keep this from me?"

"It wasn't particularly difficult," I said bluntly. "I'm a good liar. It's one reason I'll be more suitable for the Chrysanthemum than you."

"And what if you die? What do I do then?"

"If I die, it's because I've died in your place. You'll do what we all want you to do: you'll live."

"I hate you. I hate you so much!" Donia threw herself at me, hitting ineffectually with her fists. The blows glanced off my arm as I watched her, slightly baffled by the vehemence of her reaction. I began to worry she might hurt her hands.

Throughout the gardens, the restive animals stirred, rustling the greenery with their movement as they instinctively fled the noise.

Then she jerked back a step with a scream, tears on her face, and barreled for the door. There she collided with Sutera nu Impyrean, busy making her last round of the fortress before returning to her planet-bound existence.

Donia collapsed in her arms, bawling. Sutera stroked her shoulders unthinkingly, and then pulled away. "No, no, I can't indulge this. What have I told you about unseemly displays of emotion? Once you're at court—"

"I won't be at court!" Donia shouted. "Mother isn't sending me. She's sending Nemesis. That's why she's been in training with me."

My breath stilled.

"What?" said Sutera.

I stepped forward, trying to send a warning look Donia's way, but she was distraught and blind to what she was revealing to Sutera. "They're just like you. They think she's property. They're having her pose as me and risking her life like it's worthless!"

"That's treason," gasped Sutera.

The words settled in my mind like a death knell, and not for me. Sidonia had crossed a line telling Sutera nu Impyrean, and now I had to take care of this.

"Donia."

My voice, low and dangerous, seemed to break through her fit of rage. Donia stood there trembling all over, wiping at the tears on her face with her thin hand.

"Donia, we will discuss this. But first, Sutera, I have an explanation for you." I crossed the distance between us, and the Etiquette Marshal didn't think to resist when I tried to steer her out of the room with me. "You see, things are very complicated. . . ."

Donia stood rooted in place for a long moment, and then she suddenly seemed to guess what evil I intended. "Nemesis—no!"

I looked at her. I hadn't wished to do this before her eyes, but if she insisted, then let her watch.

Sutera glanced at me, puzzled and utterly guileless, a question on her lips. She never asked it.

I snapped her neck.

7

SIDONIA'S SCREAM pierced the air as I let Sutera drop to the ground, as I stepped back from the body. She rushed forward to cradle the Etiquette Marshal, shaking the older woman. "Sutera, Sutera!"

"What did you expect?" I said quietly.

Sidonia looked up at me, a horror on her face I hadn't seen since that first day before I was civilized. It was like she hadn't understood—truly understood—until that moment just what I was.

"Why?" Donia whimpered. "She helped us."

"Because you told her what she didn't need to know. She would have reported us, and then I couldn't have saved you." I drew a step closer and Donia scrambled back, still on the ground, staring up at me with abject terror.

This, I realized, was what I needed from her now. Not her adoration, not her fondness. I needed her to understand me. I needed her to finally see me the way her mother did, the way the vicar did—the way

I *was.* My throat tightened at the thought of seeing revulsion blaze over Donia's face when the blinders were finally ripped from her eyes, but I had to do it for her sake.

"Don't you understand, Sidonia?" I said. "I'm not your friend. Friends are equals. We're not. I'm not one of those tigers over there, genetically fashioned to be cuddly and bare my belly for you. I'm not here to be a companion. I'm a murderer, here to kill for you or die for you as needed. I'm your tool, your weapon—your property."

"No, you're not." Her lip trembled. "We're more than that."

"To you, maybe. But not to me. I can't feel what you want me to feel." I knelt down to hold her eyes and hammer in the brutal truth. "You *know* what I am. You know I killed one of your Servitors. Did you think I did that out of mercy? I would have done that if she'd been in the full bloom of health."

She shook her head but couldn't take her eyes from me. She was fighting with herself, not wanting to believe me—but now unable to deny it.

"I see you in the heliosphere," I said, looking inward, envisioning those services when we heard the vicar speak of Helios and the will of the divine. "You wonder about the universe. You ponder what created you, what your purpose is, what the meaning of your existence could be. . . . But I don't ask those questions, because I *know* the answers. I'm no child of your Living Cosmos, and there is no spark of the divine in me. Let me go and do what I was made to do. Don't fight this."

Donia rose to her feet, staring down at me like she'd never seen me before. She looked older than she ever had before, older than eighteen, like I'd just taken something more valuable than any material possession from her.

"I know you were forced to love me," she said, clutching her hands together. "But—but just because someone *forced* those feelings on you doesn't mean they're less important, or that *you're* less human. You're my best friend, and I love you, Nemesis. And my feelings aren't worthless just because I feel them for you. Maybe the fact that I love you whatever you are means my feelings are worth more because no one made me feel this way, it just happened. I choose to love you. I choose to care about what happens to you, and you can't take that away from me."

"You'll get over losing me."

"No, I won't." She shook her head, her eyes wide and haunted. "You mean more to me than you may ever understand, so let me tell you something right now: if you die out there, I'm going to follow you."

"I don't understand."

"If you go to the Chrysanthemum and they kill you, then I will throw myself out an airlock. I swear it."

Anger swelled in me. "Don't be stupid."

She let out a short, crazed laugh. "You don't care about what I feel, you don't care about anything but my safety, I understand that. So here it is, here is what will happen: I won't be safe if *you* aren't. You will survive or *I* will die."

I launched myself to my feet, wondering why she was saying something so stupid, so irrational. She looked at me with a sort of crazed triumph like she'd beaten me somehow, so I hissed, "Take back those words."

"No."

I seized her by those frail shoulders, those bones like bird bones that I could break and shatter so easily, and shook her so hard, her head jerked back. But still there was that insane conviction on her face, even as I roared, *"Take it back!"*

"No!"

And as her eyes held mine, wide and glorious and so self-destructively devoted to me, to me of all things. I felt a helpless surge of rage, because

I knew there was no way to tear this from her. I could break her in half, I could stomp every bone in her body to dust, and I still would never vanquish that resolve, that madness.

That was when I realized for the first time that Sidonia Impyrean—meek, fearful, shy, and gentle—could be indomitable.

So I released her, and she stumbled back several steps, still with that infuriating stubbornness and resolve on her face.

"All right," I said.

She straightened, staring at me with hope.

"All right," I said again. "I'll come back alive. I will do everything in my power to preserve my own life as I would preserve yours. I'll do it or I'll destroy this Empire trying."

Silence. I sensed something strange had shifted between us, perhaps forever. The illusions were gone, our truths bared, and yet I felt like I saw her and she saw me, and perhaps in some ways we were equals for the first time. My strength had always exceeded hers and her importance had exceeded mine, and yet here we were, evenly matched at long last. My life now held the same value as hers—because her life depended upon mine.

Sidonia straightened her garments with dignity. She looked down at Sutera, and her face tightened. Then she forced her eyes away like she couldn't stand the sight any longer. "Your nose," she said. "Make your nose your signature feature. Don't fix it. It's uniquely you."

I touched the scar tissue on the bridge of my nose, that singular mark of so much violence in my past. "How would the Grandeé Sidonia Impyrean end up with a nose like this?"

There was a sad smile on her face. "You're a good liar, Nemesis. Make something up."

8

THE SHIP that arrived to take me to the Chrysanthemum was manned by the Excess. They swarmed out like an unruly mass upon docking, their chaotic voices dominating the space.

". . . so this is the Impyrean domain . . ."

". . . always wondered what it looked like . . ."

An urgent tugging at my hand pulled my attention over to Donia. She met my eyes, and a strange emptiness filled me. This might be the last time I saw her.

It was certainly the last moment that I would be me. As soon as I stepped into the view of those Excess, *I* would become Sidonia Impyrean.

"If I could pick anyone in the universe to be me," whispered Donia tremulously, "it would be you, Nemesis."

As the last days whiled away, she'd thrown herself into helping fashion me into a better Grandeé with more enthusiasm even than her mother. We decided on my new hair color together—raven brown—and my new bronzed skin color. She chose the arched dark eyebrows and long black lashes implanted over my newly green eyes. Endless tips flowed from her about how to be a better Impyrean heir. We sat up nights as she related every inconsequential detail she could scrape from her memory about those Grandiloquy children she'd interacted with over the galactic forums, just in case I encountered those same people at the Chrysanthemum.

And, of course, I kept my nose as it was.

Donia cupped my cheeks. "You're breathtaking." Worry stole over her face. "Please come back."

I placed my hands over hers. The one person in this universe who defined me. "I will."

Then the voices swelled, and we broke apart. The Matriarch glided in, followed by a retinue of Servitors. She alone was seeing me off. The Senator had already bidden me a cursory good-bye.

She took me by the arm. "Come now, *Sidonia.*"

She'd started calling me by that name so I'd adjust. I wasn't so careless as she believed, and the name felt wrong in Donia's presence. I looked back at her as the Matriarch led me away.

"Remember what I've told you of the Excess," the Matriarch whispered in my ear.

"I remember."

The Excess weren't all like Sutera nu Impyrean (whose death we blamed on a mishap with the animal pens, whose body we shot into the nearest star because the Matriarch knew she'd want burial in the Helionic way). They also weren't like Doctor Isarus nan Impyrean, the family physician. Those two had been Excess who'd believed in the imperial system, who'd become a part of it and earned a place in it. They'd faithfully served the Impyreans and proven their loyalty, so they earned the appellations nu and nan, signifying their affiliation as male and female servants of the family.

These Excess, however, were being paid for their services. Their loyalty was not to the Impyrean family, but to the currency they'd earn from serving the Impyreans.

They were called "employees."

They were being employed, specifically, to escort me to court.

"The Grandiloquy controls all the most powerful technology, Nemesis," the Matriarch had explained to me this last week. "We have the starships and the weaponry, so we are the government connecting one star system to another. We *are* the Empire."

I knew most inhabited planets weren't optimal for human life. Few were self-sufficient, and most all of them depended upon resources from space—which the Grandiloquy totally controlled. They also depended upon technology lent to them by the Grandiloquy. In this manner, the Excess were forced to serve the Grandiloquy merely to survive.

A hush fell over the employees as the Matriarch and I rounded the corridor. The Excess stood in scattered groups, facing one another yet looking back at us like we were an alien species. I stared back at them, feeling the same way.

Just like Sutera nu Impyrean, all but the youngest of them were rife with physical defects from planetary living conditions and exposure to unfiltered sunlight. Marks on their skin, those lines called "wrinkles," excess flesh or sometimes such a deficit of flesh their bones were visible through their skin. They all had tonsures—the shaving of the very center of their scalp, leaving the rest of their hair to grow around the bald patch like a crown. It was a curious look, especially on the longer-haired women, many of whom had braided their hair to wrap in a circle around the bald spot.

Tonsure was mandatory for any Excess who wished to seek employment with an imperial family in space. It signaled that they'd converted to the Helionic faith of the nobility, or at least pretended to. If they were accepted as employees, they then received a tattoo of the family sigil on the bald patch, and from then on they had to display the sigil until they were dismissed.

There was something about the way they looked at the Matriarch, at me, that warned me there was no fondness here. They had to resent their position, forced by the Grandiloquy monopoly on technology to adopt an unwanted religion, to serve for survival. I reminded myself that these Excess had all been thoroughly screened for Partisan leanings, so they shouldn't be a threat. Partisans, after all, were those planet dwellers among the Excess who believed they would be better off freed from the Empire. They objected to the Grandiloquy's suppression of knowledge. Being a Partisan was the most dangerous treason possible, and one of Partisan leanings would never be allowed so close to the Impyrean heir.

The Excess didn't bow or kneel. They stood straight and stared back at us as the Matriarch inspected them. Some glanced uneasily at the Servitors carrying my belongings. It was well known that most Excess disliked Servitors.

The Matriarch favored them with a stiff smile and a greeting. "Hello," she said. "It is good to see you. Show me your sigils." Then, "Please."

That must have been a hard word for her to say. She never needed to use it with anyone at the fortress.

The Excess dipped their heads to display the sun-rising-from-behind-a-planet tattoo that served as the Impyrean family sigil. I saw fists curl, jaws stiffen. Some of the employees looked at one another as the Matriarch checked each of them for the sigil, and a prickling moved up my spine. Resentment hummed thick on the air.

I'd been puzzled earlier, wondering why the Matriarch bothered hiring Excess as an escort to the Chrysanthemum. They'd struck me as troublesome. Living human beings weren't necessary for *anything*, after all. Machines could be used to control a ship, to navigate, and even to repair the machines that controlled ships and navigated. Machines were used to fight wars, to develop new medicines, to contrive treatments. That was the reason humans didn't need to know how the machines operated, or the science behind their construction. The system sustained itself.

"We use employees because the Excess are expensive and perilous, Nemesis," the Matriarch had said. "Power over a machine is a given. Power over Servitors is natural if you are rich enough to purchase some. Power over the will of a member of the Excess, though—people who serve you because you have purchased their loyalty, and serve you perhaps against their inclinations or their personal liking—why, that's the most dangerous and unpredictable power of all. It attests to our strength as a family when we have a retinue of employees to escort you to the Chrysanthemum. If you didn't have employees in your escort, those at court might begin to whisper that this family couldn't afford them, or worse, *control* them. You will dismiss them from your service as soon as you've been presented to the Emperor."

Now the Matriarch finished her inspection. "Thank you, employees. I'm sure you'll serve my daughter well." She turned to me and reached out her hands. "Be safe, my daughter. May you find your way in hyperspace. Try not to die."

I took her hands, sank to my knees, and pressed her knuckles to my cheeks. "I will try." Then, that word, so strange and alien on my lips: "Mother."

We locked eyes, the Matriarch's sharp gaze and my own, for a split second as our mutual conspiracy unfolded. And then we took leave of each other. The employees cleared the way to admit me onto their borrowed starship. The appointed Servitors of my retinue followed behind me, hauling trunks of clothing and other possessions as befitted Sidonia Impyrean on her journey to the Chrysanthemum.

If I didn't have superior hearing, I might not have caught a few whispers the Excess exchanged as the airlock sealed, things they thought I would never hear:

"That's a callous good-bye," someone said. "Guess she won't miss her daughter much."

"I'm telling you, aristos are cold-blooded. They don't feel things like normal people do. Too many genetic mods over the centuries."

I didn't betray what I heard, but the words almost made me smile— an impulse that surprised me, because humor didn't come naturally to me. The simple fact was, these Excess really had no idea how callous and genetically modified I truly was.

I had only two goals going forward: to fool people into thinking I was Sidonia, and of course, to try not to die.

9

I SPENT the voyage confined in my chambers with the Servitors, reviewing everything I'd learned about the Imperial Court. I could imagine Donia pacing restlessly, waiting for the moment my ship left hyperspace and I could send her a message again.

I made myself lie in bed for eight hours just like Donia would. I made myself eat as much as Donia required. I fought the urge to move, move, and somehow get my muscles working.

It was easy forswearing exercise back when I'd been weakened by the muscle reducers. Now I felt like I was going to burst with the energy I wasn't using. I dared not indulge, or I'd undo all the work I'd put into shrinking.

Sidonia had always told me space was vast beyond comprehension, but I hadn't understood it until now. We were moving through hyperspace at an incomprehensible speed and our journey still took weeks. We were traversing but a sliver of the known galaxy. Outside the window loomed a void of darkness without stars.

Things occasionally went wrong in hyperspace. It was a rare but horrifying event for the Empire when a starship broke apart in hyperspace, and in years past, the Emperor always recognized the tragedy and issued orders for a galaxy-wide mourning period. As the tragedies grew more common, though, they became more of a secret. Terrors to hush, suppress. Senator von Impyrean believed the disasters took place because the starships were growing too old.

Such disasters didn't merely kill the people onboard the ships, they damaged *space itself.* A death zone would form in that area of space, which devoured any starship or planetary body near it. It was called "malignant space."

And malignant space seemed all the more threatening to me when I stood here, staring out into unending black, knowing at any minute something could go wrong and leave us to the same fate.

The drop out of hyperspace came as a relief. It was abrupt: the darkness simply snapped away, and light poured into the windows as we ripped into the sextuplet star system where the Chrysanthemum awaited.

There was a knock at the door, and in poured several of the employees. "Grandeé Impyrean, we've reached the Chrysanthemum. They've authorized us to approach."

"Good." Then, "Thank you," I added, remembering the Excess valued pointless courtesies.

The employees glanced at one another, and then the man in front ventured, "Do you mind if we watch from your window?"

I had one of the few view ports on the ship, as was my due.

I stepped aside so the Excess could join me in watching the approach to the Chrysanthemum. "Very well."

The starship jostled violently as the gravitational forces kicked in.

The window flooded with the blinding glare of three pairs of binary stars, all orbiting the same gravity center.

Soon a dark mass began to emerge against the backdrop of blinding white, and the ship shook its way through a gauntlet of charged weaponry floating through space, spread through the system like teeth waiting to tear into us.

"My God, we're actually here," murmured one of the woman employees. "We're going to see it."

The others nodded in awed silence. The vessel shook lightly about us the whole approach. The six-star system had such chaotic gravitation forces that there was only a narrow channel of space safe enough for incoming ships. If a great armada ever tried to attack, one of the employees explained to another, they'd have to fly in virtually single file, or get ripped apart by the stars in this system before they could approach.

"Who would ever try to attack?" I asked them.

They looked at me, surprised, since I hadn't spoken to them of my own initiative yet. Then the answer occurred to me: other imperial families.

Families like the Impyreans.

These defenses stopped any notion they might have of sweeping in and cutting off the head of the Empire by killing the Domitrian royals.

The employees knew better than to say that out loud. The man just laughed with discomfort and pointed out the window. "Well, obviously no one would."

We trembled past thousands of energy panels and stationary weapons, and then the first pylon of the Chrysanthemum slid into view. A murmur of awe stole through the employees at the sight of the Empire's greatest structure.

The Chrysanthemum was shaped like the flower for which it had been named. It was made of thousands of vessels that joined up in the very center, where the largest heliosphere in the Empire loomed. The centermost sector was made up of smaller, gently curved pylons about a great living space. It was a single vessel called the *Valor Novus* and it served as the domain of the imperial royals and visiting high officials. It also contained the Senate chambers and war rooms. All of the longer pylons were part of connecting vessels, branching out from that central starship and fanning out kilometers into space from the interior.

The Chrysanthemum in itself was massive enough to exert a gravity force without any artificial help. Every section could separate from the whole, making it possible to disassemble the entire imperial center into two thousand individual vessels.

The history I'd hastily read and the lessons I'd learned over the last few months all rang in my head, and I couldn't help thinking of what I was doing: I was a Diabolic ready to march into the heart of the Empire, where my very existence merited death. I was going to pretend to be the daughter of the Great Heretic Senator before a court of politicians who wished to destroy him. I had to deceive the minds capable of ruling over a place that looked like *this*, and if I failed, Sidonia might follow through on her threat and die along with me.

There was a dancing in my stomach that I hadn't felt in many years.

I knew at once what it had to be: fear.

Do not tromp, but glide gracefully like a swan. . . .

Sutera nu Impyrean's words drifted back to me as the strongest of my Servitors struggled to heave up the ceremonial gown I needed for the entrance to the Emperor's presence. There were employees waiting by the door to escort me, so I didn't dare relieve the Servitors of the burden.

Ceremonial gowns were intricate garments woven of metal. They compressed unmercifully about the waist, and consisted of enough gold

to weigh twice as much as the Grande or Grandeé wearing it. The ceremonial gown required an underskirt consisting of an exosuit—thin
metal bands that clasped the limbs and spine and served as a mechanized skeleton to do all the heavy lifting.

With my superior strength, I could manage without it, but again, I
had to put on a show of weakness I didn't have. So I told the Servitors
to hold it up for me, playing the perfect imperial heir letting Servitors
assist me in fastening the ceremonial garb about me. The cool metal
enclosed my skin.

Once I was wearing the elaborate outfit, I told a Servitor to hand
me the controls to the stilts in my hair. With a flick, I rearranged my
locks in a series of elaborate braids, and waited as precious gems were
woven in between the strands by another Servitor.

I surveyed the effect in the mirror. I didn't recognize this person
staring back, tall and narrow, gleaming in the ceremonial gown, raven
hair pleated and bejeweled, her skin a clear bronze lit flatteringly
wherever Sutera nu Impyrean had pigmented it.

Only the nose remained of Nemesis dan Impyrean.

I touched it to remind myself that I was still me, aware of the employees shifting their weight in the doorway, eager to get on with it.

"I'm ready," I spoke to the air.

I'd have an escort of six employees and a tail of eight Servitors
behind me for my walk from the *Valor Novus*'s docking bay to the presence chamber. As the future Senator von Impyrean, I was important
enough for the Emperor to receive in person—even in disgrace.

Whether he'd receive me with an immediate execution . . . that
remained to be seen.

10

EVEN WITH the exosuit, gliding gracefully like a swan was tricky beneath hundreds of pounds of metal, mostly because Sutera had also stressed the importance of keeping a serene, relaxed countenance while doing so. Being serene and relaxed was as unnatural to me as humor.

I forced myself to stare straight ahead as my escort led the way, though my eyes and my instincts wanted me to survey everything, everyone in the *Valor Novus*. This vessel was the centerpiece of the Chrysanthemum, the largest in size, and attached directly to the massive heliosphere. At one point, I couldn't resist peering overhead, and what I saw stopped me in my tracks.

Open sky.

The room was so large, the blue tint of artificial atmosphere drowned out my view of the overhead windows and ceiling. One pair of binary suns shone down through what had to be windows I couldn't see, and for a disconcerting moment, I felt like I had somehow ended up on a planet, not on a ship. Never before had I stood in a room where the ceiling was not visible. None of my survival skills and instincts had been cultivated for such an open and endless space. The confinement of the ceremonial gown began to grow stuffier, tighter.

The employees were looking at me questioningly, so I forced myself to move, step by step, and ignore that yawning illusion of sky. Then the great doors before me parted and I was admitted to the presence chamber of the Emperor.

All the anxiety within me calmed as my eyes adjusted to the presence chamber, as the multitudes of people came into view. They parted to clear a path to the very front of the room by the great, yawning windows overlooking four of the system's stars, and I knew with a glance which great personage was Emperor Randevald von Domitrian, because the eyes not focused on me were trained on him, including those of his mother, Cygna Domitrian—just to the right of him.

First, the Grandiloquy gait.

My employees moved to the side as well, clearing room for me to close the distance to the Emperor. Three steps, kneel. Just as Sutera nu Impyrean had instructed, I raised my eyes each time my hands touched my heart, and looked at the large man with long blond hair that trailed down about his shoulders like a mantle.

The journey to the Emperor's feet felt endless, and whispers and murmurs formed a sea of noise rippling about me as the other Grandiloquy watched. There would be time to assess them all later. For now my focus was the single man who could determine whether I would live or die.

Then I was there, kneeling before the Emperor, his black eyes fixed down on me from a face that was a study in false-youth, appearing no older than twenty but for that cold, cynical gaze. His body was towering and slab-like, the skin of his hands soft and elegant as they rose before me. I took them to press his knuckles to my cheeks.

But at the last moment, the Emperor tore his hands from my clasp and seized me by the hair.

The instinct to strike rushed up hot and fierce within me, but I held myself in an iron clasp of restraint, reminding myself that this was about Sidonia, not me. I remained as passive as a rag doll when he yanked my head backward, his eyes raking over my face.

"So," the Emperor spoke, his voice amplified to reach every ear in the room, "this is Sidonia Impyrean. How fares your father?"

The question was spoken lightly, benignly. Only his unforgiving hand, tangled in my hair, making my neck strain where he'd yanked my head back, warned me there was nothing gentle or harmless in this inquiry.

"He's well, Your Supreme Reverence." I held his eyes, hoping my gaze would not reveal the coldness of my heart. "He was so very honored you invited me to court."

The Emperor's lips curled, bitterness in his ageless face. "It was no honor, girl. Your father has committed grave heresies."

Laughter swept across the room behind me. I was taken off guard. I'd expected the true reason for my visit to remain an open secret, since that was what the Matriarch had expected.

She'd been wrong.

"I . . ." I groped for something Sidonia might say. I came up blank. So I managed, "I hope not to offend Your Supreme Reverence as my father clearly has."

"That remains to be seen. Your life will be surety against any further misdoings." The Emperor released me abruptly.

I wasn't here to die, then. Relief washed through me. The Emperor studied my retinue.

"Tell me, Grandeé Impyrean, which of these is your favorite Servitor?"

I blinked. A favorite Servitor? I'd never thought of them in terms of distinct people. All they did was obey commands. They had no capacity for individual actions.

"Come now," rebuked the Emperor, his lips twisted with humor. He pulled me up with a hand under my arm. "Everyone has a favorite pet. Behind me are three of my favorites, Hazard, Anguish, and Enmity."

For the first time, I glanced beyond the Emperor and studied the two men and a woman standing like guards behind his throne. They were all gazing directly at me, the unflinching looks on their faces like those of alert predators, muscles straining their skin, strength in every square centimeter of their bodies.

An ugly shock rippled through me.

Those were Diabolics. All of them.

The Emperor meant to frighten me with the sight of them, and it worked for reasons he couldn't guess. A terrible paranoia swept over me that their scrutiny stemmed from the fact that they could sense what I was, just as I could see with a glance what they were. There was something animalistic about them, like they were a pack of lions waiting in readiness, and I imagined they saw the same thing in me. One male was dark with rich brown eyes, the other was a black-haired man with eyes of bright blue. The female resembled me in my natural state, colorless and pale-eyed. It wouldn't surprise me if she shared much of my genetic code. We'd likely been created by the same breeder.

My gaze flashed back up to the Emperor's, my heart beating urgently. Had they guessed what I was upon first sight?

"I have a soft spot for them all," the Emperor said, eyes drilling into mine. "I couldn't bring myself to be rid of my own Diabolics, and as the Emperor, I felt at liberty to make an exception. My life is more precious than the common man's, after all."

"Certainly it is, Your Supremacy."

"Now, your favorite Servitor. Which one?"

He couldn't know what I was. He couldn't. His Diabolics would already have killed me. That's what I'd do if someone else's Diabolic neared Donia. I pointed at a Servitor quite at random.

"Excellent," the Emperor said. He crooked his finger at her, and the Servitor stepped forward obediently. They couldn't help but obey. "Tell me, Grandeé Impyrean, what is this Servitor's name?"

For an alarming moment, I came up blank. Then I mercifully recalled it.

"Leather," I said. "Her name's Leather dan Impyrean."

"Leather. That inspires an idea. Give Leather this blade," he told me, offering me a dagger.

Confused, I took the dagger from him and passed it along to the Servitor. I noticed that the entire court had fallen into silence, a strange anticipation like electricity on the air.

The Emperor placed a hand on my shoulder and whispered in my ear, "Instruct her to begin skinning herself. Starting with her arms."

I looked at him, trying to fathom what sort of demand this was. He could simply order Leather to do it herself.

The Emperor gazed back at me, his false-youth face merciless and smiling. "Do it."

So he wanted *me* specifically to be responsible for what lay ahead. Very well.

"Leather, cut the skin from your arms," I told her.

Leather obeyed. She began whimpering in agony. Then the Emperor relayed instructions to move on to her legs, and I told Leather to do so. Her skin came off in bloody peels, tears streaming down her face as she sliced at herself.

All the while, the Emperor watched my face.

It struck me suddenly that I needed to be reacting somehow. Brutality didn't faze me, because of what I was, but it would bother Sidonia.

It would bother *any* normal person. I sensed, though, that any show of fear would feed the Emperor, somehow—and perhaps inspire him to repeat this for his own pleasure.

What would Sidonia do?

I watched Leather shrieking now as she sliced her own skin off, but still obeying, her cries blotting out sounds in the court. I tried to figure out the reaction I should display. Many of the Grandiloquy looked ill. Others were discreetly averting their eyes. Still others gazed straight through Leather as though they could not see her at all. And a few others—they seemed to enjoy the sight.

Sidonia wouldn't stand here stoically.

She would yell at the Emperor and defend Leather. She couldn't stand helpless creatures being mistreated. Of course, *that* was why I was here, not her.

What else might Sidonia do? What else?

She would cry.

I couldn't cry. I wasn't even capable of it.

There was only one course of action I could take here.

So I rolled my eyes back in my head and allowed my body to go limp as though the horror had overcome me. The ceremonial garment was so heavy it gave a hearty clang when I struck the ground, and there I lay, every muscle limp, my breathing slow, the picture of overwhelmed frailty. Quite neatly, I'd put myself beyond the reach of the Emperor's brutality and neutralized its effectiveness. Perhaps this would work.

There was a split second of silence, and then a blast of laughter. "Did we overwhelm the Impyrean girl?" the Emperor crowed. "I suspect so. Where are her employees? Come forward now, don't be shy." His voice grew teasing. "No, I don't intend to skin any of you. The festivities are over."

All good humor now, the Emperor instructed them to see me to my new chambers.

I kept my eyes closed, playing the unconscious, overwhelmed thing. I was too heavy to carry in the exosuit and ceremonial gown, so my employees stripped off the heaviest parts. The mewling of Leather was continuous, and while I was prepared for my departure, I couldn't help opening my eyes a fraction to peer toward the Servitor, irritated to realize the Emperor was just going to leave her in this state.

She was crumpled on the ground, having lost so much blood she could no longer stand, her gown soaked red. The other Servitors walked past her as though she wasn't even there. It struck me how profoundly helpless a creature became robbed of free will. They couldn't even make decisions in their own self-defense. The simplest insect had that capacity, but not them.

"Will she never cease that infernal noise?" demanded a young man, striding forward to survey Leather.

I recognized him at once.

He was tall and broad-shouldered, with short coppery hair. Tyrus Domitrian's rank was betrayed only by the number of eyes fixed upon him. Just like his avatar, he looked imperfect—freckled and cleft of chin. Unlike his avatar, the madness made his eyes almost glow. Every pore of his body radiated a frantic energy, almost a delight in the scene about him.

"Why, this is so undignified. Stop this whimpering at once," Tyrus said to Leather, as though the Servitor was in any state to hear him. "It's not fitting for this company."

Leather was too lost in pain to hear him and obey, so the young man rolled his light blue eyes, pulled a slim, cylindrical weapon from his pocket, and fired a flash of light at her chest. She grew still. I knew at once that the Servitor was dead.

"Tyrus!" rebuked the Emperor. "What have I told you about killing people?"

"Yes, yes, ask you first, Uncle," grumbled Tyrus, sweeping into a bow. "But in my defense, she was irritating me."

"Oh, you," said the Emperor fondly. "She was dead anyway. Why hasten it?"

Tyrus tilted his head up, his pale-lashed blue eyes gleaming, his lips curling up in a lunatic's smile.

I recalled everything I knew of Tyrus Domitrian. I'd taken an especial interest in Sutera nu Impyrean's discussions of him after having met the madman's avatar. He was one of the great jokes of the Empire. The safest thing Randevald von Domitrian had done was appoint his lunatic nephew to be his heir. Even Randevald's staunchest foes wouldn't dare assassinate him for fear of his successor.

My eyes had opened wider without my realizing it. I only knew it when I caught gazes with a girl across the room who was staring directly at me with a cynical look on her face—the only one paying attention to me, it seemed. Her curly black hair was carefully arranged about her shoulders, her eyes keenly fixed upon me.

I forced my lids shut again, displeased that she'd noticed me. As I was carried from the room, the Emperor resumed presiding over his court. All had forgotten the brutalized Servitor.

These people truly were cruel.

But if they posed a threat to Sidonia in any way, they would discover I was crueler still.

11

VISITING Grandiloquy were housed in luxury villas beneath one of those domes of the *Valor Novus* so large the ceiling could not be seen. As soon as the employees had carried me away from the bulk of the Grandiloquy, I made a show of rousing from my faint simply so I could see my surroundings as we entered them.

The animal cloisters and gardens in the Impyrean fortress had always impressed me. Here in the Chrysanthemum, the greenery stretched so far into the distance in rolling hills that the atmosphere blotted out the most distant trees.

The disconcerting feeling crept over me just as before like we were actually standing on the surface of a planet, even though I knew this was a clear domed compartment of a vessel. The employees followed the directions they'd been given and led me to the villa assigned to the Impyrean family.

Once inside the lavish villa, I took my first easy breath since entering the presence chamber.

"Grandeé Impyrean, are you all right?" asked one of the employees.

I looked back at him. "I'm fine. Now, you all have executed your duties. You've escorted me to the Chrysanthemum and represented the Impyrean family at our best. I thank you. It's time you departed."

Surprise flickered over all the faces of the employees, but I didn't explain further. Servitors couldn't think, couldn't reason. They wouldn't notice what was "off" about me. Eventually the employees would, so now that their official duties were over, I had no need of them. They'd been seen, and I'd been exhibited as master of them.

At least this way, none of them would share Leather's fate.

At the Impyrean fortress, we'd experienced sixteen hours of daylight where the lights were full, and eight hours of evening where all lights were dimmed. The day-night cycle of the *Valor Novus* was regulated by the stars outside. It was erratic, varying depending upon which part of the Chrysanthemum faced which sun. Each of the villas had screens, however, that could block the windows and simulate nighttime. The Servitors obeyed my command to pull them down to give me a chance to sleep before the services in the heliosphere the next day—which were always conducted during those periods three times a week when all six suns were visible from the *Valor Novus*.

As it turned out, sleep was elusive, even for someone like me who required so little. The first visitor to my villa arrived with a loud announcement through the villa's intercom:

"Neveni Sagnau to see Sidonia Impyrean."

Neveni Sagnau? I laced up a semiformal gown, trying to recall the name from my training. "Sagnau" wasn't one of the senatorial names, and I couldn't recall Donia ever mentioning a Neveni from her social forums.

When I emerged to see my new visitor, I found a short girl with shiny black hair and single-lidded eyes that resembled those Sutera nu Impyrean had adopted as a fashion statement. They blended more naturally with her features, though, which made me suspect they were one of those recessive traits like red hair and unattached earlobes that were so rarely seen in people naturally. There was a crescent-shaped necklace dangling over her collar. It was a curve of metal with a razor-sharp edge, dotted with coral beads concealing its lethal nature as a makeshift dagger. Someone else might have been deceived by it. Not me.

"Grandeé Impyrean, I hope you're well." Neveni dipped to her knees, and I held out my hands. She clasped them to her cheeks. That told me this girl was certainly of lower rank than Sidonia. "I saw you faint earlier. I often suffer from light-headedness myself. I thought I'd bring you a tincture." She rose and fumbled eagerly in her tunic, then proffered a small metal phial, her eyes wide and intent on mine. "You just add three droplets to your next drink."

The electric need for some response crackled from her. I instantly grew suspicious about this girl's motives. She was too ingratiating. "Thank you."

"I'm sorry about your Servitor. That was a disgraceful way to . . ." She stopped herself just before she could criticize the Emperor. Then, "When I first came here, the Emperor was most displeased with my family as well. So you see, I understand what you must be experiencing, having to witness that."

"Do you?"

She dropped her voice to a whisper, leaning very close to me.

"We're both here for the same reason," she said softly. "We have much in common."

"What do you mean?"

"I mean that your father and my mother share a cause." Her cheeks colored. "They aren't acquainted directly, but my mother drew the Emperor's wrath when she attempted to reform our educational system. She wanted us to learn math and science and—"

I grew tense. These were exactly the sort of people I needed to avoid, but I wasn't sure whether I was at liberty to scorn this girl if she came from a great family. "I haven't heard of your family. You must forgive me."

Her cheeks grew pink. "We're not a senatorial family. My mother oversees a colony within Pasus territory."

It all made sense then. "She's a Viceroy?"

A touch of defensiveness crept into her voice. "Yes."

So this girl was one of the glorified Excess, a family lifted from the great masses by actual elections, not ancient, inherited prominence. It also meant she answered to the local Grandiloquy, the Pasus family. No wonder she was here. Senator von Pasus viewed himself as chief defender of the Helionic faith. He would never permit some lowly Excess in his own territory to commit such open blasphemies.

This girl could do nothing but tarnish the Impyrean reputation further. I would have nothing to do with her.

"Thank you for the tincture," I said, handing it back to her. "But I doubt we have so much in common as you think."

My tone was cold. She studied my expression a moment; then her face shuttered. "If that's what you want."

She knew an offer of alliance was being refused, but I couldn't see any way this Neveni girl could benefit my position here. She'd only endanger me. Donia never would have thrust away an outstretched hand of friendship, but for Donia's sake, I very easily could do so.

"If you'll excuse me," I said, turning away from Neveni, "I had a long journey."

"Of course, my Grandeé. I'll leave you to your rest." She hesitated. "If you change your mind . . ."

I shook my head and assured her very coldly, "I won't."

The following day, the entire court appeared in the Great Heliosphere for services. The imperial family—the Emperor Randevald; his mother, Cygna; his mad nephew, Tyrus; and his niece, Devineé, and her husband, Salivar—took the seats of honor in the center around the vicar.

The two spots directly flanking the Emperor were left empty, but not for long. Suddenly two of the Emperor's Diabolics filled those places, their guard duties bringing them into the most important circle of the heliosphere. I recognized the female Enmity and the dark, watchful Anguish. I didn't see Hazard among them, but undoubtedly he was nearby.

I found myself studying Enmity a protracted moment, tracing the lines of her face—nearly identical to my own—and her light hair and eyes that matched my natural coloring. Had the Matriarch's muscle treatment been less effective, and had my nose been straight, I'd have great reason to be concerned. Just months ago, we would have appeared identical twins.

She sensed my scrutiny, and her gaze snapped over to mine. I looked away quickly. I took my own position in the next row with the Senators and senatorial families, and in the following row I saw lesser Grandiloquy. Behind them, the greater among the Excess such as Neveni Sagnau. I quickly averted my eyes from her, not wanting to attract any attention from her again.

Our various Servitors all took positions in the outermost sections just behind the employees. Their heads were tattooed with various family insignias. Everyone wore the ceremonial garb for services, and the metal caught the blinding glare of the stars. I wasn't sure where to look.

That was when I noticed the eyes upon me, voices rising and falling in whispers about the Impyrean heir who'd fainted before the court. My ears could pick out the conversations easily.

". . . much taller than I expected . . ."

". . . pity she hasn't fixed her nose . . ."

". . . surely the Emperor isn't through with her already. I expected more . . ."

I lifted my chin. Donia would wilt to find herself the center of so many prying eyes, but I didn't care about these people. So long as they confined themselves to whispering about me and not threatening, I could eavesdrop on them without a care.

The vicar began the blessing and the light slanted just so, catching a thousand points along the walls, lighting a ring of sacred chalices, and the heat that filled the room surprised me. I felt sweat trickling down beneath my ceremonial garb. I dabbed at it, and felt a gaze resting heavily on me.

My eyes lifted to meet those of Salivar Domitrian, and he leaned over to whisper something to his wife. Devineé Domitrian looked at me too. Devineé and Salivar were both examples of false-youth. They were at least in their fifties but appeared no older than Donia. I knew Donia spoke to Salivar from time to time on the social forums, but only at her mother's urging. She told me that Salivar and his wife had reputations for perversity.

They both smiled at me slowly, and in that moment they reminded me of a pair of vipers coiled up, ready to spring.

They watched me throughout the service. I checked discreetly, all the while trying to put on a show of listening to the vicar. It was difficult with the sweltering heat, the presence of the Diabolics whose attention I wanted to avoid foremost, and of course, the behavior of the Emperor's mad nephew.

Tyrus Domitrian was living up to his reputation. He burst into frequent, inappropriate laughter throughout the service, and wandered from his place to survey the various Servitors as though pondering which of them he'd kill next. Were he not mad, he'd be considered a worse blasphemer than Senator von Impyrean. At some point, the third Diabolic, Hazard, materialized out of the crowd and took his arm, and Tyrus rolled his eyes, then followed him from the room. The entire assembly pretended not to notice the heir's disrespect—even Tyrus's uncle, the Emperor.

After the service, the Grandiloquy streamed out into the presence chamber to take the vapors. Servitors roved with phials of inhalants to stimulate the senses. I took one for myself and made a show of breathing in a lungful. That's when Devineé and Salivar Domitrian found their way over to me, smiling slyly. "My dear Sidonia Impyrean," spoke Devineé, surveying me, "how different you look in person."

As the Emperor's niece, Devineé was a Successor Minor to the throne, so she and her husband outranked me. I dipped to my knees before them, and they each extended a hand for me to clasp to my cheek.

"Rise, please, my dear," Devineé said, still wearing a smile. "My uncle was most unwelcoming to you yesterday."

I eyed her warily as I straightened. "It was my father's fault for displeasing him, Your Eminence. I don't share his strange inclinations."

They exchanged a look. "Oh, we are sure you don't, darling Sidonia," purred Devineé. "All this nonsense about heresy is so tedious, is it not? I care far more for the finer pleasures of life than the crude workings of politics. We want you to come to our villa tonight. Join us in our salt baths."

"Oh, they're a luxury beyond compare," spoke Salivar, pausing to draw in a deep sniff of his vapor phial. "You'll enjoy a dip."

There was something that set me on edge about these two, but these were also exactly the sort of people the Matriarch would want Sidonia to associate with. If I could befriend a pair of royals, or show myself a silly girl of some sort too empty-headed and concerned with "luxuries" to care about scientific knowledge, then I could go far in removing suspicion of heretical leanings from Sidonia.

"I'd be very happy to join you," I said. "I, too, tire of political nonsense."

Devineé's smile broadened. She blew a gale of vapor from her nostrils. "We'll send our Servitors to escort you."

I nodded my thanks, and with that, they left me. The next person I encountered was the girl with black curls who'd caught me faking my faint the day before. Her eyes locked upon mine, and a dangerous smile lit her lips. She wove through the crowd to catch up to me.

"Why, Sidonia Impyrean, how wonderful to meet you in person at last!"

She reached out her hands, and I clasped hers. She wasn't one of the imperial royals, so she couldn't possibly be of greater importance than me. I didn't kneel, nor did she. Instead we held hands in the usual way two women of the same rank did—our fingers compressed tightly until we both let go.

"Avatars are so deceptive in person," I said, at a loss. "Please remind me who you are?"

"Oh, don't play coy, Sidonia. It's insulting. Why, I always maintain

the same eyes and hairstyle," the girl said, gesturing to herself—
her icy gray-blue eyes, her curly black hair. "They're my signature.
Some of us use avatars that actually *resemble* ourselves. I'm Elantra,
of course."

"Elantra Pasus," I recalled instantly, my muscles tensing. I had to
tread very carefully around this girl. Strange to see one of the dreaded
Pasus family in person.

She was so much smaller than me. How easily I could kill her if I
tried!

"It's such a true pleasure to meet you," I said, imitating the purring
tone Devineé had just used with me. My gaze locked on her neck, so
easily snapped, and a longing filled me for the solution that a Diabolic
was designed for: simply eradicating all of Sidonia's enemies with
brute force.

Instead I had to play the refined heir and run through bland intro-
ductions. The two companions behind Elantra were Credenza Fordyce
and Gladdic Aton, both the spawn of Senators, who'd met Sidonia on
the social forums. Their families were in high favor, so they were at
the Chrysanthemum as guests, rather than glorified hostages as I was.
The employees behind Elantra displayed the sigil of the Pasus family
on their heads: a supernova. Fitting for the family that viewed itself as
the chief defenders of the faith.

"How much taller you are in person," Elantra remarked, surveying
me up and down. "Your avatar didn't represent you very well, did it?
Then again, I suppose for some, avatars are exercises in wish fulfill-
ment. . . . Though your avatar didn't reflect your *daring* choice with
your nose! Was that on purpose, or did it happen on your journey
here?"

Apart from being a Pasus, Elantra was rapidly proving an irritant
in her own right. "I had a small mishap." I touched the bump on my

nose, recalling Donia's suggestion that I retain it. For her, I would show it proudly. "I liked the effect and kept it."

"What a different sort of choice, but your family is known for such . . . different ways of thinking, aren't they?" spoke Credenza Fordyce, her eyes gleaming and intent. There was an avid sort of hunger on her face, as though she hoped I'd give the wrong answer.

"Did you enjoy the services in the Great Heliosphere? You seemed . . . rather distracted," Elantra pressed, trying to force something, anything out of me that might be construed as heresy. She wasn't very subtle about it.

"It was a long service," Gladdic said, speaking up on my behalf. His eyes were sympathetic on mine.

He was a thin boy with skin of chestnut brown, his eyes an artificially bright green. The gold woven in his hair gave him an air of delicacy, like one who'd always been well cared for. He obviously didn't seem to share the eagerness of his companions to see me slip into heresies. I'd have to remember that.

"The service was no longer than usual," Elantra said. "Or . . . or are services conducted differently at your fortress, Sidonia?"

Trying, again, to make me slip up and admit that I rarely attended them. Clever girl. She was a snake.

Little did she know—so was I.

"Oh, Grandeé Pasus, you are entirely correct. I *was* distracted during the service," I said breezily. "It's just so very exciting to be here at the Chrysanthemum. I cannot wait to experience all the . . ." How had Devineé termed it? "*Finer* pleasures about me."

The two girls broke into smiles, and there was a distinctly malicious gleam in Elantra's eyes. "Yes, I know you must already have plans to go to Salivar and Devineé's salt baths."

I blinked. Word spread quickly, it seemed.

"You should really—" began Gladdic.

"Enjoy your dip," cut in Elantra, sending him a sharp warning look. Gladdic fell silent, cowed by her. He pressed his lips into a tight line, biting back whatever he'd been about to say.

"Truly enjoy," Elantra added. "I am quite certain the Domitrians will take your mind off that dramatic scene you experienced before us all. Little wonder you were so overcome!" Her eyes shone into mine with amusement for one last moment, the accusation in their depths, *You faker!* "I must say, Sidonia, you are already quite unlike anything I ever could have expected."

I didn't have to force a smile. If only she knew. If only I could *show* her just how different I was from what she'd expected by seizing her throat and watching that smile of hers disappear. . . .

"I can't say the same for you," I responded smoothly. "You are exactly as I envisioned." Without giving her a moment to wonder about that, I turned and left them.

I was certain I'd dedicated enough time to the after-service socializing. I was just preparing to depart when Neveni Sagnau met me by the door.

"Do you have a minute?"

Irritation flickered through me. I didn't want to be seen with her. "No, I don't."

She put out a hand to stop me from walking straight past her.

"Please listen," she urged me. "You were speaking to Devineé Domitrian and her husband just now. I saw it."

"I don't appreciate being spied upon. Unhand me."

"But Devineé and Salivar are . . ." She looked around, realizing anyone could be listening to us. Then she whispered, "Don't drink the wine. I say this for your own good."

Then she tore away from me and hurried off.

I stared after her, perplexed. I could only assume Neveni was hinting about poison, but Devineé and Salivar Domitrian had no reason to kill the Impyrean hostage.

And if they tried, well, they'd find out quite quickly they'd made a fatal mistake.

12

THE SALT BATHS of Devineé and Salivar Domitrian were in the *Tigris*, just where the ship joined the *Valor Novus*. Devineé owned this entire vessel.

Again, the chamber I entered was so very large it resembled the atmosphere of a planet, blotting out the ceiling. I'd learned these were called "sky domes." I surveyed the drooping greenery and felt the thick humidity on my skin. I was going to have to get used to this. It had to be something most people actually liked, not seeing the ceiling.

"Ah, Sidonia!" Devineé called to me. She and her husband were already lounging in the salt baths. "Join us."

"The water appears pleasant," I said, stripping off my garments. A Servitor swept forward to take my clothing, and then I slipped into the warm clasp of the water. My gaze raked the lush trees drooping leaves about us, and the clear greenish-blue pools beneath them. They swirled with the light of bioluminescent creatures, there for decoration.

The two Domitrians watched my every movement, and although Sidonia would have been squirming with discomfort, something inside me rebelled at the thought of faking the same emotion. They were making no effort to make me feel comfortable, so it seemed they wished me to feel awkward. And because that was what they wanted, I wasn't going to give it to them.

"How lovely you are," breathed Salivar.

"Yes, you have a magnificent body," Devineé said.

"I know," I said.

She and Salivar both laughed.

"To think," drawled Salivar, "we've spent the last month anticipating a dip with the shy and innocent Impyrean girl, but look, my love, she isn't even blushing."

"But she is innocent," Devineé said, a sort of satisfaction in her voice. "I am certain of it." They exchanged a glance I didn't understand.

Interesting to hear that they'd been anticipating Sidonia's arrival. I didn't see what was so important about these baths, that they'd so desperately wanted to introduce her to them. All I could do was play along, though.

The water was thick and sludgy, and propelled me onto my back. The air was humid enough that I felt sticky and soaked whether under water or over it. My gaze found the clear blue of the atmosphere over us, like a cloudless sky, and I forced myself to stare up at it, trying to accustom myself to the openness of it.

Devineé watched me with a smile. "And how do you find court so far, Grandeé Impyrean?"

"Crowded, Your Eminence," I answered honestly.

"You are quite isolated in your sector of the galaxy, aren't you? Oh, how strange this must all be for you."

I found a place to balance on the side of the pool. Devineé and

Salivar both watched me ravenously, like they were toying with a mouse before devouring it.

"It's an adjustment," I admitted cautiously. "This ship is yours?"

"Oh, the *Tigris* is our own domain, but you're welcome anytime," Devineé said.

"Anytime," Salivar added, smiling.

"The salt baths were my own idea. I visited a colony where the sea was so heavy with salt, people lounged on the surface like it was grass, and I said—"

"She said, 'Salivar, we simply must have that,'" Salivar said.

Devineé trilled with laughter. "I did, and so he said, 'You wish to abandon space travel for planet-bound life?' I said, 'Stars, no. No.'"

"And so we have this." Salivar gestured about us. With the same sweep of his hand, he retrieved a jug resting in the tangle of verdant green plants.

My gaze sharpened. I was curious about what they planned. Neveni Sagnau had warned me of their wine. Clearly it would be laced with . . . something.

"Indeed, it was the finest idea we've had," Salivar added, pouring a cup of wine and handing it to his wife.

She was smiling at me with a gleam in her eye as she raised the wine to her lips—but didn't swallow. I could see that.

Salivar poured me a cup and then handed it my way. I inspected the dark red liquid, wondering what could be within it.

They couldn't intend to poison me, but they certainly wished me drugged. Sutera nu Impyrean had said that some at court liked to toy with newcomers unaccustomed to intoxicants. They'd drop a euphoric or hallucinogen into a drink and then allow the newcomer to make a fool of his- or herself. It was an easy way to liven up a party and pass idle hours.

I would have to identify whatever substance this was quickly so I could figure out the proper reaction to fake.

"A cup of wine and a lounge in the salt baths, beneath this blue sky, and all your troubles melt away," Devineé added. She raised the wine to her lips again, and again did not swallow.

I looked between them carefully.

"Indeed." I sipped my wine.

The humidity and heat made my head swim gently, but whatever they'd laced in the wine passed through my system without touching me. I drank more, trying to figure out the faint tinge of citrus, trying to recognize it. Sidonia and I had sampled such a vast array of intoxicants with Sutera, so surely I'd tasted this one before. They continued their inane small talk.

". . . services here are much more grandiose than anywhere else in the Empire . . ."

"Have you been planet-side, my dear? Oh, it's worth trying once. So many people scorn planet-side existence. Gravity bound, they say, just for the Excess, but I've learned an appreciation for it."

". . . pity your parents couldn't join us, but we were eager to meet the young Sidonia Impyrean . . ."

And then as I raised the glass to my lips, halfway empty, Salivar gave a laugh and reached out to slip it from my hand. "You drank that faster than anticipated. That's quite enough!"

"Yes, we added a little something to your drink," Devineé said, "but we don't want you *comatose.*"

I still hadn't figured out what substance it was, but I knew how to react here. I sprang out of the salt baths, certain to plaster on a look of horror. "You've poisoned me?"

"Not poison," Devineé trilled. "Something to help you relax. Try not to make so many sudden movements. You're about to get very dizzy."

Dizzy. Listless. Those were the reactions I needed to fake. I let my eyelids droop and made a show of swaying on my feet. To hide my calculation, to behave as Sidonia would, I mumbled, "Why would you do this?"

"Never fear, Sidonia. We won't do anything you'll be able to recall tomorrow." Her grin broadened, grew predatory. "The girls and boys never do."

"You may even enjoy yourself," Salivar noted, watching me with anticipation.

"*We* certainly will enjoy it," purred Devineé. She looked me over with a blissful sigh. "True youth. I can never get enough of it. Bring her over here before she collapses, Salivar."

I grappled with the situation as Salivar splashed through the salt baths, making his way toward me. This drug was supposed to take my memory, so it wasn't a recreational substance.

Comprehension crept over me.

I thought of Neveni warning me, and even Elantra's subtle taunt. This had to be a practice of Salivar and Devineé's when someone young, vulnerable, and alone arrived new to court. These were two of the most powerful people in the galaxy, yet they still resorted to drugging their conquests. They got away with it because they were Domitrians. None could refuse a dip in their baths without insulting them. No one could refuse to drink their wine.

They used their power to force this situation, and although I had the luxury of being immune to whatever they'd slipped me, others did not.

The Matriarch had advised me about sex at court. It was to be regarded as an exchange of power or a means of exerting influence, nothing more. But I could gain no power here, and though it would be unwise to resist them, everything in me rebelled at the thought of allowing them these liberties.

And then as Salivar hoisted himself out of the water, and reached out for me, he said something that cast the situation into stark clarity. "How amusing it will be, to despoil the heir to the Impyreans. This is our greatest feat yet."

Suddenly my heart stilled. This situation hadn't been intended for me.

It was intended for *Donia.*

Rage like I'd never known ignited hot and bright within me. I wrenched Salivar's arms from me and hurled him into the water. I caught only a fleeting glimpse of Devineé's shocked face before I leaped in after him, blind fury electrifying me. I seized Devineé, and in a moment I had them both by their necks. They didn't get a chance to yell out in surprise or fear. I drove their heads under water.

They began to thrash, to claw at me, but I never relented, thinking of what might have happened if it hadn't been me, if it had been Donia. My grip on their throats tightened as they helplessly tried to resist, and all I could think was that these people had wanted to rape the Impyrean heir, *my* Impyrean heir. One squeeze and I could crack both their necks, crush them, and they would heartily deserve it.

But my head cleared, and I realized what I'd done. I pulled them both up out of the water, and thrust them away from me.

They coughed and sputtered, clawing at their throats, and I felt a sinking moment of dismay, trying to figure out what I'd do. I couldn't let them live and speak to anyone of my unnatural strength, but it seemed inadvisable to commit a double murder my first full day at court.

Devineé recovered first, crawling out of the water, choking on her sobs. "What are you . . . what are you? What monstrous thing are you?"

Her flailing hand overturned a stray cup of wine, and then I knew. I knew how to deal with these two despicable creatures.

"Get back here." My voice sounded low, bestial.

She shrieked as I splashed out of the water and crossed over to her. I seized her by the hair before she could escape me and slammed her head down. She grew still. Salivar hit me from behind as he tried to defend her, and I snared him readily in a headlock and drove him to the ground.

With my free hand, I poured a glass of wine.

"This wine makes one forgetful, does it?" I rasped. "Too high a dose makes you comatose, does it, Salivar?"

"Wait, wait," he moaned.

"You have no right to speak," I snarled in his ear. "Pray to your Living Cosmos that you survive this." Then I began to force the wine down his throat. He choked on it, gagged on it, but I held his nose and forced more and more wine down his throat until he was lying limp on the ground, hazy and lost to the world.

Devineé roused. I twisted her arm behind her back, then fed her the rest of the wine.

When I was certain I'd done all I could, I threw them back to the ground. I rose and pulled on my garments, then wrung out my hair. My mind raced with thoughts about how I'd hide this, how I'd conceal what I'd done. Everyone knew I was coming here tonight! What should I do next? I didn't even know . . .

A rustling in the bushes. I froze in place as Neveni Sagnau charged out—the curved blade of her necklace in hand.

My gaze sharpened, even as this new complication registered. The wine was gone. I couldn't drug her. I'd need to drown her.

"Sidonia!" she cried, glaring at the Domitrians. The pair lay drugged out of their minds on the ground. "What—what happened here?"

"How long have you been here?" I demanded. "Are you alone?"

"Of—of course I'm alone. I just . . . I just slipped past the Servitors. . . ." She pointed backward.

So she hadn't seen. Good. She wouldn't know to fear me.

My voice was very soft and dangerous. "Come closer. I'll tell you what happened."

She just stared down at the two, stunned. I started toward her, ready to break her neck. But Neveni surprised me. She bared her teeth in a ferocious grin and then drove a kick into Salivar's side. I stopped advancing, trying to understand this. Neveni kicked him again, and then she kicked Devineé as well. She stumbled back from the two Domitrians, her eyes bright with unshed tears. She fought back tears and yet she was laughing.

"I don't know what you did to them, and I don't care. Are they going to die? Tell me they're going to die!"

"I don't know," I said, utterly perplexed by her. I found myself staring at that blade in her hand again, and it dawned on me that she'd come here prepared to . . . help me?

"They deserve it if they do. They've done this so many times," Neveni said viciously, waving the blade in her hand. "You're not the first. I wasn't either. I can't even remember my first night here, but I've seen them inviting others, and I *know* what happened to me. I wasn't going to just stand by this time and let it happen again!"

"You actually came here to stop them?" I simply couldn't wrap my mind around the idea.

"I don't know what I was going to do," she confessed, her shaking hand still clutching the curved blade. "Probably stab them, or maybe just slash Devineé's face, but . . . but I *couldn't* let them do it again." Tears spilled from her eyes now, fierce and angry, and it sank into me that this girl had come to save the Impyrean heir. To save Donia.

I could never hurt a girl who'd do this for Donia.

"Thank you. Truly, *thank you*." I wasn't used to saying those words, but I meant them.

"We're going to have to cover up . . . whatever it was that happened here," Neveni said, gesturing around vaguely. "I won't ask, Sidonia. I really won't. But listen, I know how to access the surveillance logs. I did it before I came here to make sure I could sneak in." She smiled grimly. "I'll wipe any recording of the last day or so. And you and I can come up with a story together."

I gave a stunned nod. "Together."

And just like that, I accepted Neveni Sagnau as an ally. She wasn't my choice of allies, and she'd do nothing to improve the Impyrean reputation for heresy. . . . But sometimes fate did not offer the choices we preferred, but rather the ones we must accept for lack of better alternatives.

I wouldn't kill her for now. I just hoped I never came to regret it.

13

DONIA was worried about me already, so when I spoke with her over subspace to fill her in on the events at the Chrysanthemum so far, I left out the episode with Salivar and Devineé. And the subsequent interrogation I faced.

The Domitrians had both been found the following day, comatose and undressed amid their salt baths. The Emperor learned quickly that I'd been due to spend an evening with them. Apparently, it was an open secret what Devineé and Salivar did to young people who were alone and friendless at court. Elantra's taunt played through my mind as I sat before Enmity in my villa. *She'd* known what I faced that night. She'd enjoyed the thought.

One day I hoped to thank the Pasus girl for that. But not yet.

Enmity seemed to fill the villa as she loomed over me. Neveni was trembling at my side, though I knew from my own experience that was most anyone's reaction to a Diabolic cornering and questioning them—even when innocent.

She played her part well. "I found Sidonia outside the *Tigris*. She seemed so disoriented and confused."

I nodded along, never daring to break Enmity's gaze. "I really have no memory of what transpired. Their Eminences were so kind to invite me to their baths, and after that . . ." I waved my hand vaguely. "My head still throbs so terribly. It's all a blur."

"I took her back to her chamber to sleep and stayed with her in case she was severely ill. How *are* their Eminences?" Neveni leaned forward, mock concern on her face. "We are ever so worried."

The Diabolic considered every word in dead silence, unblinking. I'd never really spent time with another of my kind. It struck me how strange it was I'd been able to pass as a person so far. Every movement, every breath this creature took screamed at me that she wasn't like the human beings I saw around me, that she was a killer and a predator and I should be alert. She had to have done everything I had to get this far, to reach the point where she was worthy of being civilized. I forced myself to blink so she wouldn't notice my fixed gaze.

Then Enmity said, "The med bots are unable to wake them from their coma. They seem to have ingested a very potent neurotoxin called Scorpion's Breath in great quantities. It's odd that you were in their company yet managed to escape their fate, Grandeé Impyrean."

"I was supremely fortunate," I said solemnly.

The Diabolic's gaze crawled between us—and then locked on me as she *really* looked. For a fearful moment, I wondered if she was seeing our resemblance . . . if she could see something Diabolic in me just as I could see it in her, or if my fragile appearance had effectively deceived her despite her better judgment.

Enmity's hand lashed out and seized my chin. I froze in place as she lifted my face into the light.

Blink, I reminded myself as our eyes held. *Do not stare. Act like a person.* I made myself swallow, fidget, just as Sidonia might do. Enmity merely studied me intently for a protracted moment, as Neveni gave a nervous laugh.

"What's wrong?" Neveni said. "Is there something on Sidonia's face?"

"You are not lying to me?" Enmity said in a dangerous voice.

My heartbeat accelerated. I knew she could feel it. But any person would grow uneasy with a Diabolic clutching them like this.

"No," I replied steadily. "Now unhand me at once." I'd managed to keep my voice soft, like Donia's, but the tone brooked no questions. I was a Senator's daughter, as far as she was concerned. She had to obey me.

Enmity had no choice but to let her hand drop. She looked between us one last time, and then she left us without another word. I did not relax after she departed, though.

"What was that about?" Neveni muttered, gesturing to her own chin.

I shook my head and didn't answer. Enmity was suspicious of me. I knew that. What she suspected, though—I could not yet guess.

"Diabolics are so creepy," Neveni said.

I smiled at her. Yes, I supposed we were.

The ceremony for the Consecration of the Cherished Dead was one of the holiest occasions in the Empire, so naturally Senator von Impyrean hadn't celebrated it unless there was company. When he allowed the celebration, the Impyreans followed the same procedure every great imperial family did: they ordered an Exalted specially bred and engineered for the ceremony, spent a week doting on the creature and treating it like something much loved, and then loaded it into a starship and shot it into the corona of a star, where it would burn to death. By handing their Cosmos a creature of true innocence and purity, they hoped to mitigate whatever sins and wrongdoing their own cherished dead had possessed when they went to the afterlife themselves.

The Emperor always celebrated Consecration Day and spent the week leading up to it trotting around the Exalted, a tiny, hairless young man or woman with no eyelashes, no coloring, and no cognitive capacity for deception, impurity, violence, or any of those nasty human impulses that besmirched real people. The Exalted had a seat of honor at every feast and every high occasion and lived like the most cosseted pet in existence.

Until Consecration Day came and the Exalted died, of course.

"Come on," Neveni urged me the morning of Consecration Day. "It's for those of greater Grandiloquy, but I can go if you take me."

Covering my crime against the Domitrians and enduring Enmity's interrogation had created a bond between us. We spent our days in each other's company.

Neveni wasn't like Donia, shy and sweet and intellectually curious. She was restless and impatient and driven to explore, and unlike her, *I* couldn't be denied entrance to most anywhere in the Chrysanthemum. I opened doors for her, and she directed our movements.

She also had an amazing capacity for gathering scraps of information or hearsay everywhere we went. The Matriarch had once said information was currency, and Neveni supplied it to me in spades. She told me her latest news as we walked to the heliosphere for the Consecration Ceremony.

"Tyrus Domitrian has already ruined the entire holiday. The Emperor's furious."

"Is he?" I said, distracted by the feel of my hair sticking up all around me.

We'd both arranged our tresses as all the attendees had, in

star-shaped haloes about our heads with effervescent essence woven in. We wore gowns of glowing gold, as befitted the occasion. Everyone we passed with dead family members to mourn had stenciled teardrops on their faces to represent the grief the years had brought them.

Neveni nodded eagerly, her own hairstyle slipping. She didn't have styling stilts like I did. "The Pasus family gifted the Emperor with an Exalted named Unity a year ago. A hand-raised one, so no accelerated growth. It was actually a male Exalted who grew up over a normal human span of life."

I raised my eyebrows. "That must have been expensive." Even Diabolics were pushed through accelerated growth our earliest years of life. It made little economic sense to feed and care for a humanoid creature before it became useful.

"Senator von Pasus can afford it," said Neveni. "And the Emperor knew he needed a top-quality Exalted because so many of the imperial royals die young. Everyone says they're sun-scorned." She rolled her eyes a bit as she said it, because we all knew the Emperor couldn't actually be superstitious about all those deaths. He knew well the cause of them.

"This year," Neveni said, "he was thrilled to get Unity. He was sure the Living Cosmos would favor him. But Tyrus ruined everything. He despoiled the Exalted."

"He *had sex* with it?"

I wasn't even a believer and the Successor Primus's blasphemy astounded me.

Neveni nodded eagerly. "He only admitted it yesterday when Unity was being prepped in the ceremonial oils. Now it can't get sacrificed because it's impure, and the Emperor's furious."

"No wonder."

Tyrus Domitrian truly was a madman. The irony was, his lechery had saved that Exalted from a hideous fate.

Neveni and I entered the Great Heliosphere to observe the fallout. Roving Servitors passed by with sumptuous trays of drinks, finger foods, and narcotics. There were bags of powder, phials of inhalants, droppers of various intoxicants to add to drinks, some ointments to dab directly on skin. Sutera nu Impyrean had shown us how to use all of them, and made us practice their use. I made a show of taking an ointment and dabbing my skin simply because I knew it would not affect me, and it might raise eyebrows if I scorned chemical entertainment at one of the greatest imperial holidays.

The Emperor had ordered Tyrus chained to the brightest window and had the UV screen temporarily stripped away so the Successor Primus could endure a full day of glaring sunburn. He was also forbidden to partake in any of the pleasures of the festival.

Tyrus's skin was already bright red by the time we beheld him, but he looked thoroughly unashamed of his public disgrace. In fact, from the smile on his face, I'd guess he was enjoying the scandalized looks from the people passing by him.

". . . I cannot help it, Grandmother," Tyrus was drawling as we neared him.

My ears picked up the conversation. I glanced at Neveni, but she was busy surreptitiously dumping out her phial of intoxicant while pretending to dab it over her wrist. After her experience with the Domitrians, it was only natural she detested anything that altered her ability to control herself.

I turned my attention back to the conversation.

"You don't know what a combination of hairlessness and innocence does to me," Tyrus said. "Asking me to refrain is like holding the rarest delicacy before a starving man and demanding he abstain

S. J. KINCAID

from eating it. It's inhuman to expect such self-restraint."

"You are a disgrace to this Empire!" scolded the matriarch of the Domitrian family, the Grandeé Cygna. "You haven't even stenciled yourself." Her own face, by contrast, was decorated with an elegant display of tears.

"Those inks irritate my skin most terribly."

Tyrus wore a lazy-lidded smile. His blue eyes were light and almost coy beneath his short-shorn copper-colored hair. His nose was long, and his chin had an unfashionable cleft that he'd never corrected. Neveni had told me he never changed any of his features, even for special occasions. Like many madmen, his outward guise seemed to be a low priority to him. He must have incurred his uncle's wrath and been subjected to this window treatment several times, if those freckles were anything to judge by. The mystery was the fact that he'd never had them removed.

"Have you no respect for your departed mother?" Cygna demanded. "Your siblings? Consecration Day is staged in honor of our dead!"

Tyrus's tone shifted subtly, some of the lightness gone. "Why, Grandmother, I should think the deaths of my parents such a tragedy, no commemoration can compare. . . . As I'm quite sure you and my dear uncle would agree."

Everyone knew the Emperor's mother had played a hand in murdering rival claimants for the throne, including her own less-favored children. Emperor Randevald repaid his mother by appointing his insane nephew Successor Primus just to ensure she never moved against him.

And now, that insane nephew had just thrown a dangerous accusation out there, seemingly without realizing it. I couldn't resist the temptation to peer back at them to gauge Cygna's reaction.

The matriarch of the Domitrian family flushed at the words. Her eyes narrowed on Tyrus. "Are you implying something, dear child? Because you speak of my own flesh and blood."

"I imply nothing. I'm merely saying, you haven't told me why I should consecrate them yet again? Look how liberally you stenciled in your own grief—I suspect you lament them enough for both of us." And then his tone changed again, adopted the drawling light-heartedness he'd used before. "Besides, what are the deaths of a few family members? My parents would have been honored to know they spawned a living God like myself."

The narrow, suspicious look on her face slackened, irritation replacing it. "Helios help me, you are a mad fool, and a blight on this family! Woe to this Empire if you ascend to the throne. I vow to the Cosmos, come that sun-scorned day, I will launch *myself* into a star!" Cygna whirled away from him and left him in his chains by the window.

Tyrus's eyes met mine, and I quickly averted my gaze. He couldn't possibly know I'd overheard that. None but a Diabolic could have discerned the conversation from so far away.

Rid of her intoxicant, Neveni nudged me to move on, and I was glad to do so. But it was too late.

"You!" rang Tyrus's voice. "Impyrean girl! Come entertain me. I command you."

Neveni and I exchanged a look; then we moved toward Tyrus Domitrian, and we both began to dip to our knees.

"No, no," he said impatiently, his restless gaze darting between us. "None of that when I am in this state. Let's not make this more of a farce than it is. We've met plenty of times, my Grandeé. But you." He addressed Neveni. "What manner of person are you? I don't know you."

"I am not Grandiloquy." Neveni rose to her full height. "I am the daughter of the Viceroy of Lumina, Your Eminence."

"Pasus territory." He closed his eyes a long moment. "Ah, of course. That woman who wished to build libraries and teach the sciences."

Neveni stiffened. "Yes, Your Eminence."

I looked at the girl sideways, wondering how she would conduct herself before a Domitrian.

"And what do you think of your mother's actions? Be honest," Tyrus said.

It was a laughable demand. Madman or no, honesty to the Emperor's heir could cost one dearly. Neveni looked at him in a way that seemed to say this, but replied very cautiously, "Your Eminence cannot expect me to speak against my own mother."

"Of course not."

"In that case," she said, growing bold, "my mother is devoted to Lumina's welfare. She intended no disrespect to your—to *our* divine Cosmos or to the Pasus family. She only wished to enhance life on Lumina."

"Planetary living is most wretched," Tyrus said sympathetically.

"Oh no, it isn't," Neveni said.

"It's not? Aren't there hurricanes and earthquakes and diseases?"

"The weather is highly variable, but so are the life-forms. There are all sorts of animals and gardens that grow themselves, and Lumina has two moons to stir the tides. It's all so very unpredictable, Your Eminence, but that makes it far more interesting than life in space."

"You speak like a Partisan madly in love with her planet."

Neveni paled, and I tensed up too. He spoke with detached curiosity, but he'd made a serious accusation and seemed oblivious to it as Neveni squirmed.

He was busy studying his nails. "But of course you are obviously not a Partisan. That would be madness. Especially here at the Chrysanthemum. That could be quite a dreadful misinterpretation of your words."

If I didn't know better, I'd suspect he was giving her veiled advice to speak more carefully. Neveni quickly said, "Obviously that would be a terrible misinterpretation, Your Eminence. Of course I'm no Partisan."

Tyrus sagged back against the window, raising his hands as far as his chains would allow so he could lace his fingers behind his head. "The stars are talking to me, and your voice drowns them out. Be quiet a moment so I may hear them. Both of you girls. Especially you, my Grandeé Impyrean. You do drone on so."

That puzzled me. I had barely spoken. Neveni and I were quiet.

"The stars say . . . They say I am particularly handsome today," Tyrus announced. "How kind of them. Do you think me handsome, Grandeé Impyrean?"

The question was ludicrous. In a court of people who modified their appearance to sheer perfection, he stuck out for being imperfect like a common Excess. For a long moment, I wasn't sure how to respond without causing offense. "The stars would not lie to you, Your Eminence."

"I think you are right," spoke Tyrus. "As soon as I am free of these chains, I vow to exhibit my fine looks before admirers near and far. . . ."

And like that, the lucidity of the Empire's heir was gone. He began affecting bizarre poses to best exhibit his muscles and looks and graciously accepting compliments from a phantom audience. Neveni and I inched back, leaving him rambling to the air, ranting about his own virtues. The light of the six suns glared through the window, and his skin continued to burn.

At that moment, there was a stirring in the crowd as the Emperor floated in above it on his antigrav chair, and then the spectacle truly began, lights flaring from the ceiling, the walls of the Great Heliosphere shifting to display scenery rather than empty space—images of royals long perished, or clips of important battles in the imperial past. Others were pictures of vessels lost to malignant space, the Empire's most revered dead.

I spotted the Emperor's trio of Diabolics. Hazard and Anguish stood on either side of the Emperor, and Enmity . . .

Stood off to the side, gazing straight at me.

I quickly averted my eyes.

"That was rather awkward," Neveni said absently as we moved toward the feasting table. "The rumors don't exaggerate. He's truly mad."

There was no sacrifice to celebrate due to Tyrus, but since the food had been prepared in advance, it was all laid out. As I watched Neveni poke at a platter of real roasted duck, the proud words she'd spoken of her planet Lumina echoed in my head.

I had to ask. "Are you a Partisan?"

I didn't care whether Neveni wanted her planet free of the Empire. I cared about whether she was clever enough to keep her sentiments a secret. If she admitted to being a Partisan, then she would have to die quickly. I couldn't trust a fool with the dangerous knowledge of what I'd done to Devineé and Salivar.

But Neveni just slanted me a careful look and asked me a question in return. "What *did* happen to the Domitrians?"

My heart gave a jerk, and I threw a look around. Was anyone close enough to hear that? No, Neveni wasn't idiot enough to speak so frankly in earshot of others.

"Let's not ask each other questions we don't want to answer," Neveni suggested lightly.

But I was no longer listening to her. No, there were no people close enough to hear us—but through a parting in the crowd, I glimpsed Enmity. She was still watching me, but she was closer now, close enough to have heard Neveni if she'd been listening.

She stood . . . as close as I'd stood to Tyrus when I'd eavesdropped on his discussion with Cygna. She began to stalk toward me, and then I knew she'd heard every dangerous syllable from Neveni's lips.

And I had no pretty lies to excuse myself. Not this time.

14

I MADE my excuses to Neveni and moved for the door, wishing for a few minutes of quiet just so I could think over my options. Enmity now knew the story I'd constructed with Neveni was a lie. She would demand another explanation. She'd probably gathered that I was responsible for the fate of the Domitrians, and I alone was responsible.

Would anyone believe her?

The chemical entertainments had begun to take effect on everyone. I passed Grandiloquy of all ages slumped on the floor, cackling as they leaned over the arms of chairs, draped back against windows, sometimes in conversation, sometimes studying their own hands like they were very fascinating to them. Doctors named nu Domitrian or nan Domitrian circulated through the crowd, tending to overdoses and adverse reactions to the narcotics.

Despite what Sutera nu Impyrean had said, I saw many people who looked sloppy. I saw many more who looked manic. Even Credenza

Fordyce was sprawled on the ground with her legs spread wide, smiling crookedly at various people who wandered past. Elantra stood above her, laughing in a giddy manner and urging her up.

I forged straight past without speaking to them, and relief poured over me as the crowd drained away, the cool embrace of the corridor welcoming me. Then footsteps sounded behind me, and I knew I had not made a successful escape.

"Leaving so soon, Grandeé Impyrean?"

I turned slowly to face Enmity. She circled me in that animalistic way and I held very still, every thought about how to behave like a real person rushing from my mind.

My twin. My shadow. Only fitting that she'd be the one to see through me.

All I could concentrate on was the predator before me. "What business is it of yours?" My voice sounded too hard, too threatening—too much like *my* voice.

Enmity did not answer, just looked at me.

"I'm very tired." Then I forced down my real feelings and faked a smile, trying to sound sincere. "What a delightful celebration. Such a pity about the Exalted."

I began to step past her, but the Diabolic was suddenly before me. Such speed, and so silently, so light on her feet. Before my muscle reduction, I could have moved like this and matched her pace for pace. I could have stood toe-to-toe with this creature and battled her in earnest.

But not now. I couldn't take on a full-strength Diabolic, yet if she figured out what I was, I had to kill her before she told anyone. I couldn't imagine how I'd manage it.

Enmity leaned in very close to me, her eyes pale and fathomless, studying me. She was so large compared to me.

121

"What do you want?" I dared to ask after an extended silence.

"I know you are lying about the Domitrians, Grandeé Impyrean."

Denial. That was the best thing I could do. "I already told you—"

"That Sagnau girl said it. I *heard*. Your story was a lie."

"My story? I have no story. I told you, I have no memory of what happened!" I hoped I sounded hysterical, afraid. In truth, I was trying to figure out whether I was strong enough to kill her with my reduced strength. I would need surprise.

Something animal and strange shifted on her face, and she tilted her head to the side. "There's something very different about you. I can't determine just what it is. Not yet."

So she hadn't yet figured out that I was like her. She'd followed her gut instinct and pursued me out here, but even now, even looking so closely as this, she couldn't determine with absolute certainty that I wasn't a person. In fact, she had to be doubting she'd even heard what she believed she had or she'd be twisting my ligaments right now, trying to force a confession from me. How, after all, could the Impyrean heir cripple two Domitrians her first day at court?

The realization emboldened me.

"I don't have time for this nonsense, you inhuman thing. Now move aside and let me pass."

She didn't budge.

"I said move aside!" I repeated, adrenaline thrilling through my veins. I wanted to move her aside. I wanted to lash out. I had to bite back every aggressive impulse roaring within me.

And then . . .

And then a voice: "Is everything well here?"

The words, unstudied and very human, finally succeeded in disrupting this strange conversation. I looked over at Gladdic Aton, the young aristocrat I'd met with Elantra and Credenza that first day.

Enmity dipped her head. "Yes, my Grande Aton."

"Yes," I said, turning away from Enmity.

Gladdic's careful, bright green eyes met mine, some emotion in their depths that I couldn't figure out. "May I escort you back to your villa, Grandeé Impyrean?"

I nodded and let him stride over and place my arm onto his. "Lead me from here."

I did not look back at Enmity again. I felt her gaze scorching my back every step that drew me farther from her deadly attention. For now.

It took Gladdic time to muster the nerve to speak. "I'm afraid I've displeased you," he said.

I looked over at him. "What do you mean?"

"When I told you at that social forum that we should keep our distance from each other, you know that wasn't about . . . about *you*, don't you?"

What was this?

"My father is a close ally of Senator von Pasus," Gladdic said. "It doesn't matter to me what your father believes, but my father is vehement on this matter. I'm not at liberty to just associate freely with you, as much as I wish I could! I just hate that I've caused you offense."

"Why would you think I'm offended?" I said slowly.

"Because." He blinked, guileless as a child. "Because we haven't spoken at all. Even in private. I thought you'd find more pleasure in meeting me in person." He looked down at the ground, a faint flush coming to his cheeks. "Your manner has been so cold toward me. I deserve it, I know, but it causes me great pain."

I gawked at him, and then caught myself and smoothed the shock away. So Donia must have behaved very differently toward him when they interacted over the galactic forums than I had since coming here.

"I'm not angry with you. And you've caused me no offense. I . . ." I groped for an explanation. "I simply don't want to create any new difficulties for you or for myself." That much was true.

He swallowed visibly as we drew down the path into the vast sky dome where our villas awaited. "I've been giving it thought, and I don't think it would harm anything if perhaps, just from time to time, we associated at . . . at public events. Do you?"

We reached my villa, and I turned to meet his earnest eyes, fixed on me in desperate appeal.

The realization struck me: Gladdic was infatuated with Donia. And clearly she'd done nothing to discourage him.

I extricated my hand from his arm, knowing Donia hadn't filled me in on something here. "Yes, I don't believe it would do any harm to see each other more often."

Donia had some things to explain.

"You met Gladdic?"

Donia didn't say it with much intonation, much excitement. It could have been because she was borrowing her mother's avatar to speak with me over the galactic forums, and it was hard for anyone with the Matriarch's cold, cynical voice to express excitement over anything.

But as I stared at her, using Donia's customary avatar to speak with her in turn, I sensed there was something more to it.

"You dislike him?"

"No," Donia said quickly. She crossed her arms.

I'd been filling her in on whatever I could tell her about the Chrysanthemum. We had to be very careful speaking, since there could be people eavesdropping. We were doing this under the guise of being mother and daughter, checking in on a private virtual forum.

"He seemed very fond of . . . of me," I told Donia. "And I knew nothing about this." That perplexed me the most, because Donia had never kept secrets from me.

"Because there's honestly nothing to tell. Look"—she shrugged—"I've always known I'd . . . that *you'd* have to marry and make an alliance with another great family someday."

"Yes."

"Gladdic Aton is a nice, intellectual, patient person." She sighed. "As good as anyone."

"But *I* don't care for him," I concluded. "So I needn't be civil."

"No! Be nice."

"I do care for him, then?"

"No, Nem—Sidonia. I like him for a potential spouse, uh, for you more than I like anyone else. But that doesn't mean I like him for a spouse. I don't like anyone for a husband, really, but I do like Gladdic more than anyone else. Do you understand?"

"No," I said frankly.

"Just remember that I . . . that *you* have to marry someone, so it might as well be Gladdic." She closed her eyes a long moment. "His parents are ardent Helionics. His family is beyond any suspicion. If I—if *you* associated with him, then you would be much safer. So it's up to you"—she looked at me intently—"to keep him interested in marrying you." She dropped her voice. "Please do it. For me."

I frowned at her. So Donia didn't love this boy, but she planned to marry him and had obviously interested him in marrying her. She wanted me to keep him interested in marrying her, even though she had no emotional attachment to him.

"How far do I take this 'niceness'?" I asked her.

"Just talk to him. Be affectionate if you can."

"Do I have sex with him?"

"No!" she flared. "Don't do that."

"Are you sure? It makes no difference to me whether—"

"I said *NO*, Nemesis! I don't want him to touch you!"

Her words were so vehement, they caught me off guard. We were both silent a long moment, looking around as though worried about eavesdroppers. She'd used my name in her anger. But there was no sign anyone was tapping into our discussion, and besides that, it was too late to fix the mistake.

"I won't," I said soothingly. "I won't do anything."

She drew and released a shaky breath. Then, "Just . . . he likes to talk. Just be a good listener. That's all he really needs. Be as nice as you can. But nothing more. *Nothing* more. All right?"

"All right."

After signing off, I stared at myself in the reflective surface of the console. Still with the raven hair Donia preferred, still with my same nose. She'd reacted so negatively to the very suggestion of intercourse with Gladdic. That was the moment it occurred to me: Donia was jealous. Terribly jealous. She cared far more for Gladdic than she'd let on.

It still perplexed me that she hadn't told me about him, but I was capable of reading between the lines. If she wanted to marry him, then I'd do my best to evaluate Gladdic to see whether he was suitable for Donia. If he was good enough for her, truly so good as she believed, then I'd do everything in my power to improve relations between the Impyrean and Aton families. If it helped remove suspicion of heretical leanings from Sidonia, even better. I could do that much for Donia.

15

ENMITY BEGAN following me. Evidently the Emperor required only two of his Diabolics at his side at any one time, which gave her plenty of opportunity to tail me through the Chrysanthemum, monitoring me for any further suspicious actions.

She was clever about it, lingering far enough away from me that an ordinary person would never notice her presence. She conducted herself as a Diabolic on a standard patrol of the Chrysanthemum, not as a hunter in pursuit of prey. Only the most paranoid mind could have connected the two of us. That she was always near me would seem a mere coincidence.

But never to me.

I became acutely aware of my every movement, my every breath, wondering how much of my true self I'd betrayed to her already. The only thing I could think to do was play the best possible Grandeé: engage myself in frivolity and hope she lost interest in me.

However much training I'd received from Sutera nu Impyrean and the Matriarch, I didn't have a true social instinct. I had no impulse to seek entertainment or make new friends, but I needed to behave in a certain way to blend in seamlessly—I *needed* to behave as though I wanted to participate in court activities. The more I did this, the sooner Enmity would have to accept that her suspicions were imagined.

This was where Neveni proved most useful.

She hungered for experiences. So far we'd wandered every garden in the *Valor Novus* and spent a long day hiking five kilometers and back down Berneval Stretch. It was the longest pylon jutting out from the Chrysanthemum, with few people and a great number of automated machines going about their tasks. It wasn't a glamorous stretch, but Neveni insisted we had to do it, since it ended abruptly at a wall where those who ventured that far scrawled their names.

I saw the names and sigils of most of the young Grandiloquy there and knew this was some rite of passage for court. There was the quasar of the Aton family, the supernova of the Pasus, the solar eclipse of the Fordyces, the six stars of the royal branch of the Domitrians, and even the black hole sigil of the nonroyal branch of the Domitrians—the Grandeé Cygna's side of the family. We added our names to the wall, and I carved in the Impyrean sun rising from behind a planet.

Neveni, somewhat defiantly, plucked off her necklace and used the blade to etch in the twin moons of Lumina. "If the Grandiloquy don't like it," she said, "they shouldn't have brought me here."

Another evening, we joined Gladdic gambling over the creature fights. Various Grandes and Grandeés exhausted their currency commissioning genetically engineered beasts for an arena in the pits of the *Tigris*, and most of the time, their creatures were killed at the first engagement. The others lost money wagering on the losers, and heartily enjoyed the bloodshed in the meantime.

This was one of those harmless public occasions Gladdic had mentioned when we could pass time together without censure. He spent much of the evening—even during his own creature's fight—catching my eye and sending me discreet smiles. I forced my lips to curve and return them, not sure that I could ever capture Sidonia's softness and warmth.

Gladdic's creature won the match, so he excused himself to run down and check on his animal's health. Neveni took the opportunity to tell me, "I really want to participate in this sometime." Her voice was hoarse from cheering on the hybrid bear-tiger she'd bet on two matches ago. "We should order a creature of our own."

I looked at her skeptically. "And you're hoping I'll pay for this."

"Come on, Sidonia. Don't you want to try it just once?"

For some reason, the idea made my stomach roil unpleasantly, though I couldn't say why. It wasn't as though I was fazed by the sight of such savage brutality. Buying a creature seemed a very typical Grandiloquy thing to do, and my goal was to appear as normal as possible. I gave her the money and left commissioning the beast in her hands.

Neveni's creature was ready within a week, tailored to the genetic code she ordered and raised with an accelerant to full size. As soon as it was ready for its first match in the arena, she invited me down to the corrals to view the creature with her. I invited Gladdic.

Neveni led us into an area in the bowels of the arena where an overpowering stench mounted in the air.

Gladdic murmured and pulled a scented jar of oil from within his sleeve. He dabbed a droplet beneath each nostril and offered the jar to us. Neveni took some as well.

I shook my head. Cloying perfume bothered me far more than the stench of animals.

As we neared the corrals, Neveni chattered about her new creature, and Gladdic questioned her from his own experience with tailoring creatures for the fights. I tuned them out, listening carefully until I discerned the familiar, smooth tread of Enmity following behind me. I wondered if she was growing bored yet.

My thoughts were still on her as we stepped into the corrals, but then my eyes took in the whole scene before me and I found myself jerking to a stop, something giving a horrified lurch within me.

I couldn't move for a long moment. My gaze trailed about me, tracing the rings of harsh fluorescent light denoting invisible walls. The roars and sounds of the creatures floated to my ears, melding with the sudden buzzing in my head. An uncanny sense overcame me that I'd stumbled backward to another time.

My hand reached out for the nearest fluorescent ring, skimming the prickling force field separating me from a tiger hybrid. I could see the creature, but it could only see me if I chose to make the field transparent. I knew this without asking.

Once I'd been the creature on the other side of those force fields.

The hand of memory gripped me in place. These had the same build as the corrals where I'd spent my early years. I remembered people drifting past, gawking in at me like this. And here I was on the other side.

I didn't realize I'd stopped by one of the pens, staring inward at it, until I felt the touch on my arm.

My hand flew up to Gladdic's throat on instinct, but I didn't squeeze. I recovered my wits just in time. My eyes met his, my breath coming quickly, and I pressed my hand back to my side. "You startled me."

Confusion washed over his face. I knew I'd done something distinctly inhuman.

"Where is the creature?" I said to distract him, forcing a smile.

"Mistress Sagnau said it's right down here."

I followed Gladdic, feeling like I was moving through a swamp, feeling like Nemesis dan Impyrean standing here completely visible in a skin that didn't fit, where surely any moment now someone would see I was an imposter.

We reached the pen where Neveni's animal awaited. All the other animals about us were pacing restlessly in their confined space, growling or agitated. Neveni's creature sat on its haunches with its leg raised, its head bent down to lick away at itself.

"Oh, come on," Neveni said, looking around despairingly.

Gladdic muffled a snigger. "I think it's enjoying that."

"Hey, stop that!" Neveni called, and whacked her palm at the force field. She let out a yowl of pain when her hand rebounded off with a shock. "Oh no, what if it does this in the arena? This is going to be a disaster."

"At least it will enjoy the last few minutes of its life," Gladdic joked.

I found myself staring over my shoulder, back at the muscular woman who'd just stepped into the corrals—the Diabolic following me. Enmity, too, was looking around with recognition on her face.

I felt a curious wrench in my chest.

For the first time, I looked at Enmity and saw not a complication, a foe, someone who might kill me or someone I might soon have to kill.

I saw a person . . . no, a *creature* who was just like me. The same past, the same experiences, someone who in different circumstances could have understood that side of me that was unfathomable even to Sidonia. I knew exactly what she had to be feeling and thinking, because I was feeling and thinking the same thing.

And then her gaze met mine and I averted my eyes quickly.

Enmity and I were twin sprouts from the same soil, and she could never know. Never. Because she would kill me for it.

Neveni was tense as we waited by the ring for her creature's turn to fight. She'd named it Deadly before seeing it, a name that was sure to become a joke if the beast went out there and resumed cleaning itself rather than fighting.

"This is awful," Neveni lamented as we sat there. "I added lion and bear. Did you two see any signs of lion or bear or did I get all dog?"

"It was larger than most dogs," Gladdic said. "It had some fur around its neck."

We watched Neveni's beast placed into the pen just beside the arena, ready to fight in the next list.

"We're going to be a laughingstock," she told me.

"I funded you," I told her. "I didn't order it. *I* won't be the laughingstock."

The dismay on her face told me I'd said the wrong thing.

Softer now, I spoke, "If you truly fear it will lose most terribly, then let's pull the creature out now."

"Why, Sidonia, that would be a terrible overreaction."

Elantra Pasus glided down and settled herself on Gladdic's other side. Her retinue of employees and Servitors trailed behind her—among them Unity, the Exalted despoiled by Tyrus Domitrian.

Neveni and I both tensed. Gladdic's dark skin paled a shade. "Elantra."

"Gladdic," she greeted him, looking him over in a questioning way—and I recalled suddenly that Gladdic wanted to avoid displeasing the Pasus family. There seemed to be a silent warning in her eyes, I swore it, but then she addressed Neveni. "Most *everyone* is embarrassed by their first beast's showing in the arena."

"Oh?" Neveni's arms were tightly crossed over her chest. She had as much reason to be on edge around a Pasus as I did. She was only here because her mother had incurred Senator von Pasus's wrath.

"Of course," said Elantra. "You simply need to do more research next time and make sure you're using a quality breeder. The cheaper ones water down their animal strains with too much dog. Let me guess: you weren't even provided with a warm-up animal, were you?"

"A warm-up animal?" Neveni said warily.

"Chum," I said quietly. Chum helped an animal learn to kill.

Or a Diabolic.

Elantra laughed. "Silly girl, you can't just dump it in the ring and expect it to know what to do. A quality breeder would have told you that. They're supposed to supply another, weaker animal. Your animal kills it, gets the taste of blood in its mouth, and then it's ready for a real match. Your little dog is going to be torn apart if you don't warm it up first." She tilted her curly-haired head to the side, her smile coy. "I can easily supply some. I happen to have extra today."

Neveni was still rigid, but she forced a tight smile. "I suppose that would be better than sending him out there to lose."

"I'll be meeting the Successor Primus in his box, so why don't you head over there with my people? I'll join you very shortly," Elantra said. Then, to Gladdic, "And you're planning to sit with me, aren't you?"

Gladdic shifted awkwardly. "Yes, yes, of course."

I looked at him, surprised by how easily cowed he was. He claimed to care for Sidonia yet dared not displease Elantra by refusing her. My opinion of him dropped.

Elantra's smile just widened at his ready agreement. "Go with her, then," she said, her voice honey sweet. It wasn't a suggestion but an implicit order.

Gladdic didn't look at me. He turned to accompany Neveni.

Gladdic and Neveni departed along with Elantra's Servitors and her despoiled Exalted. This, I realized, was a power play. Neveni looked to be part of Elantra's retinue now. Gladdic, ostensibly my companion for this match, had simply deserted me at her command. A Pasus was sweeping in and claiming her territory from an Impyrean.

I was still tempted to lash out at her, but that wouldn't be appropriate, so I decided the best reaction was to play oblivious.

"How very gracious of you, Elantra," I said, and smiled. "Neveni's creature will surely profit from this."

"Oh, I feel immense responsibility for those Excess from our territory." Elantra gave a pleasant trill of laughter. "Though of course, Sidonia, I have no grudges if you truly value that Excess as a . . . friend." She said that last word with a note of distaste. "I'll send her right back here."

"You are all kindness," I said simply, waiting for her to reveal why she lingered with me.

"You two are so very close," Elantra noted, looking between me and the box of the Successor Primus, where Neveni, Gladdic, and the others knelt to greet the arrival of Tyrus Domitrian. "It's unusual at the Chrysanthemum to see two strangers so rapidly in each other's confidence the way you two have been since . . . Oh, ever since that unfortunate incident with Salivar and Devineé, I believe?"

"She was very kind to help me," I said tonelessly. "That night is still such a mystery to me."

"Oh yes." Her eyes glittered malevolently. "But hopefully it's one that can be solved soon . . . for your own peace of mind. After all, Devineé and Salivar have awakened."

My heart gave an unpleasant jerk. "Have they?"

"Yes. It will be ever so interesting to hear what they have to say, won't it?" And without giving me another moment to contemplate the threat in that, Elantra rose and glided away from my section. She reappeared in the box of the Successor Primus, where Neveni and Gladdic both awaited. I watched Elantra draw Tyrus's knuckles to her cheeks. Apparently, she was intent on showing herself gracious to Tyrus even after he'd ruined her family's gift to the Emperor.

So Salivar and Devineé were awake. That didn't mean I needed to worry. Neveni recalled very little of their assault on her from a far lower dose of Scorpion's Breath. I'd force-fed them enough to hopefully obliterate months of their memory.

My heartbeat calmed at the thought.

A great roaring swelled around me. Below, in the arena, Deadly had been unleashed. He trotted out into the center of the arena, his tail wagging, his ears back, his nostrils quivering as he sniffed the air. I rose to see better, a nameless tension gripping me; then I caught sight of Elantra giving a wave to someone near her side.

Her employees scooped up the Exalted and tossed the startled young man into the arena with Neveni's creature. The crowd gave a collective gasp, and even Tyrus Domitrian—despoiler of the innocent creature—lurched forward as though to catch the boy, but missed. The Exalted crumpled down on the rocky ground, his bald head gleaming in the light. For a few moments, Unity crouched there, dazed. Then he stood and looked about with eyes of infinite innocence.

So the Exalted was the chum Elantra intended to feed to Deadly.

I found myself clenching my sweaty fists, understanding washing through me. The Exalted had been bred to be defenseless, to think no evil, to understand no evil. He wouldn't have any instinct to run or defend himself before he was ripped to shreds. Yet unlike a Servitor, he had the cognitive capacity to understand death when it came. He had to—because the Exalted was supposed to appreciate his fate when he was sacrificed.

My gaze returned to Elantra, to her smile as she disposed of the Exalted who had caused her so much inconvenience. Neveni's hands were clapped over her mouth, and Gladdic's head was bowed to avoid seeing the slaughter. At Elantra's side, I saw the Successor Primus who'd been the one to despoil that Exalted.

Tyrus was staring down at the boy, aghast.

I found myself studying him for a long moment, a strange thought coming to me: he didn't want the Exalted killed. Curious that it would matter to him.

My eyes were drawn back to the arena, where Deadly stalked about the helpless Exalted, but did not attack. The beast sniffed at the air, then turned away disinterestedly.

I saw Elantra point to an attendant down in the ring. She whispered something to Neveni.

And the attendant lifted a firearm and shot it at the beast. Forks of electricity enveloped Deadly for a moment, sending him yowling and yelping, running in frantic circles.

And suddenly I couldn't breathe. I couldn't.

They shocked the beast again. And again.

I couldn't see the arena, I could just see that helpless girl they'd thrown in my pen in the corrals. That little girl who'd shivered in the corner and then grown desperate enough to reach for my food. I drove her back, I screamed in her face, and she shook with tears of terror. But I didn't strike her. I didn't touch her. I looked at her for a long time, trying to figure out what this tiny, helpless thing was, and now I couldn't breathe thinking of her as I watched them torment the beast below me.

In the arena, the beast yowled again with another electric jolt, and now he was barking furiously, growling at tormentors he couldn't reach, frothing with mounting rage that would soon express itself on something, on *someone*, and my stomach tightened as all I could think about were those shocks I'd received, the ones that hadn't stopped until I couldn't see, couldn't hold back, couldn't do anything but lash out, but strike, but tear and hurt and kill, and then she was dead, dead at my feet, the first human being I'd ever killed. . . .

And then Deadly was running for the Exalted, and he didn't look pure dog anymore, but he looked like a lethal, heavily muscled, born-and-bred killer. The Exalted let out a whine and covered his face with his hands, just like the girl had when I'd finally moved on her. When she'd realized I was going to kill her, that I was a horrifying monstrous thing with no pity, no reason, no mercy, and I didn't know just what was taking hold of me right now as I remembered that day, but I hurled myself over the wall and dropped down into the arena.

I landed there on the rocks, aware of the hush that fell over the entire watching arena, aware of the confused whimpering of the young Exalted, and the terrifying, slavering growls of Deadly. Both the Exalted and the beast looked to me, the newcomer interfering in the natural order of things, and my sanity returned in a sudden thunder of horror.

I'd just done something Sidonia never would. Something she would never dare. I'd thrown myself down into the fighting arena before all these people. This was madness. Insanity.

The furious creature rounded on me, the new threat, and another terrible thought struck me.

If I fought this creature, I exposed myself before all these people. Before Enmity, out there in the crowd somewhere, who'd identify a Diabolic's strength and movements with a single glimpse.

Yet if I didn't fight this beast, it would kill me.

16

I DREW a breath and looked up at the crowd, all these eyes on me, ready to betray me. I could do this. I could. I'd stay entirely true to Donia's capabilities, and I would still defeat this creature. I wouldn't move like a Diabolic. I wouldn't fight like a Diabolic. I would still win this.

Hands were reaching down, people in the crowd eager to win favor from the Impyrean heir by rescuing her. I saw Gladdic and even Tyrus Domitrian reaching down for me. Elantra hung back, watching me with cruel interest.

Neveni tore off her necklace. "Sidonia!" She tossed it into the ring, where it landed with a faint clack.

Even amid the collective horror at my predicament, the crowd murmured, scandalized. Neveni had just broken a taboo by openly revealing her necklace was a weapon.

I moved for it, certain it could help me.

But Deadly blocked my way, his nostrils quivering, his growl deepening ominously. Despite Neveni's kind gesture, there'd be no help from her.

I backed slowly from the creature as it stalked me. I kept its attention on me, the larger and more dangerous thing in the arena with it. Hatred and hostility radiated from the beast. I reached down and furiously tore strips from my gown. If this animal truly was mostly dog, then it would attack by latching onto the first limb in reach. I kept my eyes fixed on it as I encased my left arm in protective cloth. Then I bent down to pick up one of the stray rocks from the landscape.

"Come at me, animal," I whispered to it.

Deadly's growling sounded more bearish by the second. I needed this over with. I took a sudden step to the side.

With a thunderous roar, the animal sprang forward, a mass of muscle and flashing sharp teeth. It closed the distance faster than any pure canine could hope to, and I thrust out my left arm, bracing myself for the moment those teeth dug into my skin. The great mouth clamped around my flesh; then I dragged it toward me, blind to the pain, as its jaws compressed. With my free hand, I crashed the rock down into its skull.

It would have been easy for me to crush its head if I'd used my full strength, but I was Sidonia, so it took three light blows at my hands. The animal collapsed, going limp on the ground. I jolted back a step and unwound the fabric from my left arm. The teeth had torn into it, but I only had faint, bloody nicks on my skin.

I caught my breath and tossed the rock aside. Dead silence pervaded the arena. When I looked up, I saw hundreds of shocked, staring eyes. My mind went blank. I was going to have to explain why I'd done this. How could I explain myself? How could I put into words the impulse that had led me to intervene, to stop this, when I didn't understand it myself? Donia never would have done this.

Wait.

My thoughts cleared.

No, Donia *would* have done this. Not by jumping into the arena like I had—but beforehand. She would have acted the moment Elantra tossed down that Exalted. Or perhaps even the moment Neveni asked for funding to order an animal of her own.

"Have you people no shame?" I shouted at those staring faces. I crossed over to the Exalted, curled up and frightened, and gathered the frightened boy in my protective arms. I made a show of stroking Unity's trembling back, just as Donia would have. "Is something wrong with you? What pleasure can you possibly take from watching this helpless creature torn apart? Are we savages?"

Whispers and murmurs filled the air.

I caught eyes with Elantra, and she stared hatefully back at me. There was a look on her face of bare contempt, and I knew she was already interpreting my actions as a move against her, against the Pasus family.

And then, to my profound shock, Tyrus Domitrian raised his hand for silence. The noise of the crowd faded, and the Successor Primus gazed down from where he stood, his expression clear and lucid for once.

"Grandeé Impyrean, you've entertained all of us with an unexpected spectacle. Don't we agree?" He looked about, and laughter rippled through the crowd. Tyrus caught my eye. "I think as a reward for your valor, we can give you that Exalted to take under your protection."

I released the boy quickly. I didn't want that. "No."

"No?" Tyrus's eyebrows shot up.

"The creature, Your Eminence. The beast. I want the beast. I paid for it. I want it back. It fights no more in your . . . in your savage entertainments."

It was only in that moment that I understood myself, understood what had driven me to throw myself down between the hunter and the prey. It wasn't the Exalted who resonated with me, despite my easy lies to the crowd while playing the part of Sidonia. No, it was the creature about to kill the Exalted, this beast fashioned like I was to kill mercilessly, and driven to it even when it resisted.

I wouldn't let it happen. Not again.

Instead I would make it mine.

My body shook with excess adrenaline as I was finally lifted out of the arena, as I was ushered down to the animal pens to await Deadly's return.

I expected Neveni to hasten back to my side, but the one who appeared was Gladdic. His dark hair was askew within its golden wraps, and I expected him to fret, to worry.

Instead, he said, "Why would you do such a thing?"

"Excuse me?"

He jerked a step toward me, then moved no closer. "Sidonia, that was scandalous! You're not doing the Impyreans any favors by behaving so irrationally. My father will never let me associate with you after this!"

Anger swelled in me. I tugged my sleeve up to expose the light gashes on my arm for the nearby med bots, and suddenly found myself thinking of Gladdic so meekly obeying Elantra and slinking off to join her.

For that matter, that very first day at the Chrysanthemum, Elantra had alluded to the salt baths, and Gladdic had begun to speak, then stopped. He'd been ready to warn me of what would come, I realized now, but then Elantra had silenced him. And he'd *let* her silence him.

"So to avoid scandal and preserve my reputation," I said coldly, "I should simply have allowed that beast to be tortured and that Exalted to be ripped apart?"

"It's not like it's a person," Gladdic said.

I surveyed him clinically, seeing him in a new light. Not just an outwardly fragile, delicate young man, but inwardly.

This pathetic weakling was unworthy of Sidonia.

"Just leave me, Gladdic."

"Sidonia—"

I wanted to strike him. I turned my back to him instead. "I said *leave*. I have nothing more to say to you."

Coward that he was, Gladdic did not argue, did not object. I listened to his footsteps slink away from me. I realized I was shaking all over with anger. When movement sounded behind me, it occurred to me that he'd come back for a last word. I ripped around, ready to snarl at him, but then my heart froze.

It was Enmity.

The Diabolic studied me in the bright fluorescent light of the force fields. Med bots still tended my bruised arm. I shoved them aside, bracing myself for the moment she closed the distance and killed me.

She'd seen me in the arena. She'd seen everything.

I'd tried my best to move like Donia in the arena, to conceal my strength, my speed. But from the way she was looking at me—like she could see nothing else—I suspected with a great swell of dread that I'd failed.

But Enmity made no move toward me. She just studied me like some strange curiosity. "Do you believe what you said to him?"

"Believe . . . what?" I said warily.

"What you said to that boy, just now. You believe saving that crea-ture was the right thing to do?"

The question caught me off guard. All I could say was, "I couldn't allow that to happen. What was going to take place in that arena was . . ." I couldn't properly explain away the strange compulsion I'd had to intervene. All I could say was, "It was wrong."

Enmity looked around us, seeing the pens, this place that so resembled the corrals where we'd both been raised. Where we'd both been the creatures on the other side of the force field.

"Perhaps I've misjudged you, Grandeé Impyrean. Given what I am, compassion is something very strange to me." Her cold-eyed gaze found me. "But I'm not blind to its value. You struck me as an oddity from the moment I first interacted with you, and now I sus-pect this is why. I simply didn't understand someone so . . . kind."

With those words, she seemed content that she'd solved the mystery that was Sidonia Impyrean and withdrew from my sight. I stood there as the med bots flew back over to heal my arm, trying to fathom that I'd won her over because of what I'd said to Gladdic. In intervening for a nonperson, a creature like Enmity, like me, I'd done something so like Donia, it explained away her suspicions about me.

And from that day forward, Enmity followed me no more.

My actions sent scandalized whispers through the Chrysanthemum. The Grandiloquy of more tender feelings who'd privately detested the animal fights found ways to sidle up to me and whisper, "I thought you were very brave, Grandeé Impyrean."

Others cut me. When I neared them, they made a point of turn-ing away and dropping their voices in hopes of concealing their conversations. I'd made an unseemly public display of condemnation for a popular pastime, after all.

I read nothing into it until one evening after services in the Great Heliosphere, when the Grandiloquy assembled in the presence chamber to take the vapors. The heavy weight of someone's gaze rested on the back of my neck, and I turned—just in time to see the Emperor's eyes on me, and the Grandeé Cygna leaning over to whisper in his ear.

That's when I chanced a look about me, at the Grandiloquy near me, those who'd expressed sympathies for my actions in the arena. Then I looked toward the ones who'd been avoiding me, clouds of vapors flowing up from their mouths, their eyes occasionally assessing my group. I felt a shock.

They were stratified along the exact same fissure as Senator von Pasus and Senator von Impyrean's rivalry in the Senate. Those inclined to embrace my actions and gather about me were Amadors, Rothesays, and Wallstroms. All proponents of restoring scientific pursuits.

Those who took the opposite view, those who detested my gesture and began openly and loudly boasting, especially in my hearing, of the new creatures they'd commissioned, as though to make a point—they were Fordyces, Atons, Locklaites, and other Pasus allies. The most ardent Helionics.

It couldn't be a coincidence. Those families who dared not express displeasure with the Emperor openly were doing so secondhand, by taking a stance against their foes regarding the animal fights. And they were beginning to rally around me. Around the heir to the Impyrean family, the focal point of their discontent.

I excused myself immediately and fled the crowd, because this was exactly the opposite of what I was supposed to do here at court. I was supposed to *avoid* notice, not attract it!

Yet just as I reached the doorway, I glanced back toward the Emperor. He sat gripping the arms of his chair, surveying the Impyrean faction from his high vantage point, an icy look on his face.

He was a man without mercy, and now he had his enemies coalescing in plain sight.

17

I BEGAN withdrawing to my villa more often, hoping to be forgotten. When visitors who'd recently expressed their sympathies for my actions in the arena attempted to pay a call, I had my Servitors refuse them entry. I played sick with all but Neveni.

Fortunately, I had Deadly to occupy much of my time.

At first he'd been hostile, ready to rip at me whenever I approached. I forbade my Servitors to interact with him and gave him a room all his own in my villa. Then, when I was sure there was no surveillance in the room, I shamelessly used my superior strength to teach him obedience. When he came at me, I pinned him down, forced him to show his belly. When he snapped at me with his jaws, I seized him by the scruff of his neck until he desisted.

I wasn't sure at first whether a monster bred for murder in an arena could be tamed. Deadly was such a mixture of animals that approaching him as a pure dog meant neglecting the lion, neglecting the bear.

But gradually, Deadly learned to obey me. He even revealed a frivo-lous side. When I returned to my chamber for the evening, he'd scurry about me enthusiastically until I petted him to his satisfaction. Then he'd tug at the legs of my garments to provoke me into playing with him. I found that if I made my fingers crawl over the floor like small animals, he would eagerly nip at them and chase them.

The only problem he faced with being civilized was the sheer energy he needed to expend, just as I did, and the limited space in which he had to roam. The longest pylon reaching out into space served as one of the few vigorous walks we could undertake away from prying eyes.

Neveni joined me and the beast during one of our walks down Berneval Stretch. She gave a jump of fright whenever he drew too close to us. "Are you sure you want to keep it?"

"He's already becoming easier to control. He learns quickly. Oh, and I have something for you." I fished in my pocket and produced her necklace. "Thank you for this. I know you invited disgrace by reveal-ing it in public. I won't forget your gesture."

She fingered the necklace gingerly. "I don't care what everyone else thinks of me. They all have weapons of their own. They're hypocrites for acting like I'm the bad one for having this, especially after . . ." Her voice grew jagged. "After what Salivar and Devineé did to me."

I said nothing, because I wasn't sure how to console her, so it seemed best I didn't try.

"Where's yours?" Neveni said with a sneaky smile. "You have to have a weapon. I know you do. I won't tell anyone."

I didn't bother carrying a weapon. I *was* the weapon. But I felt a need to give her an answer, so I made one up. "My shoe. There's a blade hidden in the sole."

"Why didn't you use it against Deadly?"

"I'm . . . I'm not so brave as you are in the face of public censure."

Neveni laughed and poked my arm. "Says the girl who jumped into an arena to save an Exalted." She stopped. "I can't walk any farther in these heels. Go on without me, Sidonia."

I bade her farewell, feeling indulgent toward her after her recent gesture. There was something I appreciated about her, almost *trusted* about her, to the extent that I could trust anyone other than Sidonia. When Deadly and I resumed our walk, I missed her company.

But at least I could move faster without Neveni around, and now that Enmity had abandoned her pursuit of me, I could take this indulgence. I picked up the pace. Deadly perked up, eager to run as well. We weren't creatures to creep slowly and take our time.

I launched into a flat sprint. It was faster than any I'd done since my muscle reduction, and to my immense pleasure, Deadly kept up with me, electrified with energy as I was. We reached the end point far too soon, my lungs rasping in a pleasurable way, my muscles shaking off the terrible stiffness of disuse.

It took a toll on me, maintaining this physical weakness. The canine swirled eagerly about my feet, sniffing here and there. I let him rest as I studied the wall of sigils and names. There were more names there, new ones since my first visit, families from all over the Empire.

My gaze ran over the sigils idly—and then sharpened. I began studying them closely.

The Bellwethers. The Wallstroms. The Amadors. The Rothesays. The same names that had recently flocked about me. Their arrival at court hadn't invited nearly the same attention mine had, as the daughter of the Great Heretic, so I hadn't paid enough attention to their coming. I hadn't realized how many of them were newly arrived at the Chrysanthemum.

They'd been summoned here just as Sidonia had.

Every survival instinct I had began to scream at me as I studied the new arrivals on the wall. There were so many faces in the *Valor Novus*, I hadn't paid much attention to newcomers. But this wall of sigils illustrated the situation to me in stark clarity.

Sidonia's family wasn't a rare exception, where the child had been brought to court in the parent's place. She was just the first child collected from many other great families. The Emperor was gathering the heirs in his fortress.

But why? To what end?

I'd paused so long, Deadly grew restless at my side. He began making odd noises, so I turned to him. He lunged for me—but not to bite me. He began licking my cheek.

A bubbling noise escaped my lips in my surprise. It took me a moment to feel my smile, to realize what the sound was.

I'd laughed. Laughed.

I reared back from the dog, swept up his leash, and tugged him into step with me, shaken inside. My fingers roved my lips, where that laugh had come out of me unplanned, unintended.

Whatever was the matter with me?

"My moth—um, I'm worried."

Sidonia was using the Matriarch's avatar again, making her high voice and uncertain question seem all the more incongruous.

"Worried about me?" I echoed.

Donia's gaze wavered. "More or less."

Of course the Matriarch wasn't worried about me. She had to have some sources at court. She must have heard about my interference in the arena and the scandal it caused.

"All is well. Tell everyone at the fortress that. I made a rash move that I won't repeat. And assure, uh, yourself that I'm lying very low at the moment. Attention spans are very short here. Soon I'll be forgotten. Though I . . ."

"You what?"

"I don't believe Gladdic and I will be associating after this. I'm sorry." He wasn't worthy of her. I'd explain that to her someday.

To my surprise, Donia waved that off as though it was inconsequential. "But tell me about you. *I'm* worried."

And this time, I knew she meant herself.

I'm fine. I wanted to say it, to reassure her right away, but the way she was looking at me—even from behind the eyes of the Matriarch—made my chest grow tight.

If anyone could answer my question, she could.

"I'm fine. It's just . . ." My thoughts rushed to Deadly, to the way he'd licked my face. To what I'd done after that. "I've been slightly out of sorts. I'm not used to being in this position. I *laughed* at something."

"You what?" gasped Donia.

"The dog hybrid lunged at me. I thought he meant to bite me, but he was affectionate. He licked me and was so needy. And it just happened. I laughed. And I didn't mean to do it."

"Nem—uh, Sidonia, that's not something to fear."

The words set me on the defensive. "I'm not afraid."

A small smile quirked her lips. "I know. You're not scared of anything. I wasn't trying to imply that. I just meant, laughter isn't something to feel *unsettled* about."

"You don't understand. This is unlike me. It may be a sign something is wrong with me."

"Don't you . . ." She blew out a breath, obviously noticing as I did the trickiness of saying most anything while on a potentially insecure connection. "Don't you recall the day you got your Diabolic, Nemesis, and the way certain parts of her brain were made bigger? It was done so she could love you." Her voice quavered. "But you don't just build a part of the brain for one person. Once it's there, it's there. I bet Nemesis could have loved other things if given the chance. I bet she could learn to laugh at things too."

"That's ridiculous. We're talking about a *Diabolic*."

"Or we're talking about a *girl*," said Donia softly. "A girl who grew up treated like a monster, so she thinks of herself that way, a person who's never allowed herself to feel because she thinks she shouldn't—"

"Nonsense. You're being absurd."

But despite myself, I began thinking of Enmity, whose instincts as a Diabolic dictated that she pursue me, stalk me, unearth my secrets. Enmity, who'd put her own suspicions to rest at just a hint that I might possess an unusual ability to see creatures like her as people. It was as though she craved such understanding, or even needed it.

Could we really be more than I'd ever fathomed?

Donia seemed to think so. "Don't you see why Nemesis would never laugh? She was never allowed to laugh, never given a reason to laugh. I don't know what the corrals were like, but they must have been horrifying, traumatic. And I wasn't any better to her."

This time, "I" referred to her mother, of course.

"Then once she had, uh, *you* to watch out for, Nemesis took her role so earnestly, she couldn't let herself do something like laugh. If she had a chance away from all that to be her own person and learn to feel her feelings, it's not something to fear. It's beautiful. It's a wonderful thing."

Aggravation reared up within me. "If everything you say was true, if . . . if Nemesis were capable of such feelings, then there'd be no difference between a Diabolic and a person but for physical strength."

"Maybe there isn't. Not as much of one as you think." Donia firmed her lips. "That's what I've always thought. That's what I've always said."

I closed my eyes. My mind was back on that little girl in my pen with me. On Sutera's guileless expression just before I seized her. My thoughts turned to all those lives I'd taken over the years.

Doing that made me a good Diabolic.

Being a good Diabolic meant being a hideous person.

If I was a person, then everything I was, everything I had become, was profane and warped and evil. I was either a perfectly acceptable Diabolic or an abomination of a human being.

"This conversation is foolish. I can't speak to you anymore. I need to go," I said.

"But—"

"I am ending this conversation!" And I cut the link with Sidonia off and settled, shaken, in my villa. I looked over at Deadly, slumbering in the corner, and resolved to put the dog in the arena tomorrow and be rid of him. And then he lifted his head at my scrutiny and stared back at me, his ears flattening, and a crushing sensation gripped my chest as I knew I could not do it.

What was the *matter* with me? The only thing I'd ever felt something for was Donia. She was all that mattered, and now this stupid genetically engineered hybrid was making me act like an irrational idiot.

I'd even forgotten to tell Donia about the imperial heirs being collected at court, which was the whole reason I'd contacted her.

It was no disaster to wait until next time.

18

THE GRAND SANCTUM was located in the *Valor Novus*, directly beneath the Great Heliosphere. It was seldom used. It was there for the rare occasions when Senators and other government representatives arrived from all over the Empire for a Convocation. Convocations were major events, usually when a new Emperor was inaugurated. Generations might enter the Senate and pass on without attending a formal Convocation. It wasn't just Senators who convened, but all the lesser quorums of the Empire's ruling classes: Viceroys, Governors, and hereditary titleholders from families too important traditionally to lack a rank, but too poor to hold real territory.

That was why it came as a shock when I received a message that an actual Convocation was to be held in a day. I was ordered to attend as Senator von Impyrean's proxy.

I listened to the message again, trying to comprehend it. That was when the intercom in my villa announced, "Neveni Sagnau to see Sidonia Impyrean."

I turned to Neveni as she walked in. Her hair was a mess, as though she'd just stumbled out of bed and come directly to me, as perplexed as I was.

"Did you hear about a Convocation, or is someone playing a prank on me?"

"You're summoned as well?"

"As my mother's proxy." Her eyes were wide, panic-stricken. "I don't know anything about doing my mother's job. What do they mean I have to proxy for her?"

"We go in their stead." Even as I spoke, the idea confused me. Senator von Impyrean could just attend the Convocation over the galactic forums. There was no need for me to go in his place. Something strange was happening here.

"There are going to be thousands of people there," Neveni said, almost to herself. "Surely we won't have to do anything but listen."

"Right."

"But . . . listen to what?"

I shook my head, as clueless as she was.

"I tried contacting my mother and I couldn't get through." She sank down into a seat. "Sidonia, this is really strange. They can't just give us one day's notice. How does the Emperor expect everyone to get here in time?"

A cold feeling shot through me. My mind turned to the wall of sigils I'd seen down Berneval Stretch, evidence of all the recently arrived Grandiloquy.

The Emperor, I realized, had already gathered everyone needed for the Convocation in advance. He must have been planning this since before he summoned Sidonia.

But to what end?

Like Neveni, I sent out a message to my family. I tried to contact the Impyrean fortress, hoping for instructions, for guidance. For something.

But like Neveni, I received no reply.

Convocations required something more than just ceremonial gowns. They required reflective screen garb, so when all the representatives throughout the Empire gathered in the Grand Sanctum, where the gravity was specially designed to allow every square centimeter of floor, ceiling, and wall to be occupied by seats and people, our clothing itself amplified the image of the Emperor on his floating throne at the very center.

Most of the lesser Grandiloquy had to beg and borrow money for their specialized garb. I bought Neveni her own. The Matriarch would not be pleased by this expense once I got in contact with her.

There were sixty greater Grandiloquy families in total, the most powerful of the Senate and the most important territory holders in the Empire. As the representative for the Impyrean family, my seat was in the inner circle, up a precarious climb of platforms that encircled the Emperor's position. When I found my position, the stairwell retracted into the floor behind me. I chanced a look around.

The sheer scale of the Convocation took my breath. All over the spherical space, bodies moved, people shifting about, their specialized clothing flickering with the color corresponding to the section they were supposed to occupy. Somewhere out there was Neveni. Closer to me, at the next seat over, sat Senator von Pasus. It was my first time seeing the great opponent of the Impyreans in person.

I studied him, my keen eyesight able to pick out his features despite the distance between us. His hair was long and gray, signs of age on his face. Clearly he wasn't one to liberally use false-youth treatment. Perhaps it was his attempt to appear more dignified. It occurred to me that unlike many of the other Senators here, Senator von Pasus had been given enough notice to come in person from his own star system.

My eyes roved over the other representatives of great families. Senators von Fordyce and Aton were both there, but a scattering of other families were represented only by their heirs as proxies. Our Convocation garb was programmed to display our family sigils, so I easily picked out the heirs to the Amador and Chomderley families. All young, all twitchy and uneasy-looking.

There was a clear distinction, I realized suddenly. The Senators of the Helionic faction were *all* here in person. Senator von Impyrean's faction, though, was entirely absent—their heirs all here as proxies in their stead.

I clenched and unclenched my fists, knowing something was very wrong. All I could do was wait.

Then the air split with the boom of the imperial celebration music, and the great procession of the royal relatives streamed out. They took their place at the circle just inside ours.

At last, out came the Emperor and his three Diabolics.

Along with a stream of thousands of security bots.

I caught my breath and looked around as the small metallic machines whizzed up into the air and took positions throughout the room. Not firing, just positioning themselves in silent threat before each section of the room. One security bot positioned itself before each of the seats of the great families. I found myself gazing directly into the targeting eye of a small, rounded device hovering mere meters from my position. My eyes could pick out the tiny pinprick laser barrel jutting out from it, ready to slice me in two.

Yet when I peered over at Senator von Pasus, I discovered that those families in favor with the Emperor had no such security bots aiming at them. The Helionic faction, again, had been spared.

Goose bumps prickled down my spine. I could vault from this chair and swat down the bot before me, but I knew one of the other bots could easily swivel around and kill me moments later. I just had to sit here and be obedient, whatever happened. I was trapped.

The Emperor raised his arms out to the side, and immediately the images on distant clothing shifted and began to form pixels of a larger image: that of Emperor von Domitrian's face, his skin a peach shade today, his blond hair woven with gold and set in a halo about his head, his eyes glowing proudly as he surveyed his subjects. When he raised his chin, we all pressed our hands to our hearts in salute. The rippling of arms moving in unison from so many bodies momentarily entranced me.

And then the Emperor spoke:

"Beloved subjects, I thank you for arriving as representatives or proxies for all the territories of our great Empire. We convene here today to celebrate victories over our enemies, present and past. Those battles form the foundation of humanity's current greatness and galactic dominance. . . ."

I looked to the sides, the Emperor's proud countenance beaming at me from all angles, and found other people—the proxies, like me—glancing around as well, trying to figure out what was going on. Surely the Emperor hadn't gone to the trouble of a Convocation without an important reason.

And then we learned why we were here.

"Alas, despite this Empire enjoying prosperity and strength under the rule of the Domitrian family for many centuries now, we find ourselves at a dangerous crossroads. There is a malevolent ideology

157

growing like a cancer in our midst. I speak, of course, of those who seek to recover the sciences best forgotten."

I caught my breath. *This* was why we were here.

"Those who believe this dangerous new ideology aren't merely hysterics who believe malignant space is a great menace sure to engulf the Empire one day, or Partisans among the Excess who believe themselves more powerful without our benign hand to guide them. There are traitors and blasphemers from the very highest ranks of this hallowed Empire."

My eyes remained locked on him, on that small figure on his throne amid this great assembly—not the larger-than-life face staring out from the electronic clothing. All I could think of was the fissure in opinion since my actions in the arena, the way the Chrysanthemum had seemed polarized. The Impyreans were at the center of this. They were the unofficial leaders of the "cancerous" faction the Emperor detested.

"Some Senators and Viceroys have taken it into their heads that they, and not I, should make decisions for the good of the Empire. They've spread to the Excess those heresies they do not need to know. They've breached the sacred mysteries of the Living Cosmos, even against my express orders. Many of you know who these traitors are. Many of you are spawn of these traitors."

My hands curled into fists, my heart pounding. I gazed directly at the machine floating before me, poised to shoot, wondering if I was about to die.

The Emperor let the silence hang there, grow thicker. With each passing moment, it became more difficult to imagine anyone breaking it, and perhaps that was what the Emperor intended. His smile broadened over his false-youth face.

"That's why I've called you here for a very special Convocation.

You see, the errant few who spread these blasphemies—they weren't invited. In respect to the sanctity of the great families, I combed the Grandiloquy for the most suitable heirs, the ones who both represent old blood and obedience to their rightful leaders—and I summoned them all here."

I stared at him, filled with apprehension.

"Today we are gathered here for one purpose alone: some of you have proven yourselves worthy of your family power, but your relatives, alas, have not. As of today, you take over their titles, their duties. Those of you here to serve as proxies are now elevated to leadership of your families."

I gawked at him. He couldn't just say Senator von Impyrean wasn't Senator anymore, that Sidonia was instead. It didn't work that way. Even the Emperor couldn't just arbitrarily replace people like that.

And were it not for these security bots poised to slaughter us all, someone might have pointed that out already.

"And to ensure this smooth transition of titles," the Emperor went on, his smile like ice, "I've eliminated the other contenders who'd question your claim."

Everything in me froze.

I didn't understand. I couldn't understand.

Voices fanned out around me, behind me, as people made sense of his words. All I could do was sit there and think with utter disbelief that this wasn't right, that I'd misheard.

"And so I called this Convocation today so you can look upon one another," said the Emperor, "the new and old inheritors of this great Empire. And of course, so we may pay tribute to those misguided souls who are no longer here to corrupt this august assembly." He waved his hand elegantly in the air.

And then on the glowing clothing of the lesser Grandiloquy of the outer ring, the images began to flicker. An imposing space station enveloped in a sudden burst of flames. A fleet of ships swallowed up by an automated minefield. A planet swept with an explosion.

I still didn't understand what I was seeing until the Impyrean fortress appeared on the viewer, with the time stamp of the day before.

No.

Then it exploded.

I lurched to my feet, almost tumbling off the platform at the sight. "No!"

No, no, no. The word echoed through my mind, and it wasn't real, it wasn't happening.

But it played before my eyes, cruel and vivid, the fortress crumpled in on itself, sending debris spiraling out above the familiar gas giant I'd seen every day of my life with Sidonia.

I was seeing my home destroyed—*Sidonia's* home destroyed.

"No," I croaked, and I thought of the Matriarch not answering me when I'd tried to contact them.

I thought of the Impyreans not answering me.

More images of more destruction, old families and new, all powerful, cut down at the root in a sneak attack, and the Emperor's proud face soon replaced the images, his sharp-eyed gaze seeming to cut into my very soul. Cries and shouts followed the images. In the distance, people curled over with grief. Others shook with sobs. Some sat stone-faced. Some, like Senator von Pasus, looked around smugly, exempt from the carnage by imperial favor.

All I could think was, *This can't be real. This can't be happening. . . .*

"Some of you lost whole families," the Emperor announced as the last images faded, "and I assure you, they brought their fates on themselves. Those of you who came here as proxies for your relatives leave here as powerful figures in the Empire. And you will remember, forever, the misguided blasphemies that brought your families to this point. I trust you will forever regard with gratitude the Emperor who chose you for this high rank. If you do not, well, we can always have another demonstration like this, perhaps with different people in attendance and you on the screen."

I felt like the world was going to dissolve around me, because this wasn't real, it had to be a nightmare I could wake up from.

The Emperor concluded his speech with talk of a gala—a gala to *celebrate* the sudden rise in rank of so many young Grandiloquy. I could barely understand him, and I wasn't rousing from this dream.

If I didn't shake it off soon, I'd have to believe that the Emperor had killed the Impyreans.

I'd have to believe he'd done it.

He'd killed them all.

Including Sidonia.

19

IMPOSSIBLE. It was impossible. I sat in my villa, sending transmission after transmission that wasn't being answered. I ignored my Servitors and just tried to wake from this awful nightmare.

I was sending another transmission when Gladdic walked in. I hadn't heard the intercom.

"Sidonia, I am so sorry." There were tears on his face.

I looked at him, at this stranger I felt I had never met before. I sent another transmission. This time, they would answer.

"I had no idea this would happen. My parents knew beforehand, but they told me nothing," Gladdic went on. "I would have warned you. I swear it. Please believe me. I'm here for you."

"Quiet. It's some sort of game. It's not true," I growled at him. "You're interrupting me." No answer to the transmission. I sent another.

"Listen to me. I'm a senatorial heir," Gladdic said, drawing toward me, his eyes searching, urgent. "One day I'll be able to make decisions for myself, and when that happens, you'll have an ally in the Aton family. You're not alone—"

"I don't care about the Aton family. You're talking nonsense. Senator von Impyrean is ally enough for me."

"Your father is dead. You are Senator von Impyrean now. I'm sorry."

"I said *quiet!*"

He was irritating me, because he was actually standing there, suggesting what I'd seen was real and the Emperor had actually destroyed the Impyrean family while I was away. That Sidonia had died, and here I was, here to protect her, to be a sacrifice in her place, and it was for nothing. I couldn't be alive if Sidonia was dead. It didn't work that way. I'd know it somehow. I would feel it if she was dead. I would know. The universe could not look and feel normal if all reason for its existence was gone.

"Please, you're distressed." Gladdic's hand was on my arm, trying to tug me from the panel. "You should rest. We can talk about . . ."

"Unhand me."

The words came out of me harshly, and suddenly I looked at this creature with absolutely no patience or desire for his opinion.

If it was true, if Sidonia was dead—I could hardly stand to think it—but if it was true, I had no use for him. I had no reason to make nice. If it wasn't true, then how dare he say it was, how dare he try to pull me from the panel.

"Sidonia—" He tugged at my arm.

I snapped.

I launched up and drove my fist into his face. The crunch of his nose shattering beneath my blow filled me with such satisfaction that I stalked after him when he yelled out, and then I tangled my hand in his hair and hauled him toward the door.

"What are you doing? What are you doing? Stop! Stop!" Gladdic screamed, fighting my grip.

I thrust him outside.

Gladdic clutched his bleeding face, looking at me with shock.

"If you come back, I'll kill you." With those words, I closed the door behind him.

Then I sent another transmission to the Impyrean fortress.

No answer.

No answer.

I hadn't slept in five days, and the truth was beginning to edge into me, gnawing noxiously at my insides, strangling my throat. The Servitors milled about like the mindless automatons they were, going about the simple household tasks of keeping my clothes fresh for the next time I wore them, keeping up appearances. I remembered to order them to walk Deadly. Despite all the training and discipline I'd instilled in the canine, it took several of the Servitors to haul him out with them, to bring him back.

Otherwise, my thoughts were disorganized, chaotic.

I found myself standing in the center of the room, looking about dazedly. Gladdic's blood had left thick blotches across the carpet. I stared at them.

Everything felt surreal, wrong. Different.

I stepped out of the villa into the great sky dome, four of the suns pouring light down from overhead, and I gazed up at them until they made my eyes sting. I didn't know where to go or what to do.

"Sidonia."

I was ready to kill this person, whoever it was, but then the sight of Neveni broke through my insanity. Her eyes were bloodshot.

"I'm Viceroy of Lumina now, Sidonia," she whispered to me.

I just stared at her.

Her lower lip wobbled. "I called home. She's dead. The Emperor sent in troops and they killed my mother, just like that. He appointed me Viceroy in her place, but I'm forbidden to return to Lumina. I asked because—because I wasn't sure what to do. But I have to stay here. Who ever heard of a Viceroy overseeing a planet remotely? Viceroys aren't Senators. Their job is where they govern. And . . . and how am I going to explain to the Excess who elected my mother that I'm taking her place? I'm *seventeen*. It's a joke. The office isn't even supposed to be hereditary." She blinked at me. "And you're Senator von Impyrean." She broke into hysterical laughter, and I just gazed at her. "Senator Sidonia von Impyrean!"

That's when I knew with absolute certainty: this was no nightmare, no hallucination. The Emperor had done it. He'd killed Sidonia. He'd killed the Matriarch and the Senator, and he meant to replace them with the girl in his possession. Me. He wanted *me* to be the next Senator.

"What do we do?" whispered Neveni. "My God, what do we do?"

I closed my eyes, the heat of the suns hot against my skin. Now I was a Diabolic without a master. Without a reason to exist. It was a great cosmic joke that I'd come here to save Sidonia and instead doomed her. She was meant to be the proxy Senator. She'd been meant to live. But I had lived instead.

Not for long, though.

I was through. No more fake smiles, fake courtesies, no more pretending to be something soft and weak. I would shed all pretenses and wreak as much vengeance and destruction as I could before the Emperor cut me down.

"I'm going to kill the Emperor."

I realized I'd spoken aloud only when Neveni gasped. My eyes flew open, and I saw her looking around, horrorstruck.

"You can't say that aloud. It's treason! They'll take you away!"

I seized her and yanked her to me. "If you repeat my words to anyone," I whispered to her, my hands squeezing so hard around her shoulders I knew it had to hurt, "I'll crush your skull. Do you understand?"

Neveni's mouth dropped open. She nodded quickly. "I won't. I won't tell."

It occurred to me that I should kill her the way I did Sutera nu Impyrean. It would be so easy, one twist of her neck. If I didn't, she might warn them.

Something stayed my hand.

I shoved Neveni away from me and stalked off, an emptiness in my heart that I knew would linger until my final breath.

As soon as I made the decision to kill the Emperor, the frightening sense of disorientation fled, leaving a stark, direct path before me.

I would kill the Emperor. I would do it today. Immediately afterward, his Diabolics would turn on me and I would die. My life would be measured in mere hours, not even days, and I accepted it.

As soon as I formulated my plan, I knew how I would do it. I could kill the Emperor because I had surprise on my side, and I knew enough of the court's layout to complete my grim mission.

I'd observed enough to notice the Emperor's patterns. After meeting with his advisers, the Emperor liked to relax for several hours. He always proceeded down a narrow corridor toward his lounging room. That's where I'd approach him. Just outside the lounging room. I'd twist my face as though I were in tears. I'd drop to my knees like a terrified girl and shake my shoulders as though overcome by sobs.

I'd plead with him as the helpless new Impyrean heir—as the meek and timid Sidonia—to please hear the words I could barely whisper between sobs.

The Emperor, certain he'd vanquished the Impyreans, certain he had a malleable, weak girl on his hands, would wave away his Diabolics and step forward to hear my words, ready to relish every tremulous syllable over my lips as I pleaded . . . for what? What would he hope for? For a sign I feared him, or perhaps for a sign I was desperate for his favor?

It didn't matter. All I could think of was that day in court when he'd had Leather skin herself alive and the way he'd avidly watched my face. He was a man who took pleasure in the suffering and terror of others, or perhaps of young girls in particular. Either way, I'd dangle a promise of just what he enjoyed most.

And then I'd have him. I would drive a dagger into him. If he was close enough and his Diabolics far enough, I'd aim for a lethal spot that would give him several minutes of agony before his inevitable death. If I didn't have that luxury, his aorta would do.

The privy council chamber was just meeting when I slunk into the corridor. I'd always imagined the last hours of my life in wait for death would fly by as I drank in every last minute of existence, yet now time seemed to stretch on into eternity.

I wondered if Sidonia had ever received her answers to those questions she had about the meaning of life and the reason for existence, if not in an afterlife, then as some chemical burst in the brain moments before death. She told me people sometimes saw a light before they died, one that seemed to offer all the answers to all the mysteries of the cosmos. I hoped she saw it. I wondered if she was afraid. I wondered . . .

The thought squeezed me like a clamping fist.

I wondered if she thought of me, if she had a moment to wonder why I hadn't been there to protect her.

Then the door slid open, and out prowled Enmity, surveying the corridor. In the half-light, she moved like a great tiger.

Her gaze found me. "Senator von Impyrean, what are you doing here?"

We stared at each other, and I had no excuses.

She'd always suspected me. Now I was about to prove her suspicions had been right. I was her enemy. And in moments, I would be the death of her or she would be the death of me.

20

"I MUST WAIT," I told her, giving her one opportunity. "I need to speak with your master."

Enmity's eyes narrowed. "No. You'll leave this place. At once."

I could kill her and everything would still go according to plan. The Emperor would emerge from that chamber if Enmity didn't return to raise an alarm. I'd be frightened, hysterical, and he'd demand to know where Enmity was. I'd stammer an excuse—and kill him, too.

"Did you hear me? I said withdraw from here, Senator von Impyrean," Enmity said, moving toward me in a ripple of muscle, her eyes an icy, fathomless blue. "Go at once or I'll remove you."

I was going to kill her master. By the end of today, even after she crushed my skull, tore the skin from my bones, and pulverized what remained of me, her master would still be dead. Just as Sidonia would still be gone. This great awful emptiness inside me would consume her, too.

Death wasn't always a cruelty. I would have died a thousand times rather than outlive Sidonia. So I would do Enmity a kindness and kill her now.

I bowed my head, forcing my shoulders to shake, making sobbing noises issue from my throat, hiding my face with one hand. The other clutched the dagger hidden in the folds of my dress.

"I said leave!" Enmity reached for me.

That's when I buried the dagger into her side.

I was a fraction too slow to drive it through her aorta. She moved at the last moment, a full-strength Diabolic with all the muscle mass I no longer had. All trace of calmness instantly snapped away from her expression, and she thrust me with irresistible force through the air, and the wall of the corridor rushed up to my face.

My head cracked with an explosion of stars against the wall, but the pain didn't faze me. I neatly rolled over to my feet and turned to face her, and found Enmity surveying the blood hemorrhaging from her torso.

She balled up her left hand into a fist and jammed it against her side, digging a knuckle into the wound to stanch the bleeding. Then she looked up at me. "So I was right. There is more to you."

"Yes," I said. "You were right."

She exploded toward me. I dodged and slashed at her with the knife again.

It drew a jagged gash across her cheek, but she snared my arm and wrenched it behind me, twisting at my ligaments. I yelled out reflexively, my prickling fingers dropping the knife; then I jammed my heel back into her instep. Her foot crunched and she roared in pain. I whirled about and slammed her across the face with my fist, sinking one punch after another into her, then kicked her away from me.

She stumbled, still clutching a hand over her bleeding side. "You're too fast," she said breathlessly. "You're no person!"

"You know exactly what I am."

She blazed toward me and I aimed my punch at her side—but she anticipated that and whirled around at the last moment, rocketing her elbow into my face. My nose erupted in pain, and my balance flew out from me. The world upended as I careened backward. I kicked my legs hard enough to roll upright again, but Enmity was already on me, a mass of muscle and driving fists. Knuckles pounded my cheek, splintering pain through my skull. Blood blinded me, stinging my eyes, but I remembered where her legs had been and crushed my boots into her knees, feeling her kneecap dislocate with an ugly crackle.

Enmity aimed the momentum of her fall right at me, elbow first.

The elbow shattered my ribs as it hit me with her full weight behind it, and this was where my loss of muscle began to count.

She was heavy, heavier than I'd been prepared for, and her weight crushed me down into the ground as her fists began to slam madly into me, sending nauseating pain into my ribs, and then the world became a blinding blur, whirling and teetering, and when I found myself on my stomach, trying to push myself up, I could not. My arms gave out.

And then I saw boots shuffling before me, Enmity dragging herself on her one knee to limp before me. Her hand tangled in my collar and hoisted me up, but my legs wouldn't hold.

"How fascinating," she said, her fathomless blue eyes in mine. "You're a Diabolic who's undergone a very effective body modification. Whose are you?"

I bit at her arm and tried to jab at her eyes with my fingers, but my hands couldn't connect where I wanted them to, and she shook me, shouting, "Who is your master?"

"It's Sidonia Impyrean!" I shouted back at her. "It . . . was."

The words rang in the air between us, and I felt like I was crumpling, decaying, and some emotion traced the Diabolic's bloody face. It couldn't be pity. We weren't made for that. But it was something. "I understand."

She released me in a heap on the floor, and I lay there as she leaned over to pick up my dagger. The knowledge that I hadn't killed the Emperor settled in my brain, but through the blinding pain and despair, I couldn't feel anger about that.

It wasn't revenge I'd wanted, I realized then.

It was an end to the gaping void that was an existence without Donia.

Enmity knew it too.

She staggered over to me in a blurry haze and lifted the knife above me, the blade catching the light. I would be dead in mere moments and I was ready, I was grateful.

"Enmity!"

The voice rang out in the narrow corridor, and hasty footsteps beat their way over.

"Enmity, what are you doing to Senator von Impyrean?"

"This isn't Sidonia Impyrean, Your Eminence," Enmity said, not moving. "This is a Diabolic who intended to attack the Emperor."

"You're quite certain?"

"I am, Your Eminence. She needs to die." There was a moment of silence and then Enmity's sharp demand: "What is that—"

Enmity's words didn't escape her before the energy weapon lashed out at her.

The glare blinded my eyes a moment, and I wasn't sure I was seeing what I thought.

Enmity wasn't like Leather, who'd taken a single shot to the chest and died. She stumbled back from the beam, and even with the gaping wound in her side and the damage I'd inflicted, she recovered her footing instantly and roared out with anger.

She charged at her attacker, and he shot again, a continuous beam that began carving a burning path through her as she fought it, as she forced her legs to keep moving. Then a crater of blood and flesh boiled away, exposing her skeleton, her organs, and she collapsed down to the ground.

There was a thick silence, and then hands were pulling me up. "Come on."

Tyrus Domitrian's face swam into my vision.

My thoughts turned in one direction. I fumbled with numbed fingers and pried his weapon from him, then dragged myself to my hands and knees.

Tyrus gaped at me. "What are you doing?"

Enmity was dead. I was still alive. I could still move, so I'd finish what I started. I couldn't stand, so I crawled toward the doors. I didn't have time to wait for the Emperor to come to me. I'd probably bleed out first. I would go to him. A great dark haze was creeping in the corners of my vision, closing in on me.

"You can't even stand. You can't possibly think you'll kill my uncle in this shape."

"Stay . . . back . . . hurt you . . ." The words seemed to drain from me. The darkness was growing rapidly, and then the floor was rushing up at me.

21

I **WAS BACK** in the salt baths, where the water bobbed me around, floating, floating there. But everything hurt and pulsed with pain, and it was Donia hurting, weeping like she had that time she shocked herself unexpectedly on her computer console, and I couldn't make it better. We were both young, small.

"Donia. Donia!"

"Is that your master?"

The question from above me, around me, made me look up to see a familiar face close to mine. For a moment, I felt the arms holding me up, the chest against my cheek. I could see his freckles over the bridge of his nose, the pale-lashed blue eyes floating in a haze above me.

Then Donia was gazing at me wide-eyed from the animal cloisters, and she was getting too close to the tigers. I knew they were civilized, blunted by genetic engineering, but those primitive human instincts even Diabolics possess told me these animals were muscular, strong, and they could kill her with one blow.

"Don't go near them," I told her. "They're dangerous."

"You're delirious," announced the voice, and it was Tyrus Domitrian kneeling in front of me where he'd put me on the bed, where he'd pressed a wet cloth to my head. I couldn't hold myself up. My ribs were stabbing me. Waves of heat and cold swept through me. "You're gravely injured. You may die. But that's what you wanted, isn't it?" He studied me a weighty moment.

The next thing I knew, med bots were swarming over me, buzzing, faint heat from their power generators puffing my skin. My teeth were chattering, and my thoughts swarmed with Donia, the tears in her eyes when I refused to let her call me anything other than Nemesis dan Impyrean. She'd always wanted something else from me I hadn't understood, and now I never really would.

The subtleties of the way people—real people—thought and acted and felt were beyond me. Maybe it was just the corrals, growing up that way, like the worst sort of monster, maybe it had warped me even if my nature hadn't. . . .

I was puking, dry heaving, blood splattering the floor by the edge of my bed. Med bots still swarmed me. Tyrus Domitrian stood with his arms folded in the doorway, watching me. Intelligence and cold deliberation were on his face, so unlike those other times he'd laughed and mumbled to himself, and I couldn't reconcile the two images.

"Sidonia Impyrean was your master?" he said to me. I realized hours had passed. He was pressing a cloth to my head again.

The sheets felt tangled and strangling around me. I strained to understand this, understand where I was.

"They did a fine job disguising you," Tyrus said. "I suspected something was off about you, but I never imagined . . ." He smiled wryly.

"Senator von Impyrean was a man of vision, and the Impyreans were clever. They are a true loss to the Empire."

That reminded me, like a blow stealing my breath. It reminded me of where I was, what this was, that Sidonia had died and stripped all meaning from my existence and I'd failed to kill her murderer. Instead I was here, alive, and if I could have wept, I would have. But no Diabolic can shed tears, and there was no way for this hideous emptiness and grief to escape me, so I screamed.

They tore out of me, awful, wretched screams, animal screams.

It was later when I grew aware of the fire scorching my throat, the waves of heat and cool replaced by a sort of vague physical comfort. Tyrus had returned to the room.

"Screamed out?" he said in a detached way. "It's fine even if you're not. Hearing screams coming from my chamber will just reaffirm my poor reputation."

I peered at him through crusted eyelids, the pain still battering in my awareness, but when I sat up a fraction, two, I discovered there was no bright hot wrench of agony.

The med bots had fixed my worst injuries.

Tyrus held very still as I sat up farther and saw bruises on my arms where I'd been restrained—but was no longer.

"You're not going to die," he said. "You were close. I'm certain Enmity— What are you doing?"

I swayed to my feet, then shoved him aside with all my strength. I wasn't nearly so powerful as I normally would have been, and Tyrus kept his balance. My muscles felt like they were all crying out in exhaustion, sapped of vitality.

As I stepped into the next room, the door before me sealed, several expressionless Servitors stepping forward to bar my way. In my current state, they might even have been able to manage it.

"Where do you intend to go? To try to kill my uncle again?" Tyrus spoke from behind me. "Even if you get past Anguish by some miracle, you won't get past Hazard. And even if, battered as you are, you overcome those two Diabolics in a way you could not overcome one, the Emperor has an entire entourage of Grandiloquy around him, not to mention security bots and—"

"What do you want?" I growled as I spun toward him.

"Your name is Nemesis, isn't it?"

I narrowed my eyes.

"I looked up the death register from the great purge of Diabolics. There was a Nemesis registered to Sidonia Impyrean. That's you, I assume."

"What does it matter now?"

"Because I hate waste." Tyrus settled down on his chair, regarding me with a cool, calm deliberation entirely out of place on his features—the ones I'd seen so often lit with some crazed animation. "I never had Diabolics of my own. My uncle made sure none of the other imperial royals had them. Diabolics tend to get in the way when you want to kill someone, and my uncle kills family quite liberally."

I said nothing. I had no interest in what he had to tell me, unless he revealed why he'd saved me, and when I could leave.

"I'm sorry about your master," he said, watching me carefully. "But you can look at this as an opportunity."

"An opportunity?" I sputtered.

"We want the same thing, Nemesis. You want my uncle dead, I want to be Emperor—which will require, of course, my uncle's death and quite a bit of maneuvering besides. You can't achieve it on your own, and neither can I. Why don't we help each other?"

"I don't give a damn about your uncle or politics. It doesn't matter a whit to me if you ever become Emperor. He killed Donia, and now I'll kill him or die trying. Let me out."

"I'm afraid not."

I stepped toward him menacingly. "I'm not asking!"

Tyrus flicked his finger.

Bright hot vibrating tendrils snaked up my neck and into my temples, and I found myself on the ground, gasping.

"I'm truly sorry," he said in a detached, unapologetic tone. "But I'd rather not get my neck broken right now. I'll only activate these if you move toward me."

My hand flew up to my neck, where that strange feeling had come from.

"They're electrodes under your skin. It's about the only way to control a Diabolic. I want you to hear me out."

I looked up at him, seething. "I will tear your heart from your chest!"

"One day, maybe. But not now." He stepped toward the door, then waved about the frame. "You won't be able to pass through this threshold. I want you to have time to think about what I'm requesting before making a decision."

"I've made my decision!" I shouted at him, but he was already passing through the doorway, leaving me, his Servitors trailing behind him.

I rushed for it, but the blinding shock of electricity drove me back down to my hands and knees, gasping for air, my heart sputtering in my chest.

There was nothing left for me in this universe, and I wanted nothing but for this pain and emptiness to stop. I wouldn't change my mind, however long Tyrus imprisoned me here.

22

HOURS PASSED. Servitors came to soundlessly offer refreshments, food. I wanted to throw the selections in their faces. Only the knowledge that they wouldn't flinch or react at all stayed my hand. There was no pleasure in bullying mindless, defenseless creatures.

I began contemplating the doorway again, trying to imagine what momentum I'd need to work up to fling myself through before the electricity rendered me useless.

That was when Tyrus Domitrian returned.

"Restless?"

I just looked at him, imagining how satisfying it would be to crush his skull.

"I wanted you to have time to deliberate. Walk with me."

"Where?"

He angled his body so I could pass him through the doorway. "This is my ship."

The *Alexandria*, just like Salivar and Devineé's vessel *Tigris*, branched immediately off the *Valor Novus* section of the Chrysanthemum. The difference was, no one paid a call to the mad heir's domain. The entire vessel was virtually abandoned but for the machines and Servitors running it for the Successor Primus.

As I approached, he seemed to think better of letting me pass directly by him, and he began walking, so I remained several steps away from him. He never fully turned his back to me.

"You should know, I took pains to erase any trace of our DNA from the scene of Enmity's death, but I couldn't cover up the murder. There's intense scrutiny of the Grandiloquy right now, especially those who have had their families slain. Everyone's secret weapons have been confiscated. The most respectable people were publicly humiliated, being frisked by my uncle's Diabolics. Hazard and Anguish found earbobs that served as poison darts, shoelaces of razor wire, neurotoxins concealed in all manner of toiletries. . . . We Grandiloquy are a far more savage sort than we pretend."

I didn't care about any of this. I had no intention of lingering in court. As soon as I was out of here, I'd resume exactly what I'd planned before. I wondered what would happen if I crossed the distance to Tyrus and broke his neck before he could activate the electricity.

As though he knew the turn of my thoughts, Tyrus said, "You could kill me, but the electrodes will deliver a shock to your heart and stop it. I assume it's not worth dying just to kill me. Whatever would Sidonia say?"

Even hearing him mention her name flooded me with anger. He had no right to say her name.

"I apologize for keeping you confined here like an animal, but I wanted to discuss this rationally. Diabolics are engineered with the ability to think and reason. I want a chance to appeal to that reason, but I don't intend to set myself up for death. You'll find I rarely underestimate my enemies."

"And what about your friends? People must be aware I'm here. How do you explain keeping Sidonia Impyrean on the *Alexandria* for . . . for however long it's been?"

"Five days. And it's quite simple, Nemesis. They'll assume the imperial madman has abducted you. Later, you and I may devise another explanation. . . . But no one will interfere with the Successor Primus, whatever he does in his insanity."

I narrowed my eyes. "You are no madman. I see that now."

Tyrus's gaze wavered. "No." He turned away from me, and we strode past great windows looking onto the bottom of the Berneval Stretch. "Most of my family dies young, usually at the hands of other family members. I figured out as a child that my only hope for survival lay in a projection of weakness, so I began to fake insanity."

"And people have always believed this."

"A palatable lie is easily swallowed. The Domitrians aren't a well-loved dynasty. It's an open secret that my uncle has squandered the royal coffers, spending liberally on his own pleasures, and now he seeks to tax the Excess to pay back the deficit he's caused. He hides behind his faith to justify repression of the Excess, just as my grandfather did, and his mother, and her father before her. We Domitrians have been a toxin poisoning this Empire for centuries."

Reluctant curiosity overcame me. "You've truly feigned madness for half your life?"

"A frightened child can manage all sorts of feats to preserve his existence. If I hadn't, I've no doubt I'd be dead now too, rather than heir to the Empire. It required more effort in the beginning, especially when the med bots could not 'cure' my ailment, but lately I need only make an outlandish gesture publicly now and then, and people believe.

That's how I'll explain the five-day abduction of Sidonia Impyrean."

My mind roved over what else I'd seen of him. His disrespect during services at the Great Heliosphere. "Leather," I recalled.

"A Servitor dying anyway in a hideous manner. I thought it a mercy to kill her. If it reinforced my reputation, it served us both."

"And the Exalted?"

A flicker of distaste on his face. "I'm no rapist. The sacrifices on Consecration Day are barbaric, so I told a lie and it was readily believed. Of course, the Pasus girl almost ruined my gesture before you intervened in the arena. Speaking of which . . ." He wheeled on me. "What did happen with my cousin and her husband?"

There was no point lying. "I force-fed them their own wine."

His lips quirked. "Fitting."

We stepped into a room with a clear glass floor, and beneath us was a great sky dome. A sense of disorientation crept over me as I stared downward at the blue sky I seemed to be standing upon. The room below us consisted of walls of shelves that vanished into the blue atmosphere, the sun shining up between them.

"Do you know what those are?" said Tyrus, gazing downward. "On those shelves, in stasis fields?"

"No."

"Those are valuable artifacts called 'books.' They're ancient repositories of knowledge bound in a mobile fashion."

"Are those some type of . . . of scientific texts?" I said, thinking of Senator von Impyrean's forbidden materials.

"Some of them," he said with a half smile. "The databases lost in the supernova were electronic. Those that weren't wiped out by the supernova were deleted with merely a few flicks of a button. These books, however, contain knowledge in actual *physical* form. Many of them were taken from Earth when the first colonies were founded,

THE DIABOLIC

and over time, these books fell utterly into disuse. No one bothered to destroy them, so I collect them. It's one of my . . . eccentricities. No one raises eyebrows when a madman shows interest in such things."

I thought of the Matriarch and her "priceless" old things, all probably destroyed now along with her. Strangely, though I had no bond to her, there was a pang within me at the thought she was dead.

"Do you know any human history, Nemesis?"

"Why would I?"

"It's your history too. Every strand of DNA in your body originated on Earth."

I'd never thought of it that way, but I still didn't see why this should interest me. I gazed at him flatly, waiting.

Most people grew unsettled under that stare. *A predator's gaze*, the Matriarch told me. Too direct, too unblinking for a human being. I'd trained myself out of staring, but now I had no need to hide what I was.

Tyrus studied me in return, not calculating but thoughtful. A youth who'd faked madness and maneuvered himself to the second most powerful position in the Empire in the face of the constant threat of death.

I suspected suddenly he would never fear me.

"Human history," Tyrus said, "is a repetition of patterns. Empires rise and then fall into decadence and decay. Time and again. Ages ago, human beings progressed technologically at an exponential rate. We expanded into space; we left Earth and traveled the galaxy. And then the same thing happened that always does—we grew lazy. We had technology we stopped learning how to use. We let machines think for us, act for us. The supernova and the rise of the Helionic faith merely worsened a problem that already existed. Our ancestors sought knowledge, but we, their descendants, glorify ignorance. If you scoured this entire Empire, you wouldn't find a single person capable of repairing the technology our ancestors built for us."

"Why is it necessary for people to possess that skill?" I said. Machines handled everything.

"Because this can't last forever," Tyrus said. "Our technology is aging. More of it shuts down every year and can't be brought back online. When our older ships malfunction, they tear apart space itself. We *need* a scientific revival, yet we do not have one because the Grandiloquy—because my family—knows any intellectual revolution inevitably leads to political revolution."

Tyrus's words exactly echoed what Senator von Impyrean had believed. Those beliefs were the reason the Senator and his family were now . . . were now dead.

Pain struck me at the very thought.

I couldn't bear to hear more of this.

"This doesn't interest me, Your Eminence," I said harshly. "Diabolics aren't philosophers."

"I merely want you to understand my aim: I want to become the Emperor not for myself, but for the future. I want human beings to become creatures who think, and plan, and strive for more, not what we are—this slothful, indolent species slowly whittling away the innovations of our ancestors, ignoring the dangers as they mount about us. But I can't be Emperor without you."

"How can I possibly help you in this?"

He turned away from me, gazing downward at the sky below us and the bookshelves vanishing into the deep blue depths. "I've survived this long by feigning madness. The Emperor has installed me as Successor Primus because he's confident his enemies will want to avoid my succession at all costs. I have to begin showing strength to convince people I'd make a suitable successor, yet the moment I gather any support, I become a threat to my uncle and my days are numbered." He stepped toward me. "If my uncle decides to be rid of me, I can't stop it. He'll engineer a situation where I can't bring a weapon. He'll try to catch me unaware or defenseless." He took my hand, squeezing hard. "And that is where you come in. You're a Diabolic hidden in plain sight. That makes you the most powerful defense there is. You can ensure I live. Be my Diabolic, Nemesis."

"It doesn't work that way. I was bonded to Sidonia."

"Then choose me. Sidonia Impyrean is gone. You're free to decide for yourself."

I shook my head. "How would I possibly stand by your side at all these occasions you suggest? If everything you say is true, the Emperor will never allow you to have a bodyguard, so how will you explain keeping me with you?"

"Because you'll be my wife."

23

I THINK if I'd been anyone else, I would have laughed. As it was, I just stared at his hard, resolved face with disbelief.

"Perhaps you are a madman after all."

Tyrus's hand tightened upon mine when I made to tear it from his. "What else do you intend to do? Perish in vain making another assassination attempt? You can change the course of human history with me."

"I have no interest in changing the course of human history," I cut in. "I've existed for one purpose. There is nothing else in this universe for me now."

"Yes," Tyrus said softly. "You had it easier when you were bonded to Sidonia Impyrean, didn't you?"

"Easier?" I echoed.

"Yes. Easier. You already knew your purpose in this existence. And now you don't. Now you have to grapple with the same questions the rest of us face—where do I go from here? What am I to do next? It's terrifying to realize your own decisions are shaping your destiny."

He spoke nonsense. Such decisions weren't for a Diabolic. "Unhand me, Your Eminence."

"There must be some way to convince you." His eyes roved over my face. "I cannot bring back the dead, but once I'm the Emperor, I can grant you whatever else you desire."

"I said, unhand me." My words were a courtesy. In a moment, I would break his arm.

He released me.

"I cannot force you into this," he said. "I won't try. All I ask is that before you destroy yourself, Nemesis, think long and hard about what you want your existence to mean. I don't believe a Diabolic passes in and out of this life just as an accessory to a real person. All of us are fated to return to the same oblivion. And you can choose what happens between now and that final hour. No one else can. Not even me."

I said nothing. He strode toward the door. "You'll find instructions on how to leave the *Alexandria* and return to the *Valor Novus*."

"And the electrodes?"

"They were temporary. I want us to operate out of trust from now on, Nemesis. The electrodes will dissolve as soon as you're at a safe distance from me. I'm sure you understand the need for the security measure."

"They're . . . temporary?"

"Entirely." Tyrus paused in the doorway, vulnerability passing over his face, just for a moment. "Let me know if you change your mind. The gala is in three days, and I'd like to announce you as my partner."

"A gala. You wish a Diabolic to accompany you to the gala celebrating the death of her master."

He smiled grimly. "Or the gala celebrating the first step toward avenging herself on a murderer. Shaping a future other than the one the

Emperor desires—that's the truest vengeance there is. Think about it."

I touched my neck and watched him leave.

The walk from the *Alexandria* was brief, and as I stepped into the crowded pavilion of the *Valor Novus*, I received an array of startled looks. I knew they were wondering what Sidonia Impyrean had been doing on the vessel of Tyrus Domitrian.

I ignored them and headed back toward my villa. The world felt sterile and overwhelming. No longer was I in the grasp of murderous resolve, but no longer did I have the purpose of protecting Sidonia to direct my steps.

My gaze trailed to the aristocrats weaving past me, their hair in elaborate stilts, clad in gowns, showing off their newest skin color or facial feature, whiling away time in a decaying Empire. A strange thought struck me: all these people whispered about the scandalous Tyrus Domitrian, but I was the only one who knew the truth of his calculating, deliberate mind. He was the cleverest of these people. Maybe that did make him the worthiest to rule them.

But who was I to determine that one way or another?

He'd asked me to marry him. The absurdity of the thought struck me. A Diabolic *marrying*.

It was madness.

I couldn't adopt his cause for my own. Philosophies and ideals were for people like Senator von Impyrean, people like Tyrus, not creatures like Diabolics. I couldn't conceive of choosing my destiny. My path had been crafted for me long before my growth in a laboratory.

I would proceed as I'd planned to before. I would kill the Emperor and let the consequences fall as they would. Tyrus Domitrian's fate wasn't my concern.

I passed through the sun-drenched sky dome and into my villa, where the Servitors stepped forward attentively, prepared to take orders.

"Where is Deadly?" I demanded, recalling the creature suddenly. Immediately I felt a wash of something unsettling—*guilt*—because I'd neglected to make arrangements for the dog before leaving on my assassination mission. I hadn't even thought of him. The Servitors hadn't been given orders to feed him, to take care of him, and they wouldn't know to do it of their own initiative.

But one of the Servitors presented me with a discreet-sheet, and I found myself gazing at a message.

> *Sidonia,*
> *I've heard rumors you're on Tyrus Domitrian's ship. I*
> *put Deadly in the animal pens for you. I pray for your*
> *well-being and hope to see you soon!*
> *—Your friend, Neveni*

I read and reread the message, sinking down onto one of the plush couches. I tried to wrap my brain around this girl I'd threatened with death going out of her way for me.

Your friend, Neveni.

Imagine that.

I wadded the discreet-sheet until it dissolved into powder, thinking of how strange the universe could be.

I was glad I had not killed her.

I had to move against the Emperor again, but first I needed sleep—more of it than I'd ever needed before. My dreams were haunted by Sidonia.

Six hours later, my body still ached in places but my resolve was firm. The great, gaping emptiness still poisoned me from the inside, and I knew this would be the case until I died.

This time I wasn't caught in a haze of grief. Enmity's death had surely put the Emperor on alert about a threat to his life. That meant I had to be more deliberate this time.

One way or another, I would kill him and then die myself.

I walked to the animal pens, my thoughts on Deadly. For his sake, I was going to put him down. Whether it was tomorrow or next week, I would die soon and there would be no one to take care of him. He'd likely end up in the arena again, and he would swiftly be slaughtered. Better for me to do it.

An animal keeper with a bald head tattooed with the Domitrian sigil greeted me. "Senator von Impyrean, I trust you're here for your beast?"

"My dog. He's a dog."

"Of course. Right this way." He turned and led me down the hallway between rows of pens.

As I followed him, my gaze strayed to the other animals in their own pens, some with ripped ears, some with open gashes after their most recent fights, whose owners were too stingy to pay for med bots. Others were pristine creatures more fortunate in their owners. Then I passed the most impressive creature of all, the Emperor's own beast that he'd spent a fortune designing. He'd apparently ordered this same genetic configuration over and over, with a few tweaks each time, until he had the champion he desired. He'd called it a manticore, though it was really a mixture of bull, tiger, bear, and several species of reptiles. My mind idly flicked to the idea of killing it to hurt the Emperor, and then I saw that it was worrying at a bone.

I halted, and kept looking at it.

The keeper realized I wasn't following him and returned to my side. "Senator von Impyrean, it's this way."

But I couldn't look away from the manticore as it ripped and tore at that . . . that femur. It was a human femur. The thighbone. A thick, powerful thigh bone, and I'd seen enough open fractures to know it wasn't so fragile as a regular human bone.

"Senator von Impyrean . . ."

"Who is that?" My voice was barely a whisper.

The manticore's growling and chewing noises filled the air, its great tail swishing.

"Who is that it's eating?" I demanded, whirling on the keeper, ready to tear him apart, because I knew, I knew.

The keeper blinked at me through large, confused eyes. "Oh, it's not a person, don't worry."

I began to shake with rage and horror. My stomach churned. I knew. I knew.

"The Emperor likes his manticore to eat fresh meat whenever possible—"

"Who. Is. It."

"It was his Diabolic, I believe." At the look I sent him, he said quickly, "She was already dead."

"Begone from my sight."

"But . . ."

"Begone before I tear you apart!" I screamed at him, and he scuttled back.

I pressed myself up against the force field, drinking in the horror of what I was seeing, and the manticore noticed my scrutiny and glared up at me with menacing eyes. I wanted to thrust through the force field and rend it to shreds of flesh and pulp, but I knew this fearsome creature could kill me easily. My vision clouded with the haze creeping in over me as I saw Enmity in those last moments, that fight she'd put up, that magnificent final charge she'd made as Tyrus's weapon tore her apart. Enmity, who'd appreciated compassion. Who'd come from the corrals just as I had.

She'd died for Randevald von Domitrian. She'd spent her life to her last breath, to the last twitch of her muscle fibers, defending her master against his enemies and championing him, and in reward he'd fed her body to his manticore.

Fresh meat.

I wanted to scream. It rose in my throat, the blinding scream of fury at the fate that said I was worth so little, that everything I felt and everything I was, was just an adjunct to a real human being, because I was more than this. She was more than this. We were more than this.

I'd accepted for so long that I wasn't a real person, and I never would have questioned it but for the pain I felt now. How could a creature that wasn't real experience the depth of anguish I'd experienced since Sidonia . . . since Sidonia . . . since she . . .

I crumpled to the ground, dry, choking sounds ripping from my lips, as close to tears as I would ever get—because whoever told the first machine to create a Diabolic had also told it not to give us tear ducts. They decided to fabricate me that much less human than them, and yet they didn't take away my capacity to feel pain, just my ability to express it.

My fingers tingled against the force field. I felt like I could burst through it and kill this beast, watching the manticore tear at Enmity's remains, because this would not happen to me. I would not just disappear into a void as though I'd never existed. I would not accept that I was less than these people just because they'd designed me that way.

I felt and I raged and I hurt and they could not take that away from me. Sidonia was dead and I would never get over that, but it wouldn't be my end, no, no. No, I would stand back up and I would exist as Nemesis the Diabolic and I would make my own destiny in spite of them.

I would be a Diabolic who forged a new future. Not just for myself, but for all the *real* people too. And in that way, I would have the truest revenge of all: I would make my life mean something.

When I returned to the *Alexandria*, Tyrus met me again above his library, the blue sky beneath his feet and the suns glaring up at him, casting great shadows on the ceiling above, and then my shadow joined his, and at the angle we were standing I stretched taller, longer, until we were one blur, one force above this universe.

"Have you changed your mind?" he said, taking my hands.

I didn't dip to my knees or bring his knuckles to my cheeks. I violated every protocol there was and stared directly into his eyes.

"I won't be your Diabolic. But I will be your Empress."

24

MY FIRST Senate session was the morning of the gala. I hadn't been trained all my life for this task, not like Sidonia, so the only person I could consult about it was Tyrus Domitrian. I sent a Servitor his way with a discreet-sheet, asking him what would be expected of me.

His reply came shortly:

> —*Sit anywhere you wish in the second ring to the front.*
> —*Put in more than fifteen minutes' face time, less than thirty.*
> —*No need to venture opinions.*
> —*Anticipate how my uncle wishes you to vote and do as he'd wish you to do. That is vital at this stage.*
> —*There is nothing to fear.*

I crumpled up his discreet-sheet until it was powder, faintly insulted by that last reassurance.

The Lesser Forum was an unimpressive room. Few Senators attended in person, mostly assigning advisers to monitor the proceedings over the galactic forums. When they needed to make speeches, they'd appear via avatar. Those of us who were now the Emperor's prisoners at the Chrysanthemum had no excuse not to attend, though.

So I sat there in utter silence as speeches were given in the Lesser Forum, mostly concerning things I had no interest in: agriculture, the price of commodities, contracts for galactic transport. . . .

And then the real issue came up: a resolution committing to the forcible removal of Viceroys from any colony of Excess that embarked on educational reform without the Emperor's consent.

This was aimed at places like Lumina, Neveni's home planet, and against people like Neveni's late mother.

I knew exactly how the Emperor wished me to vote. I voted for the resolution. As did every other Senator. It seemed we were all ardent Helionics now. None of the new Senators dared risk the fate of their predecessors. The vote was unanimous.

As the Senate streamed out into the antechamber, where prominent men and women in the Empire—moneyed but not officeholders—awaited them, my eye was caught by an unexpected visitor causing a stir by the far entrance.

It was Tyrus.

Whispers and murmurs stirred around me at the sight of the surprising royal appearance. I felt eyes float between Tyrus and me, because word had spread rapidly of some peculiar business going on between the heir to the Empire and the new Senator von Impyrean.

Now we were going to clarify just what that business was. He drew toward me and took my hands.

"My love, will you permit me to send some attendants to help garb you for tonight?"

I grew aware of all the eyes on us. "It would be my honor, Your Eminence."

Tyrus pulled my knuckles up to his cheeks, his eyes on mine, and pressed his cool lips to the pulse point of my wrist. "I'll count the minutes."

And then he retreated, and suddenly I was standing there in the middle of the busy room, at the other end of any number of speculative looks.

I turned and navigated my way from the room. I moved toward the chambers of the visiting Excess, wanting to speak to Neveni personally before she heard the rumors.

When I appeared at her door, Neveni just goggled at me for a moment; then she swept me into a fierce hug.

The gesture took me off guard, and it was a long moment before I remembered to return it.

"You're back! Are you well? Did you get my note?"

"I did," I said stiffly, pulling away from her. "I wanted to thank you for taking care of Deadly for me. Will you need me to get you an invitation to tonight's gala?"

Neveni stumbled back from me, staring at me, slack-jawed. It dawned on me then that something was wrong with her, and then a flush hit her cheeks. "What, that's it?"

I frowned.

"Nothing else?" Her eyes grew shiny and glassy. "Sidonia, where have you been for the last week? What happened to you? People said you were kidnapped by Tyrus Domitrian and . . . and all sorts of horrible things! And the way you were acting before you left, I thought you'd done something reckless."

"I didn't."

Tyrus and I had discussed our plan. We were going to officially reveal ourselves as a pair at the gala, but I wanted to reveal our connection to Neveni early.

"In fact," I said to her, "Tyrus Domitrian and I are now involved."

"In-involved?"

"Yes."

"Romantically?"

"Yes." He'd given me a description to recite, so I did it, hoping I looked sincere. "I was with him for five days of blissful courtship on the *Alexandria*—"

"With Tyrus? Crazy Tyrus Domitrian?"

"Yes, and we're attending the gala tonight. If you'd like to come—"

"His uncle killed your family!" she shouted. "I was afraid you'd been killed too! What are you doing, Sidonia? Are you insane? You think I want to go to a gala and dance around all night with those people?"

She burst into tears.

I stood there utterly out of my depth in the face of her torrent of emotion, her anger and fear and sorrow. She'd always been eager to latch onto me in the past for all the opportunities I gave her at court. It hadn't even occurred to me that she'd react any differently today, yet now it seemed obvious that of course, she would.

I hadn't thought to place myself in her shoes.

I simply hadn't had enough empathy to do so.

"I'm sorry, Neveni."

"I don't care if you're sorry. I don't understand you! Your family is *dead*. Don't you feel anything?"

"Of course I do."

I could tell her how it hurt me, how I thirsted for some relief to the pain of losing Sidonia. I could tell her of my deadly fight with Enmity when I'd sought the Emperor's blood, of the true nature of my deal with Tyrus. I could tell her these things and maybe she would understand, but these weren't all my secrets to share anymore. They also belonged to Tyrus, and I had no right to assume such a risk for both of us.

So I tried another tactic. "Come with me to the gala," I urged her. "Perhaps it will take your mind off your mother being dead."

But my words, my attempt at sympathy, just upset her more. "Just leave me be. I don't want to go to some sun-scorned gala. Don't you realize what it's celebrating? It's celebrating the murder of the people we love!"

It was true. That was the purpose of the gala. I dropped my gaze, unable to meet her anguished expression.

"Oh God," Neveni sobbed, "all I want is to go home. My mother is dead and I clearly don't even have a friend here anymore! Go back to your new love affair with Tyrus Domitrian. I hope he makes you really happy, Sidonia. Some loyalty you have to your parents!"

She ripped away from me and retreated into her bedroom.

I stepped back out into the hallway, blinking at the stark lights glaring down at me from the ceiling outside the visiting Excess quarters. I'd finally declared myself something more than I'd always thought, more than a mere Diabolic, but there was a great gulf of understanding I had to surmount before I could truly step into the role of a real person.

In uniting with Tyrus, I'd just forfeited Neveni as an ally for good. I'd lost the closest thing I had to a friend.

25

AS I WAITED for Tyrus's attendants, I did push-ups in my villa, relishing the burning pain of my muscles being used again. I knew exercise meant risking undoing the hard work the Matriarch had devoted to disguising me, but all I could think of was my weakness in the fight against Enmity. I never wanted to feel so useless again. The physical activity provided a glorious relief from my thoughts, which swirled with apprehension over the course ahead of me. Whenever I wasn't thinking of the dangerous venture I was about to undertake with Tyrus, my thoughts took a darker turn, toward Sidonia.

Donia smiling at me that first day in the lab, the feel of her heartbeat against my palm, the first moment something cracked open within me and the capacity to love poured in . . .

The very thought of her made me wish for death, so I tried not to think of her. Exercise helped.

So I was all the more annoyed when the intercom sounded through my villa: "Employees of Tyrus Domitrian to see Sidonia Impyrean."

I shoved myself up with one push of my hands against the floor and stalked to the doorway. There, I saw my Servitors had already opened the doors, as they had to do automatically whenever a representative of a royal paid a visit to someone of lesser rank.

A flurry of men and women poured through, their hair twined elaborately about the Domitrian six-star sigil tattooed on their heads. At the very front was a man who clearly wasn't an employee, but rather a member of the Excess taken into the Domitrian house due to his loyalty. He still had his hair, and he'd colored his skin in stripes like some odd animal. He gave a trilling laugh at the sight of me.

"Greetings, Senator von Impyrean. I am Shaezar nan Domitrian." He dipped ostentatiously to his knees and caressed my knuckles against his cheeks. I wanted to pull back straightaway from his soft, perfumed grip. "We've been sent by the Successor Primus to attend to you in advance of the gala."

"So I understand. What preparations do you have in mind? I already know how to dance." Although I'd struggled at times to learn it under Sutera nu Impyrean, that had merely been because I'd been undergoing muscle reduction at the same time. Now I was perfectly confident I wouldn't falter a step.

"That's not His Eminence's concern," stated Shaezar delicately. "He wishes you to be sufficiently bejeweled and ornamented as befits a partner of the Successor Primus."

"I have jewels."

He raised thin eyebrows etched with tattooed golden lines. "His Eminence seems to think you may need assistance choosing the proper ones for this occasion."

Because Tyrus knew what I was now. I sighed. "Very well. Let's get this over with."

I thought it would take an hour at most, but the attendants hustled around me well into the afternoon, fussing over every strand of my hair, mending each split end, weaving in shades of gold, light brown, and darkest scarlet into my raven locks; then all my hair was arranged into small braids for optimal flow during the dancing. I found myself watching the attendants, perplexed to see the sheer amount of time that could be expended on something so fundamentally unimportant. As a Diabolic, I was attentive to small details, yet I wouldn't have noticed one way or another if someone had split ends.

Perhaps Grandiloquy noticed details such as this that I did not. The attendants unveiled tray after tray of elaborate jeweled head-dresses, brooches, and necklaces that would have been too heavy for Sidonia's neck.

For all the Emperor's efforts to confiscate hidden weapons, items such as this could be wielded quite easily against an opponent. I studied the necklaces, imagining the effect they'd have if swung against someone's skull.

Of course, weight wasn't an issue. The gala was going to take place in a ball dome, a zero-gravity environment, which enabled the Grandiloquy to bedeck themselves even more than usual without even requiring an exosuit. These same attendants would pick the jewels now and then garb me with them in the minutes before the gala began.

They whispered and murmured among themselves, paying little attention to my preferences, especially when they figured out I was just pointing at random to certain items, eager to get this over with. It wasn't an attempt to be belligerent: everything they presented to me looked alike. When I tried pointing at the largest, most sparkly items instead—figuring *those* were the right ornaments for the partner of the Successor Primus—Shaezar laughed.

"Too gaudy for you, Senator von Impyrean! Those are for

Grandeés of lesser rank trying to prove a point."

Apparently, I had poor taste. My other suggestions were laughed off just as readily. Two attendants undressed me so they could tend to my skin, injecting glow just below my eyes and above my jawline, then adding additional pigment to the skin beneath my cheekbones. They even added highlights and shades to my nose in such a way that when I beheld it in a mirror, it gave the illusion of being straight, the bump barely visible.

Under their ministrations, my skin was rubbed with scented oil as beauty bots lasered away every last blemish. They chose a delicate silken gown, stark white and optimized for maximum flow and ripple in a zero-gravity environment. Because the shoes were designed solely for zero gravity rather than walking, they were elaborate wraps that trailed tassels of gemstones. I examined the impractical implements, recalling Sutera nu Impyrean's instructions regarding these: the trick was not to swing them so hard the tassels would injure someone, or even myself.

Unless I *wanted* to injure someone.

The last additions were a series of jeweled loops for my arms and thighs, the elegant magnetic steering rings used for navigating the ball dome. Angling them in different positions to each other achieved the effect of pushing one's body around in the air.

"Would the Grandeé like a massage to relax before the event?" inquired Shaezar nan Domitrian solicitously as the attendants packed up to move my jewels closer to the ball dome.

"I'll relax well enough if you leave me in peace for an hour. I assume we're done?" At his nod, I asked, "How much do I pay you?"

He shook his head. "This is Tyrus Domitrian's treat. I've never seen the Successor Primus smitten. Not with anyone, but it seems you have won His Eminence's heart."

"Yes, he's . . . we're very enchanted with each other," I intoned, hoping I sounded convincing. Then I mercifully freed my hand from Shaezar's perfumed grip.

His behavior seemed odd, so fawning. Even as the important personage, Sidonia Impyrean, I'd never been treated in such a manner.

But Shaezar nan Domitrian was just the first to react to my new elevation to love interest of the Empire's Successor Primus. He wouldn't be the last.

26

THE BALL DOME was tucked into the embrace of Langer-horn Reach, one of the long, curving pylons. The Dome resembled the Great Heliosphere, with a mass of open windows looking out onto space and private chambers for Grandiloquy branching off the larger whole. The crystalline material was more decorative, some-how, glistening in the light and casting glowing prisms about us.

My Servitors and Tyrus's attendants carried the clothing I'd don. They dressed me in the private waiting chamber off the ballroom floor as the dome detached itself from the larger structure of the *Valor Novus.*

The ball dome propelled itself away from the Chrysanthemum, shaking lightly with the gravitational forces as it moved to a more picturesque location in the six-star system for dancers to enjoy as they cavorted. Soon the ball dome settled into orbit around the smallest of the six stars, just by a purple and effervescent pink gale of nebula dust, with a view of a gas giant and its eight moons, all starkly beautiful things to provide an endless array of scenery against the vast darkness of space.

The opening strains of music pervaded the air to tell the first dancers to take their positions. That would naturally be the Emperor and his latest courtesan, a cousin of Senator von Canternella. I moved into position at the great one-way window of my chamber and held on to the ornate bars ready for me.

And then the gravity was deactivated.

A shock jolted through me at the sensation of lightness, like every cell in my body was floating upward. My braided hair drifted up in fine tendrils about my head, the rippling fabric of my gown like an underwater plant bobbing in the garden lakes.

And then out in the center of the great dome, two figures glided in from different directions. The Emperor and the Grandeé Canternella. Malice surged hot and poisonous in my veins as I watched him, this man who'd killed Sidonia. Their hands reached for each other, and then they clasped together with practiced ease as a slow, enchanting melody filled the air.

To take my mind off visions of vaulting out there and tearing out his rib cage, I forced myself to study their technique as dancers. The Emperor and the Grandeé swirled in circles about each other, and then twitched their arms to propel themselves back, almost in unison. They both wore flowing gowns that gave them a look of flower petals opening to the sun, and a steady stream of globular pools of effervescent light began to bob through the weightless air toward them.

One trick of zero gravity, Sutera nu Impyrean had warned me, was avoiding bumping into the scenery. Floating ripples of light, even floating pools of wine, served as pleasurable decorative touches, but they could easily ruin expensive gowns and cause embarrassment if an unwary dancer blundered into them.

Whoever had released the bubbles of fire did so carefully, though, and as the Emperor and his partner's dance picked up its tempo, they were well clear of the fire spheres.

And then the glass began to slide up before me. The second tier of dancers was being summoned to the floor—the Successor Primus and his partner.

Me.

I felt uneasy because Tyrus and I had not practiced the movements of dancing in zero gravity. This was a significant moment, revealing myself as his partner and confirming any rumors that had begun circulating about us, and I didn't wish to make a fool of myself now.

But there was no time to second-guess my course. Tyrus caught my eye from where his own glass partition had slid open, his short, coppery hair floating about his head, his white garb twining in tendrils about his muscular body. And then we both dove out, Tyrus in a graceful fall, me in a flip through the air. The walls of the crystalline ball dome circled in my vision as I flipped and turned.

He'd practiced this all his life and I'd only seen vids of it, but physical activities had always been effortless for me, and controlling my zero-gravity plunge proved the same. Just as I neared the center of the great dome, Tyrus reached me and caught my wrists, and together we floated downward in a ripple of stark white fabric, flashing jewels, his eyes intent on mine as the world moved around us.

I couldn't see anything but him, yet I felt thousands of eyes upon us, intent, questioning, surprised, seeing the Impyrean heir and the imperial heir together. And then Tyrus and I both twitched our arms to activate the magnetic steering rings, and he released one of my arms to spin me against him, to dip us both. Up was down and down was up, and my hair swirled in my face and the gown rippled like white fire. Tyrus's skin glowed in the light of a floating bubble of actual fire that skimmed so close a hot draft brushed my neck.

And then the next tier of dancers were summoned to the floor, and Tyrus and I floated up to the Emperor and Grandeé Canternella.

The Emperor's skin was a pale white today, without so much as a freckle, his blond hair casting him like a wraith against the scarlet garb he and his partner wore. He and Grandeé Canternella drifted toward us, and Tyrus's grip clutched me tighter as we found ourselves in a circle at the center of the vast dome, prisms of light from the outside stars dancing about us along with the globs of fire. A gas giant swirled below us and a stark purple nebula formed a sky above us.

"Grandeé Impyrean," spoke the Emperor as Grandeé Canternella peered at us inquisitively. "How ravishing you look tonight."

I felt myself choking on a sudden rush of aggression. My grip tightened on Tyrus so hard he visibly winced, and then he squeezed my hand once in warning.

"Doesn't she, though?" Tyrus said airily. "She wished to take to her chamber in mourning, but I said to her, such beauty cannot be left to spoil in isolation."

The Emperor smiled indulgently. "It's about time you attended an imperial gala, Tyrus. I was surprised at your choice of partner for this occasion. . . ."

The words rested uneasily on the air a moment, and I clenched my jaw. Yes, he was surprised Tyrus had taken an Impyrean to a gala celebrating the destruction of the Impyreans, among others.

"But now I see you've chosen a partner who dances most magnificently," the Emperor finished.

As he spoke, all I could think of was how close he was to me, how easily I could propel myself to him, abandon this charade, and splinter his skull. I didn't see Hazard. I didn't see Anguish. I was one of the only recently disgraced Grandiloquy here. The others would only be permitted to dance after the Emperor had retired for the evening. He wasn't so foolish as to put himself in arm's reach of those whose families he'd recently killed.

As Tyrus's partner, I was the sole exception. His mistake.

I could kill him now.

I could kill him *now.*

Tyrus seemed to sense my feeling, or maybe he could feel the tension in my body, because suddenly he was burying his head in my neck, his breath sweet against my skin, his arms wrapping around me, strong and steadfast. I knew I could break them in a moment, and as he propelled us from the Emperor with a lighthearted farewell, I seriously considered it.

"Don't," he said.

"He's right here," I rasped in his ear. "Right here!"

"And then what?" His pale eyes leaped up to mine. "You will die and his vision of humanity will continue to flourish, especially once a civil war erupts as the Grandiloquy rise against the Empire falling into the hands of a madman."

Tyrus cupped my cheek, then moved his grip to the back of my neck, urgent. His touch felt rough against my skin, his hands calloused from whatever physical exertion had shaped his musculature. "This is the first step of a series," he said, very low. "You will get exactly what you wish in the end if you are patient, and it will be for the best for all of us. *Please* trust me."

I thought of Enmity's body in that pen, and the words that had echoed in my head since then. *I am more than this. I am more.*

Stiffly, I nodded, then permitted him to move me farther from the Emperor. As we spun, his gaze fixed intently on mine. "Justice will be done," he said quietly. "For Sidonia—and for all the rest, too. For the entire Empire."

I found myself staring at him, struck by the way his pale eyes glittered in the light of the floating fires. What an odd person he was, who so gladly assumed an obligation and responsibility for trillions— not only those now joining us, an ever-increasing number of dancers launching aloft into zero gravity, but for the faceless strangers across the galaxy, multitudes who would never speak his name. Indeed, most of those who did speak it cursed him as a madman. Yet still he wanted to better their lives.

An odd feeling swam through me then. With my entire being, I yearned for his conviction. It was the same conviction—I realized now—that Senator von Impyrean had felt for spreading the sciences. *There are things more important than whether one person lives or dies.*

The Senator's faraway words drifted back to me as Tyrus's thumb stroked my cheek. It was a display, of course, for everyone looking upon us who could not possibly guess the true nature of our association, the true content of our discussion.

Tyrus believed in a cause and wagered his life for it. And he invited me now to do the same, even knowing I was a Diabolic. It was hard for me to understand what it was to have a cause, to have belief. But I wanted to know.

I began to catch eyes upon us, so many eyes, and past me danced Elantra Pasus and Gladdic Aton. She looked at me piercingly and smiled when I caught gazes with her, but there was a trace of anxiety in her face at seeing me with the Successor Primus. She had good reason to be nervous.

"This is vengeance for you, too, isn't it?" I said to him suddenly.

I thought of his family, dead at the hands of his uncle, his grand-mother. Two Helionics, firm believers in the current system. Yet Tyrus meant to ascend and undo everything they'd fought to protect.

"In a sense." His lips curved. "I can't say I haven't considered that a side benefit."

When the first strains of the Frog and the Scorpion began to play, I recalled learning this dance with Sidonia. A rush of grief swept through me, and Tyrus must have seen it in my eyes.

"Are you well?"

I swallowed it down. "I know this dance."

"You dance with incredible skill."

"Of course I do."

He laughed. "I find your modesty most delightful."

His tone was teasing, but I saw no use in feigning modesty. I was the physical superior of every person in this room, and zero-gravity maneuvering was all about balance, coordination, and grace. This came easily to me.

We lapsed into silence as he danced the frog to my scorpion, throw-ing me, propelling himself to where I was, as I slid down his body, as I spun about him, the twining flaps of our clothing tangling together like anemones.

"Do you know this parable, then?" he said breathlessly as we drew together again. "It's an old fable, the tale of the frog and the scorpion."

It came time for the harsh, discordant beats in the song, and I lashed at him. Tyrus reared back, catching my arm and spinning us both. The dancers rotated in my vision like hundreds of spokes on a vast wheel. When we were back together again, my back pressed to Tyrus's chest as we spun in circles, he told me the story.

"A scorpion needs to cross a stream. He asks a frog to carry him across on its back. The frog asks, 'How do I know you won't sting me?'"

The scorpion assures him that if he does, they'll sink under the water and they'll both die. That's reassurance enough for the frog. The frog agrees to carry the scorpion. They get to midstream, and then the scorpion stings him."

He reeled under another lashing movement from me, and as part of the dance, each blow produced spins of less energy, the chords of the music growing weaker, dying out. The scorpion was stinging the frog to death, condemning them both to die. Tyrus and I faced each other again, ready to drown beneath the waters of the river together.

"The frog asks the scorpion why it stung him," Tyrus finished. "And the scorpion replies, 'It's my nature.'"

We fell silent and dipped down, drowning together as the music died away.

Later our heaviest outerwear was removed and we took a rest in one of the refreshment rooms, enjoying the return of gravity. Service bots brought drinks our way. Before us, the dome still hummed with dancers against the crystalline windows and the expanse of space, many of the lesser Grandiloquy permitted to join the floor now too.

Tyrus ran a finger around the rim of his glass, his blue eyes narrowed as he surveyed the dancers. Then he spoke. "Tonight was the first step. For them to see us together. I told you the frog and scorpion fable for a reason."

I looked at him. It seemed like Tyrus did little without a reason.

"Nature does not simply reform." He tapped the edge of his glass. "A lion does not grow stripes, nor does a cheetah sprout horns. A scorpion does not cease to sting. If I am to shift my image before the galaxy, there must be an explanation for the shift that makes sense to people. It has to be you, Nemesis."

"Me?"

"*You* will be the moderating influence on me in public. We need a ready explanation for my changing ways, and that reason will be *you* gentling my character. As the Senator von Impyrean, you're already an ideological focal point. This will merely take that a step further. What I need is some occasion to do something significant to demonstrate I am changing . . . a moment to offer people a glimpse of how the Empire might be under my command when I am influenced by *you*."

I said nothing. This wasn't my way of planning, of thinking. He was the deliberate person full of far-reaching schemes. I knew how to act in the moment. "What do you intend to do?"

"I have to think of something significant to demonstrate our new dynamic. Something that will be spread widely, discussed, repeated." He drained his wine and rose to his feet, adjusting the white of his tunic over his muscular arm. He held out a palm to me. "We should return to the dance."

I set aside my goblet and took his hand, felt the strength of his grip as he pulled me up.

Tyrus searched my face intently, a cool, detached young leader, as alien to me in his calm and calculated manner as my instincts and inborn aggression were to him.

"The next time we're together publicly, I'll need to kiss you. I thought I should tell you this in advance so you're not startled. I wouldn't like a broken neck."

The idea did startle me. For a moment, I almost protested. But my own unease puzzled me. His logic made sense. Why should I mind such a trifling piece of showmanship?

Nevertheless, I thought to warn him: "Affectionate gestures that come instinctively to most humans don't come naturally to me. I'm not sure I'll know how."

"Nemesis, if you can dance so well as you do, you can kiss." Tyrus's mouth quirked, his eyes tracing my lips. "A kiss is just about adjusting to the movement, the rhythm of another person. I suspect you'll find it more natural than you could ever dream."

For some reason, I felt suddenly unable to hold his gaze. Outside, in the dome, long lines of dancers twined together like glittering vines, and the beauty of the dance made a fine excuse to turn away.

27

THE NEXT few days were a dizzying whirlwind of activity. Just by appearing at the gala with the Successor Primus, I achieved a new status at the Chrysanthemum. It began as soon as a decent hour rolled around the next morning. Suddenly my intercom began announcing an array of visitors, higher and lesser Grandiloquy both.

"Credenza Fordyce for Sidonia von Impyrean."

"Ivigny von Wallstrom for Sidonia von Impyrean."

"Epheny Locklaite for Sidonia von Impyrean."

And the announcement was always followed by some prominent personage along with their entourage, who'd dip themselves into the chairs of my villa and openly stare at me, at my Servitors, at my possessions, while they made inane conversation. Small talk wasn't an easy skill for me, so I mostly focused on not staring fixedly back at them in a way that would make them uncomfortable. They seemed too focused on promoting themselves to notice any behavior on my part.

"You do recall that social forum three years ago, don't you, my Grandeé, when I remarked on your fine avatar?" said Grandeé von Fleivert.

"Such a sturdy, handsome group of Servitors," said Credenza Fordyce. She had made a point of snubbing me until now and seemed stiff in her new role as acolyte. "You really *must* tell me what you feed them."

"Food," I replied. "They eat food."

"Food. How interesting!" she trilled.

I looked at her. She looked at me. The silence thickened.

"I must give mine far more food," said Credenza, her smile brittle.

But those visits weren't nearly so awkward as the moment Senator von Pasus called on me, trailed by Elantra, a poisonous, limpid smile on her lips.

". . . pleasure to make your father's acquaintance, oh, twenty years back. Or was it twenty-two?" spoke the Senator von Pasus, his stentorian voice booming through the room.

"It was twenty-two, Father," said Elantra. "You've told me as much."

"Yes, twenty-two years back. We both ascended to leadership of our families at the same time." Senator von Pasus's face relaxed into a smile. "I was quite sorry to hear what happened to him. Believe it or not, I rather enjoyed our clashes in the Senate. It's my deepest regret we opposed each other on the fundamental issues of our day. We could have done great things together in different circumstances." He cleared his throat, stroking at his short, neatly trimmed beard. "My point is, my dear, I know when to let old disputes pass. It can be difficult to feel without the guidance of a parent."

Elantra's smile was like plastic. "My father and I are happy to lend some help."

"Indeed," her father added. "You are still very young, dear. You can't possibly have had time to learn all the niceties of holding office." He paused. "For instance, dealing with the Excess in your territory. You simply take for granted they'll learn from your example and see things your way, but oftentimes they can prove tricky. Why, at the oddest times, some rascal among them might goad his fellows to defy his betters—to convince them they are entitled to more say in matters. . . ."

"Like Viceroy Sagnau?" I said pleasantly.

He stuttered into silence. Elantra's eyes flashed spitefully toward her father, as though she'd warned him in advance this would happen and he'd disregarded her.

I didn't care that I'd just broken a taboo by calling the Senator and his heir's attention to the Viceroy who'd defied them in their own territory . . . the woman who had ended up being killed along with the Emperor's Grandiloquy enemies.

That could only have been Senator von Pasus's work. The Emperor had no reason to strike out against a mere Viceroy, whatever her views. Neveni's mother could have posed no threat unless Senator von Pasus specifically asked for her inclusion in the great purge.

Senator von Pasus straightened, recovering his dignity. "That province, Lamanos—"

"Lumina," prompted Elantra sweetly.

"Lumina. Always troublesome. A rocky planet with an unusual ability to self-sustain, so their leaders grow egos. That Sagnau woman was a demagogue misleading her people. The majority of the Excess are too blinded by propaganda or simply ignorant to see how much they require the Empire, and how they profit from Grandiloquy patronage." He leaned closer to me, his gaze sharp and cold in the lighting of my atrium. "But they have been taught a grave lesson. There is no planet so safe or hole so concealed that it can escape the Grandiloquy's reach. Strength is the only thing the Excess respect, and they will be cowed after this, you mark my words."

Days later I was invited to my first private dinner with the Domitrian family.

Tyrus pulled out a chair for me at the table in the Emperor's presence chamber. The Emperor had yet to join us. His chair at the head of the table stood empty.

As I settled next to Tyrus, I felt the sharp weight of his grandmother Cygna's harpy gaze, assessing me. She'd been born to another branch of the Domitrian family back when the Domitrians were more numerous, less inclined to die young. It had been the wrong branch of the Domitrians. They sported the black hole sigil rather than the six stars of the royal Domitrians.

Instead of having a chance at the throne herself, Cygna had to resort to marrying the heir. When her marriage to Emperor Lotharias grew turbulent, she sought to rule through her favored child, the current Emperor. She was also the person who'd masterminded the disposal of Randevald von Domitrian's rivals for the throne.

To my displeasure, Cygna was joined tonight by Salivar and Devineé, both recovered but not quite in top form. They both offered polite smiles, but their faces looked pale and slack, their eyes clouded, as though they didn't truly see the room before them. Drool trickled from the corner of Salivar's mouth. A Servitor stepped forward to dab it away with a silken handkerchief.

Tyrus leaned toward me, making a show of toying with the jewel hanging from my ear. I felt the warmth of his breath against my ear as he whispered, "They remember nothing. Devineé can't speak clearly. Salivar still forgets his own name."

"So severe?"

"Scorpion's Breath has to be used in moderation. Any higher dose and it becomes a potent neurotoxin."

I felt a wave of cruel satisfaction as I looked at the Emperor's niece and her husband again, remembering what they'd had in mind for Sidonia, what they'd done to Neveni. They fumbled clumsily with their utensils, fighting with their own food, struggling to scrape it from the plate.

Tyrus gave a light flick to my earring. "Try not to enjoy it so visibly. Grandmother misses nothing." Then he eased away.

Indeed, when I looked to Grandeé Cygna, I found her eyes pinned to me. She hadn't missed my pleasure.

"Does it amuse you to see the condition of my granddaughter and her husband, Senator von Impyrean?"

I spoke hastily. "Never, Your Eminence. If I smiled, it was merely because I recalled how kind they were to me before . . ."

"Before their affliction and your *total* memory loss."

This woman had killed her own less-favored children. I had no doubt she'd kill me if she ever suspected what I'd done to Salivar and Devineé.

"Yes, Your Eminence," I murmured. "Such a tragic night."

Grandeé Cygna gave an impatient tug of her mouth. "How did you and my grandson come to associate, then?"

Tyrus covered my hand with his own. There was a subtle tension in every line of his body. "I've told you this story, Grandmother—"

"I wish to hear the enchanting tale from the young lady herself."

For a moment, my mind was blank. Then I recalled the idle excuses Tyrus had provided me for our new association.

"I was distraught after the events of late, as surely you understand." I sipped my wine to give myself time to recall Tyrus's story. His hand still rested over mine, his thumb rubbing back and forth over my palm, small theatrics to evidence his supposed affection. I found it distracting but fought the urge to withdraw my hand into my lap—for that, too, would not escape Cygna's notice. "His Eminence encountered me in my distress and led me to the *Alexandria*. He diverted me with these beautiful antiques called books, and one thing led to another."

Then I thought to punctuate this anecdote with a smile at Tyrus, hoping no one noticed my cold, empty eyes. He smiled back.

"Ah, of course," remarked Cygna. "The library won you over. Tyrus keeps those on hand for stars know why, but clearly *you* share your father's love of knowledge, then."

The words were dangerous. She was trying to catch me making a mistake. "No, learning is not my passion, Your Eminence," I said quickly. "The books were simply . . . very pretty."

"Ah, but that content inside can prove most dangerous." She sipped at her wine. "All this desire to learn . . . I don't understand it. Learning is an absurd use of time, if you ask me, especially when one can simply consult a computer. You should be very careful, Senator von Impyrean. You wouldn't wish to fall for the same wayward philosophies as your father."

I clenched my fist beneath the table. "No, Your Eminence, I would not."

"What surprises me," Cygna went on, "is that my grandson has become enamored of an Impyrean. I had no idea he had such leanings. I believed he gathered those books as an eccentricity, not due to an appreciation for intellectual curiosity."

It was a dangerous inquiry, and Tyrus handled it well. He chuckled, then leaned back to gaze up at the ceiling. "Well, Grandmother, in truth I have no desire to *read* those books. I simply thought they might hold the answers as to why I am so elevated above the ordinary man. I have so many questions. Why does everyone watch me without being blinded by the gleaming light of my transcendent nature? Why do I have access to the divine wisdom of the Cosmos when others cannot hear the same voices I do? What is it about my humble form that makes me so much more than an average man?" He drew my hand to his mouth then, eyes on his grandmother. His lips were startlingly warm against my skin. "Though here Sidonia von Impyrean has quite provided the answers for me."

A thin eyebrow rose on Cygna's false-youth face. "Oh?"

"Indeed. She states that I am not in fact the Living Cosmos expressing its will through my humble human form, but rather a product of Cosmic creation like any other person."

"I have told you this numerous times," snapped Grandeé Cygna.

"But, Grandmother, it is so much more convincing in her sweet voice." He reached out and stroked a thumb across my bottom lip. "Haven't I told you so, my darling?"

Did he need to keep touching me like this? But as I met Tyrus's eyes, I understood that he was only carrying out his plan: he was painting me as a moderating influence on his madness. Grandeé Cygna gaped at him a moment, her wineglass in midair. "Well." Recovering herself, she sipped delicately. "Well, Tyrus, you can count me all astonishment."

It was then I knew she believed him.

Of course she did. She'd credited his charade as a madman for all these years. Why would she not believe this new twist on it?

The lights shifted above us, taking on a golden hue that turned the finely stenciled carvings on the wall into a glittering tapestry of lace. In strode Hazard. Then the Emperor appeared, flanked by security bots and trailed by his other Diabolic, Anguish.

The Emperor, I noticed, wore full body armor.

"My son. Kiss me." Cygna tilted up her sharp chin.

The Emperor's smile was granite stiff. Clearly it vexed him to have supreme power and still receive orders from his mother. But, mindful of decorum, he bent down to press a kiss to her smooth cheek.

"How pleased I am to find us all assembled here," the Emperor announced as he straightened. As his roving gaze passed over me, a smirk pulled at his lips. "I must commend your taste, my nephew. Senator von Impyrean is all loveliness."

I'd debated returning to my natural coloring, especially since seeing Enmity's body in that manticore pen. There was a vindictive, spiteful part of me that wanted to rub in my resemblance to the Diabolic the Emperor had so easily disposed of as I worked toward his destruction.

But I hadn't done so, fearing his Diabolics would consider the resemblance far too close to constitute anything but a shared DNA template. Instead I'd chosen dark red hair and skin of stark white—the better to go with Tyrus's natural reddish hair color. We now looked like a matched pair.

As the serving bots brought in dinner, the security drones began buzzing about the table in circular rotation. Meanwhile, as was customary, the other members of the Emperor's family took turns tasting his food before he tried it himself.

He paid little attention to Tyrus's taste test, I noticed, but stared very intently at Grandeé Cygna as she sliced off the thinnest sliver of his succulent ham. He shook his head when Salivar and Devineé were given their portion by their attendants. "It would almost be a mercy if they ingested poison at this point, wouldn't you say?" Satisfied that none of his food was about to kill him, he dug in heartily.

"A vulgar remark. We should all pray for their recovery. There must be some better med bots out there somewhere, wouldn't you think?" Grandeé Cygna took the smallest bites of her food, eyeing the security bots with distaste. "This noise is intolerable. Must they circle us this entire meal?"

The Emperor's smile was chilly. "Why, Mother, you can hardly blame me for being overcautious. A week ago, I had three Diabolics. And now I have but two."

The image of Enmity being consumed by the manticore filled my brain. I tightened my fist around my cutlery, and I fought the temptation to vault over the table and drive my fork through the Emperor's eye.

A commotion near the doorway saved me from that impulse. The Emperor's security bots buzzed toward the entrance, and Anguish pivoted, his great muscles tensed.

In strode Senator von Pasus, his cheeks flushed, his gray hair disordered as though by the frantic tug of hands.

The Senator sank gingerly to his knees and said, "My apologies, Your Supreme Reverence, for interrupting you at your meal, but I have urgent news."

The Emperor sighed and rose to greet the Senator. He reached out his hands, allowing the Senator to press his knuckles to his face. Then they exchanged words even I couldn't pick out amid the buzz of the security drones.

Whatever they were, they caused the Emperor to pale. "Find that girl. Get her down here. This cannot stand," he snapped, and strode back toward the table.

At my side, Tyrus made a show of examining his fingernails. But where our shoulders touched, I could feel the alertness that gripped his body. Devineé and Salivar continued to drool and stare vacantly at their plates.

The Emperor loosed a venomous laugh. "This is a delight. Truly, an amusing turn of events." He turned to Cygna. "The Luminars have declared independence. They have expelled all imperial officials from their system."

Cygna's cheeks grew gray. "They cannot do that."

"And yet they have done it. They demand—*demand*, I say—the return of the Viceroy's daughter. Neveni Sagnau."

Neveni. I sent Tyrus an urgent look. He was still exhibiting total disinterest and did not catch my glance.

"I'll send the girl back to them," vowed the Emperor. "Oh, indeed—I'll give them her head in a box."

28

A GREAT KNOT of anxiety tightened around my lungs. They were bringing Neveni here, likely for her execution. They'd kill her right before us, and then . . . then, no doubt, they would calmly resume their dinner.

I dug my fingers into the swell of Tyrus's bicep. He looked at me questioningly, his light eyebrows raised. I could feel Hazard's gaze burning into my nape, but the others were distracted: Anguish was keeping a predatory watch on the doorway, while the Emperor and his mother had retreated to the corner to whisper fiercely together. If there was any chance of saving Neveni, I *must* speak to Tyrus— now, in private. I must get us both away from the Diabolics some- how. Their hearing made it impossible to speak to Tyrus here without being overheard.

There was another way.

I leaned toward Tyrus.

"Shh," I said, and snaked my hand around the back of his neck, across the breadth of his shoulders, so surprisingly muscular. His brows drew together. He watched me narrowly now, and my heart tripped, began to beat faster. I wasn't sure just how to do this. I had to make it look convincing.

I pressed my lips to his.

For the briefest moment, he went very still. Almost, I despaired. I pressed my mouth harder to his. *Understand me. Understand, now.*

Slowly he touched my face, his calloused fingertips settling very lightly, almost questioningly, against my cheek. And then, suddenly, he did seem to understand. He took control, his lips moving beneath mine, gentling the kiss, making it persuasive. His lips stroked over mine, then wandered across my cheek, until at last he nuzzled my ear.

"Are you all right?" he breathed.

I turned my face into his hair. He wore some rich spice. "No," I whispered.

He pulled back then and put a smirk onto his mouth. Taking me by the hand, he rose. "Grandeé von Impyrean and I must . . . speak among ourselves a moment," he said, to the people at the table not listening to him. To Hazard, whose steely expression did not waver, he sent a lecherous wink.

He drew me with him out of the room, into a curtained antechamber lit by firelight. The parlor stood ready for after-dinner recreation, stocked with trays of colored powders and phials of inhalants.

Tyrus cupped my cheek and leaned close to me, his voice barely audible. "I know that Sagnau girl is your friend, but I can't play any role here."

"There must be some way to save her." I balled up my fist against his tunic. "If you can't do something for her, no one can."

Tyrus brushed a stray lock of hair from my eyes, then watched himself trace its path along my cheekbone, presumably for the security cameras. "This is important to you."

"*Yes*. If you don't intervene, I'll do something myself—at any cost!"

He seemed to look inward a moment before a smile crept over his lips.

"You are inspiration itself, Nemesis. Return with me now."

He led me back toward the presence chamber and I followed, utterly uncertain about what he meant to do but hoping he'd fix this, he'd make it work. I wasn't comfortable trusting someone else to play an active hand in resolving something I could not.

Tyrus escorted me to the table with a flourish, his chest puffed out in the swaggering way he used only in moments of pretend madness, that crazed smile back on his lips.

"Uncle, I have a most brilliant idea!"

Cygna snorted. "Tyrus, now is not the time—"

"It's 'Your Eminence' to you, Grandmother, as I am the Successor Primus." Tyrus kept his attention fixed on his uncle.

Cygna's grip tightened on her wineglass, and the Emperor's lips twitched a moment. He enjoyed seeing his mother disrespected by his heir—as Tyrus no doubt had foreseen.

"My new love has never before set foot on a planet," Tyrus continued, "and indeed, I grow restless for some planet-side pleasures myself. Give the Sagnau girl to me, and I will resolve this situation."

Grandeé Cygna sputtered a laugh. "Will you? You think to resolve an imminent rebellion?"

"I do." Tyrus raised a grandiose salute to his uncle. "At the very least, the attempt will provide some diversion. If the Sagnau girl proves uncooperative, I'll behead her later."

"Oh, do send him." Cygna's sharp eyes glittered like knives. "This will prove most *diverting*, indeed. The madman, quelling the Excess!"

With an indulgent smile, the Emperor lounged back in his chair. "Tyrus, Tyrus . . . You know so little about power and its exercise. What can you do by going there? The Excess respect strength. They are challenging us, so the only response is to crush them."

"My uncle." Tyrus dropped to his knees, still wearing that crazed grin so at odds with what he was truly trying to achieve. "You must understand, this Sagnau girl is dear to my Sidonia, and Sidonia to the Sagnau girl. I believe with Sidonia's help, she can be persuaded to quell this rebellion with minimal expenditure of treasure. If I'm wrong, then I will take the consequences on myself."

"Oh ho!" Grandeé Cygna leaned forward. "You will accept responsibility personally?" She looked at her son. "Do send him. You selected him as your Successor Primus. Give him this opportunity to . . ." Her smile was like a hungry cat's, as though she found the prospect of Tyrus making a fool of himself simply too delicious to hide. "To show himself for the man he truly is."

The Emperor rubbed a finger over his chin in thought. "I suppose it would save some expense if Tyrus were to persuade the Luminars to meet with him in person. In fact, he might"—a gleam stole into his eyes—"*talk sense* into them. Dear Tyrus, I will tell you *just* what I want you to say." Then the Emperor looked to me. "What say you, then, Senator von Impyrean? Do you think it in your power to use this lowly Sagnau girl to erase our new troubles?"

I couldn't see Tyrus's plan yet, but I firmed my resolution and thought of how much Sidonia would have wanted to avoid needless killing in a situation like this. "Yes, Your Supreme Reverence. I feel certain we can fix this situation."

Servitors and swarming security bots appeared, a flustered Neveni Sagnau between them. Her hair was messy, her face drawn from her recent grief. She didn't have the solace I had in my plans for destroying the Emperor. She had only herself to rely upon.

Then again, maybe Tyrus had plans for her, too.

"Mistress Sagnau," said the Emperor, "your people are in turmoil. You'll accompany my nephew and the Senator von Impyrean to your planet Lumina."

Hope ignited in her eyes. I realized in that moment how desperately homesick she must have been.

"You'll quell your rebellious populace," said the Emperor, "or you'll be responsible for all their deaths."

Like that, the joy on her face was gone. Then I knew the weight of the task that Tyrus, Neveni, and I had just undertaken. It would fall to us to save countless lives.

29

IT WAS the first day of our two-week journey to Lumina. Tyrus stood in my chamber, staring out into the starlit void outside the *Alexandria*, which had detached from the larger Chrysanthemum, seemingly leaving a great empty gash in the side of the *Valor Novus*. Deadly was penned into the next room and periodically began barking through the door.

"What are you thinking?" I asked him.

His forehead creased as he pondered his plans for what lay ahead of us, his busy mind turning its wheels. He caught his balance as the ship jostled into hyperspace and the stars vanished outside. Then he turned to me.

"I'm known as a blasphemer. That may aid my case on Lumina. The Excess, as you may have heard, largely believe in older religions. They only perform Helionic rituals when the Grandiloquy demand they do so. However, if I do play up my sympathies for their . . .

blasphemies . . . other troubles will await me down the road."

"You'd alienate future support among the Grandiloquy."

"Precisely." He looked me over where I'd stretched my legs out, parallel with the floor, and seemed to realize something. "Wait, have you been balancing on your hands this whole time?"

Since we were in my private room, I decided Tyrus would simply have to put up with my exercise. I'd positioned myself on the floor and lifted my legs up parallel with it, balancing on my knuckles. Rather than respond to him, I tucked my legs in, swung them up behind me, and pushed into a handstand.

"You are so strong," Tyrus murmured. He circled about me slowly, until his legs drew into sight again. "And this requires no effort on your part?"

"Minimal." It just felt good. "I've actually been avoiding physical exertion ever since taking Sidonia's place. I gain muscle so easily."

"I devote two hours every day to maintaining my strength."

So that accounted for his muscular arms. "Such devotion to your vanity."

"If it was about appearance, I'd have them grown for me by a beauty bot. I exercise because I don't wish to ever feel weak."

Startled, I cast him a sidelong glance. I understood that anxiety all too well. But I had not expected the Emperor's heir to feel the same.

"We have many idle hours ahead of us on this journey," Tyrus said. "I'd be very interested in a mock combat with you sometime."

"You'd lose."

"We can arrange a handicap. One arm tied behind your back."

"Tie both. You'd still lose, Your Eminence. I don't want to injure you, and I promise I would."

"I'll take the risk."

"If this is about testing yourself against a Diabolic, you should know I'm not a good gauge of Diabolic strength. I've had much of my muscle mass removed."

He gave me a slow smile. "Well, then. Our handicap is already in place."

"Not enough of one," I said, then hesitated. "I am still a Diabolic." The bots had shaved my bones until I looked like a human girl—but I would never be one in truth. How odd that he seemed to forget this.

Odder yet, the idea pleased me.

"So you refuse to fight me?" he said.

Uneasy now, I shoved myself up into a flip and landed on my feet. His eyes widened. "Oh, well done," he said, as though I'd performed some great feat.

"Very well," I said. Why I should feel angry, suddenly, I could not say. "If you wish to experience defeat at my hands, I'll not deny you." It would make a fine lesson for him about my nature. "Do you want me to pummel you now?"

Tyrus laughed. "Not until after services. Best if it doesn't seem like Sidonia Impyrean beat me into respecting the Living Cosmos."

His words gave me an idea.

"Your Eminence," I said, realizing it, "Donia is—" I caught myself, pain lancing through my chest. I swallowed down the emotion and forged on, "Sidonia *was* very devout. Yes, she shared her father's interest in science, but she was also very faithful about attending services."

He raised his eyebrows. "Yes, I've heard this about her."

"So why don't we use that? You've suggested I play the positive influence on you in public, so why not this way? You can cater to the Luminars with your lack of faith, but cater to the whims of the Grandiloquy by attending services at *my* urging. The Grandiloquy will accept your being a blasphemer if you seem prepared to be an ardent Helionic when urged to it."

"Very clever," Tyrus said, grinning at me. "You will be seen convincing me to attend services despite my disinterest. Word will ripple through the Domitrian employees on this ship and reach the ears back at the Chrysanthemum. . . . More of Sidonia von Impyrean exerting a positive influence over the madman."

So that was what we did.

On a sparsely populated ship, services in the heliosphere were odd things. The highest-ranking figure always stood in the center closest to the vicar, with those of lesser rank fanning outward. That left Tyrus in the inner ring by himself, and me alone in the next ring, and then Neveni. In the outside rings were a scattering of servants, employees, and then Servitors.

Several times during the service, Tyrus stirred restively and made as if to leave. Each time, as befitted my role, I breached protocol by stepping forward to put a hand on his shoulder, conspicuously "reminding" him of my wish that he stay.

He answered each chastisement by smiling at me over his shoulder, showing everyone how indulgent he was of his new love. I could feel the eyes of the employees cutting into us, already silently composing reports for whoever might be bribing them at the Chrysanthemum. There would be many willing to pay for scraps of intelligence gathered during the journey with the Domitrian heir.

Neveni, for her part, stared out into the black void with glassy eyes, silent and immobile.

I caught up to her after the service. As she stepped back into the corridor toward her chamber, I called, "Take a meal with me?"

We hadn't spoken since I revealed my relationship with Tyrus, and that bothered me more than I wanted to admit.

Neveni half turned but would not meet my eyes. "I'm not hungry."

I groped for something to say. "Are you pleased to be returning home, at least?"

"Was it you who intervened for me, Sidonia?"

"I told Tyrus you could help matters. You could calm the unrest."

Neveni gave a hopeless laugh. "So that falls to me. How am I going to do that? My people know the Empire and the Helionics stand in the way of progress. The Empire takes more from Lumina in taxes than Lumina gets back from the Empire. In fact, what *does* the Empire even do for us? Provide security? Against what? The Empire is our greatest strategic threat! The Empire with its decadent Grandiloquy, and its ancient ships spreading malignant space everywhere!"

I looked around to affirm that nobody was eavesdropping on this dangerous talk.

"And on top of all this, the Emperor added insult to injury by killing my mother, the woman Luminars elected as leader." Neveni's voice shook. "It's no wonder there's unrest. My people were all disenfranchised, stripped of any pretense of choice. Am I supposed to tell them that none of their grievances matter?"

"I don't know what you should tell them," I said slowly. "But I know that you're the only one who stands a chance of fixing this. The Emperor has no mercy, Neveni. He'll raze the planet before he'll let it leave the Empire."

"He'll *try*." A strange gleam stole into her eyes. "Even if I help the Emperor, nothing stops him from summoning me back to the Chrysanthemum afterward to kill me anyway. Nothing stops him from razing my planet sometime later when we're not on alert anymore. Right now we're in a position of strength. If we leave, other planets will leave too. They'll fight with us. I don't have much incentive to help your beloved Tyrus. In fact, I'm going to tell you something very personal." She leaned toward me, defiance on her face. "I don't believe in the Helionic faith. I think it's nonsense."

Startled, I glanced behind us toward the heliosphere, making sure no Domitrian employees were about to hear us.

"I don't believe the Cosmos is some divine, living entity that intentionally created us," Neveni snarled. "I think space is a void and the Cosmos is a thing and *God* created us. God created the Cosmos, too. That's what my mom raised me to believe." Her face crumpled. "I didn't listen to her very often, and if I could take that back . . ."

Her voice hitched, and then she drew a shaky breath to firm herself.

"Sidonia, whatever we did on the Chrysanthemum, however many functions we went to or however many pretty outfits we wore or however much money you gave me, I'm not a Grandeé. I'm not like you. I'm not born and raised in space or favored by the Empire. I'm one of them. I'm one of the *Excess.*" She spat the word.

Only then did I realize that this word—this word I'd heard countless times, and repeated without thinking—was a slur. *Excess.* It implied that the vast majority of human beings were useless and insignificant.

"I know you will never believe it," I told her softly, "but I don't care if you're a heretic. I don't care about any of that."

But this was clearly not the response she was looking for. "Two weeks ago," she said with a bitter smile, "that would have made me very happy to hear. I would've felt like I was accepted by the Grandiloquy. Like I belonged. I used to want to belong. I was so angry with my mother for—" She broke off, mouth twisting. Then, "I used to wonder, *why* did she defy Senator von Pasus? But now I know. Now I see her for what she was, Sidonia: a hero. I'm going to be the daughter I should have been while she lived."

She left me without another word.

As I watched her go, a sinking feeling weighted my chest. It had never before occurred to me that she might refuse to help us. But I was no longer sure I could rely on her. She was too angry, too heavy with grief, to be a predictable player in this complicated game.

30

AS WE NEARED Lumina, we slowed down to carefully navigate past the patch of malignant space an imploding starship had left several years before. Tyrus headed to the largest window on the *Alexandria* so he could gaze out at it with his own eyes.

I joined him, curious about this phenomenon that seemed to fill people with such dread.

The sight surprised me. Malignant space resembled a ribbon of light against the vast starscape. However much I tried to tell myself I was looking at something dangerous, it merely appeared to be a band of glowing energy, like a vast solar flare. I said as much to Tyrus.

"Oh, it's deceptive in appearance." Tyrus pointed. "That light? It isn't coming from malignant space. Those are the hydrogen gases of stars that have been ripped apart by it. The light is being drawn into the ruptures—eaten, you could say. We're seeing the death of solar systems, Nemesis. *This* is what frightens the Luminars. They're three light-years away from here. We've used the same engines over and over for thousands of years, and we've now made ourselves forget how they even work. This right here is the end result of our ignorance: a problem we cannot solve."

I gazed again at the dead stars forming a virtual gash in space, pure light with edges of lurid purple. Now, it seemed, I could see something terrible in it. I knew I was looking upon oblivion itself.

"To think of all the time and thought we put into perfecting chemical pleasures and worship of the stars," Tyrus said. "And yet this happens more and more often, and we simply turn away. Many of the Grandiloquy would ignore this until there is no place to flee, no space free of this malignancy."

A bitter note stole into his voice.

"In some ways, we deserve this. . . . But all the others who are going to suffer for our actions don't. If I can stop it, I *must*."

He turned away from the window, a vein flickering in his forehead.

"I've seen enough. I can't look upon this anymore. Would you like to spar again?"

His stamina amazed me. "Have you recovered from the last time?"

"I'll welcome the distraction."

The first time Tyrus and I fought, I kept my hands joined together behind my back. It swiftly became evident that it would have better for him if I'd restrained my legs instead.

He moved quickly for a regular human. I was impressed by the power behind his punches, and had I not been swift enough to dodge them all, I was certain he could have knocked me off balance.

Then I delivered a roundhouse kick to his chest and heard bones crack.

Tyrus flew across the room and hit the wall with an ugly *thunk*.

He lay there several seconds, gurgling for breath as he clutched his ribs, before the med bots responded to his vital signs and swarmed over him.

For myself, shock had riveted me in place. Now, at the sight of the med bots, my trance was broken. "Your Eminence?" I rushed over to him and peered between the swarming bots.

I had known this would happen. I had *known*! Why had I agreed to such idiocy?

When they'd reinflated his collapsed lung and knit his ribs enough for him to talk, Tyrus leaned over to hack up blood, then sat up, peering at me, wiping at his mouth with the back of his arm.

"You are extraordinary."

"What?" The word slipped from me in a stunned whisper. I had been waiting, dread-filled, but there was nothing but admiration in his voice.

He spat out more blood. "I understand the brute power, the speed, but where did you learn technique?"

I blinked. Normally I disliked any questions about my upbringing in the corrals, but since I'd just nearly killed him, I felt I owed him an answer.

"When I was developing, visual aids were provided."

"What does that mean?" He heaved himself up with a wince, the med bots still crawling over him like large insects, tending to other injuries from his flight across the room.

"There were holographics projected in the pens." I spoke hesitantly, for it was hard putting into words those memories that were best forgotten. "They were images of people performing combat maneuvers. I would watch them. There was nothing else to do. I noticed that when I imitated them, I was rewarded."

"Rewarded . . . how?" Tyrus sank down onto his haunches, letting the med bots work on him, gazing at me with avid interest. The heir apparent to the Emperor, whom I had just come close to killing— waiting to hear about *me*.

"Better food," I said in bewilderment. Why did he care about my history? "A reduction in noise."

"Noise?"

I nodded. "An unpleasant humming sound. It would decrease in volume for a time if I did something pleasing to the corral master."

"That's ghastly."

Yes. It had been. "It worked," I said quietly.

He was scowling. "As far as I understand, Diabolics have a superior neural capacity to duplicate movements they've seen visually, but I had no idea such training was done under duress."

"It worked," I said again, and reached out a hand to him. Tyrus grasped it and pulled himself upright.

"Again?" he asked.

I gawked at him. "Now? After you nearly—"

"I feel quite better," he said. "I know what you can do now, and I'm prepared. We'll go again."

Had he learned nothing from his close escape? Perhaps he truly was demented. Fortunately, I was not. "No."

"Nemesis, I insist."

That stubborn look was becoming very familiar to me. "Not unless you wear body armor." He had refused it before.

"Very well."

"And I won't kick you," I added.

"That, I won't agree to. I must learn to absorb blows." He wiped at the blood crusted on his forehead from his tumble. "I've taught myself much of this combat. I've never had a sparring partner willing to risk injuring me. I welcome the worst you can do."

Madman. "You'd best not do that, Your Eminence, or you will end up dead."

But Tyrus's insistence and conviction could not be long resisted. Finally I agreed to undergo another round. This time, despite his urgings, I did not kick, and I permitted several of his blows to land just to gauge his strength. It was considerable. One strike even drove the breath from me before I instinctively lashed out and broke his arm.

Tyrus held his face granite still, trying to hide his pain as the bots swarmed him again—tending to his broken arm, his dislocated shoulder, his splintered rib, his broken nose, his swollen lips. I watched, my teeth clenched in irritation.

"Happy now?" I asked.

His laugh sounded breathless. "Did I injure you in the least?"

"My knuckles ache from punching you."

He grinned, impossibly cheerful about the whole thing. At last the med bots withdrew, and he tested his mended arm. "So," he said with a wince. "One more round?"

"No!" I thought quickly. "I'm . . . tired."

His keen eyes glinted. "Naturally you are. Certainly you're not sparing my ego because you see I'm at the limits of my strength. It's not necessary, Nemesis, though I thank you for the gesture."

I settled onto my knees to watch this strange young man. How could I be the only person who saw him for what he was? Clever and clear-sighted, impossibly resilient, willing to absorb blow after blow in the hope that it would strengthen him even if no one ever witnessed his mettle.

Curiosity was a strange feeling. I had not experienced it often. It itched at me from the inside, until at last I had to ask.

"*Why*, Your Eminence? Why learn to spar against me? Surely you have more to worry about from poisons or knives in the back.

Strength and brawn will not shield you against them."

Tyrus tipped his head back against the wall, deliberating on his answer. The pale light from overhead caught the sheen of freckles across his face. He looked very young in that moment, younger even than his nineteen years.

"Attacks can come in any form, and if I die, I mean it to be after I've exerted myself to my utmost, defended myself with everything in me—not after I wilted because I proved helpless." His lips thinned, his gaze turning inward. "My mother died when I was eight years old. I'm sure you know the story."

"No," I said. Sidonia had been the student of history, not I.

He glanced up at me. The bleakness in his face made me regret my ignorance—made me wish I could spare him the retelling.

"It wasn't stealth or poison that got her," he said. "My mother was very prudent, very cautious, very careful. We were paying a call to a Viceroy, but Grandmother had paid him on the side. A swarm of people rushed into our villa. Mercenaries. I could do nothing."

The bitter twist to his mouth puzzled me. "Of course you couldn't," I said. "You were eight years old."

"Of course," he said flatly. Then, after a moment, he shrugged. "At any rate, they butchered her. And I hid." He looked down at his clenched fist. "I've been hiding ever since, just in a very different way." A pause. "You must think me a coward."

"No," I said, surprised. But he did not look up.

I reached out to touch him. But the impulse confused me, so I stopped myself. "It's obvious to me," I said slowly, "that you did exactly as required to stay alive. I simply don't understand why your family is so . . ."

"Murderous?"

"Numerous. Why did your grandmother have so many children if she then planned to wage a war against all but one heir? The Impyrean Matriarch always said fashionable imperial families limited their offspring to avoid this problem."

Tyrus sighed. "It was my grandfather's doing. He was short-lived—only ninety-three when he passed—but he insisted on producing as many children as he could manage. Some twisted form of masculine pride, I believe. My grandmother only consented to bear one child. That was Randevald. So Grandfather harvested her ovaries and created new grandchildren without her consent. The only limitation was that he insisted on natural birth using human wombs rather than incubators. Fortunate—otherwise there might have been a hundred more Domitrians to deal with. As soon as he began weakening with age, Grandmother set to purging all the other offspring who might compete with Randevald's claim to the throne."

"But the Emperor distrusts her. I saw that. She placed him in power and he fears her."

Tyrus managed a smile as the last med bot finished mending a great cut on his chest. "After you watch a scorpion lethally sting dozens before you, it's difficult to accept that scorpion as an ally. You cannot help but think it might turn on you next. It's one reason Randevald has never wed, never fathered children of his own. He fears they'd find more favor with Grandmother than he does, in which case he'd go the way of our other family members."

"And this is also why the Emperor favors you."

Tyrus nodded. "Grandmother despises me. I survived her purge long enough to enter my uncle's confidence, and thanks to my madness, I've retained his trust and protection. She dares not strike at me, not right now. Not unless I slip and show myself in any way a threat to my uncle. Then he might permit her to strike me down. As things stand, he's fond of me because I am his bulwark against her."

I studied him, amazed. Evidently it was a blessing that I'd never been burdened by a family. The closest I had to DNA relations were my fellow Diabolics.

"So you see why I wish to fight with you, Nemesis," Tyrus said. "If you are a terrible menace in battle, then I welcome any challenge from you. It can only make me stronger in the end, to learn from the most dangerous."

His words ignited a strange glow in my chest. No one other than Donia had appreciated what I might show and teach, rather than how I might serve.

"I'll do as much as I am able," I promised him.

And for the rest of the trip through hyperspace, my days fell into a routine. Services in the heliosphere, an occasional meal with Neveni when she felt in the mood for company—which was rare. A workout with Deadly, running around the vessel to expend the dog's excess energy. Then meeting with Tyrus and battling the evening away.

I always handicapped myself. Sometimes I used bands to limit my range of motion. I insisted that Tyrus wear body armor. Sometimes I gave him a weapon and went bare-handed. As the days wore on, he required fewer and fewer advantages.

It wasn't that Tyrus's strength matched mine. Far from it. It was that he began to figure out how I moved, how I approached battle. He anticipated me. One day, when we experimentally donned exosuits to enhance our strength far beyond the capacity of regular humans—so far beyond our ordinary strength that the difference between Tyrus and me became irrelevant—he defeated me.

I found myself pinned against the ground, one metal-clad arm crushing down over mine, metal-clad legs trapping mine, and Tyrus just above me, too far out of reach for me to head-butt him.

I assessed my situation carefully, and then I had to admit it. "I yield."

"Yield? Do you really?" He gazed at me intently, his breath rasping harshly in the chamber.

"You have defeated me, Your Eminence."

"Well. Well . . . Imagine that." He released me and stood up. This time, his hand reached down toward me and clasped mine to pull me to my feet. "Nemesis, in private call me Tyrus."

"Tyrus," I repeated, the name sliding awkwardly over my tongue.

"That's it." His smile lingered as he stood looking upon me, pleasure still lighting his face. "Without the exosuit, of course, I never would have won."

"Of course not."

"Nemesis," he said earnestly, "thank you."

Now it was my turn to smile. During our journey, he had practiced his combat skills alone as often as we had fought. I was not sure I had taught him as much as he supposed. But his transparent respect warmed me regardless. It was a peculiar pleasure to feel accomplished, important. It was gratifying being needed.

I felt entirely gracious dipping my head solemnly and saying, "You are very welcome . . . Tyrus."

That night, after I had returned to my chamber and inspected the bruises splotched over my skin, it occurred to me that I hadn't thought of Donia for several hours. I hadn't felt that need to scream and collapse into myself in days.

And it wasn't just because I had vengeance to console me.

No, it was something more than that. I closed my eyes, the image of that lurid flare of light burning behind my lids. Malignant space. I saw now the true threat Tyrus wished to stave off. On humanity's current course, there was oblivion in wait, ready to consume, to destroy everything.

I could play a part in stopping that.

I could. A Diabolic. A being who was made to live and die for only one person, yet my life could influence the fate of trillions.

I folded my bare knees and buried my head against them, and whispered words that would never be heard.

"Thank you, Tyrus."

I loved Sidonia still, but my early life with her had been chosen for me.

From here, I chose for myself. And I wanted to help him claim his throne—and deal with a very real threat. That was my new meaning, my new purpose, and it made my life worth living again.

31

THE JOLT as we dropped out of hyperspace jerked me from a sleep filled with restless dreams about the Matriarch scolding me for forgetting Sidonia. The turbulence made Deadly bark excitedly. I rose from my bed to calm him, then glanced up at the window and felt my stomach drop out from under me.

The planet Lumina loomed large, larger than I'd ever seen any body in space. We intentionally plunged into the grasp of its gravity. There were continents, purple oceans, and swirls of white and gray clouds. The vessel shook around me as we drew closer and closer, and then the bright purple of the atmosphere had us in its clasp.

I didn't realize that my fingers were gripping Deadly's fur tightly until he nipped at my hand. I released him, my heart drumming frantically in my chest, then forced myself to look back up at the window, where the purple of atmosphere deepened and deepened.

In the distance the great snowy peaks of mountains rose into view, and the gravity about me shifted as the vessel released its own gravitational hold, relying on the pull of the planet's mass to provide anchoring for us. A disconcerting feeling of lightness popped through me. Buildings rose into view, and the ship jostled to the ground.

Dead silence wrapped about me as the engines cut off.

We were on the surface of Lumina.

I'd never been on a planet before. I sat down next to Deadly, scrubbing my fingers through his tufts of fur, feeling nauseous. All I could picture was the bare space above the planet with its cosmic rays and deadly asteroids, and no starship walls or force fields to protect us from those hazards, just a minutely thin sheen of atmosphere and a magnetic field.

How could people stand to live on planets with such paltry defenses? Every day on a planet meant exposure to radiation, to damaging starlight, to deadly microorganisms. One asteroid of sufficient size could kill everyone on this planet if it struck . . . yet the Excess endured it so gladly. Relished it, even.

My door slid open, and Tyrus strode in.

"I've spoken with the representatives of the rebels. They've agreed to enter negotiations. We're to be housed in the Capital."

"We won't stay here?" I said sharply, bounding to my feet.

"No, we'll stay in the dignitary compound. It's a gesture of trust, Nemesis. We leave the Servitors, though. You know how the Excess feel about them."

I felt rooted to the floor for a moment, but Tyrus was moving easily down the hallway, so I forced myself to leash Deadly and follow him.

We stepped out of the causeway of the ship, and I stared down at my shadow, still sickeningly aware of the vast, infinite open space overhead. The atmosphere was lighter here than standard, so I had to step lightly to stop myself from leaping. As soon as I inhaled the air on the surface, I felt breathless. There were so many scents, strange smells, and the air was as hot and humid as a great open mouth. My skin crawled with the grimy sense of exposure to countless bacteria, yet Neveni almost danced when she ran from the ship.

There were dignitaries waiting, and Neveni eagerly threw herself into someone's arms.

"Dad!"

He embraced her warmly, and I came to a stop just behind Tyrus. The world seemed to flicker into darkness about us for a moment, and when I looked up, I saw that a fat grayish mass of water vapor had squelched the rays of the sun.

"We should get inside before it rains," spoke one of the dignitaries, casting Tyrus a cool glance.

I sharpened to alertness. My gaze roved from one face to another, seeing similar degrees of dislike, distrust, and even hatred on the countenances of the dignitaries. Tyrus would have a difficult task persuading these people to trust him.

Neveni's father, now in possession of his daughter, sent the most malicious look of all toward Tyrus—the scion of the family that had killed his wife.

Tyrus was too clever to miss it, but he smiled with a look of bland pleasantness, ever the actor. "I agree. Senator von Impyrean is new to planetary life. I feel bad weather would be asking too much of her on the first day."

Blood rushed to my cheeks as I realized how transparent my discomfort had been, but when Tyrus held out a hand to me without gazing my way, I realized this perhaps was just his excuse to exit this awkward moment.

I took his hand and allowed him to draw me forward.

"Sweetheart, I'll send you home," Neveni's father said to her.

"I think it best if the acting Viceroy Sagnau remained," Tyrus interjected.

The dignitaries about us looked at him with varying levels of disdain. "She is not an elected officeholder," said one. "Aristocrats may place children in positions of authority, but we have laws here."

"Yet she is the single representative of your system whose authority my uncle currently recognizes," Tyrus said. "No negotiations will be acknowledged by my uncle without Mistress Sagnau present."

Angry grumbling met this pronouncement. Neveni stepped forward and said, "I'll attend."

"Neveni—" began her father.

"I've been at the Chrysanthemum among the Grandiloquy for months," Neveni replied to him with dignity. "There is no reason I shouldn't listen as my planet's fate is decided. Dad, please let me stay."

One of the dignitaries spoke up. "In this case, we'll begin straightaway, Your Eminence. Should we escort your paramour to her chamber?"

I looked at Tyrus sharply. Was it wise for me to be separated from him? Hadn't he brought me with him for protection?

He considered it a moment, then seemed to decide on something. He caught my eye and shook his head slightly, indicating that I should do as they wished. "My darling, take your rest."

Misgivings roared within me. This seemed a mistake. But I turned to follow my escort. At the last moment, Neveni crossed the distance and embraced me.

"Thank you for getting me home, Sidonia," she whispered in my ear. "I hope you know that whatever happens, I appreciate your friendship."

Later, alone in my chamber, the phrase that troubled me most was *whatever happens.*

◊

Tyrus didn't return all evening, and I roved the residential wing of the dignitary compound, trying not to dwell on the bare-naked sky out the window. It was slightly less uncomfortable inside, yet I was still acutely conscious of how contaminated planetary life was, and just how much cosmic radiation my body was absorbing every moment spent here.

Strange to think that primitive humans all originated from a place like this. And survived it.

Deadly picked up on my restlessness and grew agitated. There was nowhere indoors to take him to void his bowels, so at the direction of one of my attendants—a Luminar with a full head of hair who eyed me distrustfully and answered in monosyllables—I reluctantly led him back outside.

The sky was now black, no stars visible, the only lights from the distant buildings and the occasional slide of the moons peeking out from behind thick cloud cover. Golden lights lit a path through a thick garden, but it was like no garden I'd ever seen. Moss climbed up the trees and seemed to consume the branches, and dead leaves crunched beneath my feet. Plant fronds looked tangled together like combatants in battle.

There were numerous gardens in the Chrysanthemum and the Impyrean fortress, but they were all unnatural, carefully engineered things. These had grown themselves, with only splotches of deliberation in the occasional geometric arrangement of flowers here and there. The plants all seemed at war with one another for space, for sunlight. It was chaos. Between this and the humidity of the air, I couldn't understand how people lived with such unpredictability.

And then a droplet splashed my skin.

Deadly flattened his ears and growled. I froze in place. More droplets hit my skin, and I knew the source had to be those vaporous clouds above us. Rain. I'd heard of this phenomenon. The gardens in the Impyrean fortress had sprinklers designed to simulate rain. And then, as though a faucet had been turned on, water began streaming all about us as though from a million tiny fountains. The unexpected soaking took me by surprise, and as I pulled Deadly with me back toward the villa, wind began to blow the water into my eyes.

Wretched, wretched existence. Sutera nu Impyrean was right, this was . . .

A blinding flash split a tree apart, and then came a rumble of deafening noise.

An explosion. We were under attack! I threw myself down in the sloppy mud, Deadly's leash dropping from my slack grip. I squinted up against the driving rain to see another blinding flash that seemed to light the whole night, and more ground-shuddering roars. Deadly took off, yowling in fright.

My heart tripped in my chest, because I'd never been in such chaos. I could take on an individual attacker, but these weapons were more powerful than I could contend with. For a moment I didn't know what to do. Questions chased through my mind. Who was attacking? Was it coming from space? Was it coming from somewhere else? What manner of weapon was this? Who was the target of this attack?

Tyrus.

Of course. Tyrus!

The thought of him electrified me with panic. I had to go to him! I flung myself to my feet. The wind felt like it was whipping at my face, and the trees about me writhed as though in pain, the battering water hitting my skin, and all I could think of was that I'd allowed us to be separated and these Luminars could be doing anything to him in the middle of this attack.

I would protect him somehow. I would find him cover.

◊

Just inside the diplomatic council chambers, I encountered him. He took one shocked look at me, saw my muddy gown and frantic expression, then swept forward and engulfed me in his arms.

"My love, what's the matter?"

"Tyrus, were you hit?"

He stepped back. "What happened to you?"

"There's an attack in progress." I ran my hands over his body, inspecting him for injuries. His muscles tensed beneath my touch. "We need to find shelter right now!"

"What manner of attack?"

"Weapon fire from above. I don't know what sort. It flashed brightly through the sky. Listen! You can hear it now!" I flinched as the roaring sound pervaded the air.

For a moment, Tyrus just stared at me. And then he began to laugh.

What was amusing about this?

"I apologize, uh, Sidonia." He cupped my face. "I forget you haven't been planet-side." His voice dropped as he reached out to smooth my wet locks from my face. "And you haven't had the schooling to understand what you saw. You must have been frightened." He looked over his shoulder to address the dignitaries with whom he'd been in negotiation. "May we adjourn for a time? I have something I must show my beloved."

They looked as confused as I felt. But Tyrus remained calm, unflappable, and when they agreed to adjourn, he placed my hand in the crook of his arm and laid his own hand over it as though I were something fragile, in need of guidance. It was such a foreign gesture that I didn't know how I should feel about it. He escorted me back outside.

I moved closer to him, because Tyrus might be relaxed about the dangers but I was not. I was ready to throw him down and protect him at the first sign that his confidence was misplaced. The weapons still flashed through the sky, but when I pointed them out, Tyrus shook his head and resisted my efforts to pull him back inside. "Those aren't weapons. Do you trust me?"

I considered that. I trusted him to the extent that I was able to trust anyone. I gave a nod.

He led me farther out into the rain. As we stood there together, amid the flashes and great rumbling, he pointed toward the sky.

"This is weather!" he said, shouting to me over the sounds. "We're in a storm. These flashes aren't weapons, they're natural electrical discharges called 'lightning.' This is part of planetary living."

"This lightning is normal?" I gaped up at the blinding forks of fire. I'd heard of rain, but *electric* flashes? "People live with this? But . . . I saw a tree split in half! It's dangerous!"

A great wind swept over us, tousling his hair as he laughed. "There *is* danger to lightning. I don't deny it. But there is also such beauty in it, isn't there?"

I found myself gripping his hand tighter, trying to see these flashes as he did. Yes, perhaps there was some majesty to them. They lit the dome of the sky, exposing the bruised banks of clouds. "Yes," I said at last, a prickle moving over my skin. It *was* beautiful. How extraordinary, how strange.

I glanced toward Tyrus and startled. He was watching me, not the sky. His hair was soaked, plastered to his head. Water streamed down his square jaw, sluiced across the cleft in his chin.

A strange idea struck me: now that I had learned to see it, I might glimpse beauty anywhere. Even, perhaps, in another's face.

I swallowed and looked away. The rain still beat about us, but now the worst of my fears had receded, I became aware of other sensations: my gown clinging to my limbs, heavy and soaked; Tyrus's skin, so warm and damp against mine. From the corner of my eye, I caught the twitch of his lips, a smile quickly caught back.

Was he silently mocking my ignorance? "What is it?" I said warily.

He reached up and slid his hand through my wet hair, smoothing it out of my eyes. "It hadn't occurred to me something might worry you. I thought Diabolics were . . . fearless."

"I am," I said. But as soon as I spoke the words, I recognized them for a lie. I'd been trained to seem fearless, but I'd never truly transcended the emotion.

He stroked a hand over my arm. "Regardless. I'm sorry I wasn't there to explain earlier."

His expression looked strange to me. After a moment, I realized that it was gentleness I saw in his eyes—a truly unguarded look, from a young man who was always on the alert for danger. He was still stroking my arm, and I realized that he was trying to comfort me. *Me.*

He knew what I was. Yet he sought to reassure me anyway.

I glanced behind us but saw no one watching. This wasn't a show of affection for outside observers. He was simply attempting to comfort a Diabolic.

Moreover, he knew I had lied about my fearlessness, but he did not judge me for it.

An odd lump formed in my throat. I rubbed at it, but the feeling did not ease.

The rain died down and the lightning ceased. "I need to find Deadly," I murmured.

We fell into pace in a companionable silence. The moons emerged at last from behind the thick cloud cover, shedding silvery rays over the earth, sparkling on droplets that clung to the lush green vines. *Beauty*, I thought again. Wild and uncontrolled, like the lightning. I didn't know whether I admired or mistrusted it.

Then the light caught Tyrus's tired face, and I thought of those tense dignitaries we'd left behind. "I can find him on my own," I said. "You needn't look with me."

"I'm eager for the break. Besides, I'd rather that creature not maul one of the Luminars. It wouldn't assist in negotiations."

"How are things going?"

His lips smiled, but the rest of his face did not. "They're skeptical. Only natural, of course. With that malignant space nearby, they're worried they won't have a planet in a few decades. The Grandiloquy won't hear their concerns. Senator von Pasus's most helpful suggestion is that they consider evacuating this planet. . . . The Luminars are furious over it. I'm contending with several vehement holdouts, but I am hopeful we may be approaching a deal. Your friend Neveni will remain Viceroy in name only. They will retract their declaration of independence for now—until my ascension. And then, once I am Emperor, I will revise the policies on scientific education, and they will be allowed access to anything we can recover that may assist in containing the problem."

"And they'll accept this bargain?"

Tyrus looked away, some trouble creasing his brow. "I hope so. Otherwise, I have delivered us into hostile hands."

Hostile? I stared at him, willing him to meet my eyes and speak frankly. How hostile?

"There's your dog. Quickly," Tyrus said, springing forward in pursuit as he clapped his hands. Giddy with relief, I charged off in pursuit of Deadly, the question of Tyrus's negotiations receding, for a brief moment, to the back of my mind.

32

THE LIGHTNING and thunder returned several times throughout the night, disrupting my sleep. Every time the rumbling resumed,
I jolted upright, my heart hammering, convinced for a split second
that we were under attack. Then my conscious mind reminded me of
Tyrus's words. Lightning. Just lightning.

After sleeping so erratically, I did not instantly snap awake when
someone stepped into the room, even after Deadly began barking
from his pen. The attendants assigned to me had drifted in and out
during my stay, though they'd avoided me since I'd accosted one the
day before while trying to locate Tyrus.

The mattress dipped beneath a new weight. A hand touched my arm.

"Sidonia."

I sat up so quickly, Neveni jumped.

"Oh, it's you," I said breathlessly.

Neveni, her face grave, did not return my smile.

"I don't pretend to understand your sudden feelings for Tyrus Domitrian," she said. "I can only assume it's a reaction to your grief."

"Grief?" I rubbed my eyes, trying to clear the cobwebs of sleep from my mind.

"You lost your entire family. You're alone in the universe now, and I can't possibly imagine how painful that is." She squeezed my arm. "That's why I've argued your case to the others. They know who your father is and what he tried to do—the way he tried to pass information on to the Excess. For that reason alone, they've agreed that you won't be judged, even though you are an Imperial Senator."

I was on my feet so quickly, I wasn't aware of deciding to stand. "What do you mean, Neveni?"

She flinched at the way I leaned over her, but rose with all the dignity she could muster, her dark eyes glittering with resolve. "Lumina has left the Empire. We're not going to be persuaded otherwise. We're through with imperial domination. We may not have the Emperor on hand to punish for his crimes against our people, but the Successor Primus will make a fine stand-in."

I spoke in a growl: "Oh, no, he won't."

"It's already done." She shrugged. "They took him during the night. He's been tried, judged, and will soon be sentenced to be execu—"

I struck her.

Neveni shrieked as she tumbled to the ground. Before she could recover her footing, I seized her by the hair and pulled her up. "Where?"

"Help!" she shouted. "Help!"

The doors parted and in swarmed guards who'd obviously been prepared for just this occasion. My eyes ran over them. Four. No projectiles, just clubs. Obviously they believed they didn't need guns to take down Sidonia Impyrean. Their mistake.

"Help me!" cried Neveni.

I tossed her aside and vaulted forward. The first one put out his arms as though to catch me. The condescending smile on his lips disappeared when my roundhouse connected with his face. He flew backward into the wall. The next one was in my grasp before he glimpsed me nearing him. I flung him across the room so hard he splintered a glass table. The other two came at me together. I ducked their reaching arms, then whipped about to seize them both by their tunics. I smashed their heads together.

When I wheeled on Neveni, she staggered backward, wide-eyed and pale. She looked around at the carnage, her jaw slackening.

"You . . . you're not human."

"No," I said. Here it was, then: the danger I'd rushed to protect Tyrus from last night had come today. "Where has Tyrus been taken?"

She protested, of course. But our negotiation was short. I made it clear that if she tried to escape me, I'd snap her neck. Defeated, Neveni led me through the hallways, shooting me betrayed, tearful looks.

"I don't understand. What are you?"

There was no point in lying. "I was Sidonia Impyrean's Diabolic."

"A—a Diabolic? Like Enmity?" She goggled at me. "That's impossible."

"Obviously it's not. I deceived you."

"How can you be alive?"

"Sidonia Impyrean saved me from the great purge. Then I came to the Chrysanthemum in her place." My voice grew bitter. "To protect her."

"I don't understand! Why are you helping Tyrus Domitrian? If what you say is true, you have more reason than anyone to want the Domitrians dead!"

"I do. But *not* Tyrus." For he was a friend too—a friend who relied on me. And I feared for his safety as I had never feared before. I could not have prevented Sidonia's death. But Tyrus's fate was in my hands now.

We tore out onto the street outside the compound. "It's too late," Neveni panted. "They pronounced sentence here. They must have already taken him for execution."

"Where?"

"The Annex of Central Square."

I raised my arm. "Where is that?"

"You'd hit me again?"

"If I must."

Neveni spat out blood. The last time I'd struck her, I'd only held back a little. "Sixty blocks that way." She jerked her head down the street.

"Blocks?" I repeated, trying to figure out what she meant.

"Sections of sidewalk between cross streets. Sixty of them."

"If you're lying—"

"Why bother? You'll never get there in time."

"Neveni." I stared at her, thinking quickly. "I've valued your friendship too. I'm sorry." Then I struck her so fast she had no chance to feel fear.

I propped her unconscious body out of the street. I turned around and launched myself in the direction of the square, running as fast as I could, knowing it wasn't fast enough—knowing that as soon as she regained consciousness, she'd send her people after me.

I should have killed her. It would have been better to have killed her.

Hovercars whipped past me. The third time I was nearly run over, an idea occurred to me. I climbed up the fireslide of a building, then launched myself at a car as it whizzed past, digging my fingers into the cracks of the frame as a great torrent of wind nearly ripped me off. Frantic eyes gawked at me from within. I reared my legs back and kicked as hard as I could. The first kick bounced off the glass. The second one cracked it. The third, and I scraped my way through shards of glass into the interior.

The occupants yelped and scrambled away from me. I must have made a terrifying specter—spattered with blood, wearing a bedraggled nightgown.

"Take me to Central Square," I said. *"Now."*

Central Square was accessible only to pedestrians. A great crowd of patriotic Luminars had already amassed outside the Annex—a single, solitary tower of twisting palladium—for the excitement of seeing Tyrus Domitrian, Successor Primus of the arrogant Empire that presumed to rule them, robbed of his life. Vast screens loomed over the crowd, ready to broadcast the execution. The sheer numbers in the square staggered me—more people than I'd ever seen in one place.

As soon as I'd observed how the controls of the hovercar worked, I took them over and directed the vehicle straight into that crowd, blaring the warning siren. People scrambled out of my way. I could not figure out how to stop the vehicle. On a deep breath, I directed it into the wall of the Annex, then braced myself.

The vehicle slammed to a stop. Amid the tremendous crumpling of metal, I felt a cone of silken softness envelop me. I clawed my way free of the safety net, then kicked my way out through the window, crawling out like some grotesque newborn creature from its broken shell.

The collision had done double duty: it had opened a gap into the building. I thrust myself through that gap, clawing into the tower where the elites of Lumina were gathered, prepared to see the execution firsthand on a stage at the other end of the room.

The first guard noticed me. He shouted an alarm to the others, and the guards aimed their weapons. Bolts of energy flared toward me from all sides. I flipped back through the air, not dodging so much as shoving and leaping through the nearest spectators the way only a Diabolic could and hoping my unpredictable movements would save me.

The scattering of elite Luminars shouted in fear, crashing into one another in their haste to escape my vicinity. I leaped onto a man's shoulders, then used the height to propel myself onto the stage at the front of the room where Tyrus was being held. More guards stood posted here, aiming their weapons my way, but I ducked down and tackled the nearest, stripping away his weapon, which I then aimed at his colleagues. They fell in rapid succession.

I rounded on the dignitaries surrounding Tyrus. They had him forced onto his knees, ready for his death.

I would kill all of them or die myself.

One shot to Neveni's father—not a death shot for him, though, for she was my friend. But as for the others—

"Wait!" called Tyrus. "Don't kill them."

This was no time for mercy. I cast him an impatient look. "Why not?" In one quick move, I swiveled my weapon toward him and shot his handcuffs apart.

Tyrus gave a startled jerk as his hands snapped free, and he clambered to his feet. I circled around behind the dignitaries so the guards below the stage couldn't target me.

"Best to kill them," I said. "We'll keep Neveni's father alive as a hostage, to aid our escape—"

"No." Tyrus's gaze roved over the officials. "In return for sparing your lives, will you hear me out one last time?"

What was he *doing*? I looked at the remainder of the Luminar elites who hadn't fled, to the guards steadily approaching from below the stage with their weapons raised high. What could Tyrus possibly say that he hadn't said already? These people had proven treacherous, devious. They had sneaked in during the night to seize him for his death. They deserved no more chances.

But Tyrus had already turned away from me, addressing the

dignitaries who'd moments before encircled him, now standing with their hands raised, helpless. "One last appeal to your reason. I know you did not request my presence. I came uninvited, and if the Luminars wish to dispense justice upon my family through me after I speak once more, I will allow it. Willingly."

The dignitaries stirred. I grew aware of a few people trickling in through the gash I'd made in the wall. Neveni herself came scrambling inside, her own guards following. Clutching her head, she scanned the room. As our eyes met, I could see the betrayal and anger that contorted her face.

Neveni's father conferred with another man, then said, "Very well. We will hear one last appeal, on the condition that you submit yourself to any justice we mete out."

Tyrus nodded. "Then we'll put our weapons down and discuss this."

Put our weapons down? I bit my cheek hard to contain my rage. He meant *I'd* put my weapon down, and I wasn't about to do that. They'd been about to execute him moments ago. What was he doing? They were going to kill him!

Tyrus looked at me in silent appeal, and there was an intensity to his eyes that pleaded with me to trust him. Trust his judgment. Could I trust him in this? Could I let this happen?

My hands shook, but I forced myself to do it. I set my weapon down.

Now we were both of us at the mercy of the Luminars.

33

I FOLLOWED as if in a daze as Tyrus and a handful of dignitaries retreated together into a more private room. I stood as close as I could to Tyrus, and others were careful to give me distance. There was blood on my tattered nightgown, and I knew I'd revealed before the elites of Lumina that I could not possibly be a real person.

Tyrus faced imminent death, yet he calmly took a drink and settled himself before these Luminar dignitaries as though he commanded them—as though he'd called a sedate meeting, not a brief tribunal before his doom.

"I have approached this incorrectly," he told them. The faint golden light poured over his skin like honey, casting dark shadows into the swell of his muscular arms, over the calm dignity of his face. There was no trace of anxiety on his features, and young as he was, he looked an Imperial Emperor. It was a wonder anyone had believed he was mad. "I came here to give you reassurance that I'm nothing like my uncle, when you have no reason to trust me. You still have none."

Hearty agreement rang out about us, and I saw the flashing of hostile eyes.

"I expected you to blindly accept my assurances that I would grant you independence. But why would I keep my word once I was Emperor? Once I was secure? So let me make my case."

He reached a hand under his tunic and pulled out a thin metal phial. Then he placed it calmly on the table before him.

"You ask me how I differ from my uncle. *This* is my uncle's way. The Domitrian way. I've had this on me all along, even as your people seized me, even at the trial this morning where I was not even allowed to speak, to make my own case. Do you know what this is?"

Dead silence hung over the room. I could tell from the looks on the faces around me that nobody else knew either.

"Surely some of you know imperial history. My uncle certainly does, and he hoped to repeat it. My great-grandmother once used a bioweapon just like this to handle a rebellion on Fortican."

A stirring rippled over the room, and several Luminars jerked to their feet as though prepared to spring from the room. A phrase sounded from many lips: "Resolvent Mist! Resolvent!"

"Yes, it is Resolvent Mist. And if I wished to deploy it," Tyrus said, raising his voice but not shouting, "wouldn't I have done it already? I faced *death* at your hands and yet I was not going to use this and risk murdering thousands of innocent people. That is my uncle's way. And yes, that is the Domitrian imperial way, but it is *not* my way!"

Silence fell over the room. I drew closer to the phial and examined it without touching it. I recalled suddenly the sly look on the

Emperor's face when he agreed to let Tyrus speak to the Luminars, when he said he'd tell him *exactly* what he should say to them.

"The Emperor sent you here to deploy this . . . this bioweapon, didn't he?" I murmured. "He didn't want you to negotiate."

Tyrus gave a thin, bitter smile and plucked it up in his hands, his pale eyes tracing the smooth metal contours of the phial. "No, he had no desire to resolve this peacefully. He wanted an example made of the Luminars. He specifically asked me to gain entry to this planet, and then, upon landing, to unleash this Mist just as my great-grandmother once did to her opponents. There are enough spores in this phial to wipe out this entire province. You and I would have been safe. We received immunity against it along with our standard planetary inoculations before leaving the Chrysanthemum. The Luminars, though, would have faced a most terrible fate."

"Are you threatening us?" Neveni's father spoke, his voice wavering.

Tyrus fixed him with a steady gaze. "Isn't it clear to you yet that I am *not*? I was sent here to use this, but I would never use it. Not even at the cost of my own life. I have *already* shown you this. You meant to kill me, and I waited to die, but I still did not use this. I've no intention of continuing the old ways! I came here to resolve this conflict with words to spare this planet from the plans my uncle has for it. Whether you kill me today, or whether I walk out a free man, this phial will remain unopened, unused." He leaned forward. "But if you do agree to let me live, I can promise you one thing: you will never face a threat of this nature again. I intend to return to the Chrysanthemum and seize power from my uncle. Then I am going to dismantle the Grandiloquy's grip over this Empire and free you from their influence forever."

I caught my breath, hearing Tyrus so openly speak treason. The Luminars murmured, stunned by the words, but let him speak.

"I saw your malignant space. I know well the threat you face at some point in the near future," Tyrus said. "I *know* why you wish to secede. The Empire has been suppressing the technology, the knowledge you need to preserve yourselves, and this suppression has been done solely to preserve the power of the Grandiloquy. Those who question this repression are labeled blasphemers, heretics, because that is the Helionic faith of the nobility—a religion wielded as a cudgel by small, petty men with no true belief of their own. And yes, I can say this with certainty. I was born of these people, raised among them. Their religion is their tool and nothing more."

Neveni burst forward out of the gathered group of elites, her eyes shining with distrust. "And why would *you* be any different? If you do as you claim you will, you'll just damage your own power."

"What's the alternative?" Tyrus said. "Wait until malignant space is everywhere? Wait until we cannot turn in any direction without encountering our own oblivion? Stagnation is death, Mistress Sagnau. Rather than let myself go down in history as just another coward, burying himself in pleasure with his hands over his eyes, hiding from the realities before me, I want to be the one who takes the first step to change it."

"And how would you make that happen?" jeered a voice.

"My uncle has already given me the means of undermining the Grandiloquy. He's stripped many of the great imperial families of their influence and taken it for himself. He can now move arbitrarily in the Senate without anyone to check his power. I can use the power he's seized—the mandate he's forged for himself—and take actions over the objections of the Grandiloquy. And I swear to you, I'll do so."

"How do we know you speak in good faith?" said Neveni's father. "You could ascend to power and change your mind."

"Very simple," Tyrus said. "You have here words of high treason I've spoken to you. I admit to you that I do plot my uncle the Emperor's death. In fact, I even admit to you that I am helping a Diabolic pose as Senator von Impyrean and concealing her in the Grandiloquy, though it is high treason to even possess a Diabolic." He gestured to me.

I received several startled glances. Neveni swallowed hard but didn't look my way.

"I have given you all," Tyrus said, "each one of you, nearly a dozen witnesses, the ammunition to readily destroy me whether before or after I am Emperor, because who among the Grandiloquy will tolerate my authority over them once they see what I intend for them?"

Murmuring spread through the crowd.

"I am choosing to trust you with my most dangerous secrets," Tyrus said, his face glowing with conviction, "because we do share a cause. We are united in this. We want the same thing. Now, will you allow me to walk out of here and follow through on my plans, or will you strike me down here? I am at your mercy."

He spread his arms, and I fought back the temptation to leap in front of him and shield him from them.

And one by one, I saw the hands about me release weapons, fall from the holsters where they'd been clutching guns. Then Tyrus calmly took another drink, and it became very clear to me: he would live. The Luminars had been won to his cause at last.

We sat together by the window of the *Alexandria* as it rose from the surface of the planet, and I stared down in amazement to think Tyrus Domitrian had indeed resolved the situation. At least as far as the

Emperor was concerned, the planet Lumina had rebelled, and Tyrus came to it and talked them into staying part of the Empire. He didn't know how, and he didn't know what Tyrus had truly said, what machinations he'd performed—and he never would. It would seem an act of political genius on Tyrus's part.

Before our departure, Neveni had come to see me. She stayed at a careful distance. Then she remarked, "You must know that most people—most Excess like me, I should say—don't really care for genetically crafted humans. They're . . . they're like the Grandiloquy warning us we aren't necessary. We can be replaced."

So that was why the Excess found Servitors repulsive. And Diabolics had to be something more abhorrent than that.

Neveni's voice hitched. "Nemesis, I know creatures like you tend to . . . to kill people, so it must mean something that you never hurt me. Between that and what I know now you must have done to Salivar and Devineé, I might forgive you one day for your lies."

I hadn't missed the way she called me a "creature." "I regret that hurting you was necessary. . . . But, Neveni, I still don't regret hurting them."

She smiled. "Good." Then her smile faded. "All I want to leave you with is a word of warning. Tyrus may be the enemy of your enemy, but he is still a Domitrian. Never trust them. Not any of them. They are a family of killers and liars. He may not have deployed that Resolvent Mist—but he still brought it with him. What does that say about him?"

With that, Neveni and I took our leave of each other, perhaps forever.

Now as the purple ocean and the vast continents and mountain ranges and clouds grew smaller and smaller beneath us, I looked over at Tyrus, my mind swirling with the days we'd passed down there. He was contemplating the phial of Resolvent Mist—the order from his uncle that he'd defied. The old ways, disregarded.

"I am amazed by you," I remarked to him. "You think ten steps ahead of others."

Tyrus released an unsteady breath and tucked the phial away with a trembling hand. "Perhaps I just make it seem that way. I didn't anticipate they'd storm my chamber and take me off for execution this morning. When it happened, I thought I was dead. I thought it was all for nothing. And then you came."

It was then I noticed that his whole body was shaking, excess adrenaline spilling into his system. For his part, he gazed at me, taking in every particle of me, awe and amazement on his face.

"Nemesis, you are absolutely extraordinary. I had braced myself for imminent death, and there you exploded upon us like some avenging angel . . ." His voice caught. "I have grown used to the idea that human beings die or they betray and I could only rely on myself, but that's not true anymore. I feel I can trust you. That may seem so small an admission"—his eyes grew shadowed, his voice hoarse—"but from me, it is the greatest compliment I can ever give."

I flushed, because I knew Tyrus had lost everyone he loved as a child. I had glimpsed his pain when he'd spoken of his mother's death. I knew he'd grown to adulthood constantly threatened by death at the hands of his own family, trusting only his own wits for his survival. His words meant something significant, something important, and I didn't need him to explain why.

The way he was looking at me now . . . no one had looked at me so. I felt unable to return that look, but when my gaze dipped, I found myself staring instead at his mouth, and my face felt hot, my mouth dry.

His thumb brushed over my cheek. "Look at me," he said.

I took a sharp breath and pushed away these unsettling sensations. When I looked up, his keenly intelligent eyes seemed to pierce me, to stare into my very depths. "You are extraordinary," he said softly. "Is it selfish that all I can think now is that I want you for myself?"

I stuttered around the words. "Want me . . . how . . . ?"

An odd smile curved his mouth.

And then he kissed me.

34

THERE WAS no one around to see us—no one to fool into believing he cared for me. But his lips were pressed to mine, his mouth soft and warm.

Bewilderment gripped me and held me perfectly still as his hand slid through my hair. As he rubbed his lips over mine, a strange melting feeling ran down through my limbs. His clever fingers knew that, too. They chased the sensation, smoothing down my neck. He was not weak. I could feel the power in his grip as he wrapped his fingers around my neck. But there was no threat in it. It felt sweeter than any touch I had ever known.

His mouth grew more demanding. My hands somehow found their way to his body, testing the density of his muscled upper arms. Below us, the planet was receding, the darkness of space enveloping us, dizzying. I leaned against him. Every part of me seemed to be awakening, thrumming to life. I hadn't realized it was possible to feel this way. I was made a stranger to myself in this moment, the mundanity of everyday reality no longer imaginable.

Suddenly his body seemed a wonder. I ran my palms over his feverishly hot skin, over his broad chest. He stepped into me, putting my back against the wall. Over his shoulder, I spied the curvature of Lumina shrinking away, the stars expanding in all directions.

His mouth opened mine, and I tasted his tongue.

This! This was living. This was being alive, being human.

I never wanted it to end.

But at last, Tyrus pulled back, searching my eyes intently with his own. My legs felt unsteady. Such weakness should have alarmed me, but it felt, in this moment, trifling, a distraction from the revelation unfolding here. I stared back at him. I had never truly seen him before—so it seemed in that moment. A hundred details announced themselves, demanding my attention: the flecks of pale green in his gray-blue eyes. The intensity of his gaze, the way it felt as though he were staring into the depths of my being. How had I never smelled the scent of his skin, or noticed the strength, the skill and confidence, of his hands? My fingers trailed down the swell of his bicep, and my very skin seemed to spark with the contact.

Now, at last, I knew what it meant to be intoxicated. I could see why other people felt giddy and dazzled, inclined to foolish laughter. Perhaps I even understood the lightning better: my awareness felt electric, expanding to encompass the entire universe.

Tyrus smiled, a crooked secretive smile, as he drew my chin up and pressed his lips to mine again.

Yes.

We found our way to his plush lounger and sank down onto it together, our bodies never parting, locked together like two magnets. Was this wise? I could not say. A curious but wonderful fog filled my brain. It felt *right*. That was all that mattered. A sensation of utter wholeness spilled through my being.

After long minutes, Tyrus traced his finger over the bridge of my nose with its bump.

"How did you get this?" he murmured.

"Fighting in the corrals." I studied the cleft in his chin, the arrangement of his freckles. "You don't self-modify like the others."

"Waste of time. Why? Do you think I should?"

I thought about that. "No. I've come to identify every one of your aspects as the signature I use to recognize you. The freckles, the hair, the chin . . . Your eyes."

Such extraordinary eyes. They never wavered from mine. "You observe me," he said.

"I observe everyone. But yes, especially you."

I saw him fight a smile, and lose. He buried his head against my shoulder, letting out a long breath that raised goose bumps on my skin. I combed my fingers through his coppery hair and felt the tension still bracing his muscles, the fatigue he was fighting to conceal. "People need sleep after stressful ventures," I said softly. "Take yours."

Tyrus pulled me around so I fit against his chest, then eased me down so we lay together, his breath tickling my neck. I had never before slept so closely to someone—but after a moment, I found I didn't mind. It was peaceful, to be held like this.

His lips traced the back of my neck: "Good night, Nemesis."

I smiled, though he could not see it. I smiled at the bare room, and the cold, unfeeling starscape out the window, and I lay in perfect contentment, listening as his breathing grew deep and steady.

I felt the last thing from sleepy myself. The feel of his body against mine would not allow for it. My skin thrummed all over, every bit of it curious to explore the person pressed against me.

Very carefully, so as not to wake him, I twisted around to study Tyrus. The silvery starlight flattered him, gilding the sharp thrust of his cheekbones, the proud square of his jaw. I brushed my fingertips over his arm.

The strangeness of the moment dawned on me. Diabolics were not designed to desire. But I could find no other name for this electrified, hungering awareness of him.

A curious pressure expanded in my chest. I had not been bonded to Tyrus. There was no genetic cause for what I felt, what I was experiencing.

It could only be my humanity. Pure, inborn humanity.

Donia had been right. I'd had it in me all along.

I swallowed hard against a swell of feeling. I wanted to rouse Tyrus, to thank him as he'd thanked me for saving his life, because in so many ways, he had saved mine also.

Very gently, I touched his face. He needed more sleep than I did. And there was a certain unusual pallor to his appearance. His near execution had taken a greater toll than he'd admitted, I thought.

And so I let him sleep after all.

As we dropped into hyperspace, the silvery light outside vanished into pitch blackness. I rose quietly, stealing one last look at him before leaving the room.

Everything looked different to me: beauty, appearing at every mundane turn. The sleekness of the consoles lining the hallway; the graceful flutter of my gown around my ankles. I felt as though I were moving in a wondrous dream. My shadowy reflection flickered across a console beside me, and for a moment I stopped to consider it. I wondered at this smiling creature. She looked nothing like the flat, empty-eyed thing I'd seen in the mirrors at the Impyrean fortress.

She was *alive*.

In my chamber, I clapped my hands together, waiting for Deadly to rouse so I could do that thing he liked where I danced my fingers over the floor like they were small animals and he barked at them. My gaze found the pitch darkness out the window, and I marveled that even the void could be beautiful in its emptiness. Then my creature shuffled languidly forward.

I stared at him a split second longer, long enough to register the glossy sheen to his eyes, the way he seemed to be dragging his limbs rather than bouncing with easy power. His tail thumped once, half-heartedly, and then his legs collapsed from under him.

"Deadly!" I dropped down beside him, and it was then that I felt him vibrating, shaking, his body both stiff and far too lax in points, and I knew something was very wrong.

I fished out the case of med bots Tyrus and I used during sparring practice, then flipped up the lid. They swarmed out and flew over to Deadly, flashing their alarm lights—but then they retreated without treating him. Whatever was wrong with him was beyond their capacity to fix.

He was heavy, but I swept him up in my arms and charged out into the hallway. It took me a moment to think of where Tyrus's physician was, but I succeeded in waking him as I pounded on Doctor nan Domitrian's doorway.

He glared at me balefully for waking him up over this, but prodded at Deadly as I held him still. "Did he ingest anything on the planet?"

I looked at him blankly. I hadn't been with him every moment, not when we were separated during the lightning storm. "He may have."

"If the med bots can't help him, I don't know what you expect me to do. This is the danger in taking your pet to a strange planet. There are any number of pathogens and microorganisms in a wild environment that you won't encounter in space. He's not bred to be invulnerable."

Worry gripped me. "He'll recover, though."

"Senator von Impyrean, these beasts were made for fighting. No one engineered them for longevity."

"There has to be a way to heal him! He can't just get sick like this."

At that moment, something on the doctor's belt buzzed. He glanced down at it and then moved to the door. "I have to attend to something else. I'm very sorry that there's nothing I can do."

I glared after him. Then Deadly began to shake harder, thrashing, and I pulled him to me.

"Stay calm. I'm here to protect you. Be calm." I didn't know where the words came from, but they passed my lips like a chant. I took him to my chamber, at least somewhere familiar to him.

His eyes rolled back over and over, the whites taking on a sickly yellow sheen. Only occasionally did his gaze focus on me and stare helplessly, as though Deadly wondered why I wasn't making him feel better. All I could do was stare down at him in mute horror as he shook and then thrashed in my arms, a strange choking sound coming from his lips, foam frothing at his mouth.

I'd been so careless. I thought he'd enjoy being on a planet, having new things to smell, new places to explore. This was my fault. Better to have left him to die fighting in the ring than to let this happen.

I couldn't weep. All I could do was pet him behind the ears and hope he knew I hadn't abandoned him, but soon his seizures were continuous and his gurgling sounds unending, his tongue clamped between his teeth. That was when reality sank in: I couldn't let this go on.

I wrapped my arm around his neck and tightened my grip until his kicking legs went still.

"I'm so sorry," I whispered to him, still clutching him tightly.

I did not let go. His body grew stiff and cold in my arms. I still didn't know whether he'd eaten something on the planet or caught some disease, and it opened up a pit in my stomach to think this could just happen, that life could simply be stolen away.

And while he'd been suffering in my chamber, I'd missed it. I'd been with Tyrus.

Tyrus.

I needed to see him. I needed to hold him again and be taken back to that place of contentment where death meant nothing. I wrapped Deadly carefully in a blanket, then rocketed down the corridor.

When I stepped through the door of his chamber, voices reached me. Tyrus and Doctor nan Domitrian's.

"Easy does it, Your Eminence."

Retching sounds.

A cold haze swept over me. I remembered the doctor being called away, someone summoning him. Oh. *Oh.* Oh no.

Deadly wasn't the only one sick on this ship.

35

TYRUS straightened up, abashed, when he saw me in the doorway. He looked grayish, sweaty. "Sidonia, best stay back. I don't want you getting ill."

Horror filled me. I thought of Tyrus dying just like Deadly. I looked at the doctor, aghast. "What's wrong with him? We received inoculations before going to the planet. How is he sick?"

"Just some planetary fever," Tyrus answered for him.

"What is that?" I cried.

"An umbrella term." The doctor shook his head. "I told you how microorganisms thrive in natural environments, and space dwellers have little exposure to them. Those inoculations I gave you before you left couldn't cover everything. His Eminence never takes precautions when planet-side, so he always catches the local bugs."

Tyrus grimaced. "And believe me, I always vow to listen to you next time, Doctor."

All I could do was stare at Tyrus, looking so wan already, just hours after I'd left him. Now that I thought of it, his skin had felt warm, feverish. Why hadn't I thought to wonder if he was getting sick?

Tyrus saw the look on my face. "There's really no cause for concern," he said gently. "It will pass."

"Drink this. I'll return to check on you shortly," the doctor said to Tyrus, handing him a glass of some steaming concoction.

I remained rooted in place at the foot of his bed, stunned and stupid. Why had I never noticed before the fragility of living beings?

"You're not feeling ill yourself, are you?" Tyrus sipped at his drink, his face waxen with sweat. "It struck in my sleep, but I did notice a few aches and pains earlier."

"I rarely fall ill." My voice sounded toneless, detached. I felt strange indeed, like I'd come untethered from myself.

Had I told myself, earlier, that I was seeing him clearly at last? Now all I could see was his fragility: those bones, so easily broken and that skin, so easily ruptured. Deadly had been engineered for strength, designed to fight and survive—but that had not saved him, either.

What arrogance to forget, even for a moment, my difference from Tyrus. I was the deadliest creature ever engineered, and he was a fragile human being. I would live and thrive while others broke and shattered.

"The doctor told me your dog is ill. Is he all right?" Tyrus's voice sounded hoarse.

I stared at some point over his head. "He wasn't a dog." Now I sounded harsh, unfeeling, as a Diabolic should. "He was a fighting beast engineered to kill. That's all." My vision blurred, and I blinked hard to clear it. "He . . . It died."

"Oh." His voice was soft. "Nemesis, I am so sorry."

"It was just a creature."

He frowned. "But you were fond of him." He reached out a hand. "Come here."

I recoiled. "No. Just rest."

His mouth tightened. He tried to sit up, to come to me—and failed, collapsing against the pillows.

I hid my fist in my skirt. Fought with everything in me the urge to go to him, to help him. "Rest," I said again, backing away from him.

This time, he did not protest. "I'll come see you when I've recovered," he rasped.

As I walked back to my chamber, I felt strangely drained. Gone, dead, that flight of fancy that had powered me down this corridor so recently. I had recovered my senses now, returned to the brutal, stark reality where I was a Diabolic and Tyrus was but a vulnerable, fragile being, just like Sidonia had been.

Sidonia. I pressed my hand over my mouth and jammed back the rough sound that wanted to emerge. I had the strength of four men, yes. But I did not have the strength to endure another loss like that one. Having a heart that burned with emotion meant having a flame that could be doused in an instant by forces you could not fight, perils you could not see. To care was to be helpless in the worst possible way.

As I entered my chamber, I vowed to myself: I would never experience that weakness again.

Tyrus's planetary fever stretched on for a week. I knew he couldn't be dying, because Doctor nan Domitrian spent as much time eating as ever, rather than cloistered in the Successor Primus's chamber with him.

I didn't visit Tyrus again, but he never truly left me. He intruded into my thoughts, images of him infiltrating my inward vision. When I slept, when I exercised, when every minute crawled by during the day, I found myself picturing Tyrus, hungering for Tyrus. It was as though I'd sampled some narcotic and grown instantly addicted. I could not purge the longing from my system.

When Tyrus finally emerged from his sickbed, I felt acutely attuned to the changes in him, for all that I tried to focus elsewhere. He was visibly thinner but in good spirits. Eagerness glinted in his eyes at the sight of me. I found reasons to turn away from those eyes—to avoid him even as he continued to plague my thoughts.

One day as I did pull-ups, I discovered him watching from the doorway. "You can't avoid me forever," he said.

I trained my attention to the spot between his eyes, willing my vision out of focus. "I don't know what you mean."

"What's the matter? I know something's wrong."

I dropped to the ground to do push-ups, pretending to ignore him. It felt like turning my back on a supernova. He blazed in my awareness. I felt his presence to my bones.

"It's because I kissed you, isn't it?" He strode over and stood before me. "You're anxious."

"I am not anxious." I forced the words out with a sneer as I shoved myself upright, a sheen of sweat dampening my skin. He was close enough that I could feel the heat radiating off his body. "I am irritated."

His eyebrows jumped. "Oh?"

"I'm not like you. I can't feel what you can, Your Eminence."

A small smile crooked his lips. "I would beg to differ. You seemed entirely full of feeling when we left Lumina."

"Did you think so?" I was pleased with the indifferent tenor of my voice. "Then I must apologize for misleading you, Your Eminence."

He grasped my arm, his touch scorching me. "Tyrus, damn it. I've told you to call me by name."

"That's not appropriate."

"To hell with propriety, Nemesis! We've never been about that."

"We've never been about anything!" I ripped free of him and turned away. "I am not a person, *Tyrus*." I spat the name at the wall. "I can't feel love. I can't be a paramour or a lover or a companion. That's not what I am, it's not what I'm capable of." I wheeled back. "You expect me to be more than I am. You're asking the impossible."

He said nothing, but his face had gone pale. So soon after his recovery, the sight alarmed me—and alarm was not what I wished to feel. I wished to feel *nothing*, as a Diabolic properly should.

He closed the distance between us and pulled me to him roughly, his mouth finding mine. The kiss was forceful, demanding. His arms banded around me, tight and powerful as they pulled me against the lean expanse of his body.

For one stupid, unforgivable moment, he overcame me again. The feel of him, after so many days spent hungering for him . . . Like being woken into a dream, I had the sense I was rising outside myself. This was what I had wanted. This was all I had wanted. . . .

And it could be lost in a moment.

The black, choking fear freed me from my daze. I shoved him away. "*Enough!* You ask too much of me. Would you ask a dog to create artwork? Would you demand that a Servitor compose poetry? I cannot *do* this. I am incapable of real feelings for you. I will never be what you want. Let it go. Stop this."

Tyrus's expression cooled, that careful mask sliding back over his face. He studied me a moment in that unnervingly calm way that seemed to penetrate all my defenses.

Then he nodded. "Very well," he said quietly. "I won't force my affection where it's unwanted. From now on, I'll leave you be."

"That's all I ask." I turned away from him and resumed exercising. I was painfully aware of him until he finally left.

We did not spar again, nor did we speak outside of bland courtesies for the rest of the journey. Tyrus became so remote and chillingly civil that it would have been easier if he'd shown anger to me. Every time we stood together in a room and that glacial coolness froze the air between us, I tried to tell myself that this was what I'd wanted. I had no interest in—and no business feeling—such unsettling, aching emptiness.

Yet I could not will it away.

Perhaps Tyrus and Deadly had not been the only victims of Lumina. This unsettling need that had flared to vibrant life as we left that planet seemed like a fatal illness.

But I *would* heal from it. After all, I was a Diabolic, and Diabolics had no souls. Everyone knew that. I would never again be such a fool as to doubt it.

36

TYRUS AND I returned to the Chrysanthemum to find a celebration being thrown in his honor. The Emperor himself strode forward to greet us as the entire *Valor Novus* hummed with celebrants wearing gleaming ceremonial garb.

"The man of the hour!" The Emperor laughed heartily and drew Tyrus into the warmest of embraces. "You must regale us all with tales of how you quelled this rebellion. Did you release the Resolvent Mist?"

"Oh, this?" Tyrus calmly held up the phial. The crowd gasped and recoiled. They recognized it. "I know you ordered me to use it, but after discussion with my lady love . . ." He put his arm about my waist, drawing me against him. "Well, she persuaded me to a new view of the Luminars. 'Beloved,' she said, 'they are reasoning creatures. So reason with them!'" He offered a wondering smile to the watching crowd. "Can you credit it? On her counsel, we simply . . . talked it out."

The Emperor's expression had darkened now, and no wonder. With the audience of Grandiloquy listening avidly, Tyrus had just undermined his uncle's own policies. The Emperor had ordered him to kill the ruling Luminars. Tyrus had chosen instead to spare them.

"You took a great deal of authority onto yourself," the Emperor said mildly, an edge of danger in his voice.

"Forgive me, Uncle." Tyrus released me and dropped to his knees, catching up the Emperor's hand and pressing it to his cheek. The silence was absolute, the crowd about us holding its breath. Then Tyrus said the fateful words, "I only thought—Lumina is a wealthy province, and with the royal coffers running dry . . ."

A collective gasp rolled through the crowd at the casual airing of such a dangerous state secret. The Emperor paled.

". . . it seemed prudent," Tyrus continued, "not to start a full-scale conflict with them. Not when I could use the powers of persuasion to talk them down." He hesitated, feigning confusion as he peered up at his uncle. "I assumed Your Supreme Reverence would approve. Do you say I acted wrongly?"

The Emperor glared down at Tyrus, the cords of his neck bulging, rage barely leashed. I looked beyond him and found the Grandeé Cygna watching closely, an unpleasant smile toying with her mouth. She was no fool. She grasped precisely how much Tyrus had publicly undermined the Emperor just now. But could she possibly divine Tyrus's deliberation in doing so? And if so, would she use this occasion to whisper poison in her son's ear about Tyrus?

The Emperor yanked his grip from Tyrus's, then took a slow survey of the room, encompassing all the Grandiloquy who'd just heard open discussion for the first time of the Crown's dire financial straits . . . who'd just seen for the first time that the Emperor bayed for blood while the Successor Primus advocated moderation and reason. . . .

I caught Tyrus's eye and exchanged a level look with him. How cleverly he'd arranged this: securing a great victory that ensured he'd have a significant audience upon his return, and waiting until then, only then, to make his first true move against his uncle. Not for one moment had he played the madman today either. He'd officially abandoned that ruse. And as my eyes darted back up to the Grandeé Cygna, I saw from the mounting confusion on her face that she'd noticed it too.

Under the weight of so many eyes, the Emperor finally mustered a sick smile. He drew Tyrus to his feet. "How you have surprised me, my nephew." Despite his gracious tone, his eyes looked cold and unforgiving.

"Senator von Impyrean is a gentling influence on me," Tyrus replied with a shrug. He pulled me back to his side. "I would be lost without her."

"So I see."

There was no warmth in the Emperor's voice, and his face was like a mask of death when I glimpsed it again. A great apprehension raced through my veins. This moment marked a turning point. Whatever eventual confrontation Tyrus would face with his uncle, whatever deadly battle he would wage to usurp the imperial throne—this moment marked its beginning.

It surprised me how relieved I was to return to my villa for the first time in weeks. As I walked toward it, I even relished the controlled beauty of the sun-drenched sky dome, nowhere near so daunting after standing on the surface of an actual planet and experiencing its fearsome weather.

Here at the Chrysanthemum, all was deliberate. No insects swarmed the air but those designed for the garden. No humidity thickened in the lungs. There were no plants wrestling together in random, chaotic dysfunction. The only organisms that acted here without deliberation were the human beings.

My gaze fell on Deadly's favorite tree. A pang wrenched through my chest.

My thoughts still lingered with him when I stepped inside my villa, so I didn't immediately notice the changes. They registered as my eyes adjusted to the dimness, though: a Servitor tending a new jasmine plant, an unfamiliar gown being hemmed by another Servitor.

Every muscle in my body tensed. I held very still, listening. Someone was here. I heard a footfall that sounded nothing like the monotonous, even plodding of my Servitors. Someone stepping a few paces, stopping, turning about.

I stalked toward the next room, where the intruder lurked. Whoever it was, they would give me an explanation—or they wouldn't have long to live for this trespass.

I moved through the doorway.

And Sidonia spun around, relief on her face. "There you are! I was getting worried."

Blank shock stopped me in my tracks. I gawked at this mirage. It was a trick—it must be. Sidonia was dead. But this girl—

She had altered her coloring, given herself pale skin and hair, light eyes, a very rudimentary attempt at subterfuge. But her template was clearly Sidonia's.

I didn't believe in ghosts or specters. But I could find no other explanation. I stood dumbly as she crossed to me, threw her frail arms around me, and buried her head in the crook of my shoulder.

"Oh, Nemesis, you're well!"

The smell was Sidonia's. Her favorite lavender oil. This wasn't real. Surely it wasn't real. I was going mad!

I lurched back. "I've lost my mind."

"No, no, you haven't." Donia's eyes welled with tears. "It's a long story. But I'm here now, Nemesis. I'm all right."

I swallowed. Reached out to touch her—and gasped and snatched back my hand when my fingers closed on warm, living flesh. "Tell me," I whispered.

When she reached again for my hand, I recoiled. Hurt flashed through her face. "Won't you come closer?"

"No." My voice sounded so small. I was afraid of her—afraid she'd prove a dream.

"The last time we talked," she said, "you were nervous. You'd laughed. Remember? And it troubled you."

I exhaled. That was a universe ago, an eon long past. Back then Deadly yet lived, and Sidonia was a subspace transmission away, and Tyrus was only another stranger, a madman in the crowd. . . .

"I knew you'd be mad at me, so I didn't tell you I was coming." She gave a short, unsteady laugh. "I didn't tell Mother and Father, either. We still had Sutera nu Impyrean's identity chip, so I used it to steal aboard a supply vessel, then created orders sending her here as your Etiquette Marshal. I thought I would check on you, make sure you were all right, and then leave. . . ."

My knees gave way. I fell to the floor, unable to look away from her, unable even to breathe.

She knelt across from me, her expression fraught with feeling. "And then I heard our fortress had been destroyed."

"Donia." I murmured the word in wonder. It was her. She was here. She was alive!

"So I came here—but you were gone, Nemesis. I was so worried about you!"

"Donia!" The word ripped from me, and I plowed into her.

Donia cried out as I bowled her over, pulling her into a hug. And then she was laughing against me, the loveliest sound in all the universe. *She's alive, she's alive . . .*

I realized I was shaking, making a sound in my throat like sobs, and I knew Donia was alarmed. She tried to pull away, but I wouldn't let her, I couldn't let her go. And then she gasped, "Nemesis, you're too strong, you're hurting me."

I loosened my grip on her at last. She took hold of my face in her small hands, and her eyes shone into mine. "Oh, Nemesis, I've missed you, too. Have you been well?"

It took a moment to muster my reply to this ridiculous question. *"No,"* I said.

She smiled sadly. "Nor have I."

But that was going to change now. For both of us.

Donia was here. She was alive. I could ask for nothing more of this existence, this universe. I couldn't question that there was something greater than me that was kind and fair and benign, just as the vicars claimed in the services at the Great Heliosphere, for now I had this proof with me. The light of the stars would never bless a Diabolic, but in that moment, I could have wholeheartedly thrown myself into worship of the Living Cosmos for restoring Donia to me.

I would never allow her to be taken away again. Even as the thought settled in my mind, a dark edge of worry crept through me. She was alive, but she would not remain so once she was discovered here. If people learned that she was the real Sidonia Impyrean, she'd face execution for the treason of sending me in her place—and I'd face execution for taking her place. Tyrus would be questioned as well. The Emperor would crack down on his nephew, and families like the Pasuses would eagerly clamor to eradicate the last hint of Impyrean influence.

But what was the alternative? Sidonia could not hide as my Etiquette Marshal while waiting for the Emperor's death. She was by all rights a galactic Senator, her father's heir.

For the next several days, I mulled over this problem. I did not leave the villa, perfunctorily dismissing Tyrus's every message or summons. After such a confusing and tumultuous period, it seemed all the strangeness and ambiguity of my universe had disappeared, replaced by a glorious profusion of rightness: she was here again and I was her Diabolic and my purpose was crystal clear once more. I'd wondered how the universe could keep existing after her death, how I could go on without her. But it turned out I didn't need to.

Donia wanted to know everything of my life at the Chrysanthemum, so I recounted all the details as carefully and dispassionately as I could. I told her of alienating Gladdic, and to my surprise, she smiled and said tenderly, "Oh, Nemesis," as though it didn't matter to her in the least. It roused a faint smile from her to hear of Elantra's failed attempts to get me to voice heretical sentiments. Her face became drawn with sorrow as she heard of that fateful day that had condemned her family.

I had to stop speaking for a while because tears began slipping down her cheeks, and then it became a matter of being silent and stroking her shoulders while she wept again for her loss.

Embraces had never come naturally to me. Back in the Impyrean fortress, they'd always felt like a strange dance movement no one had adequately choreographed for me. But I had started to learn the way of it with Tyrus, and that skill served me well now as I put my arms around her. "It's all right," I whispered, and at last her tears slowed.

"Tell me what happened after that," she said, wiping her cheeks with the heel of her hand.

I didn't wish to revisit that time. The memory of those awful days after her supposed death felt like a blade digging at my core, shredding marrow and ligaments.

"I was distraught," I said stiffly. I struggled to detach myself from the memories, as if they belonged to a stranger. "I moved against the Emperor."

Donia gasped.

"His Diabolic, Enmity, fought me. She would have killed me, but for . . . for the Successor Primus. The Emperor's heir."

Donia's eyes widened, doe-like and amazed. "Tyrus Domitrian?"

"Yes. He killed Enmity." I was whispering now, though no one could hear us. Tyrus sent his own bots to sweep my chamber for surveillance twice a day. "He and I have come to an understanding, Donia."

As I filled her in on our scheme to redeem Tyrus's reputation, to put him in a position where he could strike against his uncle and get away with it, Donia leaned her head against my shoulder.

"We'll avenge your family," I told her.

"Oh, Nemesis, this sounds dangerous. I can't lose you, too."

"You won't."

But she was right. It was dangerous. That hadn't troubled me before, but everything would have to be reconsidered now that she was here. I couldn't continue to present myself as Sidonia von Impyrean now—not when it meant usurping her rightful place. My deception had to end. But if I waited to do so until Tyrus was Emperor, it would fall to him to make an example of me.

I took a deep breath. I'd accept that price gladly. I had always known it was my duty to die for her.

"What is Tyrus Domitrian like?" Sidonia asked me.

The mention of him made my skin feel hot and tight. I found myself looking away from her, oddly fearful that my expression should betray me. "Clever." My voice remained neutral, at least. "Exceedingly clever. Very deliberate in all his actions."

"Is he . . . can you trust him?"

Yes. But that certainty felt more foreign to me, in her presence. "As much as I can trust anyone who is not you."

"Will you tell him about me?"

"No."

My word came out sharply. Sidonia straightened, looking at me worriedly.

"You," I said, cupping her chin, "will stay in here and reveal yourself to no one until I've figured out a plan. I can't . . ." My mouth grew dry, my heart twisting. "I cannot risk losing you again."

"I know."

"It would destroy me."

"I know." She threw her arms around me, and I felt her tears against my skin. "I love you, too, Nemesis."

I sighed. Those were words I could never say, but Donia understood my heart. And when it came to her, I did have one. If Tyrus had been carrying me across the river all this time, then I was turning scorpion and returning to my true nature—protecting Sidonia at all costs. She would always come first, even if it required me to sting him.

37

THE SEEDS of distrust, once sown in the mind of a tyrant, flourished rapidly. After our return from Lumina, the Emperor never again looked so indulgently on Tyrus. For his part, Tyrus stealthily accelerated his campaign to undermine his uncle's authority. He was careful, though, always acting in ways that only the most paranoid mind could consider deliberate.

He made offhanded comments here and there about murdered enemies of the Emperor, casually mentioning their names in the presence of relatives who likely still grieved them. He threw out more references to the crown's bankrupt state, especially before the Empire's most fervent gossips. He also hosted a party for Grandiloquy who abhorred animal fights, on the occasion of the Emperor's manticore facing off against Senator von Fordyce's prized tiger-and-bear hybrid. "Sidonia has taught me a better way," Tyrus pronounced grandly to his guests, cupping my hand where it rested in the crook of his arm. "It is downright uncivilized to glory in blood sports." He leaned close to me, brushing a finger down my neck, his lips curving. "Isn't that so, my love?"

Those Grandiloquy opposed to the fights were the heirs of families that shared a particular political alignment, so his gesture was all the more dangerous.

Tyrus's party was well attended. It had to vex the Emperor that his manticore's triumph went unwitnessed by so many. Yet it wasn't a treasonous offense. It wasn't something he could publicly blister Tyrus over. Nothing Tyrus did could be formally punished.

The Emperor was oddly silent at the next family meal Tyrus invited me to attend. He slouched in his chair, his mouth pinched into a tight white line as he waited for his family to taste his food. But when it came Tyrus's turn, he leaned forward, watching with the intensity he had once reserved only for his mother.

"Try another bite from the other side," he told Tyrus, after Tyrus sliced off a sliver of the boar meat.

Tyrus obliged and was about to pass the plate onward, when the Emperor said, "Now flip it over and try the bottom."

Cygna looked between the two, her eyes sharp. "There will be none for you, my son."

The Emperor watched Tyrus. "Do it."

"Of course, Your Supremacy." Tyrus sliced off an overlarge chunk of the meat and made a show of relishing it. "Exquisite. You do get the best cuts."

That irritated the Emperor. "Pass it on now." He surveyed the remains of his boar. "Why, you've ravaged it! You've devoured half my meal."

Tyrus's manner was all innocence. "My apologies. Did you not instruct me to sample every aspect, Your Supremacy?"

"I have a poor appetite tonight, anyway," the Emperor growled, yet he dug into his cut voraciously.

Prickling hostility radiated from him for the next awkward half hour. Tyrus chattered to his grandmother in a show of oblivious good cheer. His light mood seemed to darken the Emperor's countenance further.

Later, as we walked back to my villa, Tyrus pointed overhead. "Look," he said. "No suns."

I looked up, startled to see naked space. The sky dome faced none of the six stars. It was a rare sight.

"Enjoy it while you can," Tyrus said. "Soon the six stars will all be in close proximity to one another. That's when my uncle will throw the Great Race. Last time, he virtually bankrupted himself."

"How?"

Tyrus chuckled. "He sank an armada's worth of money into a bet on a single pilot. Then, during the very first stretch of the race, that pilot had an accident—his ship was clipped by another, and both pilots were knocked out of the race. Randevald lost everything." His smile faded. "He was furious. He had both pilots, their families, and their crews executed."

A grim silence settled between us. I thought of the Emperor ordering Leather to skin herself, and a chill swept over me.

"He begins to distrust you," I warned Tyrus.

He looked at me calmly. "Yes, I know. I've seen him more in the company of Devineé and Salivar, impaired though they are. He means to unsettle me by showing them favor. I suspect I will shortly need you more than ever."

"I am always on guard, Tyrus." I had more motivation than even he knew. He was the guarantee for me now that Sidonia would be restored upon his ascension, that she would have a friend in power. And also . . .

I wanted him to prevail.

It made me uneasy how much his fate still weighed on me. Donia was back. My thoughts should turn only to her. But late at night, when she was sleeping, it was Tyrus I thought of most.

I cared about his well-being. I cared too much.

He was searching my face closely. "You've been quite restored in spirits lately."

"I was unaware my spirits had declined."

He sighed, then came to a stop, facing me. "Nemesis." His voice was low and steady. "We had some uneasiness between us on the ship. But I want you to know . . ." He touched my face very lightly, as though I were fragile, breakable. "It was never my intention to make you feel uncomfortable. I am sorry."

My stomach twisted. I didn't wish to speak of what had happened between us on the ship. If I could have disowned the very memory of it, I would have. Despite myself, I noticed how close he was, his lips so near mine. So very close . . .

Why couldn't I put back to sleep the strange desires he'd awakened?

"What happened on the ship," I said unsteadily. "It meant nothing, of course." Tyrus had just survived a near execution. He'd been grateful to me for saving him. No doubt he had reevaluated his feelings after I'd driven him away. He had seen them for the madness they were.

"Nothing," he said evenly.

"Good. So what happens from here?"

"From here?" He lifted his eyebrows. "I continue as I've done. Small gestures here and there, never anything to justify retaliation, but enough provocation to draw out the worst of my uncle and exhibit the best in me. And, of course, the best means the nobler side of me, drawn forth by the Grandeé von Impyrean." He gave me a wry smile, which swiftly faded. "My grandmother is the greatest obstacle right now."

"Why?"

"She is the poisonous adder whispering in my uncle's ear. She could advise prudence, caution. She could spread rumors about me to others. I've never known how to neutralize her influence."

"You will think of something."

His lips curved. "I hope your faith in me isn't misplaced." He hesitated, studying my face, seeming to wrestle with the urge to say something. But after a moment, he shrugged and stepped back a pace, and said with neutral formality, "Good night, Nemesis."

Every time I was away from Sidonia, I returned fearing that she might have vanished—simply faded into the mist like a shade, lost again, dead. But so far, my nightmare had yet to be realized. When I returned to my villa to find her waiting, relief washed through me. Still alive. Still not a phantom or a delusion.

She was content to remain in virtual isolation, partly out of fear, but partly due to her natural introversion. I'd asked Tyrus for books from the *Alexandria* about old Earth. His Servitors had delivered several full bookcases to me.

"You have an interest in history now?" Tyrus had asked.

"Sidonia finds the books pretty, and they're supposed to be the way you won me over. . . . So I must pretend I want to use them to decorate my villa."

The volumes fascinated Sidonia. I always returned to find her studying them, her eyes wide, fingering the priceless old pages with the utmost care, using a bot to translate the obsolete languages she called "Latin" and "Russian" and "English."

She told me eagerly about all the theories she was reading. "There was this extraordinary explanation about why time *itself* is distorted the closer one gets to a black hole. I'd never really examined why that might happen before, but . . ."

I nodded along without absorbing a word she said, my thoughts drifting to Tyrus. The memory of kissing him intruded in idle times. And then the intercom chimed:

"Cygna Domitrian to see Sidonia von Impyrean."

I froze. Sidonia cast a frantic look between me and the door. She knew all about the Emperor's mother, of course, but neither of us had dreamed she would visit me here.

Cygna had not waited to be admitted. She was already striding inside, as the royals were permitted to do.

I was on my feet in a shot, and Sidonia ducked her head to escape notice.

I dropped to my knees in respect. Cygna had recently refreshed her false-youth, and today her hair was a twining mass of curly brown tendrils, her eyes lashless over her cut cheekbones, her lips freshly plumped. Her hawkish gaze passed over me to Sidonia as she held out her hand for me to take.

"And who is this?" she said as I pressed her knuckles to my cheek. "No Servitor, but no employee."

"I am . . ." Donia stopped abruptly. She'd been trained to be the highest-ranking person in a room, to answer for herself. Pink stole over her cheeks as she recalled that I was her, and she was one of the Excess. She bowed her head. "Forgive me."

"This is Sutera nu Impyrean," I said. "She's an Etiquette Marshal who's been with our family for a long time."

"Indeed. How fortunate she came to keep you company after your family's tragedy."

"She trained me in conducting myself here. I am always indebted to her. It was kind of her to come."

"She may leave us," said Cygna.

Donia found her feet and cast me a worried glance before making for the door. She feared to leave me in the company of this harpy, but the greatest relief for me was seeing Sidonia escape the range of Cygna's poisonous attention.

Cygna gazed after Donia as my Servitors prepped a divan for her, laying out pillows and turning on the antigravity plates, positioning it at the centermost spot in the room. After she sat, I lowered myself on the chair across from her, fraught with apprehension about what she could be doing here.

"You have proven a most ameliorating influence on my grandson," Cygna said formally. "It inclines me to feel great curiosity about you, Senator von Impyrean."

This woman was closer to Tyrus in disposition than to the Emperor. I knew Tyrus's careful, calculating deliberation could only have come from her. I forced myself to think of every tell the Matriarch had ever pointed out in my demeanor—my unblinking, direct gaze, my empty expression—and willed them away.

"I am very fond of the Successor Primus," I said simply.

"This surprises me greatly. I always believed Tyrus to have a certain weakness of mind." She never looked away from me. She could have been the Diabolic for the directness of her stare.

"I have seen his instability, Your Eminence, but I've found he can be reasoned out of it."

"Another surprise. You can count me all astonishment, my Grandeé, that you have learned so much of my own grandson, insights I had not gathered myself. Do tell me, what does he mean by antagonizing my son?"

The question, so direct, caught me off guard. "I—I don't know what you mean by that."

Her smile sharpened. "I—I—" she echoed, mocking me. "I've never heard you hesitate in your speech once, girl. How amusing to see you are capable of it." She rose as I grappled with what to say to her. "I have never favored Tyrus, I've made no secret of that. His mother would never have been born if it had been my choice. Before her brain damage, I wished my son had appointed Deviнеé as his heir. I had no say in her existence either, but she at least resembles me. Now I find myself in the awkward position of having an imbecile for a granddaughter, so I must look more favorably upon the madman. . . . Though under your influence, you have made that easier. I must understand the motives behind his actions recently." She considered me for a thoughtful moment. "You and I could be friendly, Senator von Impyrean. I am a woman of great influence in this Empire."

"Are you asking me to inform on Tyrus for you?" I said.

"If you wish to put it so bluntly, so crudely, then yes. That's exactly what I'm asking. It's best for all concerned that I know exactly what is going on within my family."

"Ah. So you have Tyrus's best interests at heart." The skepticism had crept into my voice. I couldn't hide it.

Her eyes narrowed. "I've always had my family's best interests at heart. Whatever rumors you may have heard about me, I've only been interested in ensuring that the strongest of my blood took the reins of this Empire. I've only wished to support the most qualified heir."

"Then perhaps you supported the wrong one."

The words were out of my mouth before I could question them. The Grandeé Cygna's gaze sharpened, and I realized I could not win this conversation. "What do you mean by that?"

"Only that I love Tyrus." It was a lie, of course, but as I spoke it, I felt myself redden. I had never spoken those words, even in playacting. They felt clumsy on my tongue. "My loyalty is to him," I added through my teeth. Barring Sidonia, that was entirely the truth. "You cannot make a spy of me."

"You reject my hand of friendship?"

I did not wish to offend her. But I saw no alternative. "Under the conditions you wish to offer it, yes. I do."

"Fool girl." Her voice grew glacial cold. "I have never liked you."

"Then I've certainly decided rightly."

My remark gave her no pause. "There's always been something very wrong about you," she muttered. "I can't put my finger on it yet, but I will. And in the meantime—" Her mouth twisted. "Don't imagine yourself irreplaceable. I assure you, I can find a compliant girl to put in your place. . . . And so will my grandson, if I decide he's to look elsewhere."

I stood up, towering over her at my full height. "Then it seems we have nothing more to say to each other."

She straightened, the picture of dignity, this murderess who'd killed so many of her own children. We gazed at each other another taut, dangerous moment, and then she took her leave without a word.

I had just made an enemy.

38

I DID NOT relax until I was sure the Grandeé Cygna was gone, and then I rushed into the next room to check on Sidonia. She'd been leaning against the door—eavesdropping, it seemed. "Why didn't you just tell her what she wanted to hear?" she asked me, looking bewildered. "You could have agreed to spy on Tyrus, then told Tyrus about the proposition. That would have been the most strategic thing to do."

I paused, taken aback and then irritated by her question. The feeling puzzled me into a brief, startled silence: I had never felt irritated with Sidonia before. She was the scholar, the wise one, the real person who knew things I didn't. I wasn't used to having to explain the obvious to her.

"Because," I said slowly. "I couldn't do that to Tyrus."

"Why not?"

Suddenly my muscles ached—burning with the need to exert

themselves, to move, to labor until exhaustion. I stalked past Donia, striding along the perimeter of the room, breathing deeply to school my thoughts.

"It made me angry," I said, "that she wanted to use me against Tyrus." Donia did not know Tyrus. She could not understand. "She's his enemy, you know. His own grandmother. If she had her way—" I heard the tightening fury in my voice and bit back my next words.

"Nemesis." Her soft voice called me around to face her. She had crossed her arms, hugging herself. I saw her chest rise and fall on a deep breath. "You . . . you care about Tyrus, don't you?"

For the second time today, I felt my face burn. Suddenly I could not hold her gaze. "I didn't say that."

Footsteps padded over the carpet. Then her cool hand stole over mine, squeezing. "I'm glad."

Her words only aggravated me further. There was no cause for *gladness* in my feelings for Tyrus. They were an inconvenience—and by all rights, they should also have been impossible. The only human who I should care for stood in front of me now, holding my hand! And yet now I was fraught with irritation even at her, and it was over him, and I felt so foolish for this.

I took a hard breath through my nose before speaking again. "Are you truly glad? Don't you think it's a betrayal?"

"A betrayal?"

"Because I—I feel this for someone else."

Her face clouded, and her smile was small and shaky. "I'm just glad you're feeling things. More importantly, you're *letting* yourself feel things. It's all I could have hoped for you." She looked away quickly, her frail collarbone standing out against her skin. "I've only ever wanted you to be happy."

I swallowed. I did not deserve such compassion. "I live for *you*, Donia. Not Tyrus."

"Maybe I just want you to live for yourself," she said softly.

Donia believed it was an unquestionably good thing that I'd come to care for Tyrus. I didn't agree with her, especially when I appeared for the next Domitrian family dinner. I came as Tyrus's guest, while Cygna invited . . .

Elantra.

"Sit beside Tyrus, my dear heart." Cygna spoke more sweetly to Elantra than she had ever done with her own blood. Elantra glowed with the attention, and delicately took the seat on the other side of Tyrus.

Tyrus did not seem displeased. "An unexpected pleasure to see you, Grandeé Pasus," he said to her.

The only secret I had kept from Tyrus was Donia's restoration. I was simply waiting for the right moment to reveal it. Certainly I had wasted no time, in the wake of Cygna's visit, to go to the *Alexandria* and inform him of our conversation.

He had joined me that day in the great study off his library, beneath the vast window that looked over the underside of Berneval Stretch.

"So my grandmother likes the effect you've had on me," he'd remarked, examining the starscape thoughtfully, his fingers steepled beneath his chin. "But she dislikes you."

With Sidonia's remarks fresh in my mind, I'd felt the need to apologize. "I should have cooperated with her. It was foolish of me to openly scorn her."

His eyes jumped to mine then, his expression intent. "Why did you refuse her?"

The question sliced more deeply than he could have known. I felt the knot tighten in my throat again—the weight of my concern for him and the impossibility of admitting I was indignant on his behalf. "I don't know."

Tyrus studied me a piercing moment. Then a smile pulled at his lips. "This is actually good news, you know."

I knew nothing. I felt sore and miserable, as though I had battered my body in hours of intense exercise. "How so?"

He rose and turned away from me, folding his arms as he gazed out at this small corner of the universe that he stood to inherit. "If my grandmother wishes to influence me, it means she's decided I'm worthy of being influenced. It means I've elevated myself in her eyes sufficiently that she wishes to invest some effort in me. That, or my uncle has diminished in her eyes."

Alarm sharpened my voice. "Even if her favor is shifting, you *can't* trust her."

His laughter was husky. "I'd never trust any of my own blood, Nemesis. It's the Domitrian nature to lie and betray, but Grandmother is the most powerful woman in this Empire. With her on my side, there's little my uncle can do to me—openly, at least." He threw a hooded glance over his shoulder. "If she wishes to place a new companion at my side, she's attempting a reconciliation with me. On her terms, naturally."

"She did tell me she's only ever wanted the most powerful person in your family on the throne," I said reluctantly. I hated the very thought of helping sway Tyrus toward cooperating with Cygna.

"Yes, that's the way she is. She favors those sprigs that are fully formed. She's not a gardener who looks to cultivate; rather, she hacks freely at any new growths. Were Devineé still of full mind, Grandmother would strike me down for my recent presumptions. Instead she sees no choice but to favor me over them." He shrugged. "If she plans to entice my interest with another woman, then I will see who it is she thrusts my way and consider whether to accept the gesture. After all, our own association ends as soon as I'm in power. That was our agreement, right? So I'll stand in need of an Empress."

I looked away from him. "Yes. You'll need someone capable of forming an attachment to you." Someone other than me.

And now I knew which someone his grandmother had in mind.

As we all sat in the presence chamber, my disquiet mounted into a low roar as Elantra reached over to casually touch Tyrus's arm in conversation. Grandeé Cygna's sharp gaze was fixed on them, and I felt a rush of hot anger like poison, an urge to crush all their skulls, to tear Elantra from her seat and bash her head into Cygna's.

I fixed my eyes on my wine goblet, trying to fight it down. I might be a Diabolic, but I was not an animal.

Still my heart pounded like a drum, and my cheeks felt like they were burning with hot blood. I felt at war with myself—furious with Tyrus for his evident comfort with the situation, and furious with myself for the temptation to keep his attention solely fixed on me. I wanted to slap away that smile he gave Elantra.

People spoke so reverently of affection. For me, it seemed a torment. I couldn't believe people enjoyed these feelings. How could someone relish this excruciating need to secure a claim on another human?

I could feel Grandeé Cygna watching me. She was watching to discover the effect of her machinations. I could vividly imagine vaulting over the table to break her neck. What a glorious crackle her dry old bones would make!

I contented myself with baring my teeth in a smile. Then I redirected my attention to the Emperor.

He'd altered the usual seating arrangement to draw Devineé to his side.

She still had a vacant gaze, and occasionally a Servitor swept forward to dab at stray food on her chin or drool on her lips, but none of this seemed to disturb the Emperor. He drew her into a one-sided conversation, occasionally draping his arm about her like some parasitic root. My survival instincts began to kick in again, began to focus. As I thought over the last few days at court, I realized that the Emperor had positioned Devineé beside him at services in the Great Heliosphere. He'd also called down to her gaily from his position on his great throne, and roused vacant smiles from her.

I looked at Tyrus, still engaged with Elantra. My mind raced with sudden suspicions. Tyrus had been subtly moving to undermine his uncle, and had therefore lost his favor. He'd also been shirking his madman image in order to project more strength of mind.

The Emperor had made Tyrus his heir only because he believed him weak—mad and useless. Tyrus was weak no longer. The Emperor believed Tyrus to be out of favor with Cygna. Tyrus might no longer be her foe. Now the Emperor had a potential alternative, a genuinely weak heir due to the brain damage I'd given her: Devineé. He could slide her into Tyrus's place.

Tyrus was aware of this—but did he appreciate his peril too? I saw him casually reach out to caress Elantra's wrist.

I had to look away.

After all, there was little point protecting Tyrus from the Emperor only to end up murdering him myself.

39

DONIA came upon me in the villa pounding my fists into a column of carving stone. I'd bought it for her because it was structured to crumble easily with tools, and I believed that occupying herself with artwork between books might please her. Instead I was breaking it apart while imagining Tyrus and Elantra cavorting, and taking grim pleasure in my own pain.

"This will amuse you," I told Donia flatly. "I believe Tyrus intends to take Elantra as his Empress."

"Not Elantra Pasus!"

"Yes, her. The Grandeé Cygna has chosen her as his future wife and Tyrus isn't objecting. He believes cooperation will make his grand-mother inclined to support his ascendance."

"He's told you this?"

I turned, my heart galloping in my chest, my knuckles stinging and bloody. Images flashed through my head of the vapor room after dinner. I hadn't felt the phial of intoxicant I'd inhaled, and the Grandeé Cygna had abstained, but Tyrus and Elantra had felt it. So had the Emperor, who'd inhaled three and then climbed up one of his platinum statues to feign riding it like a horse.

Mindful of Grandeé Cygna's watchful gaze, I'd attempted to make a fool of myself, too, spinning in place and forcing mock-giddy laughter to my lips. Meanwhile, Tyrus had twirled Elantra around the floor, dancing to some imaginary music that only he heard. The sight had riveted me. They made a pretty picture together—he so fair, tall and broad-shouldered; she, vibrant with her tumbling dark hair. Emperor and Empress, yes: the Grandiloquy would approve of this pairing. Elantra and Tyrus looked designed for each other.

Suddenly I could bear no more. I left them like that, Cygna's gaze on my back as I departed the chamber.

Now, thinking on it, the bile surged up in my throat again. I turned back to the slab of stone, smashing my fists into it, taking satisfaction in how it crumbled.

"Elantra is the Pasus heir. That means she's a direct threat to you . . . to us," Donia noted, watching me brutalize the slab. "Are we in danger if she becomes his Empress?"

"No." The question surprised me. I turned back to her, feeling foolish for not having seen that possibility—foolish and then ashamed. I was Donia's protector. Why hadn't this been my first thought?

I took in the sight of her, totally alone in this universe but for me. My rage and dismay evaporated. I had no right feeling so miserable when I'd already been granted a miracle, the greatest one any Diabolic could hope for.

"No, Donia, there will be no danger. Tyrus is strong. He'll control the Helionics, not the other way around. I'll help him survive to that point, and this will be the reward I'll ask of him: your restoration.

Your safety . . . and a pardon, of course, for the deception."

Her brow knit, and she stepped toward me. "What about you? What will you get?"

"Your safety, as I said."

"Nemesis, there must be something you'll want for yourself."

"I don't want to stay here at court," I blurted. Yes, escaping this place was all I required. The sooner the better—but certainly before Tyrus took the throne. The prospect of watching the Emperor Tyrus and the Empress Elantra, ruling together, scoured through me like poison. I couldn't bear it. It would suffocate me.

I was *jealous*.

The realization dawned on me like a shock. *That* was the ugly emotion tormenting me.

Donia's face softened. "Senators have never needed to live at the Chrysanthemum before, and I can't imagine we will have to remain here once Randevald von Domitrian has perished." She took my hands in hers, making a tender inspection of my bleeding knuckles. "You and I will go back and oversee the restoration of the Impyrean fortress. It will be like it was before."

I nodded. Longing filled me for that time when life was simpler, when my days were occupied by tending to Donia and exercising and dreaming of nothing beyond what I already had.

"You and me," she continued softly. "Will you like that, Nemesis?" She raised her eyes to mine, a great vulnerability on her face that I did not understand. Could she truly imagine I would ever refuse her?

"Yes. I would like that." I stepped back from her to survey the damage I'd wrought on the stone. "I meant to give this to you so you could chisel it. There's plenty left."

Donia stepped past me to inspect the stone and reached up to touch the indentations I'd left. "I don't want to." She smiled at me. "I like it this way, the way you've marked it."

I looked at the stone, fragmented and cratered by my rage and jealousy. So this was a visual representation of a Diabolic's affection, then: an ugly, broken, blood-spattered stone.

40

THERE WAS a Senate meeting the morning of the Great Race. I knew how the Emperor wished me to vote: I was to approve the resolution to raise taxes on the Excess on frontier planets. According to Donia, those Excess traditionally enjoyed lower taxes as an incentive to live on the perilous fringes of imperial territory.

But as everyone now knew, the Emperor's coffers were running dry. He needed money to make up for the wealth generations of Domitrian Emperors had squandered—the wealth he had virtually hemorrhaged. Even those protected from his taxes would now face the burden of supporting the royals.

But Tyrus's Servitor had brought me a discreet-sheet with his own set of instructions.

Vote against the resolution.

So I voted as Tyrus asked.

I wasn't the only Senator to do so. I wondered as I looked around the chamber just how many of these people had voted against the resolution on Tyrus's instruction. It was a daring move after the recent purge, so they could only have taken the risk of doing this with a sense someone would be protecting them from the consequences of defying the Emperor.

This would be a mighty blow to Randevald von Domitrian, indeed.

I couldn't help but wonder how many blows Tyrus would inflict before the Emperor finally struck back.

After the vote, I took the magnetized tram down Cartier Stretch, the pylon opposite Berneval Stretch. This one was less run-down, designed more for wandering adventurers, with beautiful gardens, artificial streams, and frequent sky domes. At the very end was the largest of its sky domes, with vast windows overlooking the stretch of space where the racecourse was charted.

Around me, the other Senators heading to the race quietly discussed the story Tyrus had told me of the race five years ago—the pilots and their crews and their families who were all executed after the Emperor lost his bet. No one envied the pilot favored by the Emperor this year.

Apparently, the Great Race took place whenever the six stars of the system drew into close enough proximity to be reached by a single ship. The vessels competed to loop each of the stars at the fastest speed possible, drawing as close to the stars as they dared. The sixty racers— mostly hailing from the Excess and sponsored by Grandiloquy—spent years prepping their ships and honing their skills. They came from all over the Empire to compete for the great pot, a financial reward large enough to purchase a small moon.

In years past, the Emperor had sponsored the event. This time around, Tyrus had done so. His generosity must have seemed far more benign to the Emperor when he had initially offered it a year ago, before he had roused any suspicions, much less announced the

S. J. KINCAID

Emperor's dire financial straits. Now the gesture had to strike the Emperor as a deliberate and public taunt, for it suggested that Tyrus had more liquidity than he did.

I sat with Tyrus on the levitating platform reserved for imperial royals. Tyrus's fingers were steepled, his muscular arms propped on the arms of the chair. Elantra was banished down with her family on the lower platform for greater Grandiloquy. She threw Tyrus several bright smiles, one of which he returned, but he seemed too preoccupied to notice her continued flirtation from below.

The crowd about us thrummed with excitement. Tyrus had sunk funds into providing the chemical entertainments and the doctors necessary to treat overdoses. A tray was presented to us by a Servitor. I made a show of inspecting it for something of interest; it would be expected of me to partake.

No alcohol. No opiates. Nothing that could possibly sedate. Only amphetamines and euphorics that enhanced alertness.

I cast a veiled glance at Tyrus, wondering if there was a reason he'd selectively forbidden some substances.

Tyrus's smile reminded me of a lazy cat. He leaned closer to me and dropped his voice. "I want people to remember this day. Nothing that clouds the mind."

He had something planned, then. "Did you lay money on anyone?" I asked.

"A virtual fortune on Dandras Tyronne," Tyrus said agreeably. "And you?"

It surprised me that Tyrus had spent so liberally, despite knowing how much his uncle had lost the last time these races took place. It seemed very unlike him. Perhaps he knew something I didn't. I contemplated the betting screen at the foot of our chairs. "I'll bet on Dandras as well."

314

Tyrus grabbed my wrist before I could put in my bet. "Your money would be more wisely spent elsewhere."

I threw him a confused look. He *wasn't* very certain Dandras was a winner, then? I couldn't figure out his intentions.

So I placed a small bet on another pilot, one chosen at random.

The Emperor arrived with his pair of Diabolics. The holographics began to burst about us as the cheering and roar of the crowd throbbed in the air. The Emperor was escorted to his seat above ours. A sea of arms waved as people pressed their hands to their hearts in salute. He looked about the crowd with lines of anger on his face, because he clearly had just heard about the Senate vote he'd lost. He gave an irritable thrust of his hand to signal the launch.

Like that, the ships docked near the station propelled themselves off into the black void toward the first of the six stars, a red dwarf they'd slingshot around to gain momentum.

A screen dropped down to show us the vessels once they disappeared from our view. The image switched frequently from one satellite to another spread throughout the six-star system.

The race would last for hours, growing more exciting with time as the speed mounted and the racers skimmed nearer and nearer to the stars to gain more proximity points. Some racers would miscalculate and were pulled in by the gravity of the stars and destroyed. The six-star system was filled with chaotic gravitational forces, and even flying through it at standard speed was dangerous. Many of these racers would die today, but as long as they didn't falter in the opening stretch of the event as the Emperor's champion had last race, they wouldn't bring disgrace upon themselves.

Trays were passed through the crowd, with substances and foods and souvenirs. People had modified themselves to adopt the signature facial features of their favorite racers from their star systems, and they cheered whenever the screens flashed to the vessels of their champions.

Tyrus didn't speak much, his eyes fixed on the nearest screen, expectant, almost as though he was in wait. He still held my hand over the crook of his arm. His grip began to tighten on mine. I looked down at his muscled forearm. It wasn't like Tyrus to reveal his anxiety so plainly. I followed his gaze to the screen. Dandras Tyronne's vessel was closing in on the starship of a racer called Winton Travanis.

And then it happened.

There must have been a shift in gravity, some turbulence, it was hard to say. But Winton's ship swerved and clipped Dandras's, and immediately both vessels went spiraling off to the sides, disqualified.

And at the very onset of the race too.

A cry went out throughout the crowd, and everyone surged to their feet, and then Dandras's ship was caught in a gravity field it could not overcome and ripped apart with a flowery blast of fire.

Silence dropped over the crowd, and eyes moved to the Successor Primus. Everyone had seen the vast sum he'd sunk into his bet on Dandras. I searched his expression, wondering how he'd react to this.

Tyrus sat in the seat with his arms folded now, staring straight ahead with a gaze of stone. This was virtually the same thing that had happened at the last Great Race. The imperial heir, like his uncle, had dedicated his money to the fortunes of one racer—who'd then been taken out by a blundering competitor before even reaching the first star. Everyone knew what happened next for the surviving racer responsible for this accident. Disgrace. Execution.

"A pity." The Emperor's voice floated down, and Tyrus looked back at him. "I do hope you weren't cleaned out by that."

"I bet more than I would have wished to lose," Tyrus replied softly.

But there was still a lethal calmness to his face, none of the dismay I'd have expected at this loss.

"Pilot error." Malice throbbed in the Emperor's voice. Enjoyment shone in his eyes as he gazed down at Tyrus. "I'll leave it to you to dispense consequences for this."

Tyrus sank back into his seat beside me, and I found myself watching him closely, his face a chiseled, unreadable mask, betraying no emotion.

He'd *told* me not to bet on Dandras.

The offending pilot, Winton, obviously knew what happened to those who dared obliterate the fortunes of a Domitrian. When the competing ships reached the next star, his vessel had already abandoned the star system. He was fleeing rather than risk punishment at the Chrysanthemum.

He didn't get far.

Eager to win favor with the Successor Primus, some of the lesser Grandiloquy launched their own ships after him. Winton's damaged ship could not escape. The mercenaries arrived in the last hour of the race, the offending pilot between them. Word spread quickly through the crowd. Tyrus stood and returned to the *Valor Novus*, and half the crowd abandoned watching the last stretch of the race. In any case, the excitement had wound down now that most of the racers were disqualified or destroyed. The winning racer had vastly outstripped his competition and had an easy journey to the finish line.

Seeing the Successor Primus's wrath toward a pilot would be vastly more entertaining for most everyone than the inevitable conclusion of the race.

Tyrus kept my hand in his grip as we approached the Justice Hall of the *Valor Novus*, the crowds that had trailed us already scrambling eagerly into position against the walls, ringing us.

S. J. KINCAID

"Do I need to urge you to exercise restraint?" I asked him, thinking of my usual part in our public performances.

"Not this time," Tyrus said. "Let them all see my response."

We strode up to the man on his knees, a frightened-looking Excess with the imperfect skin of a planet dweller. Dread was written on his face, as he knew what had happened to the last person to cross a Domitrian in exactly this manner.

Tyrus gazed down at him for a long moment, then raised his hand for silence from all the onlookers, who'd begun murmuring excitedly, speculating over just how many people would end up executed this time.

"You were in that most grievous accident I witnessed earlier. Why did you flee?" Tyrus demanded. He loomed over the kneeling man, looking every bit a fearsome Imperial Emperor.

"I was afraid, Your Eminence. It was an accident. My navigation malfunctioned. Please." Winton flung himself down to the ground. "I know Your Eminence must have my life, but please spare my family. Spare my flight crew. They are guiltless."

Tyrus said nothing, letting the plea hang there a moment overlong, allowing the suspense to build. I could picture the Emperor himself tuning into this on a screen rather than watching the rest of the race.

"Get up, man," Tyrus said.

Winton raised his head, his eyes great and fearful. "Your . . . Your Eminence?"

"I said get up. I have no intention of executing an honest sportsman like yourself over what was clearly an accident. That would simply be barbaric."

Whispers and murmurs of disbelief rippled about the hall.

"There will be an investigation of this incident, and if anyone is deemed to be at fault, they'll be banned from operating in this sport again," Tyrus said. "As for you, you will pay a visit to the dead man's family and personally bring them a sum I will donate to them for their loss. Can I trust this duty to you?"

Winton swayed to his knees again, his hands clutched together. "Yes, yes, Your Eminence! Yes, you can!"

Tyrus raised his hands and allowed the man to reverently pull his knuckles to his cheek. "And of course, I intend to hold a service in the Great Heliosphere for those lost to this valiant endeavor. I expect you'll attend before you depart?"

"Yes, gladly. Gladly, Your Eminence!" And he pulled Tyrus's knuckle from one cheek to another in his exuberance. "You are merciful and great and just . . ."

"Take your rest." Tyrus stepped away from him. Then, to the mercenaries who captured him, "Thank you for locating our wayward friend before he could do anything rash. You'll be well compensated for your services."

As Tyrus spun around to stride out of the Justice Hall, I heard the swelling of voices, the amazement, as people beheld the mercy of a Domitrian. *This* Domitrian. It was such a stark contrast to his uncle that I could see the possibilities lighting across people's faces, the hope about what our Empire could become under such a younger, fairer ruler.

I caught up to him, understanding *exactly* what he'd done. He'd undercut the Emperor again, in another of those subtle ways that could not be directly attributed to hostility, yet served to undermine him all the same. He *intended* to lose that fortune just to exhibit his graciousness in defeat. I breathed very softly, "Well done."

Tyrus's gaze flickered over to me, and for a second that inscrutability of his wavered, revealing something I'd seen in his face when Elantra tossed Unity into the ring. "I don't deserve praise, Nemesis.

I've done something quite monstrous. The vessel was supposed to be disabled, not destroyed."

I hadn't given any thought to the man who'd been killed in the accident. The ends had always justified the means in my mind, but Tyrus's eyes were clouded.

"I'm not a gentle soul by any means. I long ago accepted that there would be blood on my hands if I followed the course I've chosen. But I hadn't expected to murder an innocent man today."

"Tyrus, if *I* allowed myself to be troubled over the innocent blood on my hands, I wouldn't be able to function. At least you can make amends for what you've done."

"Yes," he said. "*Yes.* His family will be well compensated. I'll see to them as best I can." He drew a jagged breath. "I must live with this, Nemesis, so I will. I will live with it."

We lapsed into a thick silence as Tyrus pondered the man whose death he'd unwittingly caused, and I pondered Tyrus's maneuver. Between this display and the vote earlier today, his subtle provocations of the Emperor could not be ignored much longer.

Randevald von Domitrian would take his vengeance for this. It was only a matter of time.

41

AN OMINOUS lull followed in the days after the Great Race. The Emperor made no remarks publicly about Tyrus going behind his back to turn the Senate vote against him, nor did he raise an eyebrow when Tyrus—of his own initiative—sold several of his own colonies and then gave surprise Advent gifts to all veterans of Imperial wars.

Advent gifts were a long-outdated tradition in the Empire, one the Domitrians hadn't bothered with for hundreds of years. They were secure enough in their power that they didn't require the loyalty of those Grandiloquy who controlled the most powerful starships and war machines that waged violent conflict on the frontiers.

It was the most openly hostile move Tyrus had made against the Emperor, and he called me to his side virtually full-time. We sat together in his solarium on the *Alexandria*. It was a sky dome with a verdant garden he'd recently had seeded with some foliage he'd admired on Lumina, and an artificial river powerful enough to drown an unwary swimmer.

"I'd planned to eventually install you in a chamber on the *Alexandria*," Tyrus told me, gazing down into the rushing water, "but as circumstances are, it wouldn't do."

"I wouldn't want to sleep on the *Alexandria*, anyway," I said bluntly. I was thinking of Sidonia, hidden in my villa, and how I didn't want to abandon her for so long a stretch.

Tyrus looked at me with an unreadable expression for a moment. "It's so unpleasant in my company?"

"No," I answered, too quickly.

"In any case," he said, "Grandmother might take it amiss. She's intent on the alliance between me and Elantra."

"She wishes you to wed a snake."

"A Helionic," Tyrus said with a smile. "At least Elantra will fit in well with my family. All true politicians are vipers."

I felt an unpleasant churning at the thought of Elantra Pasus as Empress. Or rather, Elantra Domitrian. People tended to take the name of the more powerful family in a marital union. It was how Salivar Fordyce became Salivar Domitrian.

"How long will we stay side by side?" I asked Tyrus. "Eventually you'll have to publicly renounce me if you wish to cleave to her. It's not like I can masquerade as Sidonia von Impyrean forever."

"But you must. No one can ever know what you've done."

"Or what? You'll face questions for concealing me?"

He turned to me abruptly. "Or *you* will be in danger," he bit out. "It's high treason to impersonate a Senator."

"So?"

"I'd have Grandiloquy clamoring for your execution. As a new Emperor, I'll face a struggle building a base of power as things are. I can't guarantee your protection if my own allies stand against you."

My shrug seemed to spark his temper. His eyes narrowed; he stepped toward me menacingly, then seemed to think better of it, withdrawing a pace and taking a long breath. "I won't allow you to face that," he said hoarsely. "You may have no concern for yourself, but I do."

Our gazes locked. Only two paces separated us. The air between us, the silence around us, felt suddenly heavy, fraught with some strange electricity.

It felt the same way as when we'd left Lumina, in those moments when we rose from the purple clouds into the great expanse of space, and he had kissed me.

I swallowed and looked away.

He didn't realize the truth: one way or another, my deception would be known once Sidonia was restored.

I pushed to my feet, miserable at the weight of this secret. Until I had met Tyrus, my duty to Donia had been my only joy. He had come between us, somehow. As much as I longed for him, I resented him, too, for the guilt he made me feel, all unknowing.

"I'll be in worse danger if I'm Sidonia Impyrean when Elantra becomes your Empress."

His hand caught my arm, pulled me back when I would have left. "I would never let Elantra threaten you," he said in a soft, dangerous voice. "Never." His expression was iron hard, and I believed him.

A shadow passed over the sunlit solarium, and Tyrus and I both looked up. The sky dome contained atmosphere, and beyond it was open space, mostly blotted out by the starlit blue sky. Yet there was something else drawing into view now. . . .

What appeared to be a large scrap of debris sailed toward us. It grew larger and larger as it neared and took on a distinct form: long and cylindrical.

It wasn't debris, I realized with shock.

It was a missile. And it would rupture this dome.

Tyrus and I both had the realization at the same time.

"Run," Tyrus said, but I was already on my feet, and we vaulted across the tranquil garden toward the door to the secure corridor beyond. . . .

A thunderous explosion jolted the entire world around us. As a jagged hole opened in the crystalline windows, the blue atmosphere roared about us, and the dome decompressed. The great wind snatched my feet out from under me. I felt myself lift off the ground—

A hand clamped on my arm, dragging me back down. Streams of blue gases ripped about me in a vicious whirlwind, stinging my eyes. I looked back and saw the blue sky draining out into the void of space around the flaming, jagged gash where the missile had struck.

"Exhale!" Tyrus shouted at me, his voice carrying on the ripping wind. "Exhale everything!"

I frantically blew out all the breath in my lungs. Tyrus's grip on me grew less sure as he strained to hold on to the tree trunk he'd grabbed, so I seized his clothing and hoisted myself up his body, seizing the tree trunk myself. Then I secured him with my free hand and hoped desperately the tree was securely rooted enough to resist the outward pressure.

It was.

The wind died away as the last of the atmosphere blew out, leaving Tyrus and me in the sudden absence of pressure.

Horror jolted through me as I registered it: we were surrounded by cold, bare space.

My heart began to beat frantically as the pressure pulsed under my skin, beneath my eyes, an ominous tingling racing under my skin. The gases in my body strained outward, and if we hadn't exhaled, our lungs would be exploding. We had only moments to escape now before we died. Tyrus's face was twisted in pain, but he tugged at the tree to propel us toward a door, pointing to it so I'd know the destination too.

Relief washed over me. Like every outward-facing room, there was a decompression closet, and the loss of pressure in the dome would have primed it to open.

We floated at a maddeningly slow pace as the tingling sensation crept up all my limbs, my ears and eyes throbbing and my skin blistering. Beside me Tyrus stopped moving and I knew he'd passed out, so I held on to him and fought the encroaching darkness of unconsciousness as my head grew light and the saliva on my tongue sizzled and began to boil along with the liquid in my eyes. The burning in my chest mounted as I tugged at everything I could find, fighting for both our lives, my ears pounding frantically with the pressure and my heartbeat, and then I was at the decompression closet.

I tore it open and thrust Tyrus inside, then pulled myself in and locked the door behind us, and with a hiss the small closet began to pressurize around us. But the atmosphere wasn't growing breathable. There was no oxygen rushing in with us. Tyrus began turning blue in the dim light, and I fumbled with hands I could only see, not feel, and tore out the oxygen mask in the wall.

Just one.

One.

I thrust it onto Tyrus's face, and then the darkness closed in and swallowed me.

42

COOL AIR rushing in. Rushing in.

Then nothing. I gasped and choked.

"Open your eyes!" Tyrus's distorted voice.

Something pressing against my face, and I could breathe again, but then, as my head began to clear, it was gone and I was choking.

I forced my eyes open and found Tyrus's face so close to mine, the long, muscular expanse of his body pressed up against me. He thrust the oxygen mask back onto my face.

"What's—what—" I murmured, my voice distorted by the mask, trying to understand this.

He pulled the mask away, and I had to hold my breath as he drew deep inhales.

"Closet . . . no air . . . take turns."

He pressed the mask to my face again and I drew in several deep, grateful breaths, and all too soon the mask was gone again as Tyrus breathed.

"Sabotage," he said, and then, "No more talk," then passed the mask back to me.

And like that, we took turns breathing in a most agonizing manner. I knew this couldn't continue forever. We could be trapped in here for hours, maybe days, before someone thought to check on us. We were lucky this closet had returned to normal pressure and temperature, but it was only a stopgap. The atmosphere was supposed to return in here so we could await rescue. If that mechanism had been disabled remotely, likely the alarm to alert others to this situation had been sabotaged as well.

I had no idea how much air this oxygen mask contained, but it already felt like it wasn't enough. When Tyrus made to tear the mask off again, I put out my hand to stop him, holding it to his face.

He shoved my wrist aside and pressed it to my face, shaking his head.

"You're valuable," I said. "Take it."

Then I thrust the mask at him.

"No," Tyrus said. He pressed in against me with his greater weight. In the limited space, I couldn't leverage my full strength, and the mask was back on my face.

I tore it off again and shoved it back to him.

Suddenly Tyrus leaned in and pressed his lips to mine, and for a moment we were there like that, trapped together with our lungs aching to burst and oxygen deprivation burning through our veins, and he was kissing me, kissing me deeply and desperately, with a fury that I could not understand.

Then he pulled back, clamped the mask over his face, and drank in a deep breath. "See?" he said raggedly.

See what? What did that *mean*? But he thrust the mask at me and my lungs were desperate for air.

"Why?" I gasped as I caught my breath. Why had he kissed me? Why wouldn't he let me endure this for him? But it would use too much breath to voice those words, and without words I couldn't comprehend him.

He pulled the mask back to his face. "Both of us," he said. "Or neither."

I could feel his heart pounding furiously, his chest against mine in the confined space, and I ached to save him, to save myself, but I couldn't do this on his terms. It seemed sometimes like we were two binary stars, circling each other but never meeting, always at cross-purposes.

When he pressed the mask to my face again, I told him, "Don't be a fool!" Then I tore off the mask and slammed my head into his as hard as I could in the limited space. The back of his skull smacked the opposite wall, and his body sagged against mine.

I took my last-ever breath of oxygen, then placed the mask securely on his face, tightening the straps so it would not fall off.

By the time he revived, the question of who would leave here would have been decided by nature.

For a moment, I could forget that this was life and death and just feel Tyrus's head against my shoulder where he'd slumped in the space that wasn't large enough to sink or fall. I wrapped my arms around him and relished the weight of his body against mine. This wasn't a forbidden indulgence now that I was about to die. I could allow myself this one moment. My mind returned to that night after Lumina when we lay together and how beautiful those fleeting hours had been before I'd turned fearful, turned cowardly.

Because that's what it had been, the thing that drove me from Tyrus. It wasn't prudence, it wasn't even duty to Sidonia, it was pure cowardice. Pure terror. I closed my eyes, cursing myself for letting fear rule my life again just as it had back in the corrals. Now I finally realized what I'd done, and it was too late to change things. The ache and burn in my lungs mounted, and I knew this would become a horror once I gave in and tried to inhale and found nothing. I longed for a chance to correct things, to set them the way they were meant to be.

And then I could bear it no longer and tried to inhale, and I couldn't, there was nothing to breathe, and Tyrus's low, steady breathing sounded in my ear as I choked and writhed and the tingling was back, all through me, a thick, heavy blackness like a swamp descending on me.

This was it. This was it.

For a second that seemed an eternity, images of Tyrus and Sidonia and the Matriarch and Neveni played through my brain like dying neurons registering their objections.

A bright light crept into the corner of my vision, growing brighter and brighter. As though I'd heard it yesterday, my thoughts filled with something Donia had told me: there was a light people saw when they died. Some believed it to be a chemical and some believed it to be the Living Cosmos calling them to the afterlife.

Diabolics can see it too, came my final thought, *so it must simply be that chemical after all. . . .*

I roused slowly. Warm arms held me against a broad chest. My vision focused sluggishly on Tyrus's face.

He was staring down at me with fathomless pale eyes, and his first word to me was a whisper. "Nemesis?"

I made a murmuring sound in my throat.

"Don't try to speak." His grip tightened. "We were rescued."

A creak in the distance.

"Pretend to sleep," he whispered.

I closed my eyes, and then a harsh, familiar voice rasped through the air.

"So it seems the silly girl might live. A foolish gesture she made."

Tyrus's grip tightened on me further. "Not everyone is like us, Grandmother. Many are better—most, I daresay."

She gave a cackling laugh. "A fine way to speak to me, Tyrus. If I hadn't dispatched my own employees to the *Alexandria*, you'd still be trapped in that decompression closet and your Sidonia would be a corpse."

"I would credit you more for your assistance," said Tyrus drily, "if I weren't fully aware you must have known this attack was coming before it happened."

"If you're implying I am responsible—"

"Oh, no. No, Grandmother. I know who was behind it. You didn't carry it off yourself, you're merely playing opportunist. You allowed it to happen without interference so you could intercede and win my gratitude. And you have it. I thank you."

"How curious," Cygna said. "You reached all these conclusions without Sidonia Impyrean whispering in your ear. I begin to suspect the rumors of her influence have it reversed."

"Of course you do."

Tyrus laughed softly and eased me down onto the bed. I peered between my lashes and saw that we were in the chamber I'd slept in on the *Alexandria* during our voyage to Lumina. Cygna stood like a bird of prey in readiness for Tyrus. They faced each other down.

"I think you've figured out by now, or you wouldn't have bothered saving me: I am your grandson. Your blood runs through me. And because of that, I, too, have figured out many things about you—such as who holds the true power in this Empire. It's never been my uncle."

"I won't endure these insults about our Emperor."

"Oh, but that's why you've tolerated me lately, isn't it? Because I see this basic truth about you, and my uncle does not. His appetites have emptied the treasury. He ignores and disregards and outright scorns your calls for prudence. He has escaped your control, Grandmother."

Silence.

"Nothing to say, I see. I know you warned him once not to appoint me Successor Primus, but he did not listen. I know he pays more heed to Senator von Pasus than to you. I know it vexes you when he watches you taste his food—as though if you wished him dead, he'd manage to survive you! He has forgotten not only what he owes to you, but how much he continues to owe to you."

"Randevald," she said reluctantly, "has disappointed me of late. I often think power is the most noxious substance in the universe. Both want and possession of it warp one's character beyond redemption."

"Grandmother, you know now it's to be open warfare between my uncle and me. Devineé is no longer fit for your confidence. I am your only alternative, and I suspect I've become more tolerable to you, have I not?"

"You have been a most accomplished actor for many years, I suspect."

"And to you, I owe that skill. I lay my truths bare before you now, one pragmatist to another. I have no unwholesome appetites, and I know well what it means to respect and fear you."

She laughed. "Oh, how Randevald must rue appointing you his successor. I warned him."

"But for all the wrong reasons. Now you see, I would never be so foolish as to disregard words from your lips as he so often does. If you wish me to be a Helionic, I will be a Helionic. If you wish me to unite with a Pasus, I'll unite with a Pasus. I would never dare to question your wisdom."

She paced away from him. I peeked at her, and my eyes caught on metallic glints in the distance. Security bots were discreetly hidden throughout the room. She was ready to kill Tyrus if she chose to. Had she saved us merely to put an ultimatum to him? Had he preempted her by laying all the cards on the table first?

"Am I to be eminently clear, Tyrus," she said, "that you are suggesting treason? You wish me to join you in a conspiracy against my own son?"

"I suggested no such conspiracy, but by saving me from his assassination attempt, you've all but offered to join one yourself."

"Tell me," she said coolly, "besides your great terror of me, why would I ever endorse you over my son?"

"Because you want the strongest Emperor, and Randevald has lost your confidence." Tyrus spread his arms. "You want the Empire to be great under the most worthy of the Domitrians, and you know and I know—"

"It's you?" she said drily.

"No, Grandmother. It's you."

The words seemed unexpected to her. Her proud chin tilted up, but she let him go on.

"And secondary only to you, there's me, the single one with the wisdom to know I'll rule at your behest. And besides that"—he reached back and squeezed my arm—"I am also fully aware that your security bots are behind you, ready and armed to kill me if I do not propose this alliance to you myself."

I didn't need more of a cue. My muscles were still dreadfully sore from the decompression, the oxygen loss, but they responded instantly when I sprang up and vaulted across the room in one movement. Cygna gave a shout of surprise as I crossed to the first security bot before it could swivel on me and fire. I twisted it just as its ray lashed out and directed the beam toward another bot, and as the third swiveled up from the ground, I flipped out of the path of its beam, seized it in my palm, and crushed it against the wall.

I looked to Tyrus, and he nodded slowly, his eyes burning. "Thank you, Nemesis."

Cygna stood stock-still, caught off guard for once, her mouth open. Then she recovered her wits. "A Diabolic. She's a Diabolic!"

"She is," Tyrus agreed.

"No wonder—" Cygna stopped. Then, "You have gotten yourself a Diabolic and disguised her as Sidonia Impyrean." She spoke the words as though the sheer audacity of the act had stunned her.

"*He* didn't disguise me," I said, adrenaline pumping through me, ready for Tyrus to command me to spring. "It was done by people now dead."

"How could you have a Diabolic?" Cygna demanded, studying me. "We never had one made for you."

"Because she's not *mine*," Tyrus said. "She's my ally."

"Ally?" said Cygna, circling me with a searching gaze. "A Diabolic without a chemical bond makes for a very dangerous ally, Tyrus. You don't know these creatures as I do."

"What would you know of Diabolics?" I said to her, my tone blistering.

She smiled, her eyes cool. "More than you might think. I knew there was something wrong about you, and now I understand what it is. So you belonged originally to . . . to that Impyrean twit?"

Anger rushed through me, but for Tyrus's sake, I did not tear her apart on behalf of Sidonia. She'd merely called her a name, and words had no power.

"If this goes forward," Cygna said, never taking her eyes from mine, "then I want no more charades with this thing."

"I will be amenable to that suggestion if you *never again* call Nemesis a *thing*," Tyrus said in a soft, dangerous voice.

Cygna looked at him sharply. "Oh, it's that way with you two?" Her gaze crawled between us, as though it had only now dawned on her that Tyrus and I had a true partnership. "How irregular your alliance must be. True attachment to a *Diabolic*, and an unbonded Diabolic attached in turn to you. How . . . radical. Well, Tyrus, I can't indulge this. If you truly mean to obey me, then you will marry where I direct you."

"Why Elantra Pasus, may I ask?" Tyrus said.

"This Empire must be run by Helionics, and neither of us can afford Pasus as an enemy," Cygna said flatly. "I don't know your true leanings, Tyrus. And I don't care. Wedding Elantra will align you with the right faction. The future of this galaxy depends upon our continued strength—not just the strength of the Empire, but the strength of the Grandiloquy. We must send a strong signal to the Excess that they will never be able to challenge us."

"Very well. Elantra it will be, Grandmother. Are we in agreement?"

Cygna let the silence stretch on, then told Tyrus, "You will have my answer very soon."

I looked at Tyrus as he nodded slowly, knowing the same thing I did: Cygna was making it clear our fates were in her hands. And she didn't wish yet to reveal whether it would be for good or for ill.

43

A CURIOUS thing about Tyrus was that no matter how urgent the situation, he remained calm in the face of mortal peril. It was only afterward that I'd see those physiological reactions others showed in distress: the blood draining from his face, the slight shakiness of his limbs.

He retreated to his private chamber on the *Alexandria* with a murmur about avoiding "outside-facing windows" for the time being. His broad shoulders looked tense as he poured a glass of wine. He took a generous swig, then whipped about and hurled the glass into the holographic fireplace. Glass shattered, and he turned on me, his eyes blazing.

"Tell me." His voice was deathly calm, entirely at odds with his expression. "What did you think you were doing earlier? We were *both* supposed to breathe! If Grandmother's people had come five minutes later, you'd be dead now!"

I stared at him, wondering how he could even ask that question. "You are a *future Emperor*. I am a Diabolic. Your life is more important than mine."

He didn't realize I hadn't just given up my own life—I'd abandoned Donia. I'd done it for him, and forfeited my role protecting her. Now he yelled at me for this?

"Had Cygna's people come five hours later," I pointed out, "you'd be dead, and all because you refused to accept that some sacrifices are necessary. Mine was. I did what was best for both of us."

"I told you not to do it!"

"You do not command me! You're not my master. We're partners. I made my decision, and it was the right one! A future ruler needs to learn to make sacrifices."

"Sacrifices?" Tyrus cried. "I've already made sacrifices. Don't tell me I don't understand making sacrifices." He raked his hands through his hair over and over. "I sacrificed *years* to pretend madness. I sacrificed my need for vengeance in order to survive long enough to make changes that mattered in the greater scheme of things. I know sacrifice!"

He whirled on me.

"And now, I've agreed to yoke myself to the wife of my grandmother's choosing. I have made many sacrifices. This one, I will not make. I *will not* sacrifice your life, and neither will you!" He stepped into my path, then reached up and clasped my cheeks, his eyes desperate. "You gave up your life for me. I can't let you do that again. I couldn't bear it if you did that!"

My mind returned to that delirious kiss in the darkness of the decompression closet, that strange shared madness as we suffocated together, death nearing.

See? he'd said.

But I did not see. I closed my eyes, and now I had no focus but the warmth of his palms cupping my face. "So you're truly to marry Elantra."

"Yes," he said roughly. "So it seems."

I jerked back away from him. "Congratulations." My voice was harsh. "I hope you have many happy years before she starts trying to kill you."

He laughed bitterly. "Ah, she'll be a true Domitrian the day she sets out to kill me." His expression smoothed. "Soon I'll be done with your services. You'll be free to do as you please. You can go far away from me."

Some black raw emotion blazed through me—too dark for anger, too sharp for hurt. I hated that he brought this out in me. I clenched my fists and forced my voice to be steady. "I'd be pleased to do so now. Step aside and let me leave."

A muscle flexed in his jaw, but he did not move. "And where will you go?"

"To my villa."

His teeth clenched. "After *everything*, Nemesis. After this whole business is done."

"That's not your concern."

"Unless you have a plan, an intended destination, it's very much my concern."

"It's not. I'll figure out matters for myself. I wish you and your future Empress much happiness." I turned away, boiling, seething inside. If only I could scrub away the memory of his mouth on mine in the decompression closet! *Why* had he kissed me? Why had he confused things further?

I wanted to leave, but something stopped me—a memory from those last moments as I suffocated. I'd finally understood that fear

S. J. KINCAID

had driven so many of my actions, raw fear. And I never wanted fear to rule me again.

So I turned back to him.

"Do you know why I want to be away from you, Tyrus?" I said in a low voice. "It's because you're making a mistake uniting with Elantra. Yes, you'll win your throne, and your grandmother will support you, but you will never trust her or respect your wife, and you will never sleep safely in your bed. You deserve more. You deserve better. I don't want to watch you do this, so I will be grateful, ever so grateful, Your Eminence, not to be here in the years ahead!"

He closed the distance between us and seized me by the shoulders, his eyes burning into mine. "*Why* would any of this bother you?"

"How can you ask me that?" I bellowed at him. "You speak to me as though I'm a person, and then you turn around and assume I'm utterly devoid of feeling! Which is it to be, Tyrus? Is it so incomprehensible to you that I could care about your well-being? That I could—"

I caught myself, horrified.

His fingers dug into my skin. "That you could what? That you could *what*, Nemesis?"

My throat felt like a knot. I couldn't speak. Those treacherous syllables wanted to escape my lips.

That I could love you.

"Nemesis," Tyrus said, very softly, "you told me on the ship that you would never experience love. You said you weren't capable of caring for me or feeling a *fraction* of the affection that I bear for you." He drew me closer, our lips a breath apart. He searched my face intently. "Was that a lie?"

A lump rose in my throat.

"Tell me honestly. Please just tell me, and if you spoke truly on the ship, I will never bother you with this again."

The words felt dragged out of me. "I spoke . . . wrongly on the ship."

His thumb stroked over my lip, his eyes glowing. "So you do feel. Can it be possible you care for me the way I care for you?"

My eyes shot up to his, the memory of his lips on mine in the decompression closet searing through my mind.

"You still do?" I whispered.

"I never stopped. I *will never* stop."

Fear coiled up within me, but I would not be a coward. Not this time.

"Don't marry Elantra, Tyrus. I . . . I don't want you to."

He broke into a smile. "Then I won't." And his mouth covered mine, his arms crushing me up against him. His hand clasped the nape of my neck, and I arched to offer him more, hugging him to me as though I could merge our two forms into one. The faint stubble on his jaw scratched my cheeks; the firm press of his lips parted mine, and our tongues tangled. Every centimeter of him felt warm and strong and magnetic, and my awareness of the room faded as I finally accepted this, these feelings I'd craved like a drug since he'd last touched me.

He swept me up into his arms and caged me against the desk as his hot lips trailed down my throat. I twined my fingers through his coppery hair, tightening my grip with a bolt of possessiveness that startled me. He was mine now, he was *mine*. And he was clever and cunning enough to preserve his life even if he defied Cygna, even if he refused her request to take Elantra.

"Do you . . . love me?" I asked him, barely daring to speak those words that by all rights shouldn't apply to a Diabolic. And then I realized what I'd said.

But before I could feel a moment of horror, he said, "Oh yes, I love you." He pulled back to fix me in his fierce and unwavering gaze. "I loved you as we rose up from Lumina and as we struggled not to fall into space, and as we stood together choking on our last breaths. You are brave and honorable and strong, and you are the only one who can see me as I am. Say you love me, too."

I felt it then, in a great crushing wave of certainty. "I do. I love you, Tyrus."

It was that calm, careful manner of his, so unlike my own. The way he saw ten steps ahead of everyone around him, so unlike my rashness. It was the way he did not see me as a creature or treat me like an animal or an inferior, though by his birth he was in fact elevated above everyone. It was the way he refused to trade a Diabolic's life for his in the decompression closet.

It was all those little acts that meant so much because no one else would ever, could ever, step into his place in my existence. And yes, I loved him as strongly as I'd ever loved Sidonia, but in a way so unlike how I felt about her. He was a hunger, a craving, a need I never knew I had.

His lips were on mine again, drawing hot kisses from me, but my mind spiraled in a different direction. *Sidonia.* Sidonia, who wanted to return to rebuild the Impyrean fortress. I couldn't fathom doing so now, but to stay with Tyrus meant to abandon Sidonia. I had to choose.

Once this choice would have been as easy as breathing. But now . . . now, when I felt complete and loved, in a way I had never known . . .

Now I could see no way to go forward.

Whatever happened, Sidonia had to resume her true identity and I had to resume mine. That was fact. That was the root and cause of the impossible decision before me.

So I told him, "Tyrus, you must know something. It may change matters."

He cupped my face gently, searching me with those earnest eyes. Had I ever seen his face so unguarded? Without that calm, careful neutrality he worked so hard to maintain, he looked younger, brighter, irresistibly touchable.

"I can't continue to be Sidonia Impyrean forever." I permitted myself to reach out and touch the freckles on his cheek, tracing a light path among them, down his sharp jaw to the corner of his mouth. "You see," I said on a deep breath, "she's still alive."

44

SIDONIA PLUNGED to her knees immediately as Tyrus walked into my villa, reaching up for his hand to draw his knuckles to her cheeks.

"Your Eminence, Senator von Impyrean is out—"

I stepped out from behind Tyrus. "Donia, it's fine. He knows."

Donia straightened, her doe-like eyes wide, and Tyrus looked her over with a stunned air, her hand still in his. "He knows?"

"Everything," Tyrus assured her. He dwarfed her with his great height, his broad musculature. "Senator von Impyrean, my deepest condolences over the loss of your family."

"Thank you," Sidonia said.

Tyrus half turned to me, uncharacteristically flustered. I felt an answering pang. Minutes ago, he had assumed that all was resolved between us. Now he knew it was not the case. "She explained your circumstances. I admit, I'm still astonished."

Donia nodded shyly. "I hope not to cause Your Eminence any difficulties."

Tyrus retreated a pace, scrutinizing the room. Fine as my villa was, it paled next to the magnificence of his vessel.

"You see," he said distractedly, "this presents us with some real difficulties. Impersonation of a member of the Grandiloquy is a capital offense. When you are restored—if there is an opportunity—well, many of the Grandiloquy have seen and interacted with Nemesis. . . . Once I am instated as Emperor, it will take time to build my strength—and I'll need their support. I can't simply present Nemesis as an imposter and expect them to dismiss it. They'll take it as a personal affront to have unknowingly interacted with a Diabolic like an equal. They'll want to see someone punished."

Donia clapped a hand to her mouth. "Oh, Your Eminence, please don't let them hurt Nemesis!" She dropped back to her knees. "You must protect her. I can't live without her."

The words echoed, reverberating with an old memory: the final weeks in the Impyrean fortress; her threat to kill herself should I die. Disturbed, I dropped down next to her and enveloped her in my arms. She never removed her gaze from Tyrus.

And he stared down at her, his expression fraught. "I will do all I can to save Nemesis, Senator von Impyrean. But this will be a moot discussion if I do not prevail against my uncle."

"But if you do prevail . . ."

He knelt, taking Sidonia's hand again. "Then Nemesis will live. That, I swear to you." His eyes moved to mine, burning with intensity.

I took a deep breath. In my bones, I knew that if I could trust in one single thing in this universe, it was Tyrus's love for me.

He seemed to see my thought, for his expression gentled. "Her life means more to me than you can ever know," he said.

Donia eased out of my embrace. "Nemesis," she said, looking

only at Tyrus, "I'll speak to His Eminence alone now."

It took me a moment to realize this was an order. "You want me to leave?"

"Yes," Donia said, without even a glance at me.

For so long, I'd been Sidonia Impyrean. *I'd* been in charge. It was strange to find myself in the position of a subordinate again. No—not simply a subordinate. I was Nemesis dan Impyrean, and Donia was my *master.*

The thought, which had never troubled me before, suddenly felt unpleasant and strange. I knew that Sidonia had never viewed me as property. Nor had we ever had a relationship where I had to follow her orders. But in matters like this, she simply assumed that her will would prevail.

Tyrus seemed to guess my thoughts. "This concerns Nemesis. She should stay."

"No," I said. Sidonia wanted to speak to him in private—so she would speak to him in private. "I'll let you two speak."

And with that, I retreated and let the two Grandiloquy speak without me.

Minutes passed. Then a half hour. I occupied myself doing pull-ups. At last Donia drifted into the room and watched me silently, a soft expression on her face that I couldn't read.

I dropped to the ground. "Has Tyrus gone?"

"Yes. I told him I'd like to speak to you in private now."

So she didn't intend to fill me in on what they'd discussed. My dismay must've been visible on my face, because Donia's brow pinched in a frown. "He's very worried about what will happen to you."

"Yes, of course."

"*Very* worried," she emphasized, then hesitated. "He . . . cares for you, Nemesis. He cares deeply."

A flush stole over my face.

She looked at me searchingly. "And you care for him, too." She bowed her head, spent a moment smoothing her skirt. "Do you trust him?" she asked finally.

"I've told you I do."

Her small hands curled into fists as she looked up. "I remember your theory about the Great Race. You said Tyrus had a hand in making that accident happen."

"Of course," I said, confused about why she'd think of that now. "He told me as much."

"You do realize Dandras *died*, Nemesis. It doesn't concern you to know that Tyrus is capable of taking a man's life?"

"It was an accident—"

"What of it? He knew the risk. He risked a man's life for the sake of a political gesture. Someone who can sacrifice one person's life so easily can also sacrifice others."

I weighed my reply carefully. Such calculations came as second nature to people like me and Tyrus, but to Donia, they must seem savage indeed. "Tyrus didn't intend his death. And I do believe intentions matter. Besides . . ." I smiled at her ironically. "I am no innocent myself. With your own eyes, you've seen me kill."

"That was different," she said softly, then grimaced.

I didn't speak the words I was thinking. *No, it wasn't.* Sutera nu Impyrean didn't have to die. She wasn't an accident.

"I only—I worry, Nemesis—"

"If you're concerned about me, don't be. My life is about protecting you, not the other way around. What *did* you two discuss? It's put you in a strange mood."

She moved over toward one of the windows gazing out into the sky dome, sunlight washing over her still artificially light hair. "Do you remember what I said before you left the fortress? I told you I'd rather die than lose you."

"How could I forget?" My voice was a harsh rasp.

Her eyes flickered back to mine. "I care about you, Nemesis. A lot. Probably . . . If I'm to finally be honest, probably the same way Tyrus does."

"I don't think—" I stopped. My first thought was that Donia had misunderstood the nature of Tyrus's feelings for me.

But perhaps she hadn't. I remembered her reaction, so long ago, to my suggestion that I further her relationship with Gladdic. I'd imagined she was upset over sharing his attentions.

It hadn't occurred to me she might be upset over sharing *mine*.

"You've been the constant in my life," Donia said, her voice hollow and distant. "When Mother would yell at me and Father would lose himself in his work, I always had you, and you were all I needed. When I was supposed to be in the social forums, finding a partner from the greater Grandiloquy, all I could think was that I didn't want anyone else. All I wanted was what I already had. I just wanted you with me forever. It's hard to see you look at him the way you do, Nemesis. It's wonderful to know you can feel that way, but it hurts me too."

"Oh." It was all I could say. I didn't know what to do. "Donia—"

Donia raised a shaky hand, bright spots in her cheeks. "You don't have to say anything. You never had a choice about caring for me. You *had* to feel love for me. It wasn't fair. You never chose for yourself, and I always knew I couldn't take advantage of that. I never would, you know. I never *will*."

"I didn't need a machine to force a bond on me. I . . . ." The words were hard to say, even now, even after the practice I had received with Tyrus. "I love you truly. You saved my life when they killed the other Diabolics. You didn't have to. You wanted me to be Nemesis Impyrean, no *dan*. I always thought that was so silly and ridiculous, but since I've been here . . ."

A wistful note stole into her voice. "What?"

"I've started to understand what you meant all along. What that was about. I finally see how extraordinary you've always been." I looked away from her. "I understand how incredible *you* are now. You're a best friend to me when by all rights, you should have been an owner to a possession. You never saw me as a thing. Not even when I did."

Donia's eyes sparkled with tears.

"Do you think there's something wrong about Tyrus?" I asked her, needing to know. "I want your good opinion. It's more important to me than anything."

She shook her head. "Nemesis, no. No, don't start doubting anything because of me. If you feel something for Tyrus, then I want you to be happy with him. I want you to have that more than I want anything else in this universe. You have to believe that."

"Why are you talking this way?" I suddenly felt suspicious. "What did you and Tyrus say to each other? You're worrying me."

She crossed the distance between us, then grasped my hands tightly and pulled my knuckles up against her cheeks. "Please don't worry about anything. We just came to understand how important you are to both of us. And he unsettled me somewhat, the way he spoke of choices."

"What choices?"

"Oh, it's hard to say. I don't think he's optimistic we can transition back to me being Senator von Impyrean without a lot of difficulty. He's worried for *you*. And I'm glad he is. I'm so glad he is. I'm sure he's thinking of a solution. Now let's stop talking about this for a bit." She clutched her temples. "I have a headache. Can you get me an opiate rub?"

Her words did nothing to reassure me. I found the ointment for her, but Sidonia was no longer feeling chatty. She settled by the window, staring out through pinprick eyes, and seemed content as long as I sat down by her side. I listened to her breathe as I used to back in the fortress, pondering our aborted conversation.

Nothing about our circumstances right now could set me at ease. I felt as though we all three dangled on the edge of a precipice, below us an unfathomable drop into a great, dark void, and I suspected even farsighted Tyrus could not spot what lay at the bottom.

45

NOW THAT TYRUS did not plan to go through with the marriage to Elantra, he had to revise his strategy against Cygna.

"Until the last minute, the very last moment, I will pretend I am upholding my end of the bargain," he explained to me.

He'd planned to dispose of Randevald first, and then Cygna. Now he meant to win Cygna's allegiance, and then betray her treachery to her son, the Emperor. Randevald would dispose of Cygna. And then Tyrus would arrange the death of Randevald, likely with some topical poison—the surest means of eluding the Diabolics.

The plan reassured me, and not just because there was no risk of Tyrus wedding Elantra. I knew Cygna was far and away Tyrus's more dangerous foe. Leaving her alive was courting disaster.

For now, we went along with Cygna's desires. Today was the day Tyrus would publicly disavow me in favor of Elantra.

The Grandeé Cygna's vessel, the *Hera*, was not so ostentatious as the *Valor Novus,* or even Tyrus's *Alexandria.* From the outside it was downright ugly, built as it had been around a hollowed-out asteroid. Yet as Tyrus and I strode in for the great reception Cygna was throwing, I realized the inside was a different matter.

Above and around us were the rugged natural features inside the asteroid: jagged stalagmites, glittering crystals, and veins of palladium, all tastefully lit and illuminated, carved elaborately in places, punctured every so often with the crystalline windows both natural and unnatural that Cygna had placed within.

"This is fifty years of work," Tyrus remarked. "The *Hera* is Grandmother's pride. It's a work of art."

"I see that." The Matriarch had told me once I had no appreciation of value, but recent weeks had taught me lessons in beauty—among other things. Looking around, I could see why this place was priceless. Love and dedication and effort had been put into this ship, and I was impressed by the effort and ambition.

"You are prepared for what must happen?" he said, searching my face intently.

"Of course."

He leaned in very close to me, his breath tickling my ear, voice so soft it was almost inaudible.

"Remember I mean none of it."

I smiled. It wasn't forced. "Tyrus, I know. Be brutal. I will smile inside."

He grinned. "I'll be monstrous."

"And, Tyrus—thank you for keeping my secret." Then, to clarify, "About *her.*"

His jaw tensed. A shadow moved over his face. "I know you are bonded to her, Nemesis. I know how valuable she is to you because of that." He hesitated in his steps, turning to me suddenly as though distracted from the task ahead. "She's the reason you planned to return to the Impyrean fortress, isn't she?"

"Of course she is."

"And you concealed her from me to protect her. I understand that." His gaze probed mine. "Nemesis, can a Diabolic's bond to a master be broken?"

"Broken?" I said sharply. "Why would I want to do that?"

"To free you of her, of course."

"I'm not Donia's captive, Tyrus. I *love* her. I would love her without the bond."

"I understand that, but Nemesis . . ." He took my hands and drew me very close. "I *know* how you express your love. I remember you giving up your life for me in the decompression closet." His hands tightened on mine. "And if the Grandiloquy discover this deception of yours, I know how you'll express it again—you'll choose her life over your own. But *I* do not choose her life over yours."

"It won't come to that." I had no way to guarantee that, but it seemed the best answer.

He pushed out a shaky breath. "Will you leave me, then? If she wants you to leave?"

"Tyrus, I—"

"It's not the time. I know that." He offered me a faint smile. "But do remember: I am a selfish person. When the day comes, I won't surrender you to her merely because she has a chemical advantage over me. . . . We Domitrians aren't ones to share."

And then he led me forward without another word. I followed, turning his words around in my mind. Tyrus and Sidonia were my entire universe now, twin magnetic poles tugging me forward. I didn't know what I would do if they pulled me in opposite directions.

We emerged into the vast presence chamber of the *Hera*, a ballroom of glittering beauty with polished walls of precious gemstones. Nameless tension stole over me as I recalled what we were here to do. There was a window of near-transparent perma-ice, reinforced by some clear substance. We took our place by that window.

The celebration was being thrown to thank the divine Cosmos for Tyrus's miraculous deliverance from the "freak" accident with the malfunctioning missile that had nearly killed him. Even the Emperor would attend later to give thanks, though only a fool would believe he hadn't been behind it.

The real reason for the party, though, was so Tyrus could disavow me and signal his obedience to the Grandeé Cygna by taking Elantra—the bride she'd chosen for him—as his future Empress.

Tyrus squeezed my hand once as Cygna mounted a great throne over the room. It was her vessel, so she was allowed it. She gazed out over the crowd within her glittering asteroid ship. It struck me how apt Tyrus's description of Cygna had been, as the one in their family most suited to rule. Though the black hole sigil of the nonroyal Domitrians loomed high above her chair, she surveyed the crowd below her with a hawkish pride on her regal features, like a ruler presiding over her subjects.

And now, Tyrus was going to publicly submit to her will by initiating his courtship of Elantra. It was a message Cygna would understand.

The Emperor arrived, with the usual accompaniment of Diabolics and security bots. His expression was disdainful as he gazed around at this celebration. He had to attend this event and publicly express his pleasure at Tyrus's deliverance from death, simply to quell the rumors that he himself had been behind the rogue missile strike. . . . Though he certainly didn't look pleased his attack had failed.

Cygna signaled for the music to start up, and Harmonids filed into the cordoned-off section of the room. I peered at these creatures, humanoid creations like I was, property of the Emperor. They were rarely seen, mostly playing their instruments out of sight. I hadn't even seen them in the ball dome at the last gala, but on the *Hera* there was no private space to hide them.

I caught a glimpse of short, rounded people, their features irregular on large heads. Some had an excess of fingers; all had wide, gaping mouths, enormous ears, small eyes. Some had overlong arms or legs, the better to play their instruments of design, and some had exceedingly short arms. One reason they were rarely seen was their aesthetically unpleasing qualities. Most genetically crafted humanoids were designed to delight the eye. Not these.

Then the music sounded from them. Harmonids were bred for one purpose: to produce music the likes of which a regular human could neither imitate nor fully appreciate. They were creatures entirely meant to entertain, and they did it exceedingly well.

Tyrus drew me by the elbow toward the dance floor, and the crowd about us cleared aside for the Emperor and the Grandeé Wallstrom to begin the first dance.

Cygna remained seated above the crowd, gazing down at us expectantly.

As the music wore on, it became time for Tyrus and me to dance. He squeezed my arm once, then led me halfway onto the floor—and stopped.

I turned to him, aware of the music still playing, of the silence descending on the crowd as they noticed something irregular about the way Tyrus was appraising me.

His eyes burned into mine for a moment, and then he reached forward and wound his fingers into my hair. I felt him unfasten a jeweled clip he'd given me and felt my hair tumble about my shoulder as he pulled it out.

S. J. KINCAID

I knew my part. I clapped my hands to my mouth, widening my eyes, hoping I'd effectively feigned horror. Withdrawal of a gifted jewel meant something.

"I am very sorry, but I must end this." He released my arm and paced away from me.

"Your Eminence, no!" I called, hoping to inject emotion into my voice. "Why would you do this? How have I displeased you?"

Tyrus shook his head. "You are all loveliness, Senator von Impyrean, but my heart has been won by another." Then he strode over to a brazier flaming in the center of a bubbling nitrogen fountain. He thrust the jeweled clip into the fire and turned around theatrically.

I collapsed to the ground, burying my head in my hands so none could see the lack of anguish on my face.

A hush hung over the crowd. Through my fingers, I saw that the Emperor and his lady had stopped dancing, both observing the scene with interest.

Tyrus reached out a hand.

"Will the Grandeé Elantra Pasus please join me for a dance?" Tyrus announced, his voice ringing over the crowd, over the tastefully muted music (Harmonids obviously knew when to adjust the volume to accommodate a scene).

Out of the crowd emerged Elantra, a vision of tumbling black curls in a rippling blue gown. Her eyes glowed with pleasure, and in that moment she looked astonishingly beautiful.

Tyrus smiled as she took his hand. In one gesture, he reached into his pocket, then swept out a jewel selected just for her: a glittering clip.

"For you, in tribute to your loveliness," Tyrus said.

"Thank you, Your Eminence," Elantra said, dropping to her knees before him. She allowed him to weave the clip into her hair—Tyrus publicly marking her as the object of his affection.

354

I inched back away from the dance floor, my head lowered as befitted the scorned lover. Curiously, the act was becoming easier and easier to feign. The sight of Elantra's pleasure, of Tyrus touching her so solicitously, made me feel slightly sick, although I knew, very clearly, that it was only a charade.

The crowd cleared aside as though I carried some contagion, allowing me to pass them. There would be no more fawning visits to the villa to win my favor. I could be thankful for that, at least. I peered up at the Grandeé Cygna as Tyrus and Elantra took to the dance floor. The music began again. Cygna's face was coldly satisfied, her thin fingers curled on the arm of her throne. She appeared the Emperor in that moment, not the blond-haired man dancing below her.

I forced myself to watch Tyrus and Elantra twirl about the dance floor. After a few minutes, my stomach settled. *Only an act.* I knew how he felt. There was no cause to doubt him. As they moved together, Elantra in bliss over her triumph, Tyrus's eye briefly caught mine, and a silent secret passed between us.

It was all I could do not to smile.

I felt the weight of someone's gaze upon me and turned to meet the Grandeé Cygna's eyes. She beckoned me over with a finger.

I hesitated a moment, wondering what she could possibly want with me now, but then I threaded through the crowd, keeping my head down like the scorned, humiliated lover. At last I reached her feet and drew her knuckles to my cheek.

She withdrew her hand from mine and caressed my hair, a sweet-smelling perfume wafting over me.

"Well done, my dear. You appear a scorned lover." She considered me carefully. "So much feeling on the face of a Diabolic! It's a bizarre sight."

I wasn't sure how to reply to that. "I'm pleased you enjoyed my performance."

"Your performance. Yes." She smiled thinly. Her eyes were too sharp and keen for her perfectly smooth face beneath coils of brown hair. "Do you know what I've been pondering ever since learning the truth about you?"

I raised my eyes to hers cautiously. "What?"

"Your Etiquette Marshal."

My heart stopped.

"Oh yes," Cygna said, seeing the blood drain from my face. "That Etiquette Marshal nestled in your villa had the look of true youth, so very unlike the Sutera nu Impyrean who once dwelled here several decades ago. And whatever could she be thinking, participating in such treason by treating a Diabolic as a Senator's heir?"

I ground my teeth together, my heart pounding furiously. "She is entirely ignorant of who I am. She had never met me before she took the liberty of traveling here to console me."

"Is that so? But you said yourself she trained you."

My heart plummeted. So I had.

"Your Etiquette Marshal is party to a criminal act. Although Tyrus has negotiated clemency for you, I take great offense to a mere Excess dabbling in imperial affairs. Why, I think I may have her detained—"

My hands flew to the arms of her chair, gripping them tightly as I leaned in over her. It was all I could do not to seize her throat. "Don't you go near her!"

Cygna did not flinch. "Ah, now *there's* the Diabolic in you." She waved her hand as though to signal someone to back off—no doubt a few of her employees had seen my move and prepared to come to her aid. I didn't even look at them.

Cygna calmly brushed aside first one of my hands, then the other. I didn't fight her. I knew better than to make a physical move on her here.

"So," she said softly, "Sidonia Impyrean lives. I suspected as much."

Anger seared me. I wanted to kill her. But it wasn't the time. We were too public. She must have come prepared for this, ready to save herself if I reacted poorly. I jerked back a step, then another.

"Oh, never fear," Cygna said drolly, reading the horror on my face. "She is safe. For now."

I turned away from her, drawing deep breaths of air that suddenly felt thin.

She rose and pressed up behind me. Her thin hand clutched my shoulder, her breath against my ear. "But tell me, Diabolic, once this is all over, you know there will be consequences. If Tyrus cares for you, how can he allow Sidonia Impyrean to live, to reclaim her identity? Surely he knows the Grandiloquy will never allow you both to escape punishment."

My voice was hard. "Tyrus will think of something. And if he doesn't, the choice is very straightforward for me."

"Of course it is. But will he truly allow your death? Truly? Because if so—why, he can't love you so very much after all. But then, I've always believed love is the most volatile substance in the universe. It erupts, it incinerates, and then it simply flames out. . . ."

I looked back at her, but Cygna stared past me toward the dance floor. I followed her gaze and found her staring at her own son, Randevald von Domitrian—the one she'd been conspiring against.

"Love betrays you, Nemesis dan Impyrean, and if you're wise, you will never forget that."

Elantra Pasus was not gracious in her triumph. In the frantic days that followed, she made certain to throw me a challenging look every time she swaggered by arm in arm with Tyrus. I played the part of chastened and rejected lover, averting my gaze from them, studying my hands.

It wasn't difficult appearing troubled. I'd felt this way ever since Cygna figured out the truth about Sidonia. I'd dispatched a Servitor to Tyrus to tell him the development, but he didn't seem to share my alarm.

Grandmother will not be an issue soon, he wrote back on his discreet-sheet. *Stick to the plan and fear nothing.*

And yet I did. I was sick with fear over what might befall Sidonia. I could never trust Cygna with this knowledge, and my mind kept idly returning to thoughts about killing her. But it wasn't the time. It wasn't. Tyrus had a plan, and Cygna had to die at Randevald's hands, not mine.

A day came, during the vapors after services in the heliosphere, when I found myself watching Cygna across the room, again contemplating the potential consequences of murdering her. Then a large presence appeared at my side. I realized with a startled jerk that it was Anguish, the Emperor's hulking, midnight-dark Diabolic.

"His Supreme Reverence wishes you to take the vapors with him in his private parlor."

"And he sent you rather than a Servitor to invite me?" I said, surprised.

"He dearly wishes to take them with you. A Servitor could not convey his urgency."

I cast an uncertain glance toward Tyrus and Elantra, both of them exhaling gentle clouds of vapor. Then I followed Anguish.

The Emperor's private vapor parlor was rarely used. He was a social creature and not inclined to isolate himself. Today, though, I stepped inside the dim chamber and found the Emperor by himself, lounging on a chair, already several phials along.

"Ah. Sidonia Impyrean. Sit." He gestured to a cushion on the ground by his chair.

I spotted Hazard behind him in the shadows, watching me closely.

Then I crossed the room and lowered myself onto that cushion. I gazed up at the Emperor's face, sloppy with his narcotic, thinking of how impossible it would have been just weeks ago for me to sit this close to him without attacking. Now that I knew Sidonia had survived him, my anger and hatred for him had cooled. I could regard him in a dispassionate way. He was Tyrus's uncle, Tyrus's enemy, the obstacle between Tyrus and the throne.

He was also a man whose age and exhaustion showed through his false-youth face, a paranoid and frightened creature eroded by power who wasn't nearly so clever as the enemies around him.

"I see my nephew has deserted you."

I looked down quickly. "He has."

"He has spoken to me of his desire to wed Elantra Pasus."

"So I hear."

He gave a harsh laugh, then sucked in a great inhale of another phial. He held it a moment, then coughed it out. "Poor taste, I say. Makes me wonder if he is mad after all. I was beginning to have my doubts."

I peered up at the Emperor suspiciously, wondering why I was here.

"You see," the Emperor said, "I've been starting to think Tyrus may have been . . . been putting on an act. He has too quickly reformed."

I said nothing.

"You would tell me, dear girl, if you knew anything. We are both of us deceived in my nephew."

"I think . . ." I hesitated a moment, remembering just what Tyrus had counseled me to say. "I think he is merely afraid, Your Supreme Reverence."

"Afraid?"

"Yes, Your Supremacy. Deathly afraid."

"Of me?"

"Not . . . just you."

The Diabolics both stirred.

The Emperor drew a sharp breath. His eyes dilated. "My mother?"

I nodded. "Tyrus was refusing her overtures," I said, clutching my skirt. "You must believe me. He was."

"Overtures?" said the Emperor sharply.

"I know little of what happened myself," I said, "but from what I heard, the Grandeé Cygna was . . . most upset with your . . . your purge of the Grandiloquy. She didn't agree with your decision."

His eyes narrowed. "Yes, she spoke against it."

"And so in the aftermath, she took an interest in Tyrus. At first it seemed innocent. She was counseling him about how to tamp down his madness, how to ignore his voices and conduct himself more winningly in public. . . ."

"Was she?" the Emperor said.

"Your Supremacy, perhaps—" began Hazard from behind him.

"Quiet, Diabolic!" snapped the Emperor, waving him back. "I will hear this. So tell me, dear girl, is this why Tyrus has behaved so differently of late? *My mother* has been whispering in his ear? *She* has been advising him?"

"Yes, and taking advantage of his instability."

I darted a quick look at Hazard's troubled expression, and Anguish's. Did they suspect me of misleading the Emperor? Could they tell with a glance at my face that I was lying?

I continued, "After the strange accident with the missile, Tyrus grew very frightened. The Grandeé Cygna told him that *you* had orchestrated the attack, and she would protect him—but only if he wed Elantra Pasus and showed himself an ardent Helionic. I think she means to place him on the throne sometime soon, though Tyrus is not coherent of mind enough to understand this for himself. He's merely afraid of refusing her, but his illness makes him so vulnerable to her manipulation. . . ."

"Yes," breathed the Emperor. "Yes, it certainly does."

Hazard laid a hand on the Emperor's shoulder. "Your Supreme Reverence, you have overdone your dosage. I think you must rest."

"I am not a child to be lectured by you," snapped the Emperor. "I will hear of this plot!"

"This isn't wise. You shouldn't listen to a word this creature is speaking," Hazard said.

"It's not a plot," I protested quickly. "Tyrus is not plotting, but a victim of—of— Stop! Unhand me!"

But Anguish had taken me by the shoulders and was tugging me back toward the door. "You must leave, Grandeé Impyrean." He used a great deal of force, far more than was warranted. Were I truly a person, he could be breaking my shoulders right now. I dared not throw off his grip and show my own strength.

The Emperor was sniping with Hazard, and Hazard was saying, ". . . untrustworthy. You can see it in her face. . . ." And their voices faded from my hearing as Anguish shoved me out of the room.

And then, outside the chamber, Anguish's black-eyed gaze met mine levelly, and I just played my role, the affronted heir manhandled by a creature. "How dare you!"

Anguish leaned very close. "Let me use language you understand: if you approach the Emperor again, I will rip your spine out."

The threat of violence made me freeze, because could he possibly have guessed what I was? No, there was no way. But before I could demand an explanation for such a naked threat, he was back inside the chamber.

So the Diabolics had been able to read the lies on my face. I just hoped the Emperor's paranoia outweighed his trust in their judgment.

I dispatched a Servitor with a discreet-sheet to Tyrus.

I planted the seeds with your uncle. His Diabolics doubt me, but he has heard my words.

Now let those seeds take root. Once the Emperor demanded an explanation from Tyrus, clever Tyrus would do the rest.

46

THAT VERY EVENING, Tyrus's engagement to Elantra was announced. I learned of it because a Servitor arrived with Elantra's missive: I was to report to her villa at dawn for her anointing.

"Anointing?" I said, staring at the sheet.

Donia snatched it from me and read it over. "Anointing is an engagement ritual. Usually people have their closest friends do it before they're getting ready to announce their union. Mother taught me how to do it, but it's elaborate. Too elaborate for me to explain."

"So I'll refuse to do it."

"No!" She paled. "That would be a terrible insult, Nemesis."

"I intend it as one," I said flatly. "I dislike Elantra, and so do you."

"No, you really can't refuse. It's a sacred rite. You could start a war with her family, and we can't afford that right now."

I didn't need trouble from the Pasus family at this precarious time. "Fine, I won't refuse, but I don't understand this. I'm not Elantra's friend. Why did she even ask me?"

"To flaunt the engagement, perhaps?" she suggested. "Listen, we'll go together. She won't object to your bringing an Etiquette Marshal. I'll whisper instructions to you."

"Dawn" was 0600, and so early that morning, Donia rubbed sleep out of her eyes as we headed toward Elantra's villa.

Elantra's Servitors opened the doors for us, and in we walked. I followed the Servitors into Elantra's bedroom, where she lay pretending to sleep.

"Wake up," I snapped at her. "Let's get this over with."

Elantra sat up, her black curls tumbling about her shoulders, and glared at me. "That is not how it's done."

Irritation flashed through me. I pulled out the silken handkerchief, and Elantra closed her eyes again, waiting expectantly. Donia had explained the first expectations of the ritual to me. I recalled this part well enough.

There was a basin of sun-blessed water by the bed. I soaked the handkerchief in it, then dabbed it over one of her closed eyes, and then the other.

"That's better," said Elantra, sitting up.

Donia peered in the doorway and mouthed what I was supposed to say.

"Congratulations to you, Grandeé Pasus, on this most glorious day when you formally pledge yourself to another," I recited.

Elantra looked between me and Donia. "Do you really need your Etiquette Marshal to remind you how to perform a basic anointing ritual?"

So she'd caught that.

"Forgive me, Grandeé Pasus," I said. "I didn't expect to do it until I had a *friend* getting married." I threw emphasis on that word.

Elantra smirked at me and rose to her feet. She held out her arms, blinking prettily. "Disrobe me."

I tore one of her buttons off tugging the silken overgown from her.

"As for why I asked you, Grandeé Impyrean, that should be very obvious."

"Not to me," I said bluntly.

Donia gestured with a finger for me to lead Elantra outside into the villa's solarium. There was a great shade hiding the sun, and Elantra stood there before it, waiting.

I stepped over to the shade and began pulling it up slowly. It was as close as we could get to a gradual sunrise playing over her skin, which was supposed to symbolize the new dawn of Elantra's life with Tyrus rising over the horizon.

"The Successor Primus and I are uniting together," Elantra said, leaning so her black hair spilled down to the middle of her back. "I thought asking you to perform this might clarify things between us once and for all. Do my back now."

I reached for one of the jars of oil that had already been set aside in readiness. "Clarify how?"

"Not that one," Elantra said sharply, seeing what I was reaching for. "That's your oil. The darker one beside it is *my* anointing oil."

I took the darker one, trying to recall the drawing Sidonia had done earlier to show me what pattern I needed to trace on Elantra's back.

It had just looked like a sun with concentric rings about it. Elantra held still before the mirror as I traced it into her skin. Whenever I faltered, Donia stepped over to my side, took my wrist, and moved my fingers for me.

"Tyrus suggested you as my Anointer," Elantra remarked.

My hand fell still on her skin. That surprised me. "He did?"

I glanced at Donia, and her eyebrows rose.

"Yes. I suppose he's trying to make you jealous." Elantra smiled unpleasantly. "That tells me he still has feelings for you, even if he may claim otherwise. Does that please you?"

Why *would* Tyrus tell her to use me? He never acted without deliberation, so there had to be a reason. Perhaps it was a gesture for his grandmother, signaling to her that I would remain important to him even if she forced a marriage with Elantra. He must have focused on Cygna without much thought about how Elantra herself would receive the request—an oversight quite unlike him.

"Of course you're pleased," Elantra said, studying me. "Anyone would be."

"I'm indifferent, really." I resumed tracing the pattern into Elantra's skin with the anointing oil.

"I suspected beforehand that he might still love you and seek me only due to necessity, but it wasn't pleasant to get confirmation," Elantra said, her eyes fastened on my face in the mirror. "I suppose he chose me over you to please the Grandeé Cygna. I accept the falsehood of his love if it's the price I must pay to be Empress."

My hand went still again, my heart giving an odd jerk. "That's . . . presumptuous." I had to say it. It was treason to discuss the Emperor's death, and Elantra was not my friend.

Elantra flashed me a spiteful look over her shoulder, her lips curling. "Don't play coy. He needs me to win the Grandeé Cygna's support. He's planning to kill the Emperor. I've even seen the poison he intends to use for the deed, a simple toxin. One unwary touch and it would soak right through poor Randevald's skin, killing him in minutes."

My hands went still again. That must have been dragged out of Tyrus, that confession. If Elantra had backed out of the marriage, the

Grandeé Cygna might have been inspired to support Randevald over him. I supposed he shared that information with Elantra to persuade her to go through with the marriage, but I wasn't pleased to hear it. She could betray us all.

Then again, Elantra wouldn't betray us if she hoped to be Tyrus's Empress. . . . But now that she'd figured out Tyrus loved me, not her, Elantra would be on guard when he ascended, ready for him to turn on her. We'd have to proceed very carefully.

"Why am I here, Elantra?" I asked her. "You didn't have to agree to invite me to this."

Elantra didn't answer that. She held out her arms for me to pull on her overshirt. Then she spun around, barefoot, and settled on the great cushion by the sunlit window. "Oh, Etiquette Marshal! Get Senator von Impyrean's oil. Now it's her turn to get anointed."

Donia selected the jar of lighter oil, the one I had to use on my shoulders and chest before I served as Elantra's escort to the vicar. Again, I didn't know the patterns I had to draw. Donia spoke up to rescue me. "I have very able hands. May I anoint my mistress? It will be faster."

Elantra never looked away from me. "She can anoint herself. Give her the jar and leave us."

Donia smiled at Elantra, her most gracious smile ever, and I wondered just how Elantra would feel if she knew her true rival was the small, meek girl beside me. "Really, Grandeé Pasus, I would very much like to do this for Grandeé Impyrean. In fact, I insist on it."

Elantra's gaze flashed to her. "How dare you insist with me! Don't you know your place?" Then the anger melted from her face, the bright flush of her cheeks fading. She tilted her head and smiled. "Very well. Since you insist, *you* can anoint your mistress."

I shrugged off my tunic and waited as Donia dipped her fingers in the oil and began brushing them over my shoulders. Elantra watched Donia's fingers move over my skin.

"To be honest," I told her, "it was very reckless of you to reveal Tyrus's plans to me. For all you know, I'm the vindictive scorned lover poised to betray him to the Emperor."

Elantra's smile was malevolent. "Oh, I'm not worried about you revealing *anything.*"

And that was when the oil jar shattered at our feet, and Donia gave a strangled cry. I spun around and met her wide, terror-stricken eyes. She raised shaky, oil-slicked fingers, and I saw that her flesh was rapidly turning a sickly gray where she'd coated her fingers. The stinging on my shoulders began at the same moment, and I knew, I knew why Elantra had brought me here—why she felt safe speaking so openly.

The oil was poisoned.

Elantra had never intended to let me leave here alive.

47

DONIA'S EYES were wide and panic-stricken on mine, and I could already see her skin mottling over her neck and chest.

I reacted at once, seizing Donia and hauling her with me toward the washroom in Elantra's villa. The skin of my shoulders burned, but I ignored it, driving Donia toward the washbasin and thrusting her hands under the faucet. I flipped on the water and scrubbed vigorously.

"Nemesis . . . can't . . . breathe . . . ," she choked out, and when I looked to her, I saw her face was growing a grayish blue.

There was a hiss, and I looked back to see the door to the washroom sealing itself shut. I launched myself to it, but the lock had been doctored—it would not budge. We were trapped.

Elantra's spiteful voice drifted over the intercom.

"It's no use," she called gaily. "It's already in your systems. I made sure to test it, just to be certain it's truly lethal. It had to sit on the Exalted's skin a good hour before he began to succumb, but humanoid creatures are always more resistant to such things. I imagine it will work far more swiftly with you two."

Enraged, I hurled myself at the door. My hand rebounded off it, sending splinters of pain up my arm. Donia choked, and I whirled around back to her. The arms of her gown were soaked now where she knelt at the foot of the sink, her skin mottled all over, and I grew aware of my urgent heartbeat like thunder in my ears, my sweaty skin, the mounting burn of my shoulders.

A cold draft of clarity swept over me.

Elantra had just locked us in.

She'd exposed us to poison. It must be the very same that Tyrus had planned to use on the Emperor.

I'd washed Donia's skin, but it was already in her system.

Sidonia might die.

"Elantra, please!" I yelled. "Elantra, please! Please, let us out. Or at least my companion. Please let my Etiquette Marshal live. Please let her go. Elantra! Elantra!"

My voice was a wail, but her taunting reply drifted into the room. "The Grandeé Cygna is supposed to arrive soon to escort her future granddaughter-in-law to the heliosphere. I suppose, instead, she'll have to help me figure out what to do with your bodies."

"I WILL TEAR YOUR HEART OUT FOR THIS, ELANTRA!"

Only silence answered me. I began furiously throwing myself at the door, knowing this was our only chance. I had to get Sidonia to a doctor. I had to get her to med bots. I had to do something.

"N-Nem . . ."

I whirled around, and everything in me froze at the sight of her. Her face was waxen, her eyes stark against her skin. She was like a rag doll slumped beneath the sink, the mottling of her neck swelling into blisters.

"Wash."

"I've washed you." My vision was blurring. I couldn't seem to look away. "I washed it off, Donia."

"You."

My shoulders burned. I thought of that Exalted, how it had taken an hour for him to begin feeling the effects. No doubt Diabolics had a similar frame of survival. Death was what I deserved for leading Donia into this trap. I didn't know what to do. I prayed to every god there might be, especially that divine Cosmos that had restored Donia to me once, to please come here, please help us, because I couldn't do this again. I couldn't bear this again.

Donia fumbled with a frail hand toward the washbasin. "Wash."

"I don't deserve to wash it off," I cried. "Donia, I hope it kills me."

"Wash," she insisted. "Please."

My brain felt numb. I splashed water on my shoulders until the stinging receded from my skin.

Diabolic physiology again. The poison was passing through me as though it had never been there. I'd trade anything to give my immunity to Donia.

"I . . . I don't know what to do," I told her. I looked at my hand, my knuckles bloody from where I'd punched the door.

Donia looked grayish blue now, the whites of her eyes red with veins. Her shaking hand closed around mine and I hunkered down against her, feeling her body like a frail little bird's, because this wasn't happening, this wasn't happening. . . .

"Love," she wheezed.

I clutched her tighter.

Her grip tightened as much as it could. Her breath was coming in raspy gasps now. "Love . . . you . . ." Then she gave a high-pitched wheeze and tensed against me and I was thinking of Deadly again and clutching Donia closely, horror thundering through my brain, because no, no, this wasn't happening. . . .

But then she wasn't breathing, wasn't moving, and I looked at her eyes like sludgy clouds, without that spark that was Sidonia, and no, no, this wasn't going to happen.

"Donia. DONIA!"

I seized her and shook her. I screamed at her. I pinched her skin, twisting it, trying to get something, trying to hear a cry, to get her to flinch, to do anything, but she was slack and limp, and she was dead, she was dead, and a scream of rage tore from me.

Then abruptly the energy left me, the strength was gone, and all I could do was rest my head against her, whispering, "I love you, too. I love you. I love you so much. I'm so sorry. . . ." Because Donia was dead, and this time there would be no miraculous deliverance.

I waited there numbly, barely moving, barely breathing, unable to comprehend how everything had gone so wrong, so quickly. I waited, hearing only the low, steady thump of my heartbeat, aware only vaguely of the burn on my skin.

I didn't understand this. I didn't understand anything about cruel, bitter fate.

And then there was a footstep outside.

I remained very still, everything in me searing with dark, molten malice. I sensed Elantra listening for movement. Then the door slid open, and she told her Servitors, "Collect the bodies. Tell Grande Tyrus—"

A Servitor reached for me and then I was on my feet and throwing him against the far wall. Elantra's scream pealed through the air, but it was too late for her, I was already upon her, and I had her by the neck, driving her backward like the helpless girl she was next to me, thrusting her down through a table, splintering it in two with the impact. Other Servitors reached for me, but I threw them away and turned all my focus on *her*.

She wailed and screamed in fright as I pinned her down, and I knew I'd just broken several of her ribs, but I didn't care. I tore at her face, I twisted at her arms, dislodging them from their sockets. And then I thrust her chin back so she'd look directly into my eyes.

"Please," she said, her eyes filled with tears.

I drove my fist through the soft flesh of her torso, and then I had it, I had Elantra Pasus's heart, and I was drenched in blood and still the molten anger and malice in me was not slaked, because nothing made sense. The organ was slick and hot in my hands and I stared at it, the body at my feet, because I couldn't understand how this could have happened.

What now?

What now?

WHAT NOW?

I dropped the heart and reeled upright, Elantra's body sprawled beneath me. Blood drenched my arms, my gown. The lights were too bright and a great buzz of noise sounded in my ears and Sidonia was dead this time, she was dead, I'd seen her die. . . .

I stumbled over to my knees and retched. Everything foul and bilious came out of me and still there was more because how had this happened, how . . .

The great thunder of panic and horror in my brain drowned out the noise of the Grandeé Cygna arriving, and then she was standing there, gray-faced and terrified for once, gasping at the sight of such carnage. And as I raised my bloody face up to look at her, she whipped out an energy weapon. "You stay back."

"She killed her," I gasped. "Elantra killed Donia."

Cygna circled about me, still keeping that careful distance, and peered in one room after another. Then the washroom. She gazed in there a long moment, then emerged.

"So the Impyrean girl was doomed after all," Cygna remarked.

And then her harsh, bitter laugh.

Laughing.

Laughing!

I hurled myself at her, but a bolt of energy tore me down to the ground, resounding through every cell in my body, and the Grandeé Cygna loomed there, weapon still raised, her hawk-like eyes on me.

"This was you, wasn't it?" I screamed, rage boiling up within me. I staggered to my feet, facing her, and the room was darkening until all I could see was her cruel, ruthless face. "You were behind this!"

Cygna's eyes narrowed. "Fool, do you think I would try to poison a Diabolic? I know whose work this is, and it's not mine. A dead Sidonia Impyrean, a dead Elantra Pasus . . . Two birds, one stone. Very convenient for my grandson."

Her . . . grandson . . .

My body froze.

"No," I said.

Cygna tilted her head. "I knew he wouldn't sacrifice you, but I wondered how he'd manage the situation." Her thin eyebrows rose as she looked over the carnage. "Now I know. It seems he chose to allow the Impyrean girl to die in your stead."

"No," I breathed.

"A dead Sidonia Impyrean means a certain Diabolic can step into her place." Cygna's voice throbbed with malice. "And of course, it's only natural this Diabolic would avenge her master's death, so Tyrus could wipe his hands of Elantra without my realizing he'd engineered her death. . . . Or so he thought. Really, it's quite insulting he thought he could deceive me. I invented this maneuver."

"You're wrong." Waves of heat and cold swept over me, but my mind was turning inward, turning around those words. I buried my bloody hands in my hair, a memory resounding through my brain.

He unsettled me somewhat, the way he spoke of choices, Donia had said to me. *I don't think he's optimistic we can transition back to me being Senator von Impyrean without a lot of difficulty. . . .*

So perhaps . . . perhaps he'd taken another course.

He asked Elantra to use me as the Anointer, knowing just what questions and revelations would follow. . . . So he could reveal to her that he still loved me without outright initiating the conversation. That led to Elantra's resolve to kill me. And when she questioned him, he showed her just the poison he knew would work on Sidonia but not on me. He knew the anointing ceremony: that a pattern would need to be applied in just the way that would require Sidonia's help. After all, a Diabolic wouldn't know an anointing ceremony. Sidonia would *have* to come help, and the poison could be hidden in the oil so easily. . . .

And if Elantra killed Sidonia, I could remain Sidonia. If I killed Elantra, he wouldn't need to marry her. It wouldn't seem to be his fault, not to me, not to Cygna. It was . . . It was just like Tyrus. A brilliant, cunning scheme.

Cygna circled Elantra's body. "He must never have intended to wed her. He didn't realize I was testing him. He failed." She propped her hands on her hips, and her lips curved in a lethal smile. "I would seek him out and punish him for this, but I would never dare rob a Diabolic of her revenge. The family will convene for a meal after services. . . . Perhaps I'll see you there?"

She moved to the door, and I didn't try to stop her. I felt frozen in place, filled with ice, numbed. Elantra's villa was quiet and still around me, sunlight spilling in the window over the blotches of blood on my gown, on the floor, and the broken body nearby. And in the next room . . . The next room! The girl I'd been created to protect. Now dead.

A great, piercing pain stabbed at my chest. I balled up my hand and pressed it to my collarbone, choking.

And all I could think of was Tyrus's vow to Sidonia.

Nemesis will live. That, I swear to you.

He'd sworn that to her.

Sworn it.

Tyrus spoke with such conviction because he'd known he could make it happen.

He'd made it happen by sacrificing her life for mine.

48

I WANTED it to be a lie.

I wanted to believe it was all Cygna's deception.

But any way I looked at it, I couldn't disbelieve Cygna. I couldn't push away my certainty that this had all been Tyrus.

I'm not a gentle soul by any means. I long ago accepted that there would be blood on my hands . . .

I must live with this, Nemesis, so I will. I will live with it.

Tyrus could live with the death of an innocent. He refused to sacrifice me. I was the one thing he dared not lose. So . . .

So . . .

Here it was. Something he *had* been willing to sacrifice.

Sidonia was lying on the bed now. I folded Elantra's sheets over her and closed her dark eyes. Her skin felt cold. She'd grown ashen, and I looked upon her for a long while, trying to understand how the Donia I'd known who'd lived and breathed and gazed at me with such life could now be this wax figure unmoving before me.

I stepped into the shower and washed off Elantra's blood. I donned one of Elantra's gowns. It wouldn't do to attract attention to myself by stumbling through the halls of the *Valor Novus* looking like the perpetrator of a massacre.

The massacre was one still to come.

A fog hung about me as I moved out into the sky dome and threaded through the crowds returning from the Great Heliosphere. I made myself think of Neveni, of the warning she'd given me once that I'd so readily disregarded.

Tyrus may be the enemy of your enemy, but he is still a Domitrian. Never trust them. Not any of them. They are a family of killers and liars. He may not have deployed that Resolvent Mist—but he still brought it with him. What does that say about him?

He'd brought that Resolvent Mist knowing how dangerous it was because he knew the power of a threat, the power of death averted. He was clever and calculating enough not to simply toss that Resolvent Mist aside or leave it on the ship.

And then he'd kissed me as we rose from the curve of Lumina. . . . Pain lanced through me like a fatal stab wound.

It was the oil that told me everything. I respected Tyrus too much to believe him capable of such a mistake, to believe he could accidentally reveal his feelings for me . . . to believe he could accidentally reveal the correct poison for Elantra's use.

My head pounded and the lights about me seemed to blur. I reached the presence chamber just as Cygna stepped out of it. She caught my eye but did not make any gesture of greeting. Instead she drew aside a few of the Domitrian employees waiting there.

The Emperor's Diabolics were not guarding the door.

Cygna was clearing a path for me, but I didn't understand *their* absence. I stepped right through the door into the presence chamber. My eyes adjusted to the dimness within the chamber, and I saw them all—Tyrus, Devineé, Salivar, Randevald—dining and drinking, streams of vapors languidly touching the air about them. Hazard and Anguish lurked unobtrusively against the distant wall.

Another curiosity. They were too far to intervene if I made my move.

But I didn't. I came to a halt as soon as they spotted me.

Their conversations fell silent. All of the Domitrians stared at me with open astonishment—Tyrus's ex-lover and an intruder. I was vaguely aware of the security bots buzzing in toward me, the only guards in the room alarmed by my presence.

"Sidonia?" Tyrus said. He took one look at my face, then shot upright. "Sidonia, what's wrong?"

What a clever actor he was! Sidonia's dying face burned before my eyes, and I just stared at him across a distance that now felt unfathomable.

He'd honestly believed he could engineer Sidonia's death and I wouldn't see his hand in it. Of course he had. If Cygna hadn't come, if she hadn't spoken, I never would have considered the possibility that it was his doing.

But now that the possibility had been suggested, it was the only one that made sense.

You'll choose her life over your own. But I *do not choose her life over yours.*

It was something a Diabolic would do—murder one innocent person for the sake of the person they most loved. I could understand it because I would have done it, but I could never forgive it.

I knew my role as Sidonia's Diabolic: to avenge this hideous betrayal. To tear out his heart as he'd torn out mine. To rip him apart. My vision blurred from not blinking, and then I had to look away because even now I could not kill Tyrus. Cygna might have cleared the way for me, but I was not her weapon. I was not even my own.

Someone had engineered Donia's murder, and it was going to be avenged, but I would act as Tyrus himself might have done: indirectly. I threw myself to the ground, to my hands and knees, prostate before the Emperor's authority. "I must make a confession to you."

"What is this?" demanded the Emperor, rising to his feet.

"Your Supreme Reverence, I have news of a plot against you."

Tyrus stiffened, and the Emperor held up his arm when his Diabolics prepared to spring on me. Out of the corner of my eye, I grew aware of Cygna moving through the doorway and coming to an abrupt, startled stop when she saw me on the floor. No doubt she'd expected to find me already standing over the corpse of her grandson.

"A plot?" said the Emperor. "What manner of plot?"

"Your Supreme Reverence—" Tyrus tried.

"I'm not Sidonia Impyrean," I shouted over him. "I'm Nemesis dan Impyrean, a Diabolic of the Impyrean household. I've been conspiring with your nephew, Tyrus, to deprive you of your life."

"Sidonia—" said Tyrus sharply.

"No, no, let her go on," said the Emperor, triumph blazing over his face. He pointed to the Servitors. "Get my niece and her husband out of the way. The rest of us will stay. I will hear everything."

The drooling Salivar and Devineé were led away by the Servitors. Tyrus started toward me—but Hazard blocked his way.

"You—you don't understand," Tyrus said, looking around, at a loss. "I think—I think perhaps she's gone mad. Let me talk to her!"

"You were mad once as well," the Emperor drawled. "I always listened to you."

"Sidonia," Tyrus said, an edge creeping into his voice, "please—"

"Don't even say that name!" I bellowed at him, my heart in my voice.

"Do you think I'm too stupid to see your hand in what happened?" I felt like I was being torn in two, and grief seemed to blind me. I could see nothing, notice nothing but the pain inside me. "Sidonia is dead. She's dead, and it was your doing, I know it was!"

"Wait a minute, she's—" began Tyrus.

"My son." Cygna spoke coolly as she joined the Emperor's side. "This is a most grievous accusation. Who knows what my grandson has planned? Before he can act, I recommend his immediate execution."

I looked up at her. Yes, she'd expected me to kill him right away. Now her face was full of tense lines—because I had not done so. I was not her tool, and I hadn't come here to play into her hands.

"And Your Supreme Reverence," I spoke, "the Grandeé Cygna is a conspirator too."

Cygna jerked. "Absurd!"

"She's been in on it from the start," I said softly. *Two birds, one stone.*

"She lies!" Cygna cried. Sheet-white, she whirled on the Emperor. But her son's reaction would not comfort her. He now wore a maniacally pleased expression: all his dreams had come true at once.

She stepped back from his smile, lifting her hands as though to shield herself from an oncoming blow. "My son—you cannot credit this! After all I've sacrificed for you, would I ever betray you?"

Tyrus laughed again, a sluggish and strange sound. He seemed to have given up on lying his way out of this. "Grandmother, it's no use denying it." He looked up at her, a sudden, expectant gleam in his eyes. "We have been found out. Our schemes are all for naught."

Cygna made a choking sound. "Why, you—"

Tyrus smiled, his eyes very cold, and I knew what he was doing. My accusation had neatly joined Cygna's fate to his, whatever it was. He would not be destroyed without seeing her meet her fate too.

"Hazard, seize my nephew," ordered the Emperor, his gaze still fastened avidly on Grandeé Cygna. "As for you, Mother—I intend to take your suggestion. *You* may act before I can stop you. There is no reason to let you leave this room."

Cygna gasped. "Randevald, what are you saying?"

He bared his teeth. "Left to yourself, you will no doubt find a way to wriggle out of conviction. No, I'll give you no chance to scheme with your allies. You will die here, now, for this shameful attempt on your own son's life. And once you are dead, Tyrus will be persuaded to testify publicly to your guilt—and anything else I wish. Anguish?" He snapped at his Diabolic. "Kill her."

Anguish and Hazard did not move.

The Emperor tore his gaze from Cygna. Tyrus, frowning, looked over too.

"Anguish!" The Emperor leaned forward. "I said, kill my mother!"

From where I was kneeling, bleak and empty, I saw Anguish cast a look toward Cygna. That look . . . it held a question.

Hazard's bright blue eyes moved to her as well.

Neither obeyed the Emperor.

I caught my breath. Why—Hazard and Anguish were looking to *Cygna* for instructions.

They weren't the Emperor's Diabolics.

They were *hers*.

They were hers just as they'd been the day I spoke with the Emperor, when I tried to cast suspicion on Cygna. Anguish had forced me from the room and Hazard had detained the Emperor—for Cygna's sake.

She'd known Tyrus and I were plotting against her.

Now Cygna's face twisted with disgust. "Randevald, how dare you doubt me? I chose you over my other children—every time, I chose *you*. And today, despite your perfidy, I chose you again—this time over my own grandson, a boy who could have outsmarted you in the cradle.

I thought to serve him to you on a platter, and what do you do? You turn on me. All these years—why, I even neglected my own safety, ordering my Diabolics to protect you instead of me. Oh, dear." She paused, smirking, as the Emperor's face slackened with comprehension. "That's right, I never told you. Their bond was never to you, Randevald. They are *mine*. But despite all my sacrifices, what is my reward?" She spread her hands. "You order my death! I see we *are* at an end. Hazard, Anguish, dispose of this traitor."

Hazard vaulted toward the Emperor, and in one movement reached out and swiped him to the ground. Anguish leaped down to smash the nearest security bot, dodging the beams of the other bots and taking them down next.

The Emperor roared in shock as he found himself on the ground, at the mercy of his own Diabolics. Tyrus stumbled back from the pandemonium. I surged to my feet, moving toward him . . . To do what? I didn't know. To protect him, to hurt him?

I didn't make it that far.

Tyrus's gaze swung toward me, alarm on his face. He flicked his finger.

And suddenly electricity spiked through me, driving me to the ground. I hit the floor, every cell in my body vibrating, and collapsed there, stunned. The electrodes.

He'd said they dissolved. They never had. They'd been there all along.

He'd *never* trusted me.

I'd imagined myself betrayed before. But now, as I gasped wordlessly, I knew the true agony of betrayal. It seared like fire along my sinews, merciless.

Moments or minutes later, I managed to turn my head and take in the scene. The Emperor was gaping at his mother, the woman he'd never understood until this moment. Then, with an ugly crack, Hazard snapped his neck.

Randevald slumped, dead.

A thick, piercing silence descended over the chamber. Then Cygna pointed to me. Hazard and Anguish were on me in moments, grabbing my arms, hauling me up between them. I didn't fight. What fight could I put up? If I resisted, Tyrus would only reactivate the electrodes. I just stared as Cygna crossed the distance to Tyrus.

The two pale-eyed Domitrians surveyed each other like foes over a devastated battlefield.

"So," Cygna said. "That was your plan with all that talk of an alliance. You were going to betray me to my own son."

"Yes," Tyrus said coolly. "But it seems you acted first."

"Of course I did. I will *always* be one step ahead of you. I suspected you were maneuvering me into a trap. So I sprang mine first. It seems your unbonded Diabolic does love you. I thought she would kill you. She had every cause. Yet she could not manage it."

"You missed the incident just now." As Tyrus glanced toward me, some emotion flickered over his face. True pain.

I touched my neck, feeling where the electrodes must be buried.

"And now here we are, at an impasse," Cygna said. "For you see, Randevald is dead, and we stand in need of an Emperor. I cannot take the throne myself, so I need someone of the blood to do so."

Tyrus looked toward Cygna's pair of Diabolics, poised to cross the room and kill him in a heartbeat.

"You were clever to try to destroy me, Tyrus," she said. "Because you were correct. I am the worthiest in this family to rule. I did so through your grandfather, and for years, I did so through my son. And now, I will either do so through you, or you will die right here and the Empire will have to content itself with a drooling imbecile on the highest throne. . . . I'd rather it were you. So many problems would ensue if I placed Devineé there now, what with the entire Grandiloquy speaking of her brain injury, but no one will challenge your claim."

Tyrus laughed. "And how can we possibly ally now? I intended to see you dead. My uncle would have followed in short order afterward. You know this."

"Ah, but I also know how clever you are. Clever enough to fear me."

He stared hollowly at the woman who'd killed his parents, killed much of his family. "Yes."

She tilted her chin up. "The rogue Impyrean Diabolic murdered our beloved Emperor today. It will be known by all."

Tyrus drew a breath.

"Won't it?" Cygna said, her voice hard. The Diabolics at my side stirred ominously, and Tyrus threw them a wary glance.

He swallowed hard, and said, "As you say, Grandmother."

"And your Diabolic will be the fire sacrifice at your coronation. A fire sacrifice in the truest Helionic sense."

Tyrus clenched his fists.

"Love or power, Tyrus?" crooned Cygna. "I know what choice I've made time and again. There's only one choice for a true grandson of mine."

And then slowly, painfully, Tyrus dropped to his knees before her, gazing up at her with his calculating eyes. "Whatever it is you wish, Grandmother."

She smiled like a great satisfied cat as he drew her knuckles to his cheeks.

Cygna spoke, "Hail to the Emperor."

Their positions were totally inverted, the new Emperor on his knees and his treacherous grandmother above him, regarding each other with the same eyes, watchful and cynical, totally lacking in love or trust.

They'd both tried and failed to kill each other using Randevald, and merely destroyed Randevald instead. Now this unholy alliance would carry forward, and this was how Tyrus's reign would always be. None of his lofty ideals or great plans would take shape under Cygna's iron fist, for she would be the true power.

I watched this with an empty heart, still acutely aware of the electrodes in my neck: evidence that my alliance with Tyrus had always been a lie. All I regretted was that I hadn't seen the true Domitrian nature in time to save Sidonia.

49

I **WOKE** back in the corrals. Or so I thought, until I heard the humming of the force field about me, and saw the bright lights glaring down from above.

I sat up slowly. Tyrus stood on the other side of the force field, his arms folded. He'd been waiting for me to wake up.

My neck stung. My hand flew up, and I felt a healed incision there. I sneered. As if extracting the electrodes *now* meant anything!

"I found it hard to trust you early on," Tyrus said quietly. "I didn't have the heart to tell you that later, when I wished those electrodes had, in fact, dissolved."

"And then you used them again."

"You would have killed me."

"I still will." I rocked to my feet, vibrating with anger. "I hate you with every fiber in my being."

Tyrus gazed back at me steadily, unmoved, untouchable. "I know what you think of me. I know what happened with Sidonia. I saw the bodies in Elantra's villa. The Pasus family brays for justice. Grandmother has ordered them banished to their system—so they don't do anything rash."

"You knew they were dead before that," I spat. "You plotted it!"

Tyrus sighed, then leaned forward, setting his forehead against the force field that separated us. "Nemesis," he said, and I heard the fatigue in his voice, the roughness, and steeled myself, for he meant *nothing* to me now. "I swear to you. It was Grandmother, not me. *Think*. She wanted to turn us against each other, so she planted that seed of doubt in your mind. She hoped you would kill me. Who else—"

"If you didn't plan it, why did you tell Elantra to use me as the Anointer?"

"I didn't."

"You told Elantra of the assassination plot! And of the means!"

He straightened, jaw squaring. "I told her *nothing*. I had no assassination plot against Randevald, not yet. I intended to follow through on our plan: to betray Cygna's overtures of alliance so I could do away with my grandmother first. *She* was always the greatest threat, not Randevald."

"So you had no wish to see Sidonia dead? You said I'd choose her life over mine, yet *you* didn't choose her life over mine. You wanted to break my bond to her."

He let out a breath through his teeth.

I closed my eyes. "Her death is the end of *everything* for me. I'll never recover. It would have been better to die with her."

"Of course you will recover," Tyrus said harshly. "You lived through this once before."

"I didn't suspect you that time."

He slammed his palm against the force field. "I *love* you," he said fiercely. "Nemesis, you are the single truth of my existence. I would *never* hurt you like this."

"But you're going to sacrifice me!" I shouted at him. "You agreed to it as soon as Cygna wished it! And you were perfectly fine with electrocuting me to protect yourself. Why should I believe *anything* you say? You pledged your love for me and so easily threw it away. Why shouldn't I believe you'd kill Donia if it suited you? 'We Domitrians aren't ones to share.' You said it."

"I am *human*. Was I jealous of your bond to her? Yes. Did I hope you'd choose me over her? Yes, I did! But I did not murder her! Grandmother knew we'd turned on her. She knew it as soon as you spoke to my uncle in front of the Diabolics. So she acted first. You *must* believe that."

I threw my hands over my face to block him from my sight, because suddenly I couldn't bear to see him—the one I'd loved, the one who'd destroyed me. So many feelings and wonders had opened themselves to me these last months, and now they burned to ashes in my heart, because they'd all been the steps leading to this betrayal. Whatever he said, whatever he once planned, he still meant to kill me. I couldn't believe anything he professed, knowing I would be the sacrifice on the altar of his power.

"Leave me," I said, my voice feeling very distant. "Go. I can't even look at you."

He was silent a long moment, then said in a tight voice, "I won't inflict myself on you, Nemesis. I will stay away. It may be safer for you, anyway."

I turned away, pain tearing me open. How dare he speak of my safety, when he planned to kill me!

"The coronation will be in a month," Tyrus said distantly. "I will have you kept as comfortable as possible until then. Don't fear for yourself. I'll plan for us both—"

My voice was a rasp. "I want nothing from you."

"Nemesis . . ."

There was real pain in that word, but he said nothing else, just let it dangle there in the thick silence.

Then, "Sidonia loved you. I saw that with my own eyes. She would have laid down her life for you."

"That doesn't justify her murder."

"It's not a justification. It's an appeal, Nemesis—an appeal to do what you do best. Survive."

And then Tyrus, the Emperor-to-be, left me alone among the animal pens, in the only place on the Chrysanthemum capable of holding a Diabolic.

Time passed slowly in the pens, surrounded by the animals. Food and water were dropped through the ceiling—fine foods, better than any prisoner warranted. A mechanical voice would chime in and ask if I wanted to shower, and then water would pour down on me from above if I said I did. A slot in the floor served as the washroom, another as a washbasin. When the sensors detected my weariness, a plush cushion rose from the floor. I never slept on it. I preferred the hard ground. At night, I dreamed of Sidonia and Deadly. I also dreamed, to my horror and self-loathing, of Tyrus.

I dreamed of him touching me, and awoke despising my heart for its betrayal.

At some point, Tyrus sent assistants down to try giving me creature comforts, but I made it very clear that I'd kill any of them who came near me.

I had no intention of basking in any luxuries, however small. I deserved none. I'd failed Donia, and I'd loved the one who might have murdered her. I wanted nothing but to pass the remaining days before my sacrifice at Tyrus's coronation without feeling or thinking. There was nothing else for me now. No vengeance to drive me this time— not when it was Tyrus I needed to destroy. I wanted to hate him, but I felt empty inside.

Tyrus seemed to sense it would insult me to visit again. He stayed clear. His assistant, Shaezar nan Domitrian, did arrive to inform me of the imminent coronation—and my imminent death.

"Is Tyrus eager to claim his crown?" I said coolly.

"I—I wouldn't know. The new Emperor has been very scarce. Busy, I think, with preparations. Is there anything whatsoever I can get you to pass your last day?" he said, hanging back warily from the force field now that he knew what nature of creature I was.

Cygna had likely followed through on her plan to spread word that I'd been the murderer of the Emperor, so I had no doubt Shaezar feared me now and wondered at Tyrus's insistence on my comfort.

"I want nothing." Then I reconsidered. "Actually, yes. I do need something of you."

A beauty bot was an odd request from a Diabolic assassin, I was sure. I had no nefarious intentions, though. I programmed the machine to strip me of the camouflage I'd worn since leaving the Impyrean fortress. An hour later, no longer was my hair colored, but I was the blank creature of white-blond hair and pale skin I'd been when I'd come into Donia's life. But for my still-reduced size and damaged nose, I appeared the twin of the late Enmity.

I didn't sleep very much. The late Emperor Randevald's manticore was several pens down from mine, and I found myself observing the wretched, neglected creature, listless now that it had no owner to unleash it in the arena for its blood sports. Beyond that were other monstrosities, all like me, all created for the pleasure of human beings.

I would be glad to leave this life.

The day of the coronation, the handlers who trooped in to retrieve me were Domitrian employees. Tyrus dared not send Servitors I could outwit, or security bots that could do nothing but kill me. They held electricity guns, ready to stun me if I refused to move of my own accord. I had to survive until I was sacrificed.

I rose to my stiff legs and waited as they encircled my pen, as they aimed the guns at me.

"You're to accompany us to the Great Heliosphere," spoke one of them, a frightened-looking young employee whose head gleamed in the light, the six-star sigil of the Domitrians stark and fresh on his head.

I held my arms out, but no one moved to handcuff me. That was a surprise. I began to walk in the familiar direction, and the employees all kept a wary distance from me.

I knew it would be simple lashing out and seizing one of their guns, turning it on the others. I did not.

It wasn't until the raucous noise mounted in my ears, the cheers of those in the Great Heliosphere preparing for the coronation of the new Emperor, that it washed over me, my sense of purpose.

I could do very little to hurt Tyrus, but I could do this: die passively at his unwilling hands. It was the cruelest blow I could strike at him and the only weapon left in my arsenal.

So I would die and I would not fight back and Tyrus could live with that until the end of his reign.

50

THE VAST, decorated crowd within the Great Heliosphere parted, and all had their hair in effervescent halos, their clothes made of glowing material implanted with light. Their faces were stenciled with the Domitrian sigil of six stars. I was escorted between them toward the vicar.

Tyrus stood on a dais above the crowd with his hair grown long and shaped in a corona of light about his head as befitted a new Emperor, looking every bit the leader of a galactic Empire.

I stared up at him in the unblinking fashion of a Diabolic, ready to die here before him.

Grandeé Cygna stepped forward, bedecked in her finest. "The murderer of my son, Emperor Randevald, will serve as the fire sacrifice to launch this glorious new era in our history!" She raised her hand for the employees to haul me closer.

I did not fight as hands seized me from behind, driving me forward, down to my knees. My eyes found Cygna's Diabolics, Hazard and Anguish, standing off by the window. They were just near the slot in the wall leading to the small, coffin-size container that would be my last home, ready to force me in if I resisted them. I could see from here that it was clear crystalline glass. I would be stuffed inside and launched into the brightest star.

"Does the condemned have anything to say?" spoke Cygna.

I met Tyrus's eyes and remained silent. He appeared a great, gleaming statue so far above me, so removed, I wondered that I'd ever touched his flesh, seen his smile. He looked as remote as the void of hyperspace.

"Long live the Emperor," Cygna said, and nodded to her Diabolics.

They crossed over to me, prepared to seize me for the final journey into my tomb.

At that moment, Tyrus raised both his hands, and the room dropped into silence. Cygna looked at him sharply, and I knew this was a deviation from procedure.

"Grandmother," Tyrus said, not looking at her, "my dearest mother to my mother, and the great root from which so much of my family has sprung—" He leaned down toward her and drew her up to his side, her hands in his. "Do you recall how once you vowed to the Living Cosmos that upon my ascension, you would launch yourself into a star?"

She stared at him a moment; then a smile pulled at her lips. "Things were very different then, Your Supremacy."

"Yes, yes." Tyrus drew her knuckles to his cheeks, holding her gaze with his pale-lashed, calculating eyes. "But we mustn't offend the divine Cosmos by scorning our vows."

The blood rushed up in my ears. I saw Cygna's face going very pale.

"Surely you are joking," she said, her voice like ice.

Hazard and Anguish realized at the same moment that Tyrus was not. Abruptly they released my arms and jolted forward—

"Now," said Tyrus, still staring into his grandmother's face.

The employees who'd come armed with electricity guns for me turned them on Hazard and Anguish and fired. The two Diabolics shouted out but charged forward, fighting the glowing currents. Their bodies hit the employees who tried to stop them, enveloping them in light as well, but employees continued to throw themselves in their path with the sort of devotion no Excess had ever shown the Grandiloquy.

And then Anguish and Hazard were on the ground, the bright, forking plumes of electricity making their bodies vibrate, dozens of employees scattered on all sides of them, already dead of the same currents that had only disabled the Diabolics. Shouts and screams swelled about me, and I turned to see the crowd writhing with movement. More employees were lashing out at Grandiloquy with energy weapons, with blunt clubs, pulling them down to the ground. Some of the aggressors were Grandiloquy, the finely dressed elites of the realm unveiling their hidden weapons and taking down targets they'd clearly chosen beforehand, clubbing the backs of heads, shooting them down with energy beams. But mostly, the aggressors were *Excess*. And then I saw a familiar face with a fresh Domitrian sigil tattooed on his head, and my heart gave a lurch.

That was *Neveni's father* taking down Senator von Farth, pinning him to the floor. I threw a glance to the side and saw a woman I recognized as another Luminar bringing down Senator von Canternella.

Luminars. What were Luminars doing here posing as Domitrian employees?

Tyrus observed it all from his dais above the room as Cygna screamed and shouted for it to stop. The employees swarmed in and tended to those disabled by Hazard and Anguish, and others swiftly restrained the limbs of the unconscious Diabolics.

No one touched me.

And then the flurry of activity, so carefully planned, was over and fully half the room of the greatest people in the Empire lay on the ground at the feet of the other half. Over them stood some familiar Grandiloquy—Rothesays, Amadors, Wallstroms. The surviving heirs of Senator von Impyrean's faction. The others who stood with their chests heaving with exertion, triumph blazing on their faces, were those Luminars posing as employees.

Tyrus must have smuggled them here for this strike.

Slack now, unresisting with shock, Cygna permitted Tyrus to take her hands again. He himself did not look triumphant so much as exhausted—a person who had just outmaneuvered a longtime foe, yet gloried not at all in it.

"Grandmother," he said very softly, "you murdered my mother. My father. My sister. My cousins. My uncles. My aunts. And yes—the late Emperor, your own beloved son." Tyrus reached out and touched her cheek, like he was marveling at a work of art. "Did you truly believe I would allow you to rule through me like an adder waiting to strike if I disobeyed?"

"I should have left you to die in space," breathed Cygna.

"But you did not, because you were considering betraying my uncle. Then you attempted to destroy me instead—so here we are. At the moment before your own fire sacrifice."

I stared up, stunned out of my stupor, to see the terror on the face of this woman who'd never feared anything.

She stumbled down from the dais, lurching away from him, and cast an urgent look around—seeing her Diabolics and allies unconscious at the feet of Tyrus's allies. He'd organized this coup in the weeks since she'd sided with him over her own son.

"I regret defiling one of our most sacred spaces with this violence," Tyrus said, "but I had to strike in the single place you would never anticipate."

"You ally with Excess over Grandiloquy!" Cygna cried, looking about the room in horror, as though she beheld an abomination.

"I ally with those who seek progress over those who enforce stagnation," Tyrus said simply. "I ally with those willing to fight for a future rather than resign themselves to oblivion. And now I give you a choice. You will go to your death, but you will have a chance to repent."

"Repent?" Cygna's voice was a whiplash.

"I am the royal Domitrian heir. I know you care for our bloodline and this Empire, so make a confession for the sake of our family before you go to your death."

"You wish me to make life easier for you before you kill me?" she said acidly.

"Yes."

"And what would I get for this? Will I survive?"

"We both know that cannot happen now."

Cygna opened her mouth like she wanted to laugh at his audacity, but then the extent of her plight seemed to sink in. A certain dimness came to her face. "I choose whether I sleep for the journey ahead of me. You will give me an injectable sedative to take as I wish. Something fast-acting."

"A simple enough request. Thank you, Grandmother, for asking me for something I can reasonably give. Now for your end of this bargain . . ." He gestured her back up onto the dais.

Cygna's eyes narrowed. She stiffly mounted the stairs and turned on the crowd, appearing torn between a fierce, unbending dignity and a need to scream for help, to panic. "I killed Randevald. The . . ."

Her voice faltered a moment, as though even the hard-hearted Cygna needed to choke back tears. "The sole issue of my womb and my most beloved son. It haunts me, and it will until the void of death claims me. I have killed many others of my family, but I've done so only for the good of the Empire, and I regret nothing."

Tyrus laid his hand on her shoulder, his face sharp and intent. "And what else?"

Cygna's mouth bobbed open and closed. She hadn't expected this. "What . . . else?"

Tyrus held her eyes as though sending her a silent message. Then he inclined his head in my direction.

Cygna's lips curled at the corners, her face cold as though she was weighing the thought of that sedative. Then she looked squarely at me, still wearing that strange smile. "If this is the burden you wish to take upon yourself, far be it from me to stop you, Tyrus. You're stumbling into your own destruction by courting these Excess, so you might as well take it a step further and unite yourself with an abomination against nature. Nemesis dan Impyrean, it was *I* who engineered the death of your master, Sidonia."

Her. *Her.* The world seemed to drop out from under me, and I felt like I wasn't breathing.

"My Diabolics unearthed your plot against me, so *I* urged the Pasus girl toward the action, and suggested the Anointing might be a wonderful opportunity to carry it out. I instructed her on just what to say to lead your suspicions toward my nephew. The fool girl didn't even understand *why* I wanted her to say such things when she was about to kill you anyway, but she did it—and never realized she was weaving her own demise. Since I wished Tyrus dead, she was useless to me." Her hard gaze moved back to Tyrus. "I trust that confession pleases you?"

A buzz filled my ears. I felt dizzy, barely able to concentrate on Tyrus's voice: "I thank you for your honesty," he said. "Would you like to be sedated now?"

"I will walk to my own death."

"I understand." There was respect on Tyrus's face. He took her by the shoulders and pressed a kiss on her forehead. "I thank you, Grandmother, for all that you have taught me."

With that, Cygna raised her chin and threw a last look around the heliosphere—at her unconscious Diabolics, the crowd of implacable foes, and at me, the one she'd intended for the death she was about to meet herself.

"I see you truly are the most cunning of the Domitrians, Tyrus," she said, delivering her last words as was her right. "In these recent weeks, I earnestly believed we were working together, that perhaps you were the heir to create a greater Empire at my side. But instead you were plotting my death. Woe to you all, for you are now ruled by a most clever fiend. The dawn of his reign sees this most sacred space littered with victims of his treachery. Quite fitting for the most pernicious of my descendants. You have brought your fates on yourselves." Her voice dropped to a whisper only I could hear. "As have I."

Her body shook so violently, I could see it even beneath her great ceremonial gown, and the sedative nearly dropped from her hand when a doctor nan Domitrian stepped forward and offered it on a cushion. She pocketed it, stiffened her shoulders, and marched toward her crystalline tomb, lowering herself into the enclosure and stretching out there as the clear crystal slid closed behind her.

As we watched, Cygna's tomb detached itself from the heliosphere and shot off into the dark, on course for the brightest star in the solar system. If it reached that star and burned, it was a good omen for the reign of Emperor Tyrus von Domitrian. If it was destroyed by the system's gravitational forces first, then lies would be spread that it had reached the star anyway.

My mind reeled, all the certainty of my imminent death ripped from me. And now Cygna's words were in my mind, infecting me with doubts, because I was utterly desperate to believe them. I wanted to believe one of the two people I loved in this universe hadn't killed the other.

But if she'd spoken just to get the sedative, if she'd lied . . .

Tyrus had told me once that a palatable lie was easily swallowed. If this was a lie, it was one so appealing, I was desperate to believe it.

Tyrus stepped down from his dais, and he was blinding like the sun itself with his halo of hair done in the Helionic ceremonial fashion, his effervescent gold ceremonial coat. But in that face that could look utterly ruthless, there was a softness, a need, and he said, "Nemesis, did you hear her speak?"

I looked up at him, so wary, choking on uncertainty. "How could I miss it?"

"I did this for you. This was all for you. The universe may deliver itself into my possession, and I'll still feel as though I've lost everything without you by my side. I am madly in love with you, and I hope to all the stars you still feel something for me."

I stammered as I spoke: "Swear—*swear* to me you didn't have a hand in Donia's death."

He pressed his hands to his heart. "Nemesis, I swear to you. I did not do it."

Still I hesitated. Sidonia's face flashed through my vision, begging me to be careful. But the temptation to rise, to take Tyrus's hand, chased swiftly after. He was everything I still wanted, yet I could not dishonor her. . . .

But Sidonia had wanted me to be happy.

The realization washed through me, and I swallowed. I thought of her delight when I discovered feelings, when I found love.

"If I ever discover this is not the truth," I warned him softly, "I will be merciless."

He smiled. "And I'd expect nothing less from you, my love. Now take my hand."

If he was her murderer, I had a lifetime to figure it out. I could avenge her tomorrow if I learned he'd done it. I could avenge her in ten years if I learned in ten years, and I'd have ten beautiful years before that. I would always mourn Sidonia, but I had survived this loss once and I could survive it again.

I raised my eyes to the new Emperor, to that figure like a gleaming sun rising high above me, offering one of its golden beams to bathe me in its glory, but not just the Emperor—Tyrus, the young man who plotted with me and confided in me and explained lightning to me and kissed me . . .

I took his hand.

His face broke into a glorious smile as he raised me up onto the dais with him. We stood above the heliosphere of Grandiloquy and Excess, and the allies of Tyrus even now clearing away his opponents—now his prisoners. His grip felt sure and strong on mine. His gaze was intense enough to set me afire. I swept my eyes over the room, seeing the battlefield where he'd finally outmaneuvered Cygna Domitrian.

This massacre was what he'd contrived in the month spent consolidating his power as the new Emperor. It must've been easier for him to gain allies as the incoming Emperor than it had been as a Successor Primus of dubious reputation. He'd worked with the Luminars and snuck them in as new employees. He'd figured out Cygna's supporters and neutralized them all at once. And he'd played along with my sacrifice in a show of submission to Cygna, planning all along that she should take my place instead.

It shouldn't surprise me anymore to find Tyrus thinking ten steps ahead of everyone around him. Someone capable of doing this had no need to kill Sidonia Impyrean just to secure my life, surely.

I needed to believe it, and so I did. I made up my mind. I chose the truth Tyrus offered me and hoped desperately it would never come to taste bitter.

The vicar was escorted in to anoint Tyrus with oils as befitted the new Emperor. But when he reached for Tyrus's hand, he found it linked with mine. And Tyrus would not unlink with me as we stood together before the Helionic vicar.

The vicar recoiled. "That's a Diabolic," he said, aghast. "I can't bless a Diabolic."

I made to withdraw my hand, but Tyrus clutched me tightly, his eyes fastened upon the vicar. "I would prefer to retain your services at the Chrysanthemum. I see no reason our aims must be opposed. But if you will not anoint her, you will not anoint me. Nemesis will be my Empress."

"This is an abomination against the Living Cosmos. No Emperor can forgo his anointing, and I *will not* bless a Diabolic!"

Tyrus just smiled. "Look around, vicar. This is a new era. And if need be, it will leave you behind."

With that, he drew my knuckles to his cheek and turned away from the vicar. There were a few sharp, indrawn breaths across the Great Heliosphere, but none dared to speak up against the new Emperor Tyrus von Domitrian. As he stepped down with me, leaving the vicar where he stood with his phial of unused, star-blessed oil, the cheering arose and pounded in our ears.

The Grandiloquy and the Excess on all sides parted for us to pass, and my heart felt like it was going to pound out of my chest, for I knew the import of what Tyrus was doing. He was not just leaving the

Helionics behind, but all those who cleaved to the old ways.

In the doorway, I roused as though waking from a dream. "Tyrus, how can this happen?" I turned to him. "You can take risks as a new Emperor, but this Empire won't tolerate you wedding a Diabolic. Even the Excess think me an abomination!"

"I'll make any sacrifice for the era I wish to enter, Nemesis," he answered me, his eyes intent on mine. "But not this one. Not you. Never *you*."

Cygna had said once that power had a way of changing people. As I stared up at Tyrus, a peculiar foreboding wisped through me. I could not know what awaited us in the months and years ahead, but I could only hope this cunning of his remained as noble, as pure as I believed it was—or Tyrus had all the makings of a most terrifying Emperor.

Then he drew me close and kissed me in full view of the Great Heliosphere.

His lips felt right: soft and warm. I twined my arms about him, Tyrus in his ceremonial garb and me in the clothes I'd intended to wear to my death.

Some might call us a monstrous pair, and they would be right. Tyrus and I were both scorpions in our way, dangerous creatures crossing the most treacherous of rivers together. Together we might sting—but we also would float.

Perhaps scorpions were the only ones who could save each other.

Whatever lay ahead, it would always be the two of us above the rest of the universe, and woe to any who dared step in our path.

ACKNOWLEDGMENTS

For some reason, I always struggle with acknowledgments. It gets trickier every single book because the number of people who should have my recognition, thanks, and gratitude only increases as my career matures, and I live in mortal terror of leaving people out.

Meredith Duran, because in addition to being an amazing sister, you are also the most amazing beta reader I've ever had. Thank you for your keen eye for characterization and your instinctive feel for the necessities of a compelling romance. I honestly don't think *The Diabolic* would have reached this place without you.

To those others I love most: Mom, Dad, Rob, Matt, Betsey, Stella, Madeleine, Grace, and Sophia.

To my agent, Holly Root: You are a wonder. You've been everything I could have hoped for in an agent, and a great guide every time I'm not sure what's happening, or where to go next. Thank you for giving me a second wind. I can't wait to see what lies ahead of us in this partnership!!

Now on to Simon & Schuster Children's folks: this is daunting. I have met such an extraordinary array of wonderful, enthusiastic, skilled folks that this list could stretch on perilously long and I'd still leave someone critical out. Some names: Stephanie Voros, Deane

ACKNOWLEDGMENTS

Norton, Alexa Pastor, Anne Zafian, Dorothy Gribbin, Chava Wolin, Chrissy Noh, KeriLee Horan, Katy Hershberger, Audrey Gibbons, Lucille Rettino, Michelle Leo, Betsy Bloom, Anthony Parisi, Candace McManus, Christina Pecorale, Gary Urda, Victor Iannone. I am sure I've missed people. I'll just say that when I've seen your offices, interacted with people at long tables, I've been in awe of all of you, and so grateful to work with you on this book.

I must single out Lizzy Bromley for that incredible cover.

And now, most importantly: Justin Chanda. Justin, every author dreams of working with an editor like you. From the first day, your enthusiasm, insight, and expertise have been so priceless to me. I eagerly look forward to all the work we're going to do together.

Some other publishing folks: my fellow YA writers, too many people to name at this point, who have provided insight, commiseration, and friendship during this process. Molly O'Neill, because we've become friends, and you were there at the beginning of my career. I'm so glad to remain connected with you always. Dana Spector, Barbara Poelle (thanks for giving Justin a heads-up!), and all the foreign publishers who have picked up this book.

And of course, thanks as always to David Dunton, Sarah Shumway, Laurel Symonds, and the other publishing folks from earlier in my career who will always have influence.

My real world people:

Judy and the Persoffs, Winnie and the Hattens, Todd, Barb and the Anticeviches.

Various friends, many of whose names I will forget to place here. Off the top of my head: Jackie, Leslie, Yae, Stephen, Abby, Tina, Heidi, Alice, Tim, Allison, Mark, Bryan, Amy.

A special shout-out to David Bishop. I may not have been right for that MA program, but your mentoring and advice truly helped me

ACKNOWLEDGMENTS

find my direction again. Thank you, and I hope to see what awaits you down the road!

Robert Graves, for writing *I, Claudius* and inspiring the BBC miniseries that inspired me to write this book!

And last but definitely not least, those amazing readers, bloggers, librarians, teachers, and booksellers who responded to the Insignia series. Thank you for your enthusiasm, your support, and the time you've dedicated to reading my work. You make everything possible!